Threefold Dread

Threefold Dread

Elodie Stirling

Eloquent Muse Press

Threefold Dread

Elodie Stirling

Eloquent Muse Press

Cover design by Elodie Stirling and Kara Buelow Cover Photo by REXANDROS
Library of Congress Control Number: 2025902021
Names: Elodie Stirling, author
Title: Threefold Dread: a novel / Elodie Stirling
Description: First edition. | Seattle, WA: Eloquent Muse Press [2025].
Identifiers: LCCN 2025902021 (print)
FIRST EDITION: May 2025
ISBN: 979-8-218-62690-7 (print)
Subjects: Crime–Fiction | Fantasy–Fiction | Suspense–Fiction | Mystery–Fiction

For my wonderful daughter and sons, Lauren, Marc, and Alec, with all my love.

"Murder will out, this my conclusion."
—Geoffrey Chaucer

The Tribunal of Blood

The air tasted of copper and old ash.

He had killed in silence before—through the muffled thud of a pillow, the suppressed crack of a pistol, the quiet slip of a blade between ribs. He knew the sounds death made. He knew the weight of a body going still.

But this was different. This was the cold burn of inevitability, the weight of a debt finally coming due.
He stood in a chamber that existed between places. Stone walls stretched upward into darkness, their surface slick with moisture that smelled of grave earth. Three figures waited beyond a circle of flickering torchlight, their shadows stretching toward him like grasping fingers.

The Tormentors did not speak in unison. Their voices came separately, each carrying a different texture of judgment.

"The first," said the one on the left, her hair writhing with living serpents that hissed in rhythm with her words. "The father's blood."

"The second," murmured the one on the right, her eyes burning like coals in a dead hearth. "The mother's tears."

"And the third," whispered the central figure, her voice the sound of chains dragging across stone. "The oath broken."

His throat went dry. He had buried those memories deep, beneath layers of cash and lies and careful planning. He had told himself that money justified all things. That survival was the only morality. That the world belonged to those ruthless enough to take it.

But the Tormentors did not care for his justifications. They cared only for the truth written in blood.

"Someone summoned us," the middle one said, and he realized with dawning horror that someone knew, but how, he had been very careful. Maybe something else could have done this—some ancient mechanism of justice that operated outside the whims of gods and men alike.

"I didn't—" he began.

"Denial is the first lie," interrupted the left Tormentor, stepping forward. Her torch flared, illuminating the bronze armor she wore, etched with scenes of children weeping over fallen parents. "We know the shape of your sins. We have been walking beside you since the first drop fell."

The chamber seemed to shrink around him. The torches cast dancing shadows that looked too much like the faces of those he had destroyed—the woman who'd caught him stealing from her shop, the man who'd threatened to expose his operation, the girl who'd seen his face and begged for mercy.

"What do you want from me?" He asked, his voice steadier than he felt.

The Tormentors turned their gaze upon him together, and for the first time in his life, he understood true fear. Not the sharp terror of a close call, but the slow, suffocating dread of a man who knows there is no escape.

"Judgment," said the one on the right simply.

"Not punishment," added the left.

"Only truth," finished the center.

She raised her hand, and the stone floor beneath his feet became transparent. Below him, he saw not the depths of the underworld, but moments from his own life, playing out like reflections in dark water. He saw the first time he'd taken a life, the thrill that had curdled into addiction. He saw the faces of his victims in the moments before they died. He saw the life he'd built on their graves.

The Tormentors watched him watch himself.

"This is where most break," the middle one observed. "Some scream. Some beg. Some try to bargain with us as if we are merchants."

He clenched his fists. He had survived worse than visions. He had survived the police, the rivals, the close calls. He would survive this.

"I am not afraid of you," he shouted

Threefold Dread 2

The serpents in the left ones hair stopped hissing. All three figures smiled, and it was the most terrible thing he had ever seen.

"Fear is not the point," she said softly. "Understanding is. You have spent your life believing that power makes you untouchable. That the world bends to those strong enough to force it. Tonight, you learn that some debts cannot be paid with gold or blood or even death itself."

She stepped closer, and he could smell the rotting grave on her breath.

"Tonight, you will learn what it means to be truly alone."

The torches flared once, twice, then died. In the darkness, he heard the sound of chains being drawn tight.

And somewhere, far away, a bell began to toll.

Chapter 1
Dixie Cove Springs 1967

It was an ordinary sunny Thursday in the Sunshine State. Colorful songbirds were chirping from the tree branches of an oak tree, as a squirrel was lazily munching on a strawberry from the garden patch.

She glanced at the clock on the kitchen wall, it was just one more hour before the next reading, but that wasn't the cause of her anxious feelings. She'd had those all morning, but assumed they were because of her pending divorce.

Kassie was a petite woman with an elfin face and more than a few cowlicks throughout her hair—making the task of styling her long, thick auburn locks close to impossible.

She pushed back the strands that kept escaping from the ponytail scarf and continued pouring the fudgy double chocolate chip batter into the muffin tin, set the oven to 350° and then the timer for 35-minutes. After removing the apron, smoothed down the cream-colored peasant top and straightened the lime green tapered pants. Kassie examined her hair in the hall mirror, sighed, and again tucked strands back into the scarf. Then sat down to wait for the timer to ring, and stared out the window at nothing in particular.

The muffins were a special after-school treat for her daughter Ruby, who had made honor roll again, and this was her favorite treat. Kassie planned to make it an early night since there was an appointment scheduled first thing in the morning with her attorney to finalize paperwork. She felt emotionally exhausted. This time, her husband, Phil, had gone too far, and she was putting an end to their disaster of a marriage. She planned to break the news to Ruby after dinner, and hoped her daughter would understand her decision.

Kassie had suspected Phil of infidelity before, but the private investigator she'd hired confirmed her suspicions. The report and photos had not been a complete surprise, but it was a rude awakening to have confirmation that there was more than one woman. However, a specific one was the most astounding. When she confronted him with the evidence, he adamantly denied any involvement and much less with many. Only this time, she had proof. She had even followed him one night and seen for herself what he was up to, and that was all the validation she needed to proceed with the divorce.

Kassie was dreading the next reading. This client had scheduled over a month ago and Kassie didn't have a phone number to call her to cancel. The only consolation was that this would be the last time she'd read for her.

Kassie was an exceptionally accurate tarot reader and sought after by many clients; some would even drive from other states or out of town just to obtain a reading from her. However, this was one client definitely not wanted or needed.

An earlier appointment had gone well. The reading hardly ever deviated from the woman's previous readings. For some reason, the client didn't trust the love offered to her by someone she had known for many years. She had feelings for him, but was unsure to proceed with a new relationship. Kassie told her that the man interested in her who always showed up in her readings as the King of Cups was definitely her knight in shining armor, and truly loved her. Kassie was sure the client felt the same in return, but for some reason she still hesitated. She liked this client, but sensed undertones of anger and resentment. The client always arrived early, was polite, friendly, and tipped generously. Kassie also liked the way the client dressed, but couldn't imagine herself wearing scarlet red—it would make her look feverish.

Kassie was about to walk into her office just off the staircase where the reading room was located, but then remembered she'd forgotten to leave a note for Ruby. Heading to the kitchen she wrote her a note, and left it attached to the fridge with a magnet. It was a rule never to interrupt when the "in session" sign was flipped around.

"Help yourself to a muffin. I'll join you as soon as the last reading is over, and we can discuss matters. Love Mom."

The front doorbell rang; Kassie opened the door and led the blonde woman to the small office where she did consultations and tarot readings.

Kassie shuffled the cards, and cut them into three piles, then back together. She reached across the table and placed them in front of her client.

"Think about your question while shuffling the cards, then choose five cards, and place them on the table face down."

The woman shuffled the cards while biting her bottom lip, picked the cards, and placed the chosen ones on the table.

Kassie flipped over the first one and slightly grinned.

"The first card is The Lovers. This card represents relationships and choices. It indicates a decision needs to be made about an existing relationship, or a choice of potential partners. Whatever the choice is, it should not be made lightly, as the ramifications will be long-lasting."

The woman smiled slyly and nodded. "Go on."

"The next card is the Knight of Wands. This man is an act first, think later type. He is impatient, impulsive, and loves action. He also has a tendency to rush into things without thinking about the consequences of his actions. He acts in haste, and often fails to be realistic. He's headstrong, and impetuous."

The woman chuckled softly, but said nothing.

Kassie glanced up to see the client's smug expression, but she knew damned well who the card represented.

"The third card you've chosen is the Knight of Swords. This guy's a powerful figure full of life and energy. Once he sets forth on his journey, there is no stopping him. He doesn't see, or care about, any upcoming challenges, risks, or dangers, but will instead charge forward into dangerous territory without any foresight or preparation."

"The fourth card is the King of Pentacles. This man is grounded and stable—often to the point of being too grounded. He thinks long-term, and likes routines. He is practical, but also loves having fine things. Not only does he care for himself, but he also takes care of those dependent on him—no expense is spared."

"There seem to be a lot of men in your life." Kassie slyly commented. The woman smoldered with resentment at the insinuation, as each new card was an accusation, accurately telling a story she didn't want told. Her knuckles turned white from gripping the arm rests on the chair, to stop herself from strangling the woman reading the tarot cards.

Kassie felt the seething resentment emanating from her client, but kept laying out the cards. The tarot told her what she already suspected, and which the client wanted kept secret.

The negativity emanating from the woman was making Kassie uncomfortable. The last glance had shown the client unblinkingly staring at her, as if trying to convey a silent message of unforgiving judgment. Mouth pinched shut as though holding back what she really wanted to say. Since this was the last reading Kassie would ever offer this client, she was going to give her exactly what she was paying for—explicit details.

"The last card in your reading is The Tower, which represents a sudden and unexpected change, upheaval, destruction, and chaos. This event will leave you shaken, and will affect you mentally and physically. There's no escaping it, especially since you've ignored the warnings along the way. This change creates chaos and destroys everything in its path."

Narrowed ice blue eyes studied Kassie. *I'm prettier and sexier than she is—why is he even with her. Look at that wild hair and unflattering attire.*

"Do you have any questions?" Kassie inquired.

"No, I don't have any questions," she replied mockingly, with emphasis on the last word. "You've covered more than enough."

Kassie didn't respond to this obvious challenge. "I'm just the messenger. How you interpret the message is up to you."

The woman crossed her arms and glowered at her suspiciously.

That's a nasty scowl. Kassie thought. "Well, that's the entire reading. And I won't be giving you any more readings."

The client looked taken aback, but didn't ask why. She reached into her purse, pulled out a twenty-dollar bill, and slapped it on the table.

"Don't worry." She retorted. "I wasn't going to ask for another."

"I didn't think so. I know that you and my no-good husband are having an affair, and you're no longer welcome here." Kassie stared her down.

Mouth falling open, she gasped. Speechless, all she could do was to give Kassie an incredulous stare.

"I…have no idea what you're talking about." The woman stammered.

"Oh I think you do." Kassie retorted. "If I were you I'd heed the warnings the cards gave you."

The woman pushed the chair back, making a loud scraping noise, yanked the door violently open, which caused it to hit the wall and leave a dent. Then stomped up the hallway, and stormed out the front door, slamming it behind her so hard it rattled the walls. "Go to hell!" She yelled as she walked towards her car.

Kassie shook her head. *That's some temper.* She walked up the hallway and locked the front door. Then returning to the office, unlocked the bottom drawer of the desk, pulled out the lock-box, and placed the bill inside. She lit incense and a candle, then picked up the tarot cards and gave them a good shuffle, trying to rid them of the negative energy they had just encountered. As she was shuffling, three cards fell out: the Ten of Swords, Knight of Wands, and Death.

How many more men does this woman actually have in her life? She wondered while reshuffling the cards, then returned them to the stack, carefully wrapped them in black silk cloth, and placed a jet-black obsidian stone on top.

The Ten of Swords represents betrayal, backstabbing, hitting rock bottom, sorrow, and misfortune. The Death card signifies a major phase in life ending, and a new one beginning, but in a romance reading, it means upheaval. The knight of wands reversed is someone extremely reckless, hasty, egotistical, and arrogant.

Feeling a sudden stab of anxiety and a quick pulse in her throat, Kassie quickly opened the top drawer, and looked for a sage bundle. Then remembered she had already used it the last time the same client had come for a reading, and had forgotten to replace it.

Making a mental note to pick some up at the Herbal Fayre Shop, Kassie got up and stretched.
Feeling tainted by the awful energy left behind, she headed upstairs to shower and wash off the bad vibes.

Chapter 2
Ruby and Giselle

Eleven-year-old Ruby and her friends were walking home from school. They were teasing each other about the boys they liked. When Ruby's block came up, the three friends said their goodbyes and went their separate ways.

She watched as her classmate Giselle walked quickly up the sidewalk on the opposite side of the street, her head bent down, with scraggly hair hanging over her face. Ruby felt sorry for her and thought of talking to her, but maybe her friends were right and she should avoid her as everyone else did.

That girl is definitely odd!

Giselle was not only anti-social, but she behaved strangely too. Giselle would come to school with no lunch and didn't buy any—then she would sit in the outdoor area and stare at the empty table while chewing on her hair. She didn't interact with any of the other students and when any of them attempted to talk to her, she remained silent as a stone, and just stared at her lap until they left.

One day, Ruby decidedly walked over to Giselle, and handed her half of her sandwich. Ruby hated cafeteria food and besides it would be an unnecessary expense for her mother, so she just prepared her own lunch. Afterward that day, Ruby began making two lunches every morning, one for her, and one for Giselle.

Giselle would devour the food as soon as Ruby handed it to her. It was as if she either hadn't eaten anything for breakfast or eaten very little, but Ruby suspected that she probably hadn't eaten at all. Maybe Giselle was one of those kids, who skipped breakfast, or maybe her parents worked and didn't prepare any for her and she didn't know how, but either way, Giselle was ravenous come lunchtime.

When Ruby's friends sat down for lunch at their usual table, Giselle remained at an empty one, even though they invited her to join them. It was the same every day; Giselle would thank Ruby for the food, quickly gobble it down, then excuse herself, and run off. One day, Ruby finally managed to coax Giselle to join them at their usual table. Giselle sat quietly not talking to anyone, and leaving after eating her sandwich.

One time, Giselle was wearing her usual cardigan in warm weather, it had gotten caught on the table edge when she stood up, and it pulled away from her shoulder, exposing a large purplish bruise on her upper arm. One of the girls asked if she'd fallen off her bike. Giselle blushed deeply and sheepishly responded. "Yeah, I guess I did." Then ran to the girl's bathroom and locked herself in a stall.

Ruby ran after her, walked into the bathroom, and heard sobbing. It was Giselle. Ruby asked if she could do anything to help, but Giselle responded, "No, there's nothing you can do, but thanks anyway."

Sometimes Ruby and her friends caught up with Giselle walking rapidly home, and joined her. That was when she learned that Giselle liked to read about the supernatural, just like her. The others had laughed, but Ruby was adamant that there were things out there that were unexplainable.

"Just like your crush on Richie!" One of the girls teasingly replied.

"Ha ha, very funny!" Ruby responded laughing.

Giselle laughed too. That was the first time anyone had seen her smiling and enjoying herself, and they all slyly elbowed each other with knowing looks. But all that ended as soon as her block came up, and her mood turned morose. Ruby suspected that maybe Giselle didn't want to go home, because she'd be all alone waiting for her parents to come home from work, so she invited her over. The reaction from Giselle wasn't one she'd expected. At first, she'd been thrilled at the invitation, but the next moment, she was apprehensive, asking what time Ruby had on her watch.

"Well, if it's okay with your mom, I don't want to cause any trouble." Giselle replied.

"Of course it's okay with my mom; I'm sure she'll be glad to meet you. Come on."

She linked elbows with Giselle and sang "Up, Up, and Away," and Giselle joined her.

They made an unusual pair. Ruby with cheeks that easily flushed, long auburn hair, aqua eyes, and the delicate features of her Irish predecessors, and Giselle with shoulder length, pale blonde hair, pale blue eyes, and fair skin that made the pallor and undereye circles stand out more than Ruby's freckles.

Giselle liked going to Ruby's house after school; it had almost become a ritual. She could stay as late as she wanted, but made sure not to overstay her welcome, unless invited to stay the night, which came in handy sometimes. Ruby's mom, Kassie was very nice, and Giselle found herself wishing Kassie were her mom too.

Giselle considered herself lucky that she now had two households that welcomed her warmly. At Ruby's, the air always smelled of freshly baked brownies and lasagna or other mouth-watering meals. There was always laughter and gaiety, and the welcoming atmosphere sometimes made Giselle's eyes tear up with longing for the same in her home.

What Ruby didn't know was that after saying goodbye, Giselle didn't go directly home, but instead to her neighbors. In fact, Giselle avoided going home at all if not necessary, and she knew perfectly well that her mother didn't expect her home, or even care if she didn't return.

On days, that Daddy didn't have a flight—Giselle went straight home as soon as the last school bell rang. Daddy was an airline pilot and worked most days. Sometimes, he didn't return home for many days when flying internationally, or when flights were delayed due to bad weather. Giselle giggled at the thought, *even weather can be bad. I wonder if mama will get angry at it and wave her fist to stop the badness.*

Mama was a stay-at-home mother, but that was all she mostly did: stay-at-home. She wasn't like the other mothers at all. No, her mother was very pretty, just like the models in magazines, and she didn't dress like other mothers either. She was always wore the latest fashions, with makeup on and her hair perfectly styled. She knew she wasn't as pretty as mama.

At last year's Christmas party, her aunty Deirdre had commented that, Giselle would grow up to be a beauty just like her mother. But Delores just retorted, "Pfft. She mostly gets her looks from her father—adequate, but no great beauty."

Deirdre had looked away, embarrassed, then started a conversation with the woman next to her, while her mother had grabbed another cocktail, and walked away. Giselle had overheard though, and it was then that she knew she was not a pretty girl, but having her mother confirm it made her sad. She knew her daddy was handsome, but he was a guy and she didn't want to look like a boy.

After saying goodbye to Ruby, Giselle went home, dragging her feet to avoid getting there quickly.

A deep purplish tint had invaded the afternoon skies with the promise of rain. The sky resembled the hue of bruised skin around a black eye spreading rapidly, and her surroundings felt heavy with oppression.

Giselle wished for the hundredth time that she was still at Ruby's house. Ruby told her that her mom wanted to discuss something important with Ruby, and that she would see Giselle at school on Monday.

"I thought I told you about Mama's Night!" Delores angrily shouted as soon as Giselle walked through the front door, making her jump back in alarm.

Squinting, she saw her mother sitting in the darkened living room. The slurred words alerted Giselle she had already been at the "happy juice," as Delores liked to call it, and it was better not to argue.

The last time she hadn't wanted to go outside again and said so, things had not ended well.

Daddy had been out of town for three days, and whenever he was away, meals were nonexistent. Giselle hadn't eaten anything except the other half of Ruby's sandwich—because she had forgotten to make another for Giselle that morning, it now was late afternoon and she was famished.

Mama had told her that children should be self-sufficient; what if she and Daddy suddenly died, or some psycho broke in and murdered them in their sleep? What would she do then? Make your own damned meals, and that is precisely what Giselle had been doing. One day, there was no food as usual, and when she heard the jaunty tune from the ice cream truck coming up the street she bravely dared to ask.

"Please mama, could I have a quarter for an ice cream? I'm hot from running around, and ice cream will cool me down." She didn't want mama to feel embarrassed for having forgotten to buy food the last time she went to the grocery store.

Her mother set the drink down, the ice cubes tinkling in the near-empty glass.

Then she grabbed Giselle's arm and dragged her outside.

The water was so cold that Giselle screamed. It was shockingly cold. Mama had turned the hose on full force and explained.

"Ice cream rots teeth. Water is free and will cool you down better than any frozen treat." Mama had hissed at her through clenched teeth.

Giselle stood on the front lawn in wet clothing plastered on shivering skin. Standing in a puddle and dripping on the concrete, she looked around, embarrassed, hoping no one had seen what had happened. But she was wrong. Next door, a curtain slightly parted, and worried eyes watched in horror at the cruel treatment of the sweetest child she knew.

Giselle quickly ran through the front door to head upstairs and change into dry clothing, when she felt her hair yanked with force from behind.

Startled by the sudden pain, Giselle yelped and turned around. She was clobbered by the raised umbrella in Delores' fist. Tears streamed down Giselle's cheeks, as her mother raised her hand again and again.

"That'll teach you to run through my clean house dripping wet. You should know better," she shrieked at her terrified daughter.

"Strip right here and hand me those wet clothes, you stupid child." Her lips pursed by suppressed fury.

Giselle hesitated, but did not dare defy the glowering look Mama was giving her. She removed the soaked clothes and handed them to her.

"The underwear is wet too; take it off. How did I get such an idiotically stupid child?

Maybe I have someone else's child, because you were switched in the hospital the night you were born, and the lucky mother got the smart one."

Embarrassed, Giselle removed her underwear, handed it to her, then ran up the stairs, two at a time, and into her bedroom, and locked the door.

The spreading purple and yellow blotches were only surface wounds; she had become an expert at covering them up with long sleeves and pants. The real wounds were within—the feeling of betrayal and the breaking of trust. She knew parents were supposed to protect their children from harm, and not hurt them.

Giselle kept hoping that Mama would become loving and caring like the mothers she saw at school dropping off classmates and kissing them goodbye. Those mothers baked cookies and fussed when their children got skinned knees. Mama only drank her happy juice and became angry over a scrape; because blood had stained, the clothing and more pummeling would occur. So Giselle just kept silent, bandaged her own injuries, cuts, and scrapes, and washed blood out of stained clothing.

Another time, Giselle had asked when her mother was getting more food, and Mama had slapped her so hard across the mouth that her lip was cut, then blood had dripped all over her shirt, and Mama had gone ballistic. She had gotten one of Papa's belts and whipped away because of the bloodstained top while yelling at her, "See what you've made me do!"

Mama had brusquely yanked off the shirt and burned it in the kitchen sink, and then blamed Giselle again, for having to burn a perfectly good top. But mama had already been drinking happy juice, and Giselle blamed that instead of mama, because mama had not been in her right mind.

From then on, it was yes mama, no mama, or thank you mama, with no extra comments or requests.

"Children can be so inconsiderate," Delores said and got up to pour herself another drink.

"You know I host Cocktail Nights whenever Daddy is out of town, and no children are allowed."

"Sorry mama, I forgot."

"Then make yourself scarce and go somewhere to play until the party is over, or go stay at one of your friend's houses. Children shouldn't be seen or heard! And don't slam the damned door on your way out." She yelled.

Delores limply brushed her hand upward, as if shooing away an annoying fly, while the other hand held a glass, the martini spilling over the rim. She picked out the olive with her long, scarlet fingernails and plopped it into her mouth. Delores sat in the armchair looking like a tipsy queen. Her silken robe dropped off her pale shoulder and further slipped down, exposing a full breast.

Giselle looked down at her feet, embarrassed, and then ran out the door, which slammed shut behind her.

"Damned kid always slamming the damned door." She complained loudly, to no one in particular.

Delores thought back to the reading with the psychic and worried some more, this was the very reason she'd started drinking earlier than usual.

Kassie was a well-known psychic—a very accurate one. She had never failed to provide accurate information before, and most importantly helpful advice.

This time, however, the tarot cards had given her a dire warning, and she'd been troubled all day. Then she remembered that tonight was her favorite night of the week and decided to ignore the whole thing. Dumb psychics and their stupid tarot cards—what do they know anyway?

Shrugging off the feeling of impending doom and thinking about the fun night ahead of her, she went upstairs to shower and change into more suitable attire. She laughed aloud as she turned on the shower, imagining herself walking into the supermarket in lingerie. That'll definitely give the old biddies next-door something to gossip about; damned intrusive busybodies.

Giselle watched from behind a bush as her mother drove away, and then she snuck back inside. Checking the kitchen cupboards for anything to eat that Mama wouldn't miss, she found a can of peanuts in the back.

Climbing up on the counter she reached for it, opened it, and dropped some into her hand, careful not to spill any salt or take too many to be noticeable. Then replacing the jar in the same spot, Giselle checked the refrigerator. Found and drank some juice straight from the container, then opened the pickle jar, grabbed one and ate it. There wasn't much else except for a head of lettuce and a jar of sauerkraut that she didn't like the taste or smell of, and closed the door.

Giselle went upstairs and checked the drawers in her parents' bedroom. Maybe daddy had some snacks in the drawers. She opened each drawer, careful not to displace anything, but found nothing. Then she remembered reading in a mystery story that some people hid things under their mattresses, and she began running her hand along the sides.

There was nothing on Mama's side, but feeling underneath Daddy's side of the bed, her hand bumped against something hard and cold. She squatted, reached in, and pulled out a metal object. Then gasped when seeing it was a gun and almost dropped it on the carpet. Giselle heard a car pull into the garage and quickly replaced the gun exactly where she had found it.

The kitchen door slammed shut, and Giselle become panic-stricken. She wasn't supposed to be in the house. She needed to escape quickly.

Quiet as the setting sun, Giselle scuttled towards her room, quickly went inside, and silently closed the door. Then she slowly opened her window hoping it wouldn't creek and climbed out onto the ledge. She expertly walked along the perimeter, over to the branch of the oak tree that would lead her to the others, and down to the ground. Once again, on solid ground, she looked around; after making sure Mama hadn't noticed her and ran off.

Chapter 3
Twin Pass Junction

The professor's voice droned on as he described the importance of angles and their application to calculations.

Sherry, lost in thought, stared out the window and wondered what CJ had planned for their Saturday night date. He'd told her it was a surprise, and she was anxious with anticipation.

"Miss Townsend, what are the six functions of an angle commonly used in trigonometry?"

Emily poked her friend in the back with her pencil eraser, which startled Sherry out of her reverie.

"I'm sorry, Mr. Sullivan, could you repeat the question?"

"What are the six functions of an angle commonly used in trigonometry?" He repeated with a sigh.

Sherry didn't hesitate. "They are sine, cosine, tangent, cotangent, secant, and cosecant."

"Very good, you are correct." The teacher looked pleased and continued with the lesson.

"You make the rest of us look bad," whispered Emily.

"You should actually study once in a while," teased Sherry.

Emily poked her again.

Sherry looked around the classroom. There were rows of small wooden desks with attached chairs. The desks looked slightly worn, and many of them had etchings with the scribbles of bored students. The chairs were just a bit small for the average person and allowed for little movement, so having your textbook, notebook, and pencil laid out before class began was necessary. This was the first thing Sherry did everyday as soon as she sat down, and this quirk always made Emily roll her eyes at her while shaking her head.

Along the walls were the usual diagrams, posters, and rules. The room smelled of the usual classroom scent: chalk, eraser dust, the sharp, crisp quality of fresh ink on paper, and from the students…perspiration.

The classroom felt overly warm because of the home economics ovens across the hall—filling the classroom with the cloying scent of over baked banana bread. The nauseating smell only made the already overheated day more uncomfortable. Students were squirming in their seats, and longing for the bell to ring, so they could leave the area as quickly as possible.

The windows were large and air sometimes flowed through. Students raced to get a window seat where they could watch the football team practicing, and feel an occasional breeze on their sweaty faces. The sky was clear except for a few scattered clouds, and Sherry could see a long line of exhausted physical education students lined up at the water fountain.

The teacher continued talking about angles and looked as inspired as a used tea bag.

Sherry felt herself slipping into a daydream as she pretended listen—an extremely pleasant one about CJ. Her teacher's lesson would have to become very interesting if he wanted to compete with her thoughts.

The bell signaling the end of class rang, startling Sherry out of her thoughts.

"Come on dreamy, cheerleading waits for no one," urged Emily.

CJ was waiting for her by the lockers. "Hi, beautiful, what are you doing tomorrow night?"

Emily rolled her eyes.

"Better stop doing that or your eyes will get stuck that way." CJ warned her.

"I'm rolling them to see if I can find what's left of my brain after listening to all of your lovey-dovey cooing all the time." She stuck her tongue out for emphasis.

"You're just jealous," teased CJ. "Hasn't Dwight asked you out yet?"

"Why, what has he told you?" Emily quickly responded eyes wide-open interest peaked.

"Oh, he might have mentioned a certain, pretty green-eyed brunette."

"Go on!" Emily purred.

"I'm not at liberty to say, but he's definitely interested."

Emily's eyes opened wider, and a smile spread across her dimpled cheeks. Dwight had just joined them.

"What are you all up to?"

"We were just talking about you," replied CJ.

"All good, I hope."

He looked straight at Emily, who blushed deeply.

"You know it always is." She answered bashfully.

"Anyone going to see the new James Bond movie this weekend, You Only Live Twice?" Dwight asked.

Everyone shrugged.

"Why, are you going to watch it?" Emily asked pointedly.

"Uh, yeah, I guess." Dwight replied sheepishly.

"There's also Wait Until Dark and Far from the Madding Crowd," Emily slyly suggested.

"So many choices. You know what they say; life is just a bowl of cherries." Dwight told her.

"Yeah." Retorted Emily. "And this conversation is the pits."

Dwight looked confused, not understanding why Emily was always annoyed with him. Just then, the warning bell rang, and Emily grabbed Sherry's arm. "Come on we're gonna be late for practice."

"You go on ahead; I'll be right behind you."

"Come on, Em, I'll walk you to the locker room." Dwight told her and led her away.

Sherry turned back to CJ. "In answer to your question, I'm going on a date with you."

"You absolutely are." Was CJ's vague response.

He kissed her cheek outside the locker room. "See you after practice."

Sherry sat on the bleachers watching CJ make a touchdown. Her long golden-brown hair hung straight down her back, and making her neck too warm.

If the team wins tonight's game, they will remain undefeated the entire year, and that was all because of CJ's natural athleticism. Sherry thought.

CJ had already received three scholarship offers from top schools; he just hadn't signed up with one of them yet, as he was still waiting to find out which one Sherry could attend with him. Their picture was in the yearbook under most likely to marry after HS. They had already decided: college, marriage, career, and two children, in that order.

Warren, the team's linebacker, was having a party at his house since his father was out of town. Sherry was thinking of the cute outfit she'd be wearing tonight when she felt a thump on her head.

"Hey you!" Emily said cheerily.

"Hi Em, I thought you'd left. What are you doing out here?"

"Checking out the boys, of course. You?"

"Working on homework and waiting for CJ."

"You two lovebirds are like an old married couple; it's gross."

"You're just jealous Em!"

"Of course I am you idiot!"

The friends burst out laughing while Emily contemplated the field deep in thought.

Sherry looked at her friend in contemplation. "What's wrong?"

Emily stared straight ahead and sighed. "It's Dwight. I know he likes me, but he never asks me out. I was hoping he'd ask me to go with him to the party tonight, but no luck."

"Look at him out there, running off his cute butt like a bull charging at a matador, but gets all tongue-tied around me."

Sherry giggled at her friend's simile. "I believe his position is tight end, and news flash, he's always been shy. Just because you'll even talk to a stone, doesn't mean everyone else is as outgoing. Maybe give him a little push; drop hints."

"Sherry, if I drop anymore hints he doesn't get I—might as well lift my halter top and flash him. Maybe then he'll understand."

Sherry laughed at her friend's exaggeration. "That will definitely get his attention."

"Then I know what I'm wearing tonight. My brand new lavender halter top with purple hiphuggers."

"What are you wearing Sherry?"

"I haven't decided yet."

Emily stood up. "Maybe we can get ready together—call me later."

Sherry turned around at her name being called from the parking lot. Her father was hurrying toward her. *Oh no, what's wrong?* She wondered.

"Sherry, I'm glad I found you." Your grandmother fell and fractured her leg, and your mother and I are driving over to stay with her for a few days until she's out of the hospital, and we can set up in-house care. Also, your mom and I are going to need you to babysit your sister until we get back."

"Sure, dad, how's grandma doing?"

"She's stable. Well come on, quickly, grab your things. I'll drive you home."

Reluctantly, Sherry gathered her schoolbooks and notebooks and jammed them into her bookbag. She looked across the field and saw CJ standing there with his palms facing up and a questioning look.

She mouthed. "Call me" while making the phone gesture with her hand, then followed her father to the car.

As soon as practice was over, CJ ran to the locker room, yanked off his shoulder pads, and pulled out a dime from his pants pocket. Then, slamming his locker shut, he ran in the direction of the office; the pay phone was next to the entrance.

As soon as he returned, Dwight pounced on him.

"Well, I did it!" Dwight exclaimed excitedly while grabbing both CJ's arms and shaking him.

"Did what?" CJ asked distractedly.

"I asked Emily to go to Warren's party with me."

"Oh." CJ replied distractedly.

Dwight looked at his friend quizzically. "Really, man, you've been busting my balls for months about asking Emily out, and all you can say is oh!"

"Sorry, cool man. I'm glad you finally grew a pair."

Dwight looked at his friend worriedly. "Okay, what's wrong? Spill!"

"Sherry just told me she can't make it to the party tonight because her grandmother is in the hospital. Her parents are headed two towns away for a few days, and Sherry needs to babysit her sister."

Dwight nodded. "Bummer. Sorry man. I know you had big plans for tonight. But why don't you go ahead with them anyway?"

CJ looked at Dwight as if he had lost his mind, not comprehending what his friend was trying to tell him.

"Look, man, don't flip your wig. Just drive over to her house and do what you had planned for tonight."

CJ stared at Dwight as if seeing him for the first time. "You're right, I should just go over there, but I had it all planned out. I made reservations for dinner, and then planned on stopping by the party afterwards with Sherry."

Dwight patted him on the back, "Just get going, and land that chick."

"I think I'll do just that," CJ told him with conviction.

"See you later, dude, and good luck." Dwight patted CJ on the back.

"See you on the flip side," responded CJ.

Whistling, CJ headed for the showers but didn't notice Warren lurking around the end of the lockers. He had heard every word and wasn't happy. His tightened jaw, flared nostrils, and clenched fists stirred anger within him, as he smoldered with resentment.

He used every ounce of willpower he had left to stop himself from punching the locker. Warren took his time getting dressed, waiting as a freshly showered CJ went to his locker to get dressed.

"Hey man, are you coming to the party tonight?" Warren asked him.

"I planned to, but now I'm not so sure," replied CJ while pulling on his jeans.

Warren gave him a wounded look. "Really, man, you're gonna stand up the whole team?" This party's mostly for us after we get the big win tonight."

CJ smiled and said, "You're such an optimist. How can you be so sure we'll win tonight?"

Threefold Dread 20

Warren shook his head. "You're the best player we've got; how can we lose?"

"Alright, I'll try and stop by later." CJ replied

"Groovy, see ya tonight." Warren happily replied.

Chapter 4
Dixie Cove Springs

Fury made her cherry-red Mary Jane's strike the ground in heavy clomps. She'd barely made it to her car before her anger erupted. Like a child having a meltdown, she pounded on the steering wheel with her fists and screamed obscenities into the empty car.

"Who the hell does she think she's fooling?" She yelled. "She's probably smugly laughing at me. I'll kill her!"

Pulling a flask out of her handbag, she took a long swig; the amber liquid flowed smoothly down her throat, and felt herself begin to relax. She smoothed down the collared floral mini dress then started the car.

"If others disrespect you, you have to take matters into your own hands to make them respect you." She said aloud.

Her mother had drilled that into her, and her father had beaten it into her after he'd found her in the backseat of her boyfriend's car in tenth grade.

After a prior abusive relationship, she vowed never to let another man manhandle her ever again. Instead, she always had the upper hand, and controlled her relationships.

She sat in the car for a long time before coming to a decision, and then with her mind made up, drove off. She knew what she had to do, and there was no time to waste. She hadn't driven all this way to be insulted. To think she'd left the warm arms of her lover to attend this appointment made her even angrier.

She parked and went inside. After placing a wide-brimmed hat upon her head, she slipped into a raincoat. Before leaving, she remembered something. Walking over to the closet, she reached for the box hidden in the back, and rummaged inside until she found what she was looking for. Grabbing it tightly in her hand grabbed a bottle of red nail polish. Satisfied, went to the mini bar, and grabbed a miniature skewer from last night's cocktail discarded in an ashtray. She smiled, knowing the plan was complete.

Looking out the window to make sure no one was around; she got back into her car and drove up the street.

She drove back to Kassie's house, but parked two blocks away near an empty lot then walked the rest of the way. Sneaking behind bushes and trees, and making sure there weren't any Nosy Nelly's around. She looked through the kitchen window. Seeing no one there, she carefully turned the doorknob, and a sinister smile spread grotesquely upon her beautiful face. Hiding her shoes beneath a bush walked inside barefoot.

Once inside, after listening for sounds and footsteps, and hearing and seeing none, carefully opened kitchen drawers and found what she was seeking—the sharpest knife and dishwashing gloves next to the pristine sink.

Cracking open the door leading to the hallway, she tiptoed past the reading room and turned the sign around, and then crept towards the stairs. Taking one-step at a time and hoping none creaked, but one did, and she froze. Flattening herself against the wall, she waited listening, but no one called out, and then continued upstairs until she heard sound.

There were two rooms. The first one's door was open, and she peered inside. It appeared to be a child's bedroom, with a desk underneath the window and a bookshelf next to it overflowing with books. There was a well-worn teddy bear on the neatly made bed.

She continued to the only other bedroom and held her ear to the closed door.

She heard the shower running and a radio playing. She cracked the door open and heard a woman singing the part of Tammi Terrell to "Ain't No Mountain High Enough" alongside Marvin Gaye.

Yeah, there definitely ain't no mountain high enough for you!

She silently closed the door then hid behind the curtains.

Chapter 5
Ruby

Ruby hurried up the street, trying to keep pace with her friend who was walking in a state of urgency. She was just as anxious to get home. That morning her mother had told her, she had something important to discuss with her. The friends said their goodbyes, and Giselle headed towards Miss Tisi's house, while Ruby headed straight home.

Ruby was nervous about the talk with her mother. She had known for quite some time that her parents weren't getting along and suspected their discussion would have something to do with that. Two weeks ago, while she was in her bedroom, finishing her homework, her mother was in the kitchen arguing with her father, and their raised voices could be heard throughout the house.

"Your name is perfect, Phil, since you're a damned philanderer." Kassie spat at him in fury.

"Aw, come on, babe, don't be like that. You know you're the only one for me." Phil responded with an innocent look on his face. A look Kassie had come to know very well throughout the years—the one he always gave her when he had been caught messing around.

"This is the last straw, Phil. I want you to move out–today!"

"But babe, give me a chance to explain?"

"Don't you babe me, you cheating asshole. This isn't the first time and it won't be the last. Let's go over the facts, shall we? This morning when I was doing laundry, there was lipstick on both sides of your shirt collar, and it also reeked of expensive perfume."

"Babe that was your perfume and lipstick. You know, when we got romantic last weekend?"

It rankled her every fiber of her being whenever he called her babe, and yet he continued calling her that even though she had told him it annoyed her.

"We both know I don't wear perfume, and when have I ever worn garish red lipstick?"

At a loss because he had run out of excuses, he just stood there dejectedly and shrugged.

"I followed you last week, to a house blocks away where a woman was waiting at the front door; you kissed her while grabbing her ass."

"That was a house party, and the hostess was giving me a friendly kiss on the cheek as a welcome." Phil explained.

"Really? Then your cheek must have changed positions, and if you call a French kiss a friendly one, then you're dumber than I thought." Kassie retorted.

"Okay, you've caught me. I did have a one-nighter, but it will never happen again. I promise."

"You're a damned liar Phil, but it will happen again, with her or with someone else. I don't know and I could care less, because you will no longer be here."

Ruby rounded the corner and neared her house. She felt a strange sensation in the pit of her stomach as she walked through the gate. Something wasn't right. She hoped her mother and father hadn't gotten into another fight. They'd been fighting a lot lately, and it made her feel so awful she'd leave the house and go to the park up the street until just before dinner. It ended the same way every time: with her father storming out and threatening that he'd never return, and her mother telling him not to. But he always returned, and each time her mother took him back.

This time he'd been gone for two days, and Ruby wondered if he was home, and the two were fighting again. Maybe that was what her senses were picking up the closer she got.

When her mother gave tarot readings for clients, Ruby would sometimes listen outside the door. The cards never lied and told a story that clients sometimes didn't want to hear. But her mother told them exactly what the cards wanted them to know.

One client had been over often for readings, but didn't seem to like what the tarot cards had to say. The last time, the woman had yelled at Kassie that she wasn't giving her an accurate reading, and demanded that she reshuffle the cards again. Kassie had complied and reshuffled, and the cards picked out by the client were the very same ones as before.

Ruby listened intently as her mother gave the reading.

"The first card is the Three of Swords, which indicates a sorrowful experience and grief. It will be a time of tears and regret. If you are in a relationship, this can point to a breakup, a conflict, or some kind of separation."

"The Lovers represents relationships and choices. You will need to make a choice about an existing relationship, and you may end up choosing one partner over another."

"The Seven of Swords represents deception, lies, trickery, cheating, and a lack of conscience. This card also signifies mental manipulation, tactics, scheming, and cunning. It means that someone is being deceitful."

"The final card you've chosen is The Tower, which is associated with sudden, unforeseen change. Expect the unexpected; this could be a warning of upheaval. It also represents danger, crisis, chaos, and destruction, which can be unexpected alteration and this, is usually scary, profound, and unavoidable due to prior actions. This negative event will be like a bomb going off in your life. This coming change seems to be brought on by your actions. And because it is next to the Knight of Wands, he may be involved in the reason for this change."

The woman had then thrown the fee on the floor and stormed out the door. She yelled she'd never come back and would tell everyone what a fake Kassie was, but Ruby knew her mother was no fake. Kassie had predicted many occurrences in the lives of her clients, and they were always grateful to be prepared before anything happened, but not this woman. Ruby resented the implication that her mother was a fraud, and it made her angry.

Besides reading for clients, Kassie was also a consultant for the police department. They called for her services whenever they were stuck, and were always provided important clues to help them solve difficult cases.

Ruby opened the kitchen door and smelled the baked goods wafting through before entering. Slowly closing the door, so it wouldn't slam and disturb her mother who was probably in a reading, she let herself into the kitchen. Reading the note on the fridge, Ruby poured herself a glass of milk, placed a muffin on a plate, and carried both to the table.

She hung her book bag on the back of the chair. Then tiptoed halfway up the hallway and saw the sign on the door. Satisfied all was as should be, she returned to the kitchen, and started on homework.

Looking up at the clock, it was now five; she hadn't noticed how long she'd been working on the essay. Standing up and stretching, Ruby took the plate and glass to the sink, washed both, and placed them on the side to dry.

That's strange she thought. Readings never took more than twenty-five minutes, thirty at the most. It had been almost two-hours since she had come home from school.

Walking up the hallway and seeing that the sign was still on the door. She softly knocked using a knuckle, just in case. No response. Ruby called out to her mother. Still no response. She cracked the door open and saw that the office was empty.

I guess she forgot to turn the sign around before she stepped out.

Ruby went back to the kitchen to collect her things. That's odd, mom starts dinner promptly at 5 o'clock on the dot every day, but not today.

Threefold Dread 26

"I wonder where she could be," Ruby worried aloud.

She headed upstairs to take a shower. Afterwards, she checked the hallway saw that it was getting dark, and turned on the lights, then went back downstairs, and turned on lamps. Deciding to surprise her mother when she returned, she went to the kitchen, and began pulling out pots and pans.

After dinner was left cooking, she went back upstairs to her room and noticed that her parent's door was shut. Their door was never shut unless they were sleeping, but nobody was home. Maybe her mother had a migraine and had been asleep all this time and she had neglected to check on her. Feeling terrible for not having thought of that earlier, Ruby lightly knocked on the door.

"Mom, are you awake?"

No answer.

She knocked again and repeated the question, but still no response.

Ruby opened the door slightly, but the room was too dark to see anything.

"Mom, are you here?"

No response.

After switching on the night table light, lying on the bed was her mother. Ruby walked towards the bed and was about to wake her, when she saw a knife protruding from her abdomen, and the blood soaked sheets.

Next to her mother was a little carved doll.

Ruby began to scream and scream.

Chapter 6
Twin Pass Junction

As soon as CJ and Dwight walked through the front door, a round of applause echoed throughout the house. The party was in celebration for the football team beating their rivals for the first time in three years. Their quarterback Caleb had made eight touchdowns and 302-yards, leading his team—the The Dragon Warriors to an 84-0 victory.

Everyone was applauding, except for one. He stood in the back against the wall, slinging back his third beer and glaring at CJ. The girl next to him put her arm around his shoulders asking if there was something wrong. He gently pushed her away and walked towards the cooler to extract another beer.

It was only seven thirty, and already most of his classmates were either drunk, or high, or both. Sweaty teens coiled tightly together, were slow dancing to The Young Rascals "How Can I Be Sure."

Warren's house was packed, and couples lined the stairs, making out. Beer bottles decorated every available surface. The stereo blasting the latest tunes was deafening, and haze from cigarettes and weed hung in the air like a heavy fog. Strings of colorful lights hung across the living room, illuminating the furniture like a kaleidoscope, turning slowly when viewed. Popcorn and chip fragments were ground into the carpet and crunched with each footstep. The song changed from slow to pandemonium with psychedelic rock from Jimi Hendrix, and dancers jumping chaotically to the music. The smell of spilled beer, a cloying mix of hair products, cigarette smoke, sweat, and strong aftershave permeated the room.

CJ went to the rec room and watched a couple of his teammates trying to get the perfect shot while avoiding the eight ball. Picking up a disposable bowl of pretzels, CJ made his way back towards the front entrance. His friend Dwight, whom he had arrived with was nowhere in sight. He looked around, wishing Sherry was there with him.

The previous week, they'd had an argument after Jaimie passed by him and pinched his backside. He had been waiting for Sherry to drive her home after football practice, and she had just come around the corner of the locker room. CJ baffled by the incident just laughed it off, but Sherry didn't find it funny at all. She was furious and wondered why the school slut was touching her boyfriend inappropriately.

Deciding he'd had enough, CJ searched for Dwight, but couldn't find him anywhere and assumed that his friend, who was on a mission to confess his feelings, had caught up with Emily.

Throwing the empty bowl into the trash bin CJ decided to walk home. A party without Sherry was no party after all. Just as he was exiting the front door, someone yanked him back in, and he turned around. Readying himself to fight off a drunken fool, instead he found Warren standing in the doorway.

"Hey CJ, where are you off to? You're not leaving this early, are you? It's barely eight o'clock. You haven't even had anything to drink."

CJ looked at his teammate and nodded. "Yeah, Sherry couldn't make it and I'm lost without her. I gonna call it an early night."

Warren wasn't listening; instead, he turned CJ around and led him back into the house and towards the kitchen; then reached in the refrigerator for a beer bottle, snapped off the top, and handed it to CJ. "Stop being such a certified candyass and have some fun."

"Drink up, buddy; the party's just starting." He patted him on the back. "Come on; let's go upstairs and where it's quieter."

Reluctantly, CJ climbed the stairs behind Warren, who led him into a bedroom. Another guy he didn't recognize was waiting for Warren to continue playing Battleship. Warren introduced him as Lenny. Jaimie walked in carrying the board game Clue and was adamant they should all play that instead.

CJ sat on the bed, took a swig of his beer, and watched them play. He had almost finished the beer, when Warren took the half-empty bottle from his hand.

"Hey Jaimie, pass CJ another beer."

Jaimie quickly got up and walked to the corner of the room, opened the cooler, and pulled out a bottle of beer. She popped open the top and handed it to Warren.

"Drink up buddy. The night is young." He slapped him on the back.

CJ drank some and noticed it had a slightly bitter taste, but Warren wouldn't let up, calling him a wuss, and CJ drank some more.

CJ's eyes were getting heavy, and he tried standing up, but fell back onto the bed. He tried calling out, but didn't have the energy, and fell into a deep sleep.

Dwight had been in a corner of the patio deck making out with Emily, and he was eagerly awaiting her return from a bathroom break. He'd just seen her rushing towards him, and thinking she was just as eager to return to their earlier session, stood up to meet her halfway. But something was wrong; she was frantically mumbling something incomprehensible and gesticulating towards the rooftop. He ran towards her.

Dwight became concerned with what she'd told him and ran into the house, taking the stairs two at a time. He found CJ lying on a bed in one of the bedrooms.

Emily stood behind Dwight, biting her fingernails, and nervously watched him try to rouse CJ, but he was so out of it that he would just drop back onto the bed like a rag doll.

Dwight kept shaking CJ until he was semi-awake, but CJ just promptly fell back asleep. He had never known CJ to over-drink, and he couldn't just leave him there in that state. He'd have to get help.

Dwight told Emily to go downstairs and quietly send up Henry and Mike so they could help get him downstairs and into his car. Just as she was about to go, Jaimie stuck her head in the door and asked if everything was okay.

Dwight shook his head. "He just had too much to drink. I'll get him home, and he'll be okay."

Jaimie nodded and shut the door.

Emily returned with the two boys, who helped CJ sit up, pull on his t-shirt and jeans, put his shoes back on, and maneuver him down the stairs, then outside, and into Dwight's car.

Emily got into the front seat, and Mike and Henry, pushed CJ into the back seat and then sat on opposite sides of him, holding him up like a pair of bookends.

Chapter 7
Dixie Cove Springs

Giselle felt a rumbling sensation in her belly, and hugged her midsection. It was already past suppertime, and all she could think about was the food she'd stashed away earlier. She felt a surge of anger, imagining other children in their loving homes sitting down to a hot meal with their caring parents.

She'd been at her next-door neighbor's house—Miss Tisi, where she went almost every day. Miss Tisi ran a business making, painting, and dressing carved dolls that she sold to specialty toy stores and other arts and crafts stores too. Her sister Alee came over often to help with other crafts, and sometimes their other sister Meg helped too. Meg had once made Giselle a lovely Christmas mug with Santa Claus' face, which Giselle treasured so much that she continued using it after Christmastime.

Unfortunately, one day, her mother spotted it in her hand at breakfast, and asked her where she had gotten such an ugly mug. Giselle's pulse quickened and her stomach felt queasy, knowing her mother detested Miss Tisi. Delores had told her that their stupid neighbor and her idiot sisters were busybodies and interfering old hags, and that Giselle was forbidden from going next door. She knew that was a lie, because her mother had never actually met Miss Tisi or her sisters; she would ignore them and refuse to acknowledge their presence if they happened to be outside when she was. It was probably because Delores suspected Miss Tisi was the one calling the police.

As soon as Giselle told her that Miss Meg, her neighbor's sister, had made the mug for her as a Christmas present, Delores opened her hand and let go of the mug. Giselle watched as Santa's face shattered on the ground and into a thousand glittering fragments.

Giselle stood stupefied, watching the pieces of her beautiful mug broken on the floor, and crunch beneath her bare feet. Tears had streamed down her cheeks, which maddened Delores, who reached out to slap her head. When Giselle flinched to avoid being hit, she was smacked in the ear instead. The ringing in her ear lasted for about an hour, it hurt badly and made her dizzy, which caused her to vomit. Delores told Giselle to clean up the mess she had made, and then she turned and left the kitchen.

The following morning, there was a bloody spot on her pillowcase, which she quickly washed out in the bathroom sink, but she was afraid to tell her mother in case she slapped her other ear. She could hear slightly muffled, but the pain was still there and her ear itched terribly.

Giselle was having trouble hearing from her left ear for two whole days. She was unable to understand what others were saying and was getting into trouble at school. Her teacher accused her of daydreaming and not paying attention to the lesson. Giselle hoped she wouldn't call her home and complain to her mother. But two days later, her hearing came back, so she considered herself lucky she could hear with both ears again.

Her neighbor, Miss Tisi, taught her how to make the most beautiful things. Giselle especially loved all the decorations Miss Tisi made for the holidays, and best of all, she got to keep everything she made. She considered them her treasures. Miss Tisi's sister, Alee, had made her a little toy chest to keep them in, and Giselle made sure to keep them hidden in the back of her closet.

The last time Mama had unexpectedly gone into her room and found her playing with the little carved dolls, she had grabbed them from her and chopped them into little pieces with the butcher knife on the kitchen cutting board.

Mama told her, "Those cheap toys could leave splinters in your fingers, which could get infected, and then your fingers will have to be amputated." Giselle had been very upset, but Miss Tisi had made her more to replace the ones Mama had ruined.

Miss Tisi taught her how to paint the little wooden dolls and even how to make the tiny clothing they wore. Best of all, she got to keep the little dolls, which were perfect for the dollhouse her sister Alee had made for her. The dollhouse was two stories high and intricately carved from wood; it was kept in Miss Tisi's shed for her to come and play with so that it wouldn't be destroyed by her mother.

Night was beginning to fall, and she thanked Miss Tisi for having her over. Giselle would have preferred to stay there because the house felt like a real home should, full of laughter and hugs. She felt accepted and loved when she was with Miss Tisi and her sisters, but she didn't want them to feel obligated to feed her again. They had invited her to stay for supper, but she was too embarrassed to accept; she lied, telling them she was expected for dinner at home. But she saw the glances they exchanged with raised eyebrows.

As Giselle was reluctantly leaving, Miss Tisi put her arm around her thin shoulders.

"Well, dear, if you change your mind, my door is always open. And you can always ask for help."

Giselle nodded and ran off.

Hiding behind some bushes on the side of the house underneath her bedroom window, cautiously looked around, and seeing no one, she climbed up the tree, and then nimbly climbed through the open window. She quickly pulled out a paper bag from underneath the bed, and ate the second sandwich Miss Tisi had made for her that afternoon.

After an hour, a few cars arrived, the music was turned up high, and the party had begun.

Giselle looked out the window of her darkened room, and counted the cars parked out front: one, two, three, four, five, six…eight. She sighed. It would be another long night. She worried the neighbors would be upset about the noise and call the police again. Just as she was about to pull the curtain shut, a red truck drove up. A muscular man exited and walked up to the front door.

Sighing, Giselle ate her sandwich, and continued worrying about the noise and the police showing up. Turning away from the window, she picked up the new book she had checked out from the school library and opened to chapter four of The Boxcar Children reading by flashlight. Giselle wished her life would turn out the way the children's lives had; where a wealthy and kindly grandfather would offer her the safety of his home, and stop the craziness and terror she was forced to live whenever Daddy wasn't home, which was often.

Suddenly, the loudness stopped, and looking out the window, Giselle saw that the cars were starting to drive away, signaling that the party had finally ended. She gave a sigh of relief that the police had not come tonight. The small clock on the nightstand read half past midnight.

Peeking out her bedroom door, she tiptoed up the hall, quietly went downstairs, and was about to sneak into the kitchen for a drink of water when the kitchen door slowly opened. Panicked, she quickly ran through the hallway and up the stairs to her bedroom, and hid under the bed. Sometimes, Mama's friends returned after the party had ended, and found their way into her bedroom.

The approaching footsteps stealthily walked through the kitchen and into the hallway.

The man stood at the foot of the stairs. Hearing muffled sounds upstairs; he listened intently, and then climbed, counting each step, as if miscounting one would bring bad luck. He was a superstitious man.

He quietly opened the door. The room was empty; *Giselle was probably sent to a friend's house to be out of the way,* he thought with relief.

Giselle watched her door slowly open and saw a shadow illuminated on the floor from the light in the hallway, and held her breath. The shadowy figure closed the door, walked back up the hallway, and stood in front of the master bedroom. He heard only silence.

The man opened the door and stood silhouetted in the entryway. The room was enveloped in moonlight. There was a form underneath the sheets. He walked over to the bed, sat down next to the sleeping shape, and sighed. A long-forgotten emotion within him stirred; he had not been with her for two months, and remembering her soft skin, he slowly pulled down the sheet and saw her perfect nakedness. Desire rose as he gently ran his hand over her body. She stirred, turned over, pulled him down to her, and kissed him, her kisses becoming deeper, which he returned in earnest.

He heard water running in the bathroom and thought she must have left it running. Just let it run, he thought tiredly, and proceeded to undress.

After a few minutes, the shower was no longer running. Could he have imagined it? Maybe Giselle had returned after all.

Dammit, he thought, why is she using this bathroom? He was about to get dressed and check, but was stopped short.

Standing in the doorway was a man. Light flooded from behind him, outlining his nakedness, and casting a long shadow into the room.

At first, he was confused and thought a burglar had climbed through the bathroom window, but he couldn't imagine why he would be naked. He didn't immediately move, but slowly slid his arm over the side of the bed and reached underneath the mattress.

"Babe, where are the extra towels?"

He was dumbfounded. His mind couldn't grasp the reality of the situation, and he thought he must have misheard. Then reality shook his senses as he slipped out of bed, dropped to the floor, and crawled behind a chair.

He watched as the naked man shook his head, walked over to the bedside, and shook her. There was no response. He shook her again and repeated the same question. She slightly opened one sleepy eye, reached out to him, pulled him towards her, and attempted to kiss him. He stopped her and pushed her back onto the bed, disgusted at her drunkenness.

Threefold Dread 34

"Well, if you can't tell me where the towels are, maybe that little brat you're always complaining about knows where they are." He pulled the sheet from the bed, wrapped it around his midsection, and headed towards the door.

The man stood up, turned on the lamp behind the chair, and stared at the stranger.

The naked man stopped, frozen in place, and turned around.

"Who the hell are you?" He asked angrily, thinking Delores was playing games again

"I'm her husband; who the hell are you?"

With eyes narrowed, he spat back. "The hell you are. Everyone knows Delores' husband abandoned her and her brat months ago, and left her to fend for herself."

He raised the gun and pointed it at him. "I asked who you are!" Darius repeated, ignoring the comment.

The naked man nervously glanced around the room, trying to locate his pants, but didn't dare move.

"Look man, I don't want any trouble. This is all just a big misunderstanding."

"You're damned right it is." Darius growled.

"Delores told me she was divorced. I had no idea, man. Just let me grab my clothes and get the hell out of here."

The cold look reflected on Darius' face made him shudder. Darius tightened his grip around the handle of the cold, metallic gray revolver, then lowered the gun, grabbed the clothing on the chair, and tossed it at the man.

The naked man grabbed his pants and thrust himself into them. Delores was now fully awake and watching the scene in horror.

"Darius, what the hell are you doing?" She slurred and grabbed her head with both hands to stop the room from spinning.

"Be quiet, you drunken whore," he responded.

She was shocked. He had never spoken to her like that before.

"How dare you talk to me that way!" She got up and staggered towards him.

"I'll talk to you any damn way I please." Darius responded.

"Really? Because the man you once were would have kicked your ass all over this damn room for talking to me like that. He would also have beaten the crap out of a strange man in his bedroom. No backbone, you're just a spineless coward!" She yelled.

She advanced towards him with outstretched hands and raked her long, red fingernails down the sides of his face. He pushed her away from him, causing her to fall backward onto the bed.

"Phil!" she yelled. "Help me!"

"So, the naked man has a name." Darius mocked.

"What the hell are you doing at home anyway? You aren't supposed to be back until tomorrow." Delores stated. "This is my home, and I can come back any damn time I please."

"Oh, is that so?" She retorted. "Well, let me just tell you something, you impotent asshole."

"Impotent, huh, who do you think you just balled before lover boy returned from showering?"

She had no idea what he was saying. She'd just had sex with Phil, and then Darius appeared, angrily waving a gun.

Realization swept over Phil's face. After having sex with Delores, he had gone to shower. Then Darius returned and was having sex with his wife while he was still in the shower. The hammering in his chest made him break out in a sweat.

Darius noticed the shocked looks on both their faces. Phil couldn't believe she had lied to him, and he felt like hitting her.

All three stood staring at each other in silence, no one daring to move.

"Look, man, like I said before, I don't want any trouble. Just let me get out of here."

"No one's stopping you." Darius responded calmly.

"Both of you get the hell out of my room!" she yelled.

The throbbing in her skull ebbed and flowed like a cold tide.

"Where's our daughter?" Darius demanded.

"Staying at a friend's house. Did you think the brat was here while I was having some fun?" Retorted Delores.

Darius pressed his lips together tightly. "I want you both out now." He told them, resisting the urge to shoot her on the spot.

Phil didn't need to be told again. He ran from the room, tore down the stairs, and stumbled out the front door.

Delores faced Darius, haughtily placed her hands on her hips, and stared him down.

"I'm not going anywhere." She responded and sat on the bed, once more holding her head between her hands.

"Oh, yes, you are," Darius replied pointedly.

He picked up her scattered clothes, threw them at her, and told her to get dressed.

She refused and threw them back on the floor. Sat back down on the bed and crossed her arms.

Once again he picked up her clothing, and then grabbed her arm, and roughly pulled her down the stairs and pushed her out the front door. She stood naked on the porch. He threw the clothes at her and slammed the door. He grabbed her purse and car keys from the table and threw those out the front door too.

Delores stood there dumbfounded, but somehow managed to pull her clothes on after the third try. She opened the car door and sat inside, trying to think of where to go, but her throbbing head was making this decision very difficult. After a while, she started the car and drove up the street.

The slammed door and the silence alerted Giselle that the house was empty, but she waited a bit more before daring to exit her hiding place. Then, peeking out the door and seeing only the dimly lit hallway, she tentatively took a few steps, stopping every three to make sure not to encounter anyone, just in case.

Feeling extremely thirsty, Giselle ventured towards the kitchen for a much-needed drink. She opened the refrigerator and looked inside, seeing that the water pitcher was empty and hadn't been refilled as usual, grabbed he container of orange juice. She picked it up and shook it. Fortunately, it still had some in it. She gulped some down thirstily.

A movement from the table startled her, and she dropped the juice that quickly spilled all over the floor. Giselle froze, expecting Mama to be there, and braced herself for the violence that would ensue. But Mama wasn't there; it was someone else.

"Daddy!" She shouted and ran to him and into his open arms.

They hugged each other tightly, and Giselle, seeing tears streaming down his cheeks, started crying too. She noticed something on the table, and remembered where she had seen it earlier.

"It's alright, little one; don't worry about anything; Daddy's here now." He picked up the worried and upset child and sat her on his knee. After a few moments, he managed to compose himself, wipe his face, and then Giselle's cheeks.

"It's late; let's get you into bed."

She looked down at the mess the juice had made, and went to get paper towels to clean it up, but her father stopped her.

"Don't worry about that I'll take care of it. Let's get you upstairs and tucked into bed."

After giving her another hug, he held out his hand. Giselle held his big, warm hand, and felt safe for the first time in her own home that day. Suddenly, the front door slammed. He looked at the worried child.

"Stay here quietly until I come back for you." He whispered.

She nodded. "Yes, daddy, I will." She whispered back.

She watched as her father slowly pushed open the door and went to investigate. Giselle listened as his footsteps faded up the hallway. Soon there were raised voices, things crashing against the walls, and Mama screaming horrible things at Daddy.

Giselle knew she was supposed to stay in the kitchen until Daddy came back, but she wanted to see what was happening. With fear and trepidation, she tiptoed into the hallway, Giselle could hear the sound of blood pumping in her ears, and hoped no one else could.

"What are you doing?" Put that down! No stop!" Darius yelled.

The loud sounds from before could no longer be heard; it was a sound she couldn't identify. As she got closer, it sounded like low moaning.

Peeking around the corner, Giselle was met by a horrifying scene. Quickly, she began running back towards the kitchen to get to the neighbor's house for help. She had just turned the doorknob and was about to run outside when someone grabbed a handful of her hair, yanked her backwards, and slammed the door shut.

Then the beating began.

Delores began hitting Giselle until she was backed against the table. Eyes widening in alarm, she watched as Mama, with a crazed look, grabbed a knife from the counter, advanced towards the stunned child, and began slashing at her. Giselle held her hands in front of her to ward off the knife, and her arms were slashed. She grabbed a chair to put some distance between them and managed to push so hard that Mama stumbled and dropped the knife.

Giselle attempted to run out the door again, but Delores grabbed her arm, pulled her back into the kitchen, and slammed her face onto the table. There was a cracking sound, and Giselle found she couldn't breathe as she watched blood dying the white tablecloth a vivid red. She helplessly stood there stunned from the pain and injuries.

Delores was frantically looking for the knife. She finally located it, grabbed it, and raised the knife to stab her daughter. As soon as she took a step, she slipped on the liquid on the floor and fell back into the sink. She recovered quickly, and still holding onto the knife once more advanced towards Giselle cowering at the kitchen table.

Then Giselle remembered what Daddy had left on the table. It was next to her right hand. She grabbed the gun and pointed it at Mama.

Cruel laughter filled the room.

"Are going to shoot me? You don't even know how to use a gun, you stupid brat!"

Delores advanced towards the trembling child and slashed at her, cutting her forearm, where blood began gushing out. The terrified child pulled the trigger and horrified watched as Mama kept advancing with the knife raised without even noticing she'd been shot.

The sound terrified Giselle; it reminded her of a firecracker, but much louder. Delores kept advancing towards Giselle, and plunged the knife into Giselle's thigh. Terrorized, Giselle pulled the trigger again. The gunshot echoed deafeningly in the confines of the kitchen as she saw Mama again slip on the spilled liquid, where she dropped the knife, stagger, and fall, while clutching her head.

Giselle's mind swirled with a million unconnected thoughts as the pain radiated throughout her body. She saw the vase that a few minutes ago held Marigold, Tansy, and Lady's Slippers on the floor smashed to pieces, the flowers splayed out. The blood quickly soaked into the petals, turning them crimson-red. She thought she smelled pennies but didn't see any on the floor.

Giselle tried to focus on the meanings of the flowers from a book she had read at Miss Tisi's house. Marigolds meant cruelty, grief, and jealousy; tansies meant hostile thoughts and declaring war. What did Lady's Slipper Orchids mean? She tried hard to remember the meaning of the most beautiful of the bunch, but had trouble focusing.

She felt her eyes getting heavier and thought she was just tired, and that she should be in bed because it was so late.

As she struggled to remain standing, her breaths shallow, she remembered the meaning behind Lady's Slipper Orchids. They meant capricious beauty, but she couldn't remember what capricious meant; she'd have to ask Miss Tisi the next time she saw her. Then she lost consciousness and fell to the floor in a heap, next to her mother.

Chapter 8
Ruby

Ruby sat alone in the waiting room by the emergency room door. She got up often and paced back and forth.

Her mother was barely breathing when the paramedics arrived, but they had managed to stabilize her, and now she was in surgery.

The nurse let Ruby make a call from the nurse's station, but was unsuccessful in locating her father. Then she called her grandparents, and they were on their way, but because they lived in Miami, it would take them a while to get there.

A few nurses were taking turns looking after Ruby. They had gotten her juice and some crackers, but she couldn't eat anything. She could still feel the muffin she had eaten earlier, sitting in her stomach like a heavy stone.

She was frightened about her mother's condition, and the scene where she discovered her stabbed in bed kept replaying in her mind. She berated herself for not finding her sooner. She should have known that something wasn't right.

If Mom dies, it's my fault. She started crying again, and one of the younger nurses named Penny, the one who let her use the telephone and gave her the juice and crackers, rushed over. She put her arm around her shoulders and let Ruby weep on her shoulder.

"There there now, don't you worry, your mother's in good hands. The surgeon operating on her is a top specialist. It's lucky he happened to be here, since he was checking on a patient. He'll let you know as soon as the surgery is over."

Penny handed Ruby a small packet of tissues and excused herself. "Just let me know if you need anything." She told Ruby and went back to work.

Ruby heard sirens in the distance that got closer as they neared the hospital. She looked up when the double doors swung open, and three stretchers were wheeled inside.

A nurse ran towards them. "What do we have here?"

The first paramedic rapidly told her male patient, 32, with multiple stab wounds.

The second paramedic informed another nurse, female, 25, two gunshot wounds, one to the lower abdomen and the other left side of the head.

Threefold Dread 40

The third paramedic told the nurse, female, 11, deep stab wound right leg upper thigh and right forearm; multiple slashes on both arms.

Ruby watched open-mouthed as the gurneys were wheeled into the treatment room. The third stretcher carried her friend Giselle.

One of the nurses called "Level One and Two," and they were all wheeled in a straight line through the double doors.

Ruby didn't know what 'Level Two' meant, as 'Level One' had been called out when her mother Kassie had been wheeled in earlier, and the nurse had explained that it meant 'Immediate: life threatening.'

Ruby rushed up to Penny, "what does 'Level Two' mean?"

"It means the condition could become life threatening!" The nurse informed her.

"That was my friend from school; is she going to be alright?"

Penny looked through some papers, frowned, and then looked at Ruby. "Let's wait and see shall we. She just got here and is being attended to; let's just hope for the best."

As Ruby turned around, she saw her grandparents walking in through the doors, and ran to them, and they embraced her.

"Any news yet?" Her grandmother asked anxiously.

Ruby shook her head and began to cry. Her grandmother led her to the chairs, gently pushed her into one, and sat next to her. She put an arm around her shoulders and tried to calm her down. Her grandfather walked over to the nurse's station to ask if there were any updates.

"It's all my fault, grandma. I should have checked her room sooner." She told her between sobs.

"Ruby darling, you know that's not true. How could you possibly have known something was wrong?"

"Where's your father?" asked grandpa gruffly.

Ruby shook her head. "I don't know. I called him at work and was told he was out of town on business."

Her grandparents looked at each other and shook their heads.

Ruby saw a doctor wearing surgical clothing walking towards them. The look on his face made her breakout in a sweat.

"I'm Doctor Healy. I am sorry to have to tell you, but…"

Ruby didn't hear the rest. She felt the blood rushing to her ears and then darkness surrounded her.

Chapter 9
Twin Pass Junction

Sherry held up her hand and admired her newly acquired jewelry; there was a tiny sapphire in the gold band and was engraved inside—Forever CJ+ST.

CJ had driven over before the game, placed it on her finger, and she'd immediately accepted.

She was ecstatic with the idea that CJ had given her a promise ring, which signified a promise to take the relationship seriously. She knew that it also symbolized hope for the relationship's future development, and that was something she had dreamed about since they'd begun dating.

Her parents were still with her grandmother; they had telephoned earlier and told her she was as well as could be expected at her age. The doctor explained that she would stay in the hospital, in traction for many weeks until the bone healed. She had fractured her tibia, and that surgery had gone well. She was in considerable pain, and the nurses were icing, elevating, and resting her leg to help to reduce inflammation.

Her mother told her they would drive back in the morning, and then return late afternoon to visit grandma. That Sherry should continue taking care of her sister until they returned.

Sherry wished for the third time that day that her grandmother hadn't fallen and injured herself, and causing her to be stuck at home with her five-year-old sister, and missing the party last night.

She wondered why she hadn't heard from CJ, and when she called his house, was told by his mother that he was feeling unwell, and still in bed.

CJ tried sitting up only to fall back onto his pillow. He was overcome with extreme drowsiness, felt nauseated, and had even vomited after using the bathroom earlier.

His father had questioned how much he had to drink the night before, but CJ could only remember having a couple of beers. Besides that, he couldn't remember anything beyond going upstairs to Warren's bedroom. He didn't even recall how he had gotten home from the party; he felt very confused. Maybe he'd had a bad beer and it had made him ill. He closed his eyes and fell into a deep and disturbed sleep.

He slept all of Saturday and well into Sunday. His worried parents checked on him often, and his mother made chicken broth with crackers and brought it up to him on a tray. She took his temperature, and satisfied he didn't have a fever, left him to eat his meal.

On Monday morning, CJ reluctantly got out of bed, dressed, and found he could barely eat the small amount of cereal in his bowl, and pushing it away left for school.

Outside the classroom, he felt a slap on the back. It was Dwight. "Hey buddy, how's it going?"

CJ turned to look at him, and Dwight noticed he looked unwell.

"I stopped by Saturday afternoon, and your dad gave me the third degree. He asked me how much you had been drinking. But I told him that you never had more than one or two beers, tops. He didn't seem to believe me, but didn't ask anything else. How much did you really have to drink? That's so unlike you Mr. Clean-cut."

CJ nodded. "That's just it Dwight, I never have more than two beers, it's a rule I've made for myself. Maybe I've caught a bug or something."

"Well you were really out of it man. Emily was freaking out about you trying to jump off the roof or something. She overheard Jaimie telling someone that you were on the roof. She must have heard wrong, but I still went to check, and found you splayed out in a bedroom with all your clothes off."

CJ's eyes widened. "What did you say?"

"I said…"

"Never mind, I heard what you said, but that can't be right. Why would my clothes be off?"

"You mean you don't remember taking off your clothes?"

"I don't remember anything after watching the game of Clue being set up in Warren's room"

"The other thing is that I couldn't rouse you. It looked like you were in some sort of stupor."

CJ was bewildered. "Since I only had two beers, I can assure you that I wasn't drunk!"

Just then, he heard Sherry call out his name and turned around to greet her.

"Hey you," she said. "How are you feeling?" When I called, your mother told me you were unwell."

"I was ill all weekend. I think I caught a bug, and I'm still extremely tired today. I have to tell coach I can't make practice. Wanna hang out after school?"

"I wish I could, but mom and dad are driving over to see my grandmother. She just had surgery and is hospitalized until further notice, and my sister and I are going with them, but I'll take a rain check!" Sherry responded disappointed.

"I think I'll go back home. I don't think I can sit through any classes today."

Sherry looked at his pale complexion, and wondered what had happened at Warren's party. CJ's lips and skin were pale, his flushed face and eyes appeared glassy. Maybe he was coming down with something.

"You should probably go home–you don't look well at all." Sherry told him while reaching out and feeling his forehead.

CJ nodded. "Yeah, I'm gonna to call my dad from the office, and see if he can pick me up."

"Do you have a doctor's appointment?" Sherry inquired.

CJ shook his head. "Nah, I'll be alright after I get more rest. I'll call you later."

"Take care of yourself." Sherry said to his retreating form.

After CJ walked away, Sherry looked for Emily, and found her by the lockers with Dwight.

"You two, follow me. I want details!"

Dwight and Emily looked at each other apprehensively, and obediently followed Sherry to the bleachers.

Chapter 10
Dixie Cove Springs

Elizeus Bishop slowed his steps as he neared the front door. The lead detective, who had requested him, was waiting for him behind the crime scene tape.

"Hurry up rookie quit dragging your feet."

Zeus couldn't believe that only after sixteen weeks in the police academy, and followed by six weeks of training, he was with the senior officer at a crime scene.

The academy class work covered about three hours each of college-level criminal law and criminal evidence. He spent many hours on the range, but essentially had little physical training, and only a couple of hours of very basic defensive tactics training.

This day could not have been worse; Zeus had unwillingly been forced to attend his first crime scene and didn't feel prepared. Feeling queasy and wishing there had been a heads-up before having a big breakfast, he quickened his pace, and followed the detective inside.

"Listen rookie, forget textbook crime scenes, and just tell me what you see."

Detective Jenkins filled him in on everything discovered prior to his arrival. Zeus reluctantly followed him up the stairs.

The detective stood by the bed and looked at the blood pattern on the quilt. He stared at the small-carved doll with a tiny knife protruding from the stomach and red paint all around it.

"What do you make of this object?" He asked Zeus.

Zeus looked at the doll intently. "Well, the doll depicts the crime scene, but I don't understand its relevance; maybe it's the attacker's calling card."

"Or maybe it's a distraction because the culprit wants to throw the investigators off. Either way, it was left here deliberately for us to find." Detective Jenkins replied.

Zeus nodded and walked over to the window.

"Checking the draperies for some fashion tips, rookie?" The forensics officer dusting for fingerprints goaded him.

"Hey chief, maybe she stabbed herself for attention. I mean, she was just laying there, arms folded over her chest as if she had laid down for a nap."

"It's lying, not laying, you dimwit. She isn't a chicken." Detective Jenkins corrected him.

The detective walked over to Zeus. "Did you find anything?"

Zeus took a pen from his pocket, lifted the edge of the curtain, and pointed down.

The detective squatted beside him and nodded.

"Hey, funny boy, stop dusting for a moment and get one of the other clowns up here pronto."

The detective handed one of his gloves to Zeus, which he used to pick up a small object. It was a gold-colored bobby pin. There were footprints imbedded in the plush carpet—small, narrow ones.

Zeus then followed the detective downstairs to search for anything that may have been missed by the other officers.

Zeus noticed the kitchen was pristine. He could detect the smell of scrambled eggs with black pepper; the musty smell of old Florida houses lingering in the air.

Everything was in place, one dish and one glass had been washed and left drying on the dish rack. Even the towel was neatly folded in half and hung over the oven handle.

The counter-tops were clean and there wasn't a crumb anywhere; it seemed that someone had baked earlier. There was a pot of something burnt that resembled beef stew, but that was the only thing out of order in the kitchen.

"I wonder what she had to talk to her daughter about that sounded so serious."

"That's a good question," Detective Jenkins responded. "We'll have to get permission from the grandparents to ask."

"What's the status on the husband? Has he been found yet?" Zeus inquired.

"Not yet, we're still trying to locate him."

Detective Jenkins watched as Zeus used his gloved hand to open the back door and carefully look around before descending the stairs. He followed him out.

Zeus looked around at the carefully tended vegetable patch and carefully arranged flowerbeds.

"What is it she does for a living?"

Detective Jenkins gave him a sad look. "She's a tarot reader—a popular one. She's also a psychic who has helped the department solve impossible cases."

Zeus nodded, then walked to the far corner of the pathway leading away from the front entrance and squatted.

"Detective, take a look."

Detective Jenkins squatted next to Zeus, who had parted a clump of low bushes and underneath was another set of footprints embedded in the moist dirt.

Detective Jenkins walked up to the back door and yelled, "Mack, get out here now!"

After leaving Mack to make a plaster cast of the footprints, he and Zeus reentered the house.

Zeus asked, "Where did she do her readings?"

"Follow me."

Detective Jenkins walked towards the front of the house and opened a door with a sign that still read, "Reading in Session."

"That's curious," Zeus commented as he lifted it to look on the opposite side. "The sign was never flipped over. I wonder if this was an oversight, or was she chased through the house by her attacker. Possibly someone she read for on that day."

Detective Jenkins shrugged and shook his head.

Another cop ran up to them. "Detective Jenkins, we just received a call; there's been another incident six blocks away."

Detective Jenkins sighed deeply. "Let's wrap it up here for now. Leave an officer outside, and make sure no one enters. Zeus follow me."

Upon arriving at the new location, the officer waiting for the detective at the front door informed him of everything they had found so far.

"The family of three that live here—man, woman, and child— suffered gunshot wounds and stabbings."

Detective Jenkins looked at him. "Do we know if there was an intruder?"

"We're not sure yet, we just got here a few minutes before you did, and we're still going through the rooms."

"Very well, get some gloves and booties to Bishop; he's now on the investigation team."

The first responder nodded, walked over to the patrol car, pulled out a pair of gloves and booties, and handed them to Zeus.

"Good luck, rookie."

"Thanks Henry. I'll need it."

Zeus walked into the hallway and looked around. He chose the living room to investigate first.

The first thing he noticed was that there had been a large gathering or party. There were half-filled wine glasses and half-drunk cocktails on every available surface; the ashtrays were filled to the brim. Every inch of the dining room table was laden with trays of party food; used napkins, plates, and silverware were strewn about. The portable bar in the corner was fully stocked with a couple of bottles smashed on the floor.

The iced cake in the centerpiece was still intact, but the means to cut the cake was not on the table. Zeus searched and finally located it. The serrated cake-knife was lying on the carpet, covered in blood. The photographer was just walking in, and Zeus motioned him over.

"Hey rookie, what are you doing in here? Shouldn't you be giving out parking tickets or something?"

"And shouldn't you mind your own damn business and only photographing evidence?" Detective Jenkins retorted.

"Sorry detective, I just thought the rookie was lost or something."

"The rookie is with me."

"Dunn, get in here."

"Yes, sir, right away."

"Tell me everything you know.

Detective Jenkins motioned to Zeus.

Dunn filled them in on what they had discovered so far; Zeus listened and took notes.

"I'll check upstairs, and you check downstairs. Then we'll meet and exchange notes."

With that said, Detective Jenkins turned and walked up the stairs.

Zeus walked over to the Sylvania Record Player and looked inside. The record was still spinning, and the title read, "I Think We're Alone Now" by Tommy James & The Shondells. He half smiled to himself. *Yeah, that's probably what she was thinking.*

The husband was stabbed here with the cake knife, but by whom. Zeus wondered.

He made his way to the kitchen and saw the disarray. Overturned chairs, a table pushed towards the wall, a butcher's knife covered in blood lying on the floor, and a snub-nose revolver on the table. He noticed a bloody handprint on the door, a small one—*the child's*; it was too small to belong to an adult, and the floor was sticky with an orangey substance.

He opened the cabinets and the refrigerator, which were curiously empty given the plethora of food in the living room.

Zeus called the photographer over, and after the photos were taken, Zeus picked up the revolver and opened the chamber. Two bullets were missing, which fit in with the report of two shots fired. *But who shot the mother? Was it the husband or the child? Did the child stab the father, or was it the mother? Then which one stabbed the child? Mother and daughter were found together; was she trying to protect her daughter from the father? And if so, then why was he in the living room and the gun in the kitchen? Did she take it from him?*

Detective Jenkins entered the kitchen. "What a mess. What have you got for me?"

Zeus glanced at his notes and told Detective Jenkins exactly what he had found.

The detective nodded. "You're wasted as an ankle-jerk grunt; I'm going to put in a request to have you transferred."

"Thank you, sir. I think I'll do well, especially under your wing."

The detective nodded and said, "Follow me; the person that called this in is the neighbor," he studied his notes, "a Miss Tisi."

Detective Jenkins and Zeus walked outside, but before they reached the end of the driveway, Zeus stopped. The detective turned around and watched him. He could see Zeus's eyes darting back and forth, like someone at a tennis match.

Zeus mentally measured the distance between both houses, when he noticed the neighbor's kitchen window had a direct view of the kitchen door and wondered how much she had seen.

Detective Jenkins knocked on the front door as Zeus waited behind him.

The door was opened by a short and stout woman with a pleasant face, wearing a smock covered with paint and glitter. She reminded Zeus of a garden gnome in paint-spattered overalls.

"You must be the detectives; come in, come in." She opened the door wide. "I've just taken some cookies out of the oven and brewed a pot of tea. Would you like some?"

The detective looked at Zeus and nodded. "Sure, we'd like some."

"Have a seat." She motioned to the living room. "I'll be right back."

Tisi went into the kitchen and within moments returned with a tray laden with cups, plates, and napkins and placed it on the coffee table.

Zeus looked around the tidy living room and then at the dining room table, covered with art supplies from end-to-end.

Miss Tisi handed each a cup and told them to help themselves to cookies.

"I baked these Kourabiedes earlier–they're my favorites."

"Excuse me?" Detective Jenkins was just about to take a bite, but stopped, cookie held mid-air.

Tisi let out a guffaw. "They are Greek Butter Cookies, and an old family recipe passed down for many generations."

Zeus took a bite, while Jenkins waited for his reaction before eating his.

"Kourabiedes are a classic Greek cookie. Some call them wedding cookies, some call them Christmas cookies, but I just call them delicious! They're buttery, crumbly, and sweet, but not too sweet." Tisi informed him.

She pointed to the plate. "Don't be bashful–help yourselves."

They both nodded and placed more cookies on their plates.

"Thank you Miss Tisi; I was informed that you are quite good at arts and crafts, and that you specialize in miniature carvings that are sought after."

Tisi's face turned a bright shade of pink. "I dabble in many different things detective."

Detective Jenkins pulled out a plastic bag from his pocket and placed it on the coffee table.

"Is this one of yours?" He asked directly.

Tisi looked down at the bag and asked, "May I pick it up?"

He nodded. "Yes, of course."

Tisi gently picked it up and first looked at the front, then turned it over to observe the back.

Nodding, she placed it back on the table. "I believe so, but not the extra details."

"Which details do you mean?" Jenkins asked her.

"Well, Tisi responded, looking down at the object and wrinkling her nose, "I would never stick any sort of weapon in any of my carvings, and I certainly would never paint what I presume to be blood on my carvings either. This may be one of mine, but it certainly never left my studio that way!"

"Could you give me a list of your buyers?" Detective Jenkins asked her.

Tisi nodded and got up. "Yes, of course."

She walked towards the small table that held the telephone, opened a drawer, and pulled out a folder. She walked back over to the couch, sat down, and then pulled out the master sheet of all the vendors to whom she had sold carvings, dollhouse furniture and decorations, and handed it to Jenkins.

Detective Jenkins and Zeus read through the four sheets. Some were in town, others in different cities and states, and three were in another country.

Jenkins looked up at Tisi and asked, "May I keep these and have them photocopied?"

Tisi gave him a sly smile. "Of course, but only if you bring them back to me. They're the only copies I have."

"I'll make sure you get these back before the end of today. Detective Jenkins responded.

Tisi smiled and nodded. "Good."

As the detectives were headed out the door, a thought occurred to Zeus.

"Miss Tisi, have you ever carved any dolls for the little girl next door?"

Tisi nodded. "Yes, I have, but why do you ask?" She narrowed her eyes.

Before the men could answer, she interjected. "Fiddlesticks! If you think that darling child did this to the doll then you're sadly mistaken, I'd look elsewhere if I were you."

Zeus too narrowed his eyes and asked, "What do you mean?"

"Well," Tisi explained, "that poor little girl has been abused on a daily basis and living in fear of her mother. My door is always open to her; she is a polite, gentle, and loving child. There is no possible way that she would have done anything wrong; it's not in her nature. No, I suspect it is quite possible someone took one of the carved dolls I made for her and defiled it. Maybe someone wanted it to look like Elle did that to the doll, but I very much doubt it."

"Thank you Miss Tisi, your observation of her character helps. Here is my card, if you think of anything else, anything at all, just give me a call." Jenkins handed her his card, and he and Zeus walked back to the house next door.

Tisi stood at the front door, lost in thought, as she watched them walk away. Then she went back inside, locked the door, and made two phone calls.

Chapter 11
Twin Pass Junction

Sherry struggled to catch up to CJ, her long auburn hair whipping her face in the crosswinds. CJ had been acting strangely since the day he had given her the promise ring, he was avoiding her, and she wanted to know why. Maybe he had changed his mind about the promise he had made about to her about their plans for the future. Whatever the reason, she was determined to find out today.

After going into a full run, she managed to catch up to him and tapped him on the shoulder. He whirled around with a look on his face that reminded her of a small, startled animal sensing danger.

"Are you okay?" she asked him apprehensively.

He looked like he was about to cry and bit his lip to stop it from quivering. He hugged her and told her he'd always love her, no matter what happened.

Sherry pushed him away "What do you mean no matter what happens? What's going on CJ, talk to me! You've been distant for over a month, I feel like we're drifting apart. Have you changed your mind about the promise, because if that's it, then tell me, and you can have this ring back." She began pulling it off her finger, but he stopped her.

CJ looked at her sadly and said, "No, you don't understand that's not it at all; my feelings towards you have not changed; it's the circumstances that have."

"Then help me to understand, CJ. I've been going out of my mind with worry, and you've completely locked me out. What the hell is going on?"

"The night at Warren's party, something happened that I have no recollection of, but there have been…repercussions."

"What are you talking about? What happened?"

"That's just it; I have no idea what happened that night. I was so out of it that Dwight and the guys brought me back home, and I have no recollection of that happening either. Much less, what happened at the party? All I know is that the following morning I had a giant hangover."

Sherry was astounded. Her straight-and-narrow boyfriend was drunk at a party; she couldn't believe it. CJ never had more than one beer, two at the most—his rule.

"I thought you went with Dwight?"

"I did, but he finally admitted his feelings to Emily and they hung out. I didn't want to be a third wheel."

"What's the last thing you remember?"

"I wondered about aimlessly since you weren't with me." He said that with a sad smile.

"What else do you remember?" she smiled back glumly.

"I remember two of the guys playing pool, and then I decided to find Dwight so he could give me a lift back home, but I couldn't find him anywhere and decided to walk home. That's when Warren ran outside and made me feel guilty about leaving early. He went to the fridge and handed me another beer, and then told me to follow him upstairs, where it was quieter. So I followed him to one of the bedrooms, and the last thing I remember was a game board being set up."

Sherry looked at him, not knowing what to say. "I don't understand. What, you just passed out? Did you get injured on the field and maybe have a concussion?"

CJ shook his head. "No, I wasn't injured."

"Then what does it all mean? None of this makes any sense. Maybe you did have too many beers and got drunk."

"No Sherry that's just it; I didn't and I wasn't."

"Then maybe you ate something that was bad and it gave you a reaction. Did you go to the hospital and get checked out?"

Again, CJ shook his head. "No, my father was convinced I was hungover and that a doctor couldn't help me. So I just waited it out, but it took two entire days before I felt better."

"Why didn't you just tell me all of this and not ignore me for an entire month?"

CJ sighed deeply. "Because Sherry, it seems that something else happened that night that I can't remember."

Sherry nodded. "Go on tell me. Whatever it is I can handle it."

CJ looked so wretched and crestfallen Sherry felt sorry for him.

He looked down and in a low voice said, "I'm not so sure you can. I'm still processing it myself and can't comprehend how it could have happened without my knowing."

"What the hell happened, CJ? Spit it out already."

"I was confronted by Jaimie. She told me that I forced myself on her after the guys left the room."

"WHAT! I can't believe what I'm hearing. No way! I don't believe it."

"Neither did I. I thought Warren had put her up to this cruel practical joke, until Jaimie told me herself, and it turns out she's pregnant and carrying my baby."

"That lying slut!" Sherry said through clenched teeth. "I don't believe for one minute that you would do anything so heinous, and much less with the school tramp."

"So what happens next?" Sherry questioned.

CJ looked despondent and stared down at his shoes.

Sherry held his hand. "Tell me what else is going on."

"Warren confronted me and told me that if I didn't agree to marry Jaimie so she wouldn't become a social outcast, they would go to the sheriff and file a rape report."

"And you agreed to this? You must know this is a lie and that you're being set up."

"Do I, Sherry? When I can't even remember how I got home that night."

"What about your scholarship?"

"I'll have to forfeit that and work full time for my parent's company."

She couldn't believe what she was hearing.

"Your entire future has just been flushed down the toilet." *And my life's been turned upside down too.*

"I'm well aware Sherry, but what else can I do? I'm damned if I don't and damned if I do."

"For starters, you can demand that she give you proof of her pregnancy. And even if she gives you proof, anyone could have fathered that child."

"Don't you think I've questioned that already? I'm really in no position to demand anything. If I don't go through with this, I could end up in jail."

"Maybe that's the better option." Sherry retorted.

CJ shrugged and began to walk away.

"So that's it? We're officially over; it's like our relationship never even existed!" Sherry shouted at his retreating form.

CJ stopped, turned around, and walked back towards her. "What do you want me to say? I wish things were different."

"I want you to say that this is all a big mistake and that everything will be back to normal. That we'll be driving off together to college next month as planned, and that our future is still hopeful."

"Sherry," he held her hand, "I wish I could say that to you, but I can't. I have to do the right thing."

Threefold Dread 54

"Why don't we run away together? That way you won't have to go through with this farce." Sherry implored.

"And if I agree to do that, what happens when Jaimie and Warren file a report with the sheriff? Then I'll be a fugitive, and either get caught or have to turn myself in, and what about you? You'll be caught in a nightmare."

"I already am CJ. I already am!"

Someone tapped him on the shoulder and he flinched.

"Sorry to interrupt, but we have an appointment in exactly fifteen minutes, and need to get a move on or we'll be late."

CJ turned around to see Jaimie standing behind him, and his shoulders sagged.

Warren, who had quietly walked up behind Sherry startled her.

"Hi there Sherry! Still hanging out with this loser?" He said mockingly.

Sherry turned around abruptly and glared at him, barely concealing her irritation, and loathing.

"The only loser here is you! What the hell do you want, Warren?" Sherry replied unpleasantly.

"Whoa, what's with all the hostility?"

"I know you're somehow behind this frame-up Warren Bullard, and I'm going to get to the bottom of this. And as for you, you stupid slut, you know damn well CJ never touched you!"

Warren shrugged nonchalantly, and Jaimie hid behind CJ.

CJ gave Sherry a slight nod and walked away with Jaimie. Warren followed them, and put his arm around his shoulders. "You're doing the right thing, buddy."

CJ shook off Warren's arm. "Then why do I feel so lousy?"

"Probably because you can't control your animalistic nature." He responded, laughing."

CJ balled up his fists and sped up his pace to avoid punching Warren in the face. *Maybe Sherry's right, and there's more to this than I've been told.*

Sherry watched them walk away feeling a mixture of sadness, loathing, and anger. She wondered how she could discover the truth; because she didn't for one minute believe what Jaimie claimed happened with CJ the night of the party. There was no way her boyfriend was a rapist. She didn't know how, but was damned sure that Warren and Jaimie had concocted this plan together. But why would they do such a thing? She needed proof—quickly, but where to start?

Walking home after school, Sherry made a mental note to ask Emily who was at the party, and picked up the pace. She wanted to talk to the classmates who might help clear up what had really happened that night. *For starters, who was the older guy in the room, and why did Warren take CJ up there to hang out with just them three? Secondly, why was CJ up on the roof?*

Hearing a shout behind her, Sherry turned around to see Emily running up the block and waving for her to stop. She reached Sherry out of breath, and panting tried to get the words out.

"Did you hear?" Emily managed to say.

"Did I hear what?" Sherry responded.

"Give me a minute to catch my breath." Emily placed her hands on her knees and took deep breaths.

"CJ, Warren, and Jaimie were just at City Hall, and guess what they did there?"

Sherry crossed her arms and shook her head, but had a feeling she already knew.

"CJ and Jaimie applied for a marriage license. Can you believe it?" Emily told her incredulously. "What the hell is going on?"

Sherry looked forlorn, wiped tears away, and Emily hugged her.

"Sorry to be the bearer of bad news, but I thought you should know. Let's get you home, and I'll hang out with you for a while." Emily pulled a tissue from her purse and handed it to her friend.

Sherry sniffed and nodded, and they both walked in companionable silence the rest of the way.

Chapter 12
Dixie Cove Springs

Delores awoke feeling dazed and confused. A nurse came in to take her vitals, and then went to fetch the doctor. She looked at the vacant bed next to hers and was relieved to be alone.

Within moments, a middle-aged man wearing a white lab coat walked in.

"Hello, Mrs. Mackenzie, I'm Dr. Curtis; I performed your surgeries; how are you feeling?"

Delores looked at him bewildered. "Surgeries?"

"What do you remember from yesterday?" Doctor Curtis asked her.

Delores thought long before answering. "I remember an altercation between myself and my husband, and then he went ballistic."

He nodded. "I see. Well, you were lucky; one bullet that hit your neck barely missed your carotid artery, but the other bullet that hit you in the abdomen and caused extensive damage. Unfortunately, you will never be able to have children again."

She inwardly sighed with relief. She hoped her murderous-minded daughter would be sent to a psychiatric ward, given electroshock therapy, and stay there for the remainder of her life. She also hoped that Darius was dead. *The filthy bastard!* She hated him as much as she hated their daughter. *They could both die,* as far as she was concerned. Phil was also equally responsible for not standing up to Darius and defending her. Her desire for vengeance was growing by the minute.

Delores feigned sadness, clutched the sheets, and bit her lip. "Oh no, I was hoping to have more children in the future."

The doctor shook his head. "I'm sorry, but there's always adoption if that's an option for you."

He wondered why she hadn't asked if her husband and child were okay, so he didn't bring it up. The husband's wound wasn't fatal, but he was incapacitated. As for the daughter, she would recover from the wounds, but he wondered if her mind would be intact afterwards. He didn't like this woman at all and was anxious to leave the room as quickly as possible.

"The police asked to be given notice of when they could question you. I'll tell them to wait until tomorrow, when you're fully awake." Doctor Curtis informed her.

Good, she thought. *That will give me enough time to concoct a story to bury both my rotten husband and my idiot daughter.*

Delores slept on and off the rest of the day. When she awoke later that afternoon and was about to call the nurse to bring her pain medication, she looked over and saw a woman in the next bed.

Dammit, she thought, *why does she have to be there?*

She was a very pretty brunette, much younger than she was, and lying back watching a soap opera.

Feeling Delores watching her she asked. "So what are 'you' in for?"

"Two gunshots from a loving family member. You?"

The other woman chuckled. "Yeah, me too. What are the odds?"

"I wonder how long before I'm discharged." Delores wondered aloud.

"Well afterwards you'll be sent to rehab to recuperate from your wounds. The place is full of recovering druggies, and alcoholics."

Delores squinted, wondering if she somehow knew about her drinking, and was making fun of her. She hoped not. For her sake.

"So where were you shot?" Delores asked.

"Two shots. One in the abdomen, and another grazed my neck barely missing the carotid artery."

Delores couldn't believe it. She was taunting her. "Really, I don't see anything."

The woman half sat up using her elbows, and turned her head to reveal the bandaged area, then lifted her hospital gown and showed her the bandaged wound.

"I just thought that somehow you knew about mine, and were making fun of me." Delores told her.

"Nah, I don't care either way. I just want to recuperate and get the hell out of here. I don't have time to play games with a total stranger."

She turned towards the wall and ignored Delores.

"Don't be so touchy, I just don't trust anyone after what I've been through. I mean how would you feel if your family tried to murder you?"

The woman turned back towards Delores with a wicked grin. "Makes sense, my name's Jaimie, and you're right not to trust anyone–I did, and look where it got me–shot and almost killed."

"I'm Delores, and I agree with you. I trusted my family and they turned on me for no reason whatsoever."

"So what are your plans after rehab?" Asked Delores.

"I plan to get even with the bastard that set me up." Jaime responded.

"Sounds dangerous. You think you can manage it?" Delores questioned.

Threefold Dread 58

Jaimie laughed. "Oh yeah, I have a plan all hatched up. It's all I could think about in the ambulance. Soon as I'm discharged, I'll put it into action."

"What are 'your' plans afterwards?" Jaimie asked.

Delores scornful laughter needed no words.

Jaimie nodded and smiled. "That's what I thought. We'd make a good team."

The women talked for a long time. Both feeling that each understood what the other had been through, and how much they had in common.

Chapter 13
Twin Pass Junction

Sheriff Raymond Hayward paced in front of the jail cell where CJ was being held.

"Tell me once more what happened."

CJ raked his hands through his hair, as he explained for the tenth time what had occurred the previous night.

"I delivered a custom made living room set to a family in Key Biscayne, and because I had made good time on the road, decided to return home and not spend the night there since that saves money.

"I entered quietly through the front door not wanting to wake Jaimie since it was late. When I walked into the bedroom…" CJ looked at his feet, face beet-red.

"Go on son." The sheriff also looked embarrassed, as he had already heard what had occurred earlier, but wanted CJ to confirm it again.

"Well, Jaime was in bed alright, but she wasn't alone."

"Did you recognize the man she was with?" The sheriff wandered why CJ hadn't been forthcoming with this information earlier.

CJ looked at him. "It's a face I'll never forget."

"You've seen him before?" The sheriff narrowed his eyes.

"Yes, at Warren's party, the night we won the state championship."

"Is he a student at your school?"

CJ shook his head. "No, he's friends with Warren and Jaimie though."

"What makes you think so?" The sheriff was now very interested in this new piece of evidence.

"Well." CJ began, "The night of the party, Warren led me to an upstairs bedroom and introduced me to this guy who was with Jaimie. His name was Lenny."

The sheriff studied CJ, and remembered he had always been a courteous, polite, and an all-around nice young man. He helped his father make furniture and then delivered the pieces afterwards. CJ's father had been his friend since grade school, and he knew their household was a peaceful one, where CJ was taught manners and morals. He was sure the accusations from Jaimie were false, but he had no way of proving or disproving them without locating Lenny.

"Tell me what happened after you entered the bedroom."

"I turned on the bathroom light so I wouldn't wake Jaimie, and that's when I saw him. Saw them."

"What happened next?" Sheriff Hayward asked.

"I pulled him out of the bed and yelled at him to get out of my house. He sat up on the side of the bed, pulled his pants on, calmly walked to the chair, and grabbed his jacket. He reached into a pocket and pulled out a gun. So I lunged at him and he dropped the gun.
Then, Jaimie picked up the gun and pointed it at me, but I shifted and she shot Lenny instead. Lenny was angry, went after Jaimie, and punched her in the face. He grabbed the gun from her and pointed it at her, and I lunged at him again to stop him from shooting her. During the scuffle, the gun went off and Jaime was shot. I was trying to get the gun from Lenny, it went off a second time, and Jaimie was shot again. I was distracted by the second shot and Lenny hit my head with the gun. The shots alerted the neighbors, and Lenny ran off. That's the last thing I remember."

The sheriff shook his head. He knew CJ was telling him the truth, and he knew that Jaimie was not a good person.

"Jaimie's statement to the police about what happened differs from yours. She's saying that you arrived home angry that you had to travel and deliver furniture, and that you took it out on her, by hitting her and then shooting her. That had it not been for the neighbors, you would probably have killed her. She never mentioned another person being there."

CJ nodded. "I don't understand what's going on. I did everything she's asked of me, and now this. And I don't even own a gun."

The sheriff again narrowed his eyes. "I sense there's more to this story than what's occurred tonight?"

CJ nodded. "Yes, but…"

"CJ, I've known you since you were a boy. I've known your father even longer. Hell, he even punched Bruce Trent for bullying me in the third grade, and we've been friends ever since. Over the years, I've watched you grow into a considerate, honest, and helpful young man. I cannot believe for one minute that you are capable of committing the crimes you are being accused of, but I am duty bound to find out the truth before condemning anyone. I want to hear your side of what happened, and don't hold back anything. I want to help you, but for me to do that I first have to know everything you know. Start with the night of the party."

CJ began to explain everything he remembered from that awful night, which wasn't much.

Chapter 14
Dixie Cove Springs

On a stormy Wednesday morning, Delores arrived at Crescent Oaks Rehab. She had just been discharged from hospital, to recuperate from the surgeries, and to detox from alcoholism.

She had protested at first, denying she had a problem with alcohol, but after suffering with tremors, sweating, anxiety, on and off nausea, and insomnia and irritability, she understood the symptoms were more than just the aftereffects of surgery.

The doctor had explained that without the proper treatment for her alcoholism, she could also begin suffering hallucinations, mental confusion, and seizures. He also informed her that her liver was enlarged, and could cause life-threatening complications.

Delores had attributed the aches, pains, and fatigue, to an oncoming cold. She had been feeling hot and cold on and off with goosebumps and a runny nose, but she didn't develop a cold. After not having a drink for the weeks she was hospitalized, she was also agitated and angry.

Delores and her roommate Jaimie had both been discharged from the hospital on the same day, and on their way to same rehab.

As soon as they arrived, a nurse rushed over and told the transporters to wheel them to a waiting area, and the two women were left alone, with the nurse promising to return soon to get them sorted into their rooms.

A few minutes later, another woman was wheeled in and left with the other two. The woman with long, blonde hair and blue eyes looked annoyed.

"How long are we going to be kept waiting to get a room?" The woman asked annoyed.

Jaimie shook her head. "Who knows, these places are always total chaos. The last time I was here one patient attacked another over some medication."

Delores looked over at Jaimie. "You've been here before?"

Jaimie nodded. "Yeah, I needed treatment for a...different incident."

Delores shrugged and glanced over at the newcomer lying on the gurney next to her, and wondered what her story was. The woman turned her head towards her as if she had heard her thoughts, and glared at her then turned away. Delores didn't like this woman, and felt anger at being easily dismissed.

Jaimie looked at the newcomer. "So what are you in for?"

The woman turned towards her and winced, she bit her bottom lip over the pain shooting through her head. "I'm here because I was attacked by someone I hardly knew while working late one night." She pointed to her head and abdomen. "I suffered a concussion from a gunshot that grazed my head and another bullet embedded itself in my abdomen. If it weren't for a colleague showing up to pick up some paperwork, I'd probably be dead."

"You're lucky he showed up when he did! I hear ya. If it weren't for my neighbors, I'd probably be dead too. Why were you being followed around? Are you famous or something?" Jaimie inquired.

The woman laughed and shook her head. "Not famous, but one night I met this guy at a bar, and afterwards we went on a couple of dates, and he became obsessive. After I broke it off he began showing up everywhere I went, and I mean everywhere."

"That's creepy!" Jaimie responded. "You're not from around here are you?"

"No, I'm not, why do you ask?" The woman wondered.

Jaimie shook her head. "No reason, it's just your accent is different."

The woman smiled. "I'm Canadian.

Jaimie laughed. I've never met a Canadian before.

"My name is Jaimie by the way."

"I'm Kim."

They both looked at Delores who responded sarcastically. "I guess we'll all be great pals then. We have so much in common."

The woman rolled her eyes and turned towards Jaimie.

Jaimie smiled at her and shook her head. "You sure are a long way away from home." "This rehab was highly recommended, and I wanted to get out of the country for a while. Who knows, I might even make a new start here." Kim told Jaimie.

"What about your family? Can't you stay with them for a while, until you're fully recuperated?" Jaimie inquired.

Kim felt more alone than ever, sorrow shredded her insides. She remembered her fourteen-year-old self, working on a school essay and being interrupted by the doorbell. Peeking through the peephole and seeing a pair of Mountees standing there. She opened the door to devastation and the end of her normal world. She had to stop herself from curling into a fetal position, as she had been doing for many years whenever sadness overcame her.

She shook her head slowly. "I'm an only child and an orphan, so no parents or siblings. No other family that I know of."

"That's tough." Jaimie responded, and not knowing what else to say remained quiet. Kim planned to contact her college friend DD, who she hoped would be happy to hear from her. They hadn't seen each other in since college, but had stayed in touch. DD always the practical one could give her the good advice she needed. Kim had quite a bit of money saved up, which should help get her a fresh start in a new town. The last time she'd seen DD was when she'd married Gordon.

Kim thought bitterly that she should have made more of an effort to nurture her relationship with Erik. The four of them had been close friends, and went everywhere together on their free time. However, Erik was getting too serious, wanting to get married after graduation, but she had other plans.

She'd wanted to establish herself in the business world first, and marriage and children weren't on her mind…possibly later, much later. Maybe it was because the person she really had in mind for marriage was the handsome Gordon. She had flirted with Gordon before Eric and Deirdre joined their inner circle, but Gordon only had eyes for Deirdre—his precious DD, from the moment they'd met. Kim had only started dating Eric to try and get Gordon jealous, but that never happened.

After graduation, she established a real estate agency with Brennan whom she'd known since grade school. A few years later, she tracked down Eric, hoping for reconciliation, but he was happily married with two children. Depressed, this had led to drinking, which at first was just a couple of cocktails after work to calm the nerves, drinking late morning, and again at lunchtime. After rehab, Kim decided to start dating again, and in the path of a psycho, she'd gone on two dates with, and the one who had almost killed her.

She hoped DD would let her stay with her and Gordon when she was discharged. Together they would figure out what to do next. Maybe she could open a real estate agency in Florida. Kim thought that was a good idea and Brennan could run the office in Canada. For now, all she wanted was peace and quiet to recuperate, and afterwards, begin a new life.

After an hour of waiting, Delores was getting irritable, and about to call a nurse and ask what the hell was going on, but the fire alarm rang, and a commotion was heard in the hallway.

"It happens occasionally when one of the druggies goes haywire and sets off the alarm, hoping to get a fix of some sort during the distraction." Jaimie told them.

Threefold Dread 64

After a while, three nurses came in and removed the brakes to wheel the gurneys to their rooms.

"Don't worry about that. It was a false alarm." The nurse explained.

However, no sooner had the nurse told them not to worry, when the intercom called for all staff to attend to a code red.

"Sorry girls, but we seem to be having one emergency after another today. We'll be back as soon as this new one is handled."

After thirty minutes, one of the nurses returned and wheeled Jaimie's gurney out the door. Before they could return for the other two women, the fire alarm rang for the third time that day.

Jaimie was bored. Used to company at the hospital, she wondered if Delores and Kim had gotten situated yet. Cracking open the door to her room, and peeking out, she walked up the empty hallway towards the waiting area. Seeing no one around she slightly opened the door and peaked inside, then after a few moments, quietly closed it unseen. While walking back up the hall towards her room, two nurses entered the waiting room, and another code red was announced. More nurses ran through the doors of the waiting room. Amid the commotion, Jaimie leaned against the wall hoping to get a glimpse into the room and find out what was happening.

The nurse who had wheeled Jaimie to her room spotted her, walked over, and asked her why she was out of bed, and if she needed anything.

Jaimie shook her head. "I just wanted to know if my friend has a room yet."

"What's her name dear?"

"Delores. Delores Mackenzie." Jaimie told her.

"Let's get you back into bed shall we?"

Jaimie refused to budge, now alarmed. "Why, what's happened to her?"

The nurse pressed her lips together and shook her head. "Sorry dear there's been a complication; the staff is working to resuscitate her." That said, she turned Jaimie around by the shoulders, and led her back up the hall towards her room.

Chapter 15
Dixie Cove Springs

Giselle sat at Tisi's dining room table with her leg propped up on a cushioned chair, her bandaged arms on her lap. Tisi was taking care of her until her father returned from his flight. He aunt and uncle were out of town, and arrangements were being made for Giselle to stay with them when they returned.

This was the happiest Giselle had ever been. She was staying in an inviting home with a loving mother figure. She pretended that Miss Tisi was her fairy godmother who had rescued her from an evil stepmother.

Miss Tisi brought a bowl of homemade tomato soup with a grilled ham and cheese sandwich and set it in front of Giselle. She watched amusedly as the recuperating child hungrily dug in, and finished the meal quickly.

"There's no need to rush dear, there's more if you want some."

Giselle shook her head. "No thank you Miss Tisi that was delicious, but I'm stuffed."

"Too full for one of my freshly baked chocolate chip cookies, I made just for you?" Asked Tisi grinning.

Giselle's eyes opened wide. "Really, you made them just for me?"

"Uh huh, I certainly did."

Tisi went to the kitchen, brought out a plate of cookies and set them down on the table.

Giselle looked up at Miss Tisi. "May I?"

"Yes of course dear, help yourself."

"Giselle grabbed one and bit into the chewy, chocolaty cookie, feeling its warmth fill her insides.

"Thank you Miss Tisi for always being here for me." Tears welled up in her eyes, and she put the cookie down to avoid choking on it.

Tisi got up, sat next to her, and put an arm around her shoulders.

"I will always be here for you." Tisi felt tears well up in her eyes too, and used the handkerchief from her pocket to wipe them away.

"Now let's eat these cookies before they become salty."

Giselle half-smiled, nodded, and used the back of her hand to wipe away her tears.   Then picked up her cookie and finished it in two bites. She hoped she could stay with
Miss Tisi and never have to return to that house. She didn't like it there; she kept having nightmares from that horrible night.

There was a knock at the front door, and in entered Miss Tisi's sisters, Meg, and Alee.

They hugged Giselle and sat down to enjoy some cookies and tea.

"Do we have news for you Tisi." A delighted Meg exclaimed.

"Yes." Chimed in Alee. "Very good news."

"I'm at the edge of my seat, do tell!" A now excited Tisi responded.

"We've just returned from the development site of that new neighborhood we were considering, and the houses are already being built." Exclaimed Meg.

"Oh, the pamphlet you brought with you last week?" Asked Tisi.

"The very one." Responded Alee.

"We were shown the model house and it's just perfect for the three of us. The rooms are spacious—there are four of them: A big kitchen, attached garage, and an enormous backyard." Meg told her all excited.

"We can go tomorrow and put a down payment on the lot we have our eye on. How does that sound to you Tisi?"

The sound of quiet sobbing, made the sisters turn towards Giselle.

Tisi got up and rushed towards her. "What is it Giselle. Are you in pain?"

Giselle shook her head and gulped down a sob. She rubbed the heel of her palm against her chest. Meg and Alee were now alarmed too.

"Tell us what's wrong." Meg asked now alarmed.

Alee stood on the opposite side of her sister Tisi, and rubbed Giselle's back.

"I think I know what's wrong. Are you worried about Tisi moving away?" Alee asked.   Giselle gulped back another sob and shook her head vigorously.

"Oh dear child." Tisi spoke softly to Giselle. "Even if I moved to another house, I'd never really be far away; your father can drop you off anytime. And remember how Meg described the house—it has 'four' bedrooms, and the fourth one will be your room." Giselle nodded, at a loss for words and hugged Tisi.

The sisters looked at one another and smiled.

Ruby sat in the living room of her grandmother's house working on an essay. She went to the room where her mother was convalescing, and checked on her for the sixth time since she had gotten home from school. She knew she would never feel completely safe again, but since living at her grandparent's house after that terrible day, she had begun to feel somewhat relieved.

Giselle still wasn't back at school, and Ruby visited her at Miss Tisi's house after school. Her grandfather drove her to school every morning and picked her up from Miss Tisi's house in the afternoon. School was almost out, and the long drives would soon stop. She knew it was a burden on her grandpa, but he had insisted that she finish out the year at her school, rather than starting at a new one with only one month left. Her grandmother looked after her mother while Ruby was at school.

Ruby was glad that Giselle was being looked after, had three meals every day, and most of all was loved. She was glad her friend was away from her horrible mother, and that she was staying with Miss Tisi, whom she knew, would lovingly attend to her needs.

Her mother had known Tisi and her sisters for many years. Kassie had met Miss Tisi at the gardening center when her mother was planning her garden, and Tisi helped her pick out some plants and flowers, and then offered to help her place them.

Her mother opened her eyes as Ruby stood in the doorway watching her with a worried expression, and patted to the side of the bed.

"Ruby sweetie, I'm alright, please stop worrying." She smoothed back a stray lock of auburn hair so much like her own.

"Are you hungry? Do you want me to bring you something to eat?" Ruby asked her.

"You know what—I am hungry, and craving some of your grandmother's pot roast from last night."

Ruby gently hugged her mother. "I'll run downstairs and warm some up for you."

Kassie watched as Ruby rushed off to the kitchen. She felt lucky to have such a loving and attentive daughter, and knew by the worried looks she continuously got that it would take a long time for Ruby to feel safe again. Her frequent thoughts were how the deranged person had gotten inside her house, and why the person wanted to hurt her.

Kassie never saw her attacker. After getting out of the shower and getting dressed, she had bent down to retrieve a pair of shoes from the back of the closet, when someone had placed a pillowcase over her head, and then hit her several times with a heavy object. Afterwards, she was dragged her by her hair backwards over to the bed, and pushed onto it. All she remembered was the feeling of being punched multiple times in the stomach, a cold, burning sensation, and then the immense pain. She passed out afterwards, and then woke up in the hospital one month later.

Threefold Dread 68

The doctor had told her that she had been stabbed three times in the abdomen, and the knife had sliced her spleen and liver, but thankfully, her rib cage had stopped the knife from doing more damage. He'd performed emergency surgery to repair her punctured liver, and removed the spleen. She had lost quite a bit of blood, and was lucky her daughter had found her when she did, otherwise, she wouldn't be alive. The doctor explained she had been in a coma in the ICU for 4-weeks. The recovery process however, would be long and painful.

Shifting her position carefully, she instantly felt a sharp pain that made her gasp. Ruby who had just walked in, set down the tray, rushed over, and placed a second pillow behind Kassie's back, and gently helped her sit up.

The detective assigned to the case discovered she had been stabbed with a serrated knife. He told her that it seemed the crime wasn't premeditated, but a spur of the moment one. During the investigation, they found that one of her kitchen knives was missing from the set, that they had found it underneath some bushes outside her back door.

He'd asked her if she had any enemies, but she couldn't think of any. She did tell him that she had some clients that were unhappy with the outcome of their readings, but otherwise, couldn't think of anyone angry enough to do her harm.

Detective Jenkins asked her about her husband, whom they still couldn't locate. But she'd been adamant that he wasn't violent, a serial cheater, yes, but he'd never been aggressive or threatening towards her.

Ruby placed the tray with a bowl of pot roast on her mother's lap, then picked up the second bowl and sat down to eat. Noticing her mother's pained expression, Ruby knew she was in pain, but was pretending she wasn't. Looking at the notepad, Ruby noticed it was time for her mother's pain medication. She opened the bottle, shook a pill onto her palm, and handed it to her mother with a glass of water.

Kassie swallowed it and wished the effects were instantaneous.

"Thanks honey, remember, I'm still recuperating, and the doctor did say there will be pain for some time."

Ruby looked at her mother sadly and asked tentatively. "Mom, that day, did you have any inkling that something was wrong. I mean, you've been able help the police on countless cases, so wouldn't that also work for you?"

Kassie shook her head. "That's a question I've often asked myself. I did feel off that day, but just ignored it, thinking it was that whole business with your father."

Ruby nodded. "I think I know what you mean. Sometimes I get a feeling something's not right, but dismiss it like I did that day, and then everything goes wrong."

"Ruby, what have I told you? What happened wasn't your fault. How could you possibly have known? And if it weren't for your quick thinking, it would have been much worse."

Ruby held her mother's hand. "I know mom, but I still can't help thinking."

"No more of that talk. This delicious pot roast is going to get cold. Let's eat up." Kassie suggested.

They ate in silence, each gazing pensively out the window. However, Ruby's dark thoughts led her to make a promise to herself. *When I find out who did this to her I'll make them pay!*

Chapter 16
Twin Pass Junction

The young man slowly looked around; feeling unnerved as if he was being watched. Except for a neighbor walking his dog a block away, he didn't see anyone else. He eventually shrugged it off as paranoia. Or as his younger brother would often tell him, "you're a dork."

After inserting the key into the lock, and turning it counterclockwise, he felt the resistance. It had been sticking for a long time, and he remembered promising his dad he would lubricate the lock, but kept forgetting.

Applying pressure, he felt the key fully turn, and the click granted him entrance. He shut the door and dropped the key onto the foyer table. Then headed straight towards the kitchen, very hungry after the rigorous practice session coach had put the team through.

He pulled out a loaf of sliced bread, ham, cheese, lettuce, tomatoes, onions, and yellow mustard. Then he stacked the layers together, and pulled out a carton of orange juice.

He sat down to eat his sandwich and thought about his earlier altercation with Warren in the locker room.

Warren had been peddling enhancement drugs to the other players, and he wanted no part of that scenario. Warren had tried to coax him into buying some from him, and after that didn't work, he tried guilting him by saying, "if we lose because you choke, it's on you buddy. Remember how you scored points during the semifinals, but in the final you completely choked, and because of you we couldn't advance to the playoffs last year."

Warren was unbelievable, bringing up last year's game, which wasn't his fault. The opposing team's running back had tripped him on purpose.

He would stand his ground–absolutely no drugs would pass his lips. He'd tried to talk to coach, but he was busy and waved him away; he would try again tomorrow.

After washing up and returning the carton to the refrigerator, he went upstairs to start on his homework.

Stretching, he looked at the clock on his night table and saw it was getting late. He got up from his desk, and stretched again. Looking through the blinds, he noticed it was getting dark out. He grabbed fresh clothing and headed for the bathroom.

After showering, he went back to his room and turned on the radio. Out of the corner of his eye, he thought he saw a shadow outside. He parted the blinds and looked around, just then a cat jumped up on the window ledge, and his breath caught. He laughed aloud that a stray cat had caused such dread. "I really am a dork!" He said aloud.

He had the house all to himself for two entire days; he smiled thinking of all the peace and quiet he would get. It was Friday night and his annoying little brother was on a camping trip with his friend and family, and his parents were out of town until Sunday. The guys in the football team were teasing him that he should throw a raucous party in honor of his sudden solitude, but he declined. He just wasn't the type to enjoy loud parties, much less throw one, and especially because this would be letting his parents down and losing their trust. He was planning on having an early dinner and settling down in front of the television to watch episode six of Star Trek, the title according to TV Guide was 'The Doomsday Machine.'

His father had gotten him, hooked on science fiction, and he couldn't get enough of the subject, watching shows and reading about it.

After pulling the TV Dinner from the oven, he peeled back the foil and inhaled the enticing smells of fried chicken, whipped mashed potatoes with creamy butter, mixed vegetables, and the desert section held apple and peach slices. He poured himself a glass of juice, opened up a tray, and placed in front of the sofa. Then he settled down to enjoy his food and favorite show.

At 9:30 PM, he turned off the television set, and threw the aluminum tray into the trash bin; he washed the glass and fork, and placed them on the side.

He yawned and stretched, then turned off the downstairs lights, and went upstairs.

He planned to read a chapter from his father's copy of A Sound of Thunder by Ray Bradbury. Pillows propped behind his head, he began reading, and before long, he nodded off.

He awoke hours later, with a stiff neck and rearranged the pillows for a more comfortable sleep. While reaching out to turn off the lamp on the night table, a movement across the room caught his attention.

"Hey buddy. Did you have a good snooze?" Came the taunting question from the shadows across the room.

"Shit Warren what the hell are you doing in my room?"

Warren smiled widely. "I've come to make you an offer."

He was stupefied, *what the hell is he talking about and how did he get into the house?*

"About our chat earlier." Warren stated and cocked his head to the side.

"If you're here to try and convince me to take those damn pills you can get out right now, because the answer is still no!"

Warren chuckled. "No Mike, I haven't come to convince you of anything. I see you've already made up your mind. I've actually come to warn you before you do something stupid that you'll later regret."

"Warn me about what?"

"If you decide to squeal on me to coach or anyone else. I just want you to know that I happen to know where your little brother is camping for the weekend. These woods are full of dangers beyond your imagination. People can get spooked in the dark and think that a person is a bear, a mountain lion, or some other predatory animal ready to pounce and attack them. They usually react badly and shoot without a second thought. Afterwards, people will lament over a tragedy that could have been avoided had acted carefully."

Mike stared at Warren open-mouthed and speechless.

"Shut your mouth buddy or you'll swallow a fly. Warren teased him.

Mike shut his mouth and gathered his thoughts. "So you broke into my house to threaten to kill my little brother if I tell anyone what you're doing."

Warren laughed under his breath. "That's precisely what I'm doing. So what's it gonna be?"

"If you touch one hair on my brother's head, the wild beasts in the forest won't be the only hunters."

Warren laughed aloud. "No, seriously, am I supposed to be frightened by your empty threats. Just promise to keep your mouth shut and all will remain as is. Now say it." The last words were said through slanted eyes, gritted teeth, and malice.

Mike nodded. "I promise to keep my mouth shut."

"Good, we're all done here then. Oh and Mike, you should fix that faulty lock, anyone could get in and kill you while you sleep."

With the last threat, Warren turned around and walked out the door. Mike quickly got up and followed him downstairs, and waited until Warren walked out the front door.

Mike quickly locked the door, then grabbed a kitchen chair, and shoved it under the doorknob. Then he checked the lock on the back door and shoved another chair underneath that doorknob. He checked all the windows, opened, and relocked them.

Satisfied all windows and doors were safely locked, he made a mental note to call a locksmith tomorrow. He would pay for a new lock for the front door, and have the locksmith add deadbolts to both doors as an extra safety measure. He also wanted extra security placed on the windows. He had enough money saved up from his part time after school job at the hardware store, and besides he'd get a discount on parts.

He decided he needed extra protection before going back to sleep. Switching on the light in the hall closet, he reached for the latch and opened the attic door. Then he climbed up, reached into the rafters, and pulled down a locked box. His father had shown him where the key for the box was hidden, and reached up into a small opening between the boards, and found it. Unlocking the box, he picked up the gun and opened the chamber. Satisfied it was loaded, went back down the ladder, and closed the attic door.

He walked back to his room, and looking over his shoulder sat on the side of the bed, and placed the gun into the top drawer of his night table. Then propped the pillows behind his head and opened the book to the page he had nodded off on; he wouldn't be able to sleep tonight.

Chapter 17
Dixie Cove Springs

"Captain Mackenzie, please go to the information kiosk for an important message."

Darius Mackenzie's flight landed on schedule. After a long flight, he was anxious to get home to his daughter. Concerned something might have happened to her he broke into a sprint, and headed to the nearest help desk.

"I'm Captain Mackenzie you have a message for me?"

The woman at the help desk nodded, opened a drawer, and handed it to him. He slit open the envelope and scanned through the message, it was from his brother.

The message read: Everything's fine at home, but received an urgent call from the rehab center yesterday, and they require your presence immediately. I figured since it's on your way home it's more convenient to stop by there first. Will see you later. Gordon.

Darius wondered what had happened as he drove to the rehab center. Delores had been transferred there before his overseas flight, to receive therapy after a three-month hospital stay.

Remorse and regret had been his constant companion for the past few months. Regret because had he divorced his wife as he had been planning to do, then things might not have ended up the way they had, and regret, because their only child had experienced abuse and trauma, since he hadn't listened to his brother and sister-in-law earlier.

After pulling into a parking space, he exited the car, sighed heavily, and stood looking around. The place was enormous, with three large building complexes and well-tended gardens.

He walked through the double doors of the main office building, and gave his name to the receptionist.

"Please have a seat Mr. Mackenzie and I'll inform Mr. Parker that you've arrived."

Darius nervously paced by the window anxious for whatever news awaited him. He knew it couldn't be an insurance issue, because as a pilot, he had a very good one, and couldn't imagine what could possibly be wrong.

A short, bald man, rapidly walked up the hall, and introduced himself as Mr. Parker, head of administration; they shook hands, and he motioned towards his office.

"Mr. Mackenzie, I'm afraid I have some bad news for you."

Darius braced himself, worried her injuries had gotten worse.

"Yesterday morning, at 11 AM your wife passed away from a heart attack."

Darius sat there overwhelmed by the sudden news, and trying to calm his racing thoughts.

"But how can that be? I was told she was healing well from her injuries. How could she have a stroke at such a young age?"

"We can't say for sure, and blood clots can sometimes form after trauma and surgery, but I can tell you she went quickly, and didn't suffer."

"Didn't suffer?"

He couldn't believe she was gone, just like that, and only twenty-five years old. She had been as much at fault for the issues in their marriage as he was, but he mostly blamed himself for the way things had turned out.

Tears rolled down his cheeks as he remembered the good times when they had first been married. Then he remembered that fateful night, when they had both almost died, and now she had.

Mr. Parker looked sadly at Darius and pushed a box of tissues towards him. He left the room to give him time to compose himself, and waited a few minutes before returning with a glass of water that he placed in front of him.

Darius drank some water, and looked at Mr. Parker. I'll see about her funeral arrangements today, and let you know.

"There's no need Mr. Mackenzie, your wife left a living will in case of death for the funeral directive, she requested no memorial service; no death announcement, and that a simple graveside burial would suffice. Your insurance company was notified, and her body as per state law was transferred to the funeral home, they took care of everything. She was buried at the Eternal Slumber Cemetery."

He handed Darius a pamphlet, and on it was a sticky note with the plot number and grave section.

"I had no idea she had a living will." Darius told Mr. Parker, completely bewildered. Darius couldn't wrap his mind around the suddenness of everything.

Mr. Parker explained, "The nurses were alerted that Mrs. Mackenzie was in distress.   They tried to resuscitate her, and did all they could have to save her, but she was already gone."

They hadn't been on speaking terms after that fateful night. Both had spoken a couple of times, where she mostly blamed him for what had occurred with their daughter, as she stated, almost murdering her. What

Threefold Dread 76

Delores never acknowledged, however, was that she had almost killed him and their daughter that night. Had Giselle not stopped her own mother with his gun, Delores would probably have succeeded.

Mr. Parker shook his head and gave Darius a sad look.

"If there's anything more I can do for you, please let me know."

Darius left the building, sat in his car, and shed tears for someone who didn't deserve it.

Chapter 18
Giselle

Giselle was staying with her uncle Gordon and her aunt Deirdre while she continued recovering from her injuries. Darius had returned to work the previous week after being given clearance to fly, and was due back soon. He had spoken to a real estate agent about putting the house up for sale. He didn't want Giselle ever, stepping foot in that house again. He had planned to place half the money from the sale aside for Delores so that she could get herself another place. Darius had already spoken to his attorney to begin divorce proceedings as soon as Delores was completely healed, and he wanted full custody of Giselle.

Giselle had been having nightmares, and her aunt Deirdre had begun sleeping in the room with her. This made Giselle feel better, not completely safe, but better. Her aunt and uncle's house was quiet and filled with love and laughter, but Giselle was having a difficult time adjusting. She wasn't used to three meals, plus homemade baked goods on a daily basis, but this seemed to be the norm. She loved her aunt and uncle, but was afraid her living conditions wouldn't last and that she'd have to return to her prior home, and live with her mother after she was out of rehab, and this terrified her.

That afternoon Deirdre came to the bedroom with a plate of cookies and a glass of milk, but couldn't find Giselle. She placed both on the little table, and went through the house calling her name, but no response. Frantically, she called Gordon, who came home from work, and they searched throughout the house and the backyard too. Then Gordon remembered something Darius had told him, and checked the bedroom closet.

They found Giselle cowering in the back. Together they coaxed her out, and held her while Giselle sobbed uncontrollably. After she could shed no more tears and had calmed down, Giselle told them that Delores used to chase her with a belt, and that she'd hide in the hall closet, behind a partition. Terrified when she heard the doorbell, and thinking her mother had come to take her home she'd hidden in the closet, just as she'd done countless times at home.

Deirdre shook her head and reached out her hand. "No darling, the person at the door was the Avon lady."

Deirdre and Gordon assured her that her mother would not come to their home, and that she would never again have to return to her previous house.

Giselle gulped and nodded not quite comprehending. "But where will mama live when she gets out of the hospital?"

Gordon and Deirdre glanced at each other. "Let's not worry about that right now. Your father is due back from work later today, and he'll explain everything," responded Gordon.

Giselle took Deirdre's hand and stood up.

"Have a seat dear and have your afternoon snack. I baked your favorite cookies. Deirdre smiled at her and sat on the opposite chair."

Giselle looked down at the book she was reading: From the Mixed-Up Files of Mrs. Basil E. Frankweiler. She carefully placed the bookmark between the pages and set it aside. Before sitting down, Giselle smoothed down her pink sleeveless dress with white embroidered flowers, pulled up her white knee-high socks, and admired her brand new white patent leather shoes. She looked at her exposed arms. It was the first time she was able to wear anything sleeveless, but the scars were still visible.

Giselle gulped down some milk, bit into a cookie, and started to feel better.

An hour later, Gordon heard the front door shut and went to meet Darius to tell him what had happened.

Darius looked like he had been crying.

Alarmed, Gordon led him into the kitchen.

"What's happened?" Gordon asked worriedly.

Darius dropped into a chair, and looked up at him. "It's Delores. She's dead."

Gordon sat in the chair next to him. "How is that possible?"
"I've just come from the rehab center and was told she died from a heart attack." Darius told him sadly.

"Now I won't need to press assault charges, and I'm glad I refused to do so when the police told me I should."

Gordon got up, went to the liquor cabinet, poured finger width of scotch into a glass, and handed it to Darius. "Here this will take the edge off."

Darius took a sip, and then placed it on the table. "What will I tell Giselle? She's already been through so much; I don't think she can handle much more."

Gordon looked at him thoughtfully, and relayed what had happened just before he arrived.

"What do I do Gordon? Do I wait to tell Giselle her mother is dead?" Darius implored.

Giselle was standing in the doorway and had overheard the last words spoken by her father. She rushed towards him and wrapped her arms around his neck tightly. A tear slid down his face.

Giselle placed both hands on either side of his face, and told him, "it's okay daddy, she can't hurt us anymore."

Darius picked his daughter up, sat her on his lap, looked into her serious and solemn face, and hugged her tightly.

Deirdre who'd overheard the conversation was astonished by Giselle's response. It was then that she understood that the level of abuse her niece had suffered in the hands of that 'psychopath,' as she had always silently called her, was greater than any of them knew. She never really liked the woman, and would never wish her harm, but it was still shocking that her own daughter was okay with her death.

Deirdre would suggest therapy for Giselle to Darius, but in the meantime, she would make sure her niece experienced all the comforts of a loving home.

Deirdre sensing that Darius needed more time to himself told her niece that it was bath time. Giselle gave her father a kiss on the cheek before slipping off his lap, and skipped happily towards Deirdre, who held her out her hand, which Giselle held tightly, and led her towards the bathroom.

Gordon and Darius looked at each other astounded, and sat in companionable silence; neither knowing what to say.

For dinner, they enjoyed a home cooked meal of spaghetti and meatballs, with green beans, garlic bread, and a slice of apple pie for dessert. That night Giselle didn't need Deirdre to stay with her until she fell asleep. Uncle Gordon read her a bedtime story, and auntie Deirdre tucked her in and kissed her goodnight. Her father came in to give her a good night kiss, but looked very sad, and left quickly telling Giselle he'd had a long day, and was exhausted.

That night, Giselle dreamt of brilliantly colored fairies floating through the garden riding on ladybugs.

Chapter 19
Twin Pass Junction 1968

Jaimie was glad to be out of rehab, but not to be returning to the small town she had grown up in, and had been anxious to leave since high school. She stared out the window of the taxi, as miles upon miles of fields devoid of life passed by in a blur—just like her life.

She wasn't happy coming back to the town where everyone knew her business. She planned to grab the cash she'd stashed away, and go back to Miami.

Even though Lenny had visited her in the hospital and apologized many times for panicking that night, she still hadn't forgiven him. He'd given her some money to get her things in order. He'd also told her to stay with him as long as she liked, and that was exactly what she planned to do.

She paid the cab driver, exited the car, and quickly went around the back. She knew CJ wouldn't be home this early and feeling around the ledge of the door located the key, and unlocked the door.

She entered the kitchen, and poked her head in to make sure no one was around, then made her way to the bedroom. She grabbed her clothing and went to shower. After drying off, she slipped into her favorite tomato-red, low-cut halter mini dress, and red sandals. Afterwards, she went out to the garage, pulled out a drab brown suitcase, and packed her things.

In the second bedroom, kneeling down, she pried open a floorboard, then sticking her hand underneath pulled out bundles of cash tied with rubber bands. This was all the money she had saved throughout high school from her cut of drug sales to neighboring towns with Warren and Lenny.

Before she left, she planned to visit CJ to tell him to set up the divorce, and that she wouldn't be returning. She heard a car drive up and saw that it was Warren. He didn't even knock, but opened the front door and walked inside.

"I see you've returned to the scene of the crime." Warren said clamping his lips together in a smirk.

"You think what I've been through is funny! I could have died!" Jaimie spat back.

Warren nodded his head. "Actually I do. I knew you weren't too smart, but actually screwing Lenny in CJ's home was asinine. You had one job, to mess up CJ's life beyond repair, but you only managed to mess up yours. We had a deal, and you didn't follow my instructions. How do you plan to fix this problem, or should I just finish-off what Lenny didn't?"

A sheen of sweat appeared on her forehead, as she began replying in a quavering voice, but anger quickly replaced the emotion. "I don't know what else I can do to help you achieve your goal of ruining CJ's life. Or are you such a coward you can't do it yourself?"

Warren looked at her as if he were looking at a bug he planned to squash with his boot. Then he cracked his knuckles and rolled up his sleeves.

"Care to repeat that?" He replied through clenched teeth.

Jaimie watched as the big, blue vein throbbed visibly in his forehead. He spoke louder and faster, cursing and threatening her, while working himself up as his cheeks became reddened. She'd seen him angry before, but this was much worse. She felt a tightening in her chest, and instinctively backed away. Warren advanced towards her and then noticed the suitcase by the door.

"Going somewhere?" He asked while continuing to advance towards her.

She held her palms up and out. "Warren please! I've been through enough already." She pleaded.

"And whose fault is that?" He shouted in her face. Spittle landing on her face.

Jaimie bit her bottom lip and dared not reply. She backed as far away from him as she could, until she felt the cold hardness of the wall.

Then she felt his big hands clamp around her neck, as she pummeled his chest with her fists. Moments before she lost consciousness, she heard a car door slam next door, and then succumbed to darkness.

Chapter 20
Twin Pass Junction 1970

Calvin Jones leaned against the brick building, feeling the welcome coolness through his t-shirt that read Keep on Truckin', but unfortunately, the jeans were still sticking to his skin. It had been an uncomfortably, sticky humid day, and furniture orders had nearly tripled. He couldn't complain though, because if it weren't for his father he wouldn't have a job. Everyone knew no one hired someone with a criminal record.

He'd never left the small town he'd been born into, and had only been able to leave it behind for a twenty-four month sentence for the alleged shooting of his lying bitch of a wife. Luckily, he was granted an early release on good behavior.

The day he'd been released from prison he'd found Sherry waiting for him to drive him home. He'd been expecting his father, but she'd asked him to let her pick him up instead. She had visited him every week, and that was the only thing he had to look forward to besides his parent's visits.

His eyebrows drifted up in appreciation. Sherry walked out of the general store wearing a light blue halter neck polka dot dress with a big white bow tied on the side, and blue flats. She reminded him of an auburn Audrey Hepburn. He remembered every curve, and wondered why she was still in love with him.

She spotted him watching her from across the street and smiled.

"Hi CJ, what are you doing lurking about, it's too hot today to be out!"

He sighed and crossed the street. "It sure is Sherry."

Sherry had been his girlfriend in high school when he was the quarterback, and she was head cheerleader—a perfect couple; they were voted homecoming queen and king.

His life had been great; a girl he loved and could see a future with, and a football scholarship as soon as he graduated. Everything had been perfect, until that fateful night at Warren's party, when his life had practically ended. He'd been forced to marry Jaimie right after graduation—the only choice he'd been given, or suffer the consequences. CJ had been embarrassed and apologetic to Sherry, especially after he had given her the promise ring, but he had to do the right thing.

Jaimie claimed she was pregnant from the one time they'd supposedly had sex, and he couldn't even remember the encounter. Since Warren's father was out of town, the party was unsupervised with copious amounts of booze flowing throughout the night.

How could I possibly stop loving Caleb because of what supposedly happened! Sherry wondered as she looked at him crossing the street. She certainly hadn't. She'd become suspicious when Jaimie showed no signs of pregnancy, and then learned she had miscarried.

Sherry doubted that tramp was ever pregnant to begin with, but her friend Melissa had learned from the rumor mill, that CJ had beaten Jaimie up, and that's why she'd lost the baby. She wondered if he'd caught Jaimie cheating on him, and if that was the case, she deserved the beating, but doubted that ever happened, because CJ wasn't a violent person, and would never hurt anyone.

I wonder if CJ was driven to violence, but I've never seen that side of him. He's always been kind, gentle, and considerate towards me and everyone else.

Sherry had gone to the sheriff with her doubts and assumptions, but he'd told her that without evidence there was nothing he could do. However, if she came across any information that could possibly help CJ to let him know.

"Nothing much, just got off work and picking up food for tonight. What are you up to?"

"I was about to head over to the diner and grab some supper before heading home."

"I bought enough for two. Wanna join me?" Sherry asked.

"Sounds good to me. I'll take a home cooked meal any time." CJ responded.

"Great, meet me at my place around 7."

"Alright, see you then." He went to hug her, but then remembered he needed a shower first, and backed off."

Sherry smiled at him. CJ smiled back embarrassed.

Instead, CJ blew her a kiss, which she caught. "See you later then."

Jaimie had telephoned him earlier and asked him to meet her at the house, but he declined telling her that wasn't a good idea, and instead, she should stop by the shop where there were witnesses. She showed up looking like hell and wearing a scarf around her neck on the hottest day of the year. She was also carrying a suitcase. CJ was surprised she hadn't asked him for a divorce sooner, and before he had a chance to do the same, told him it just wouldn't work out between them. CJ just shook his head. Jaimie told him to draw up the divorce papers, handed him Lenny's address, and then walked away. She waited at the station and boarded the next bus to Miami.

Threefold Dread 84

CJ strode towards his truck and got in, but not before admiring Sherry crossing the street in his rear view mirror walking towards her car. He liked that her dress clung to her curves, and the way her hair blew around in the wind. He was lucky she had believed his side of the story, and that they had ended up back together against all odds. He drove up the road listening to Midnight Confessions by The Grass Roots. Yeah, I plan to confess to her again in time, and pledge much more than a just promise ring.

Sherry practically skipped to her car thinking of the night ahead. She was very happy CJ was back in her life. The song on the radio was Lady Willpower by Gary Puckett & The Union Gap, which she took as a sign to make sure she was clear about how she felt about him. She turned the music up full blast and loudly, sang along not noticing someone was following her.

Two blocks away from her house, she almost ran through a red light, and had to slam on the brakes. A police car turned on sirens and flashing lights, and immediately pulled up behind her and told her to pull over.

"Ah, shit!" Sherry braced herself.

"Well, well, if it isn't Sherry breaking the law."

"Dammit it Warren what the hell do you want? You know damn well I didn't do anything wrong."

His warning glare shut her up quickly.

"Yeah, I know you didn't. I just wanted to see you. Where are you headed?"

"That's none of your business."

He held up his hands in resignation. "No need to get huffy, just wanted to be sure you're okay."

He watched as she drove away wondering how to win her over, then became enraged when he thought of her with CJ.

Dispatch called him snapping him out of his thoughts, and sighing, turned on his siren, turned the car around, and sped up the road.

Sherry parked in the garage, entered through the kitchen, put the groceries away, and then ran upstairs to take a shower. She rummaged through her closet and pulled out a green halter-top sundress with pink flowers, and brown strappy sandals. She pulled her long auburn hair up into a ponytail and headed downstairs. If she remembered correctly Caleb's favorite food, was pork chops, mashed potatoes with gravy, and green beans. Afterwards, she started on his other favorite—chocolate cake with buttercream frosting.

CJ arrived at seven on the dot, dressed in jeans and a blue Lacoste polo shirt, holding a bottle of red wine, and a beautiful arrangement of flowers wrapped in lavender paper with a pink ribbon.

"What a beautiful bouquet, thank you!" She kissed his cheek then admired the flowers. "What made you pick these in particular?"

"Well, I asked which flowers had the specific meanings I had in mind, and Ruthie picked these out."

"Do you know the meanings of each one?" Sherry wondered.

CJ smiled sheepishly, "I have the meanings right here," he pulled the card from his back pocket. I had her write them out for me. I knew you'd ask."

Sherry smiled back, "Caleb Jones you know me so well. Tell me what they mean then."

CJ looked at the card and began to recite the meanings. "Red tulips are a sign of everlasting love; pink tulips symbolize happiness and confidence; Forget-me-nots are obvious, but also symbolize true love and memories, to keep hope and never forget the ones we love, and finally Lily of the valley, which means a return of happiness.

Sherry gave him another kiss and then left him opening the wine.

He looked around appreciatively. The dining room carried a happy vibe interwoven with the delicious aroma coming from the kitchen. He walked into the living room and looked around. Everything was neat and orderly and nicely decorated, but in an understated way. He could imagine sitting side-by-side with Sherry on the couch with the blue cushions, curtains closed, and lights off, watching television with a bowl of popcorn. That's all he needed, and all he'd ever wanted, cozy evenings at home in a clean house, good food, and an attentive wife, on whom he could lavish his affection. It felt like a sanctuary. He'd wanted the same lifestyle as his parents who had been married for thirty-years, and still treated each other with love and respect.

He'd gotten neither in his farce of a marriage, but he'd still expected it. Jaimie, however, hadn't been the domestic type. She'd preferred hanging out at the local bar, drinking better than the boys did, and then going home to pass out until the following day—that is if she did come home. Jaimie had never cooked a meal, and housekeeping, well, that just didn't happen. CJ had hired a housekeeper-cook; otherwise, he'd have no food, and be forced to live in filth. The housekeeper, a kindly older woman whom his mother had found for him, would sigh deeply whenever she was picking up a trail of Jaimie's clothing, and cleaning vomit off the bathroom floor, and sometimes in other places too. She'd given CJ sympathetic looks, and he was ashamed of his deplorable wife, and embarrassed that others pitied him because of her.

Whenever anyone asked him why he put up with her, he'd remember that she'd gotten pregnant, and probably the reason she resented him, and as a result drank too much. No one else believed that but CJ. He failed to see her for what she really was—a vain, lazy, immature piece of trash who expected much, but contributed nothing in return.

"There you are I thought you'd gone." Sherry appeared behind him making him jump.

"I was just admiring your decorating skills. This room is really nice, and homey and welcoming too."

"Why thank you CJ. I decorated the entire house all by myself. I enjoyed picking out, well, everything. After my grandmother left it to me in her will, I couldn't stand the old-timey vibe, so I changed practically every little thing."

I thought your grandmother lived elsewhere.

"No, that's my grandmother on my dad's side."

"The one that fell and fractured her leg that night." CJ replied, remembering that was the reason Sherry wasn't with him the night of the party.

Sherry ignored the disappointed frown on his face. "Come on, dinner is on the table." She took his hand and led him towards the dining room.

"Oh course my lady lead the way."

CJ saw Sherry had placed the flowers in a crystal vase on the side table.

After CJ poured more wine, and dessert was on the table, they sat facing each other; then both looked down at their plates not knowing what to say.

Sherry looked up and caught him staring at her. "I know we've exchanged pleasantries and chatted trivialities, while casually dating but why don't we drop the pretenses and talk like the close friends we used to be."

He stared at her a few moments, and then felt his entire body relax. "Agreed. Then you won't minding me saying that I not only like being here with you, but the funny thing is, and don't laugh."

She shook her head and with her finger crossed her heart.

He smiled at her. "I feel like I've come home."

He watched as a tear rolled from the corner of her eye.

He reached out, wiped away the tear, and held her hand. "I'm sorry if I've said anything to upset you."

She squeezed his hand, and cried the tears she thought she'd run out of years ago.

"Silly man, you're not upsetting me. These are tears of happiness."

He brushed her tears away and kissed her hand.

"I'm so sorry Sherry for all the misery I've caused you."

"I'm 100% sure Warren had something to do with whatever it is happened that night with Jaimie. I told the sheriff what I thought, and he agreed with me. The problem is there is no proof of what they did, and I've tried to find out, but have had no luck. Except…"

He sighed heavily. "After she lost the baby and became an alcoholic, it was a difficult time, and I'm sure it wasn't easy for her to live with her assailant, but I tried to give her a comfortable life."

She nodded at him. "Really CJ. You still refuse to see the evil in others. There are things you don't know, and that's why you're still defending her."

He stared at her uncomprehending. "What do you know that I don't?"

She looked at him sadly. "I'll tell you after we've finished the delicious dessert I made especially for you."

He looked down at his plate. "I can't argue with that. Dinner was amazing as always." He lifted his wine glass. "To reestablishing our relationship."

She nodded and clinked her glass to his. "Here, here."

After dinner, he insisted on helping her clear the table, and after everything was in the dishwasher, they sat in the living room with glasses of wine.

"Okay, here goes, so prepare yourself for a shock."

He looked at her solemnly and nodded. "I'm ready for whatever you have to say; because I'm at this point I'll believe anything."

She looked at him for a few moments, took a deep breath, and proceeded with the story.

"After graduation, a receptionist job opened up at Dr. William's office in the next town, and I was hired. One day, on my lunch break, I was sitting across the street at Maxine's Café and saw Jaimie walking into the office."

He leaned forward with furrowed brows. "She told me that she didn't want to go to Doc Gordon's, because he was too old. And I didn't ask who she went to instead, because she was upset and didn't want to talk about it."

Sherry rolled her eyes, with an exasperated sigh, and proceeded. "Forty-five minutes later I watched her leave. I returned fifteen minutes early so I could find out why she was there."

He nodded quickly. "Please don't tell me she had an abortion."

She raised her eyebrows and gave him a slight close-lipped smile. "CJ, Dr. Williams does not perform abortions they're illegal."

He looked at her with narrowed eyes. "Maybe she was trying to confirm a pregnancy with one of her lovers."

"I want you to know that after we were married, I never touched her. She disgusted me, and I just tolerated her and planned to divorce her after she had the baby." CJ stated.

Sherry tilted her head slightly then leaned towards him, and spoke in a lowered voice. "I looked in her chart for the diagnosis."

CJ moved towards the edge of the armchair and nodded. "Go on, I can take it."

"CJ she was never pregnant, because she couldn't get pregnant."

His eyes opened wide. "Was it because the miscarriage left irreparable damage?"

Sherry reached out and held both his hands. "No, you're misunderstanding. The reason she couldn't get pregnant was due to salpingitis, which is the medical term for inflammation of the fallopian tubes."

He shook his head, not understanding. "Um, ah, what exactly does that mean?"

She tightened her grip on his hands as if trying to transmit the answer to him. "It was because she had contracted a sexually transmitted disease, which caused Fallopian tube damage. She had Pelvic Inflammatory Disease, which is an infection in the upper genital tract, and hers had spread to the fallopian tubes, uterus, and surrounding tissues, which lead to her infertility. Most women infected with Gonorrhea have no symptoms, which is why there is no way she could have been pregnant."

CJ looked at Sherry wide-mouthed and speechless. "She told me that we should abstain from sex, as if I would even want to touch her. Afterwards, she told me she didn't want to try for another baby. She avoided being around me and started going out every night. I just thought she was depressed about the miscarriage." The last part he repeated with realization in his wide opened eyes.

"So all this time I've been feeling bad over what happened to her, and she'd been lying to me! I wonder if she lied to Warren too, or if he was in on it."

Sherry shrugged and continued holding his hands. "I assume he knew."

"Shortly after, I visited a divorce attorney, and had the papers drawn up, but then the incident happened where she was shot." He pulled his hands away from hers, sat back, and stared straight ahead.

Sherry also sat back, and in a soft voice asked him. "Do you want to tell me what happened that night? There were many rumors going on from everyone who didn't know squat."

CJ looked down at his hands now in his lap; his entire body slumped like a man about to face his executioner, and spoke so low Sherry had to lean closer to him to hear.

"I had just returned from delivering furniture to our clients in Key Biscayne. Dad had gone home for the night, and mom had made dinner, so I finished up, and drove back to the shop and dropped off the delivery truck. It was Aggies's day off and I would have had to make my own food so I went to my parent's house for dinner. Afterwards, mom suggested that I stay the night since it was getting late. I've wished so many times that I had stayed.

Around 9:30 PM, I drove back home, climbed the stairs towards my bedroom, to take a shower and get some sleep. I heard a noise coming from her bedroom, and went to check if she was okay. I walked in and found her in bed with a guy, whom I recognized as the same one at Warren's party—the one playing a board game with Jaimie. I got angry and told him to get the hell out of my house, and he got up. But after getting dressed, he pulled a gun from his jacket pocket and pointed it at me.

Jaimie was pulling on a robe, but never told him to put the gun down. Instead, she seemed indifferent with him threatening me. I lunged at him, and managed to get the gun away from him. The gun slid under a chair, and Jaimie picked it up and pointed the gun at me. The guy tried to take the gun from her hand, and they struggled with it, but it went off and shot her instead. The gun dropped next to her, they both dove for it and he got it, and they continued to struggle with the gun, it went off again, and the second shot hit her too. That's when the guy got scared and ran out the door, leaving his gun behind. I ran over to her, grabbed some towels to press against her arm and her head, and then called for an ambulance. The sheriff questioned me all night, and then released me into the custody of my parents.

"As soon as Jaimie was able to speak, she told the police that I had arrived in an angry drunken stupor and shot her."

Sherry stared at him and tightened her lips. "But what about the gun? It clearly wasn't yours!"

He wrinkled his face as if he'd encountered a bad taste or smell, and responded scornfully. "I didn't know it at the time, but found out later that the guy she'd been with was a small-time drug dealer named Lenny. Apparently, they'd been dealing drugs together. The police searched the house and found packets of drugs stashed in the closet, which she told them were mine, and that I was not only dealing them, but using them too, and the reason I was violent towards her."

Sherry held her hand against her mouth—struck silent. In a shaky voice—halting, and disbelieving she responded softly. "You poor thing, how you've suffered needlessly. Did you tell Sheriff Hayward all this?"

He looked at her sadly. "I did, but he told me that the odds were stacked against me, because Jaimie was the one shot and hurling accusations at me."

"That worthless, despicable piece of trash! She probably concocted the night of the party story, and used you as her meal ticket, and when that didn't work out as she'd plotted, betrayed you not once, but twice. And no, I'm not sorry she was in critical condition." She stated the last part with conviction.

CJ looked at her confused. "Used me for what? My parents own the shop; I have nothing she could possibly want."

She nodded her head sadly. "Ah but you're wrong. You had a football scholarship, and she thought you'd be her ticket out of town, and the reason she faked having sex with you and lied about the pregnancy."

He looked at her quizzically. "What do you mean she faked having sex with me?"

Sherry blushed deeply. "I asked the people at the party, and everyone remembered you wandering about—not drunk. And they also remember Jaimie disappearing with Warren and another guy they didn't know upstairs."

"Dwight drove you home while you were still too out of it to remember. Just how much did you have to drink that night?"

He stared out the window, and then looked at her and shrugged. "I only remember having two beers. You know I'm not a big drinker."

She gave him a sad smile. "That's exactly how I remember you. I'm guessing she put something in your drink and had everyone think that you'd somehow had sex with her. But physically, you were in no condition to even be able to ahem, function."

He looked at her sheepishly. "I agree with you. I've had plenty of time to think about what happened that night, and the night of the shooting too. And I've come to the conclusion that she planned everything to ruin my life, but for what reason?"

He wrapped his arms around himself and clenched his jaw, but tears escaped leaving trails crisscrossing his cheeks.

She hugged him and offered words of reassurance and encouragement. He wiped his face with the back of his hand, and turned to her. "I've made a mess of my life, and hurt the person I've never stopped loving in the process."

She looked at him lovingly. "I've never stopped loving you either. And I want you to know that I don't blame you for what she did. You may have been clueless about what she was up to, but you were a gentleman and did the right thing for the wrong reason, though you didn't know it at the time. Look at me Caleb, and listen carefully the shooting was not your fault it was hers. If she'd had it her way, you'd be dead."

Sherry held his gaze, then stood up, held out her hand, and silently led him to the bedroom. "Let's make a fresh start beginning tonight."

Chapter 21
Warren

Warren Bullard was a bully through and through, no exceptions. He'd bullied the weak all his life, and what better job than join the police force, where he had all sorts of excuses for the treatment of the crybabies he encountered.

He was on duty, making nightly rounds and decided to drive by Sherry's house. As he turned the corner, he spotted a navy blue pickup truck parked out front.

What the hell is pretty boy doing here? His hands tightly clenched the steering wheel.

Warren parked the patrol car further up the street and turned off the lights. Looking around and seeing no one, walked towards the side of the house, and peered through the window. He spotted them in the dining room sharing a meal. He shrugged, nothing to worry about, just old friends having a meal together. But he'd make sure it was CJs last meal in the free world; he smiled at the thought.

Dwight was off-duty and looking forward to a home cooked meal—it happened to be potpie night—his favorite. He was also happy to spend a quiet evening with his wife Emily. Saturday night CJ and Sherry were joining them for dinner and a movie.

He parked in the driveway and opened his car door, when a movement across the street caught his eye.

He quietly pulled the door closed, slid down the seat, and watched as Warren strode up the sidewalk towards Sherry's house; then stealthily walked through the side gate and closed it behind him. Dwight opened the car door and pressed it closed, then crossed the street and hid behind a couple of Cypress trees the gardeners had trimmed to look like giant pears, and parted some branches. Warren was looking through the dining room window, where Dwight could see CJ and Sherry having dinner.

Warren walked back through the gate and quietly closed it behind him, content no one had seen him. But he was wrong. Then got into his patrol car, and drove away. Dwight would have to let Sherry know that the asshole had been stalking her again; he'd also let Sheriff Hayward know. He also needed to warn CJ so he'd be prepared, just in case. Warren looked like a man on a mission—one that required vigilance. Dwight knew there was nothing worse than an unknown adversary was, but he had just become Warrens foil.

He and Mike were convinced Warren was up to no good. The altercation he'd overheard earlier with Jaime, and then tonight catching him spying might just be enough for the sheriff to set up surveillance on Warren.

For the hundredth time, Dwight thought back to the night of the party and how he had driven a passed-out CJ home. Afterwards, he and Emily returned to the party and Tracy one of the cheerleaders had given him and Emily a rundown of what she'd heard.

Tracy told them that she and her boyfriend had gone upstairs to make-out in one of the spare bedrooms, and overheard Warren and Jaimie arguing in the bedroom next door. She pressed her ear to the wall, and heard Jaimie shout, "If CJ dies it's your fault and something about the roofie. I guess Warren was pissed because Jaimie had taken a drunken CJ out on the roof, and he could have slipped and fallen, or maybe they were having sex up there. Warren must have been quite worried; after all who could blame him, CJ is the star quarterback. *Jaime is so irresponsible sometimes!*"

Dwight hadn't taken seriously, what Tracy had said she'd heard that night because she'd been a little tipsy. He'd asked CJ about climbing out onto the roof, but his friend denied ever having done so. Besides, he had no idea how he came to be undressed, when the last thing he remembered holding a beer in his hand.

Then right before graduation, CJ had surprised everyone by marrying Jaimie—the school tramp. Dwight couldn't understand why he would do such a crazy thing, when CJ was dating one of the prettiest and nicest girl in school—Sherry. Jaimie was pretty, but not Sherry pretty. None of the guys on the team could make sense out of it either. That night, Jaimie had hooked up with about three other guys, and not one of them was CJ, maybe there was some truth to the rooftop story, but it just didn't make any sense.

The gossipy busybodies started the rumor mill, and concocted various stories about why CJ and Jaimie were getting married, but none of them were true. He tried talking CJ out of marrying Jaimie, as no good could come of it, but CJ wouldn't listen to him. He'd insisted on doing the right thing, even if it cost him everything, and it had.

Dwight wondered about the wording Tracy used that night, and realized that roofie probably didn't mean a rooftop, but possibly a drug. He'd learned all about illicit drugs while at police academy that were used to drug unsuspecting females in nightclubs, but he'd never heard of a guy being drugged. Dwight thought of the state CJ was in when he dropped him off at home, and he seemed really out of it, so he concluded it was very possible his friend was drugged. Judging by the state CJ was in this was the most logical conclusion that would explain what actually happened that night.

Dwight remembered that night vividly. He had found CJ in an upstairs bedroom lying half-naked on the bed, and had become concerned when he couldn't rouse him. He'd just assumed that he'd had too much alcohol, but had mixed feelings since that wasn't like him at all. CJ wasn't known to drink more than one or two beers at the most, which was his limit. But who knew, he wasn't his babysitter, and perhaps that night he had drunk much more than he usually did that night.

He'd seemed extremely drowsy, weak, confused, and unaware of what was going on around him. Dwight and two other guys from the team, Mike and Henry had helped drag CJ down to his truck since he was unable to walk properly.

When he dropped by on Saturday afternoon to see how he was doing, CJ couldn't remember anything from the night before. It was as if his memories had been wiped clean. CJ told Dwight that he'd woken up feeling uncomfortable and confused, and that there were memory blanks about the party. He also told Dwight that he'd been vomiting since early morning, and was having trouble focusing, because his vision was blurry. Dwight had asked him if he remembered what he'd had to drink at the party, and CJ told him that Warren had gotten him a couple of beers, and that's all he remembered drinking—2 stinking beers.

The following Monday at school, Warren had chided CJ about his drunken stupor, and patted him on the back about his sexual exploits with Jaimie. CJ was walking Sherry to class, and was embarrassed by the comment, but shrugged it off as Warren being a jerk. There was no way he would have been with Jaimie, he hardly even knew her, but Sherry was very upset. She ran into the girl's bathroom and didn't come out until class was over. Then she had gone home, feeling ill.

Dwight knew something was very wrong that night at Warren's party, but couldn't quite grasp the situation. Years later, he still thought about the night that ruined his best friend's life. He wasn't sure, but he felt that bullying scumbag Warren was involved, somehow.

He crossed the street and knocked on Sherry's door.

Warren had just gone off-duty, raced home to change into more suitable clothing then jumped back into his truck, got on the highway and headed towards Key West.

There was a large shipment coming in tonight, for Mongoose, Gordo, and Flaco's operation, which, one of their girlfriends had nicknamed 'Operation Moonglade.'

Jaimie was the only one curious enough to ask what that meant, and Flaco enlightened her. "It means a bright reflection of moonlight on a body of water."

Gordo laughed, "Yeah that was because the first anagram of our names made no sense."

Mongoose chimed in, "Don't be throwing shade on my lady. It makes perfect sense, and if you two ignorant idiots don't get it, then that's your problem."

To which Gordo responded, "The first one we nixed, one because we had no idea what the hell it meant, and two because it made absolutely no sense at all.

"So what was the word?" Lenny was now curious.

Gordo and Flaco looked at each other and burst out laughing. Mongoose told Lenny, "boondoggle means to waste money or time on unnecessary or questionable projects."

"Ah," Jaimie responded, "I see what you mean, but it's partly correct."

Mongoose patted her shoulder. "See, she understands that these nightly rounds constitute as questionable projects."

"Yeah, but instead of a waste of money, it's a very profitable project, and therefore, not a waste of money." Gordo chimed in.

"Stop with the chit chat and get to work, this one's a large one." Mongoose told them.

"By the way," he looked at Jaimie, "what's with the scarf?"

Jaimie's face reddened as she glanced at Warren and she flippantly replied. "A girl's gotta look good at all times; even when she's unloading questionable sacks."

The trio looked at each other and nodded knowingly. Mongoose waited until Warren was out of earshot and whispered in her ear. "If I was you, I'd keep away from that one. If he's mistreating you, just say the word, and it will stop. I promise you."

Jaimie looked at Mongoose. He might be a dangerous drug lord, but he treated his girlfriend with respect. Jaimie gave him a weak smile and mouthed, thank you. He winked in response.

Warren, Lenny, and Jaimie were unloading the crates to an isolated area of Key Largo. Warren had discovered it by accident one day while exploring the area on his speedboat. He found an uninhabited small islet about twenty-miles west of Key West. It was about four-miles long and largely covered by mangrove. To anyone passing by, it looked like an impenetrable maze of woody vegetation, and not a place for either a picnic or a tryst. But for him, it was a place to unload contraband—lots of it.

Warren thought of himself as a pirate fighting against prohibition, except instead of alcohol it was mainly cocaine, and other assorted drugs too. It was an extremely lucrative and easy moneymaking operation of mind-altering substances; he was raking in hordes of cash. He'd been amassing money since high school and there were no limits to what money could buy, except for one thing—Sherry. Warren wondered how that could happen, but tonight was all about making himself richer. Soon he'd quit the police force, move to Miami, and live in luxury. Sherry would be awed by his wealth and leave town with him and leave loser-boy behind.

He'd met Lenny in his junior year of high school, and he'd introduced Warren to Clemmy. Lenny and Warren had been moving Clemmy's shipments until Lenny introduced him to the kingpin trio. Mongoose had told Warren he'd pay him triple what Clemmy was paying, and Warren accepted the offer on the spot.

Warren had told Clemmy that he was off to college and couldn't work for her anymore. She'd taken it well and even offered to pay his tuition, but he'd declined telling her he was offered a full scholarship from his football prowess. She'd thanked him for his honesty and they'd parted ways. She even offered to give him a job after college if his career didn't take off as expected.

"Shit happens." She told him. "Come see me when it does."

But Warren hadn't attracted a scout during their games; it was that pretty-boy asshole who had gotten the scholarship instead of him. Warren knew he was better than CJ, but for some reason the scout had not picked him. Maybe the stupid scout was attracted to CJ and that's why he offered him a full scholarship instead.

Pretty boy always gets whatever he wants: a loving family with a profitable business, the prettiest girl in school, and a damned scholarship. And what has life offered me— nothing that's what. Life had offered him an abusive, alcoholic father, a weak mother who had abandoned him and run off with another man when he was a boy, and a lesser position on the football team—left tackle. He'd always wanted what CJ had and that included Sherry.

Warren had seen to it that CJ got exactly what he deserved—the whole nine yards; he chuckled at the pun, and turned up the song playing on the radio full blast—Smiling Faces Sometimes.

Warren returned to Twin Pass Junction at 4 AM, went home, showered, microwaved a frozen dinner, set his alarm for 7 AM, and went to bed. He planned to warn CJ off before he got too carried away with his freedom, which Warren planned to end soon enough. He'd try again to make Sherry see reason, and point out that life with a convicted criminal wasn't good for her future.

When the alarm clock went off, Warren punched the snooze button so hard the clock flew off the nightstand and shattered into pieces on the floor. He sat up and still half-asleep stumbled into the bathroom. He got into his truck, tore up the road, and headed to Raelene's Roadside Diner for breakfast.

As he drove up Main Street, Warren immediately saw his target. He parked at the diner and walked over.

"Hey CJ, how's it going?" Warren asked.

CJ looked over the box he'd just opened with the claw of the hammer. "Life's great." He responded flatly, he placed the hammer on the table, and began taking the box inside the shop.

The flippant response angered a sleep-deprived Warren, and he followed him into the shop. Warren grabbed CJ's shoulder, and CJ dropped the box and picked up the hammer. Warren backed away with both hands raised.

"What the hell do you want Warren?"

"Nothing buddy, just to have a word with you.

"Well I'm busy working, so come back later." CJ proceeded to the workbench and raised the circular saw to begin cutting the mid-section of a dining room table.

Warren unplugged the saw and stood across CJ glaring at him. "You know I don't like to be kept waiting." He responded through gritted teeth.

CJ stared him down. "You might frighten others, but you don't frighten me. Don't you have parking tickets to give out to the elderly, or harass children or something?"

Warren glared at him, thinking that if they weren't in an open door shop that he could just beat him to death, and no one would know who did it.

"Just say what you have to say, and be quick about it. Like I said, I'm working."

"Alright, I'll say what I came to say. Stay away from Sherry!"

"And why should I do that? Give me one good reason."

"I'll give you two. One I'm sure she doesn't want a rapist hanging around her, and two remember that neither Jaimie nor I told the sheriff what happened that night, so if you insist on hanging around Sherry, I might just get Jaimie to confess, and you'll be arrested again. I mean you've already made an attempt on her life and she's scared of you. Who's to say you won't succeed on the second try?"

CJ who rarely got angry became furious, and balled his free hand into a fist. The other hand grabbed tightly onto the hammer he was still holding.

"You listen to me Warren. I'm sick and tired of your baseless threats. I have no idea what happened that night at your house, but there's one thing I'm sure about, and it's that I didn't go near Jaimie. She's always disgusted me, so why would I force myself on her? Hell, you probably staged the entire thing, and somehow managed to get me drunk."

"But you did because she was hysterical when I found her cowering in the corner of the room, and you passed out naked on the bed. After you were married, in a fit of anger you shot her. Then when she returned from rehab and was packing her suitcase to get as far away from you as possible, you showed up and tried to strangle her."

CJ looked straight at him. "What are you talking about?"

"I saw Jaimie before she left town and there were bruises around her neck. I asked her about it, and she told me you had walked in on her packing and became angry. I told her to go to the sheriff, but I guess she decided not to after all."

CJ stared at Warren who looked disappointed at Jaimie's decision.

"You're a lying piece-of-shit and everyone knows it." CJ countered.

"I saw her after she stopped by to ask me for a divorce. Now I know why she was wearing a scarf around her neck on such a hot day. I never went near the house, because I asked her to come here instead, in case something else happened beyond my control, and I'm glad I stuck to that decision. How do you know about bruises on her neck? I only saw a scarf."

Warren advanced towards him, but CJ raised the hammer, and he stopped.

Just then, CJ's father walked in through the side door. "What's going on here?"

"Nothing Mr. Jones, just a disagreement between old friends." With that said, he wished them a good morning and left.

CJ and his father looked at each other. "What was that about son?"

CJ looked at his father, and for the first time asked for his help. "Dad, I think I've been set up; not once but thrice, and now he's threatening to do it again, and this time I'll either be in prison permanently, or worse."

"Listen son, I'm calling the sheriff right now. This has to stop, and for what it's worth, I believe you've always told the truth, but that boy just isn't right. It's common knowledge. Why the sheriff keeps him on is a mystery to me."

"If he returns, defend yourself anyway you can, but I'll put a stop to his bullying ways if it's the last thing I do."

"I just wish someone else overheard the conversation. No one would believe me if I told them what just transpired." CJ told his father.

"Oh, I don't know about that—Raymond has never believed Warren innocent of any wrongdoings. He just hasn't been able to prove any of them."

CJ's father walked swiftly towards the back office to call the sheriff, and CJ went back to work.

However, both men were wrong. Chief Deputy Mike was about to grab lunch when he saw Warren enter the shop. He followed him and stood outside near the entrance, behind the oak tree. He could have gone in and stopped the argument, but that wouldn't be enough to stop Warren from getting even, and as usual not getting caught. No, this time he had proof of a threat, and Sergeant Dwight saw him stalking Sherry and CJ the other night. He hoped this was enough to get the sheriff to make a move. He'd waited years for Warren to pay for the terrifying threats he'd given, and he was on the receiving end of one of them.

There had been many complaints throughout the years about Warren, but he had always managed to wriggle his way out with excuses. Since there were no witnesses other than the complainants, Warren continued getting away with whatever he wanted. He also remembered one specific night in high school when Warren broke into his house, one he would never forget.

After hearing every word of the altercation, and recording it on the handheld recorder, he carried with him. Dwight headed back to the station to inform the sheriff. Lunch would have to wait.

Chapter 22
Miami, Florida 1986

Kimi Darlow was attending a party in her honor for being top real estate agent of the year. She excelled at selling luxury properties, and move the prior owners into even bigger estates that were more luxurious, and very expensive. This was her fifteenth year at the company, and even though she was a high earner, it just wasn't enough for the lifestyle she had in mind.

After rehab, she had decided not to start her own agency as a safety precaution, as this would ensure the wrong person couldn't track her down. She had settled for Picket Fences, because the agency was the top one in Miami, and outsold others monthly if not weekly.

However, she couldn't believe how much of a percentage the agency took from all her multi-million dollar sales, and there were lots of them. All she got in return from the usurpers was a frosted cake, chips, balloons, and flowers. *Pathetic!*

The decade had gotten off to a rocky economic start, with two recessions happening back-to-back, the other agents were always complaining that no one was buying houses anymore. The reason for that was that their clients were only after cheaper properties in lesser-valued neighborhoods, but that definitely wasn't her cup of tea.

She sought out the wealthiest and wooed them with her charm and beauty, which always ended in a huge sale. Some were return clients who were in need of homes for their offspring or aging parents, and Kimi never failed to impress and deliver.

The other agents at Picker Fences had given her the cold shoulder every time she sold another expensive property—weekly and sometimes more than once a week. She knew who to sell the properties, and estate sales brought in substantial growth. She'd made sure to build up her roster with only top paying clients, which mostly included drug dealers, with enough money to burn in a fireplace at Christmastime, but not enough things and places to spend it legally. Word had spread like wildfire, and not a week went by without a new millionaire client to add to her growing list.

Kimi's success had enabled her to secretly set-up her own real estate agency, but the firm didn't need to know that just yet. They would know the day after she received her commission, which was the day after their stupid little party. Who was she to deprive them of thinking they had bested her by continuing to increase the percentage of profits taken from her sales. Let them enjoy their cheap, store bought cake, because that was the last time they would profit sweetly from one of her sales.

She had already recruited her secretary—Paige with the lure of a higher paycheck. It was easy to tempt her since she had a little habit that needed a higher salary to maintain. Kimi had caught her at it one morning when she had arrived very early with and no other staff the office. Paige had already collected her client list, which she was not obligated to leave with Picket Fence Realty. The name fit the agency more than they knew—small Americana houses not worth the lot where they were located.

Another staff hire was Jaime, whom she had met during one of the worst times of her life…a time she had almost died. She knew Jaime was flaky and couldn't be trusted, but she'd been forced to hire her as sort of a partner-in-crime. That way she could keep a close eye on her, and any misstep would not be tolerated and quickly corrected.

Besides, Jaime knew the underworld quite well; having been a part of it since high school, and that connection would bring more wealthy clients with something to hide. To Kimi, they were just another ticket to an early retirement; living in a beachside mansion, and sipping margaritas by the pool.

Kimi had named her agency Pinnacle Real Estate, Brokerage and Management; she wanted the whole shebang; a one-stop shop. She had already notified her clients that the agency would be open for business the following day, and had let them know that her company would be offering property management services, which many of them were eager to know more about. She had befriended other top agents working for mediocre agencies, and lured them over to hers; after all, she couldn't run an entire company by herself. They had willingly joined her, as their gripe had been the same as hers, but there was another thing that interested her.

Every single one of them had something to hide, and she had made sure to find out exactly what those things were before bringing them, onboard, just in case. Their commissions, however, would be quite high to keep them happily working for her.

In a stroke of luck, the queen of cocaine had contacted her the previous week, asking about a property for sale in Key Biscayne. Telling Kimi, she had come highly recommended, and especially because she was discreet and tight-lipped. She had sold her the property through her own agency, and therefore, keeping all of the profit.

Threefold Dread 102

They had met on a bench at the beach, and there Clemmy had detailed what she wanted from her, apart from discretion—a way to invest large amounts of nontaxable funds. Kimi quickly understood what Clemmy required for her illegal drug business, and was trying not to show how eager she was to comply. Clemmy had been straightforward.

"Do you want to make some real money, or continue earning small change from your wealthy clients?" Clemmy had asked her point-blank.

No beating around the bush from this woman.

"I do require that all my business associations follow my two golden rules." She told Kimi.

"And what would that be?" Kimi asked her.

"Loyalty and especially keeping your mouth shut." Was all Clemmy said.

"I can definitely do that. I already do that for all my clients, and there is plenty to keep closed lipped about." Kimi confessed.

"Do we have a deal then?" Clemmy held out her hand.

Kimi nodded enthusiastically and shook her hand. "Yes, we have a deal."

Kimi stayed up half the night coming up with a plan for a sophisticated system of money laundering. She had gotten the chance of a lifetime, and was going to exploit it for all it was worth. She had already been given the Buccaneer Hotel to manage.

There was only one snag in the plan she had not foreseen, Clemmy told her she would be working alongside Jaimie Joplin. Jaimie seemed nice enough and they had met under similar circumstances, and she knew Clemmy wanted Jaimie to keep an eye on her. That was fine by her as long as Jaimie knew her place and stayed out of her way. Kimi had her eye on a sweet little condominium that was still under construction, and she wanted the penthouse. This lucrative stroke of luck had fallen into her lap, and had made her happy to the point of being giddy. This deal would take her one-step closer to acquiring it.

She arrived at her apartment, locked the door behind her, and stripped off all of her clothing, leaving a trail all the way to the kitchen. No need to worry, her maid would pick them up the next day. She opened a bottle of chardonnay, and poured a half a glass. Then purposely pushed the cork back in tightly, and placed the bottle onto the top rack of the mini-fridge behind the bar.

She walked into the bathroom, turned on the jazz station, filled the tub, added Gardenia scented oil, and slid into the warmth to soak.

"Tomorrow will be the start of my empire, and a much more profitable life." She said aloud, and smiled widely.

Chapter 23
Deirdre

Deirdre kissed her husband Gordon in the morning as he left for work, and decided to drive into Miami to shop. Dixie Cove Springs was a nice place to live, but good clothing boutiques were non-existent.

She parked her car at the mall, then wondered around from shop to shop, but couldn't find what she was looking for until stepping into the last shop. There Deirdre found a pair of shoes to compliment the outfit she'd just purchased. She planned to wear both for dinner tonight. Afterwards, she decided to have some lunch before the long drive back. Checking the menu in the window, she turned around and saw a familiar face.

"Well if it isn't the long-lost Quinn. What brings you to Miami?" She inquired.

Quinn turned towards his name being mentioned and smiled broadly. "Hello Mrs. Mackenzie! Long time no see!"

"I could say the same about you." Deirdre told him. "What have you been up to?"

"I've been busy setting up a consultation company, and I can tell you it keeps me running all over town. Are you living here now?" Quinn inquired.

She shook her head. "No, I like to visit, but am not interested in living here. There's too much going on, all the time. I'm still in the same house in Dixie Cove."

Quinn nodded. "I hear you, its non-stop action. Where are you headed, if you don't mind me asking?"

"I was actually looking for a place to grab some lunch; any suggestions?" Deirdre inquired.

Quinn smiled. "What a coincidence, I was headed to lunch myself. Would you like to join me?"

Deirdre smiled back. "Why thank you Quinn; don't mind if I do."

After they were done, and Quinn paid for lunch, he had a request, jotting his phone number on a napkin, handed it to Deirdre. "Could you please give this to Elle the next time you see her?"

Deirdre smiled widely. "I thought you'd never ask."

They said their goodbyes, and Deirdre returned to the mall and headed towards the parking garage. As she neared a designer shop, she bumped into a woman exiting in a hurry with a large bag, which she dropped.

"I'm terribly sorry." Deirdre picked up the bag and handed it back to the woman, but almost dropped it before the woman grabbed it from her hand.

"Clumsy clod. Next time look where you're going." The woman retorted then turned around and rapidly walked away.

Deirdre watched the familiar figure beat a hasty retreat. "Wait come back!"

Within moments, the woman disappeared into the crowd.

Deirdre stood rooted to the spot, had the woman not recognized her? They'd known each other since college, and she hadn't changed enough to be unrecognizable, but it was still a shock to see her after all this time. After a few moments she turned the corner and sped walked towards the nearest exit. Once inside her car, she sat for a long time ruminating before driving away.

On the drive back home, she tried to come up with different scenarios as to why she had seen this person now after such a long time, but couldn't come up with one that sounded sane. The last time they'd spoken was when she was in rehab recovering from wounds. She wondered if she should tell Gordon at dinner, or telephone him as soon as she got home.

Confusion and doubt clouded her senses, and she dismissed the thoughts as delusional. Maybe it wasn't her at all and just someone that resembled her, since she seemed different. *Oh, well, it's probably my overactive imagination.*

Deirdre turned up the radio, and sang along with Billy Joel to Uptown Girl.

After arriving home and placing the keys on the hall table, she slipped off her shoes, and walked towards the kitchen to drink some water. There was a knock on the back door, and thinking it was her neighbor promptly opened it.

There stood the ghost; there was no denying that she had been confused or imagining things. She realized too late that she should have looked through the window before opening the door.

Gordon's voice echoed in her mind, over the countless times he'd warned her to look before opening the door. He'd told her many times: DD, even though this is a safe town criminals aren't tied down to other places.

Deirdre tried to shut the door, but wasn't quick enough.

She was forcibly pushed back inside, and punched in the stomach, winding her. Then she saw the barrel of a gun pointed towards her, and tried to run, but was pulled back and spun around.

"After all these years, It's surprising to see you again. I thought earlier that I was imagining things, but here you stand." Deirdre gasped.

Still pointing the gun at her, the woman walked over to the radio and turned it on, then turned the volume up as high as it would go. The song playing was ironically
Ghostbusters.

"How…?" Deirdre asked. Stammering in confusion. "I moved long before…"

"Before…? Because I just followed you stupid." The woman smiled maliciously.

"I see you've become quite the little homemaker." The woman looked around disgusted that such a thing was doable.

"I had my eye on Gordon before you came along, and he might have ended up with me, but you threw yourself at him and ended up with him anyway. After an encounter that almost got me killed and landed me rehab, you never even bothered to visit. That hurt! Did you think only a phone call would suffice?"

Deirdre didn't know what to respond, and didn't.

"What do you want?" Deirdre asked annoyed at the unwelcome intruder.

"Why to even the score of course." The woman responded. "And to eliminate every last one of your family members, one-by-one." She informed her laughing mockingly.

The woman pointed the gun directly at her chest. "I want you to look at me, and be the last thing you ever see."

A flash and a thunderous noise echoed deafeningly in the confines of the kitchen, as she watched Deirdre stagger and fall while clutching her chest. The woman backed up to avoid the rapidly spreading cloud of blood inching its way towards her.

Deirdre's mind raced with a million thoughts. What will Gordon have for dinner tonight? Will he or our neighbor find me and call an ambulance? Why would this woman want to kill me? I've never done anything to her, and Gordon was never interested in her.

The woman stood in the doorway watching Deirdre's life slowly dwindle.

Deirdre's mind continued to think of more things she wished to accomplish, but her thinking was beginning to get hazy. Then she felt something being pulled from her hand, and her pockets being checked. She watched as the woman opened her purse rummage through it, and remove a piece of paper.

She then watched as the designer heels walked out the door and shut it behind her. She couldn't think anymore and was getting very sleepy.

I'll close my eyes for a few minutes, then get up, and clean up this mess before Gordon gets home. Feeling she could no longer keep her eyes open, closed them to rest.

After that, her world went completely dark.

Chapter 24
Ruby

Ruby had been feeling uneasy all day especially after receiving a shocking item in the mail addressed to her; it had given her a headache and left her feeling edgy. Late afternoon, her mother came downstairs looking tired and worried, which made Ruby's anxiety elevate. Maybe her mother had received the same thing too. She hoped not.

"Mom, what's wrong?" Ruby asked worriedly.

Kassie walked over and hugged her daughter. "Stop worrying I'm just stepping out for coffee. Working on the cold case of a missing woman is taxing, so I thought I'd just step out for a bite and change of scenery."

Ruby inwardly sighed that she had guessed incorrectly. She hoped her mother would date the kind Mr. Bonham, owner of the bistro who was interested in her mother. He was a very nice man and Ruby wondered if he had a son. Kassie casually mentioned how he kept inviting her out, but had declined feeling she was past the dating stage. Ruby knew that excuse was mostly because of her father's infidelities.

"Going to see Giles?" Ruby teased her mom. "I see you're all dressed up and looking fabulous."

Kassie's cheeks turned pink. "Maybe I am, and for your information, I'm having dinner with him tonight. We're just meeting up for coffee."

Ruby was not expecting this answer, as she had seen the hesitation every time he asked her out. "Well good for you! I'm glad you finally decided to start dating."

"Whoa. One step at a time; we're not dating yet, these are just dates." Kassie informed her daughter.

"Um hmm, we'll see." Ruby responded grinning.

Kassie shook her head, kissed Ruby's cheek, and left.

Finally! Ruby was glad her mom was at least trying. She was only forty-two and definitely not too old to date.

"What you smiling so widely about?" Athena had come to update her on the sales, and the status of construction on the new shop.

"Mom has finally decided to start dating after all this time." Ruby told her friend and shop manager.

"Really, that's great, and it's about time." Athena responded. "It's Giles isn't it?"

Ruby nodded. "Yes, and I approve."

"When are 'you' going to start dating again?" Athena slyly commented.

"As soon as I find someone worth dating. Not everyone is as lucky as you've been with Sebastian. So when are two having a baby?" Ruby asked pointedly.

"I've got to get back to inventory see ya later." Athena quickly responded and briskly left the room.

Ruby laughed aloud. "Thought so." She shouted at her.

As soon as Ruby's three o'clock walked in, she immediately felt uncomfortable, but shrugged it off to bad vibes from the previous reading. She made a mental note to have her assistant limit her readings to only four daily.

The blonde woman sat across from her, and Ruby felt déjà vu. "Have I read for you before?"

The woman pursed her lips, making them seem bow like. "No you haven't. You were referred to me by a client." She responded smiling only with her mouth.

Ruby didn't like this pristinely dressed woman. She was wearing a tailored white suit with a matching short skirt, a light blue silk blouse, and designer white leather pumps.

Even though she was polite and seemed friendly, something about her just didn't feel right.

Kimi studied the reader as if she were trying to extract information from her telepathically.

The reader went by the name Ruby Bloodworth, which she suspected was a professional name and not her real one. She was wearing a crimson-lined black robe adorned with golden symbols, and wore a ring with a giant gem like her namesake on a slender hand with long red fingernails. Her hair was a golden coppery red, but not the kind that came from a bottle and her face was beautiful. Kimi wondered if all of the red meant passion or anger, or a combination of both, and smiled inwardly.

Ruby suddenly reached across the table, grabbed Kimi's hands, and pulled them towards her. This sudden action startled her, and she had to stop herself from yanking them back, but didn't, as she was curious where this was going.

While holding Kimi's hands she asked "Have we met somewhere before?"

Kimi studied her face for a moment, "No I don't believe we've ever met. I would have remembered you." She responded expressionlessly.

Kimi didn't notice the dark look Ruby gave her, because she was staring at the reader's hands still grasping hers. Ruby couldn't understand why she felt such antagonism against this stranger, but she did.

"I see a darkness around you, but it's not clear what it is." She told Kimi.

"What darkness. What are you talking about?" Kimi asked, with a hollow feeling in the pit of her stomach.

"It's not clear if it's someone you're around, maybe where you work, or someone from your past, but it's definitely following you around. Maybe a previous wrong that needs to be righted and until it is, the darkness will continue following you around until then."

"That's absolutely ridiculous!" She angrily responded and yanked her hands away.

Kimi was starting to get angry at the woman's insinuations. She looked into the narrowed eyes of the psychic, and thought she saw a flash of anger. But that couldn't be possible, she'd never even met the woman, and why would she be angry with her anyway. Now she was imagining things. She had to calm down, before she experienced a little of the darkness mentioned.

"How do I remove this darkness?" She asked angrily.

"You can't. Just stay away from trouble or it will find you." Ruby answered brusquely.

Kimi wondered why that sounded like a threat, but ignored it since she really wanted the much recommended reading.

A deep frown appeared on Kimi's forehead. "Enough of this darkness nonsense just get on with the reading."

Ruby shrugged and picked up the deck of cards. "Think about your question while shuffling the cards, and then hand them back to me."

Kimi shuffled the cards, and after a couple of minutes handed the cards back to Ruby.

The first card she turned over was The Lovers. "This card represents choices. It indicates a decision needs to be made about an existing relationship, or a choice of potential partners. Whatever choice you make, don't make it lightly as the consequences will be permanent."

Kimi looked at Ruby expectantly. "Do go on. Maybe the next card will show who my lover man is."

Ruby turned up the next card. "The knight of wands is an act first, think later type of guy. He is impatient and impulsive, and loves action. He rushes into situations without thinking of the consequences of his actions. He is headstrong, and impetuous."

Kimi smiled a slow smile, thinking of a lover with these qualifications.

The next card Ruby turned over was the knight of swords.

This guy's a powerful figure full of life and energy, and once his mind is made up, there is no stopping him. He doesn't care about any potential challenges, risks, or dangers, and instead moves forward with a strong intent to succeed and win. He can be blind to the consequences of his actions, and may charge forth into dangerous territory without any foresight or preparation. He may also neglect to understand the needs of others as he fervently pursues his own goals.

"These are two headstrong guys in your reading so far. Do you know either of them?" Ruby asked.

Kimi looked at Ruby, and nodded. "Maybe one, but I hope I run into the other one soon. He sounds like lots of fun, especially physically." She winked at Ruby.

Ruby ignored the inference and turned up the following card. "The Six of Cups can represent old friends, or lost family members re-emerging in your life."

Ruby looked at Kimi, and saw a shadow cross her face, then just as quickly disappear.

The next card was the knight of cups.

"This knight showed up in a reversed position, he represents a person with an overactive imagination, and is unrealistic. He can be passive aggressive, and full of empty promises. Feelings can run hot and cold. This guy seems flaky and unreliable, so be warned."

The Tower card was turned up next. "This card is associated with sudden and unforeseen massive change and upheaval. Expect the unexpected. It also represents danger or a crisis. This change is usually scary, life changing, and often unavoidable, quite possibly because you have ignored previous warnings."

Ruby was very curious to see what the last two cards were. The next card she turned over was the Seven of Swords. "This card represents deception, lies, trickery, cheating, and lack of conscience. It can signify mental manipulation, tactics, scheming, cunning, and enemies who masquerade as friends and spies. It could mean that someone is having thoughts of being either unfaithful or deceitful."

Ruby wondered if the card meant the woman sitting across her or her lovers.

The last card was The Fool. "This is a card representing a new beginning, and an end to something from the past. It can mean an important fresh start in almost any aspect of your life. The Fool signifies

Threefold Dread 112

a new journey is about to begin. So maybe one of those two guys will go on the journey with you."

Ruby continued. "The reading implies that you'll have a tough choice to make between three men. One of these guys may be with someone else and leave that person for you, so be aware of that. Another can represent a love from your past coming back into your life, and that's what the unexpected event could mean. The last one is just for fun he is romantic, but not to be taken seriously.

Kimi smiled at this "I could definitely use a fun man in my life."

Ruby studied her and wondered what kind of journey life had planned for this woman. Because whatever it was, she was certain it didn't bode well for her future, but kept that thought private.

"Do you have any questions?"

Kimi shook her head. "No I don't think so. My business is doing great, and no enemies have popped up, so I'm good. My boyfriend and I split up, but I think he'll be back. I wonder who the other guy is though." She said thinking aloud. She snapped back to the present, paid Ruby $200, and then gave her a $125 tip. "Thanks for the reading hon it was great. I'll try to keep the darkness at bay to avoid disaster." She smirked.

She winked at Ruby then quickly got up, smoothed her skirt, adjusted her jacket, picked up her designer purse, and left the room.

As soon as she was out of sight, Ruby laid her hands on the deck, and tentatively pulled the top card.

She placed it on top of the other cards. It was The Dark Magician. She nodded knowingly to herself, that's what I thought. The energy of this card personified anger, bad intentions, hateful thoughts, black magic, or psychic attacks. But it could also represent repressed anger, degenerated into an angry presence that could be dangerous. This card was a warning to be aware of an enemy, who watched from a hidden place.

She felt there was carefully controlled anger coming from the woman no matter how hard she tried to conceal it. This client could possibly have stored up anger, and eventually it would emanate in destructive ways. Maybe the anger was subsiding from where it once reached an explosive level, which could have come from jealously, fear, hatred, or disdain. This type of person was usually the wounded one, who sank into deep despair, sadness, hopelessness, and may even express these emotions through anger and violence. It could be intentional dark magic or natural dark magic, which is done on an unconscious level through thoughts. Regardless, the focus and feeling was that an enemy lurked closely to this woman, searching for her weakness, and for an opportunity to exploit it, or maybe she was her own enemy.

Had she drawn the card before the woman left, she would have warned her to beware of things out of place, or situations that just didn't seem right. To listen to her intuition, warning her of an enemy's presence, or approach, to be suspicious of strangers at her door, or some casual acquaintance asking personal questions. She would have also warned her to take steps to protect herself, and take notice of strange dreams or nightmares. She may never see or recognize this enemy, because the work is done behind the scenes, and in the shadows.

Scary card, she thought, and for a moment considered calling the number the woman had left for her appointment, to warn her of impending doom, but didn't. For some reason, she felt that the woman wouldn't listen. Ruby had sensed a repressed anger lurking behind her fake smile, and preferred not to wake that dormant dragon. *Just let sleeping dogs lie,* was her motto, and left it at that.

Kimi climbed into her shiny new red Mercedes and smiled all the way back to the office. She wanted to grab the package Paige had picked up earlier, and take it home with her.

Kassie sat at a table by the window admiring the interior of Bistro Vienna. She raised the cup with a Viennese specialty that Giles had prepared for her, and took a deliciously long sip. The coffee was made with espresso, lightly sweetened, and topped with whipped cream, and a splash of liquor called kirshwasser—a fruit brandy distilled from cherries. He motioned that he would be right over.

The ambiance was comfortable, but sophisticated like stepping into a different place and time. The European-inspired restaurant was designed after a 19th-century Viennese eatery in the town Giles lived as a child. This was the best place in town to enjoy coffee, brunch, lunch, dinner, and desserts, especially the sweets.

She liked the carved wood paneling, chandeliers, and Mozart subtly playing in the background. Conversations were low spoken, and all tables were occupied with patrons seated at the deep brown smooth wooden tables, in comfortable velvet-covered chairs in a rich shade of burgundy. Each table had a small crystal vase containing one perfect pink tulip.

Opening the menu, she quickly scanned through the delicacies: raspberry soufflé, Swabian apple tart, cherry strudel, Marzipan Mozart chocolates, Sachertorte-chocolate sponge with apricot jam,

Kaiserschmarrn—chopped-up fluffy pancakes, served with icing and applesauce, Palatschinken—thin layers of crêpes filled with apricot jam and side of vanilla ice cream, Punschkrapfen (punch cake) a hot pink crumb cake filled with apricot jam, nougat chocolate, soaked in rum…

On the dinner page: Wiener Schnitzel with redcurrant jelly and potato salad, Tafelspitz—beef cooked in broth served sliced with root vegetables, apples, and breadcrumbs, baked potatoes and dill-cream sauce, Schlutzkrapfen, half-moon shaped pasta filled with either spinach and potato, and sprinkled with grated Parmesan…

Giles walked over with his Viennese coffee placed it on the table, leaned down and kissed her cheek, and then sat down next to her. Kassie closed the menu and looked at him.

"My mouth is watering just looking at the menu. I want to try something different every time I come here. Everything I've eaten has been delectable." Kassie told him.

Giles smiled back at her. "Then why don't we start with the Wiener schnitzel, and then we'll see about dessert?"

"I think that's a wonderful idea." Kassie responded.

After they'd finished their coffees, he stood up and held out his hand. "Come with me, there is a private room in the back I've reserved especially for us for tonight. By the way, you look beautiful."

Kassie blushed. "You're making me feel like a young woman again."

Giles squeezed her hand. "You still are."

When Kimi got off the elevator there at her door stood Warren, all 6' 2" of handsome, tanned, and muscular waiting just for her. She walked over to him and he planted a deep kiss on her eager lips. She opened the door to her apartment and they both entered, with arms around each other. She excused herself to take a shower, since she had been busy driving to appointments all day, while he ordered takeout and opened a bottle of chardonnay.

Kimi perfumed her body, and dressed in a sexy red négligée trimmed with midnight black lace. She watched as his eyes nearly popped out of his head as he handed her a glass of wine. Food arrived and while they ate, they talked about nothing in particular, each with only one thought in mind.

After dessert and banal conversation, the radio began playing 'The Lady in Red,' Warren held out his hand and they slow danced until the song was over. He then picked her up, and carried her into the bedroom.

She remembered the tarot reading earlier about the knight lovers. Damn she had been right about one of them!

Exhausted, they fell into a deep slumber in each other's arms.

That night, Kimi dreamt of a falling out the window of a high-rise condominium.

Chapter 25
Bishop and Shepherd Private Investigators

Elizeus Bishop, or Zeus as everyone called him, had just received three phone calls, and one was especially worrisome. During his years on the police force, the officers called him 'Almighty Zeus,' because he could spot minuscule clues overlooked by others, which helped solve many cases because of this ability. Working with Detective Jenkins had helped get him promoted through the ranks quickly, but that was now in the past.

Zeus wasn't a tall man, but his looks made up for his lack of height. He had thick wavy brown hair, cut short with sideburns and some gray streaks beginning to show; his clean-shaven face only accentuated his boyish good looks. He used his good looks to his advantage, especially if the perp or suspect was female; he didn't hesitate to use his charms. His eyes were the color of Cognac left in glasses long after the guest's cigars had burnt out. Some had commented that he had peripheral vision into your very soul, which made criminals confess whether they wanted to or not.

He sat drumming his fingers on the desk, as if attempting to awaken the gods of decision.

Earlier, he had received a phone call from Kassie Mason who reverted to her maiden name Driscoll after the divorce. Zeus had been the detective assigned to finding her husband after she had been stabbed nineteen-years ago. The officers investigating the crime scene had been quick to deduce that anyone could have attacked her, and her husband who was supposedly out-of-town was no exception.

The police had been quick to accuse Darius of attacking his wife, after she told them she had intervened when he was attacking their eleven-year-old daughter Giselle, and that she had stabbed him in self-defense. But after studying the crime scene and questioning their neighbors, Zeus didn't believe Delores Mackenzie's story.

The sergeant wanted to charge the husband for attempted murder and child abuse, but Zeus disagreed, and Detective Jenkins agreed, as many clues lead to her being the instigator.

As soon Delores was able to talk, she accused her husband. Saying that he had chased her and their daughter with a knife, and to protect herself and Giselle, she'd somehow managed to turn the knife on him, and stabbed him instead. Then both had run to the kitchen back door to summon help.

When they'd questioned Delores why she thought her daughter had shot her, she told them Giselle probably thought she was Darius come to kill them.

That statement didn't sit well with Zeus for a few reasons.

One, her husband was found lying in the living room stabbed in the abdomen, incapacitated, so he couldn't possibly have been chasing her and her daughter to the kitchen.

Two, the daughter had defensive knife wounds on both arms and hands, and a knife protruding from her leg when they found her slumped on the kitchen floor, and Delores' prints were taken from the knife.

Three, the neighbors stated that every time the husband was out of town, the wife held wild parties and had seen men leaving at late hours, which backed up the husbands story about the reason he kicked her out of the house.

Four, the next-door neighbor told him that the little girl was constantly abused by the mother, which she had witnessed many times. The child was never fed, and the poor little girl tried to cover up the multitude of bruises left by her mother's beatings, which she and her sisters had witnessed various times as well.

Zeus believed the husband's statement that he had kicked his wife out of the house after finding her in bed with a man named Phil. That Delores had returned, still drunk, and started yelling and throwing things at him. Then she grabbed the knife left on the table to cut the party's cake, stabbed him, and then went after their daughter. The last thing he remembered before losing consciousness was hearing a gunshot.

Zeus and Detective Jenkins had shown the captain all the evidence collected at the crime scene, and the witnesses' statements. They were waiting for the wife to recuperate, so they could arrest her for attempted murder and child abuse. However, they were unable to do so, because she died soon after being sent to rehab.

Zeus met Freya Shepherd when she was promoted to detective, and was partnered up with him. At first, he thought she was too inexperienced, but soon came to realize that Freya was another version of him. Together, they shared a special set of skills, critical thinking, attention to detail, problem solving, great at communication, and emotionally stable, but her computer and writing skills were much better than his were. Together they were referred as 'the dynamic duo.'

A year later they began dating and two years after they were married. They discussed what they would do future wise, as they didn't want to stay in the force forever, and came up with a plan. After consulting with Detective Jenkins, he liked the idea of opening a private investigation agency, and the detective even worked with them on cases until he retired.

Freya walked in chatting away about her day then walked over to her desk and placed a stack of files on the left side. Zeus watched as she sat down and began going through case files.

Freya was as beautiful as when he'd first met her, if not more. The golden highlights in her brown hair made the tips appear fiery from the afternoon Sun shining through the window.

She looked up feeling his gaze and smiled. "How was your day?"

Zeus walked over and kissed her cheek. "Lovely to see you too honey." He responded with a smile.

"Well, I received three phone calls from three different individuals that are all connected with a perplexing case from nineteen-years ago that remains unsolved."

Freya listened to his list of why he believed the mother was guilty, and the father was innocent. "But what does all that have to do with the calls today?"

Zeus explained. "Because I have a feeling they are somehow connected."

"How can they all be connected to something that happened nineteen-years ago?" She wondered.

"I don't know yet, but that poor abused child was probably left with a long list of issues."

Now she was intrigued. "What kinds of issues?" She asked as she closed the file and gave Zeus her full attention.

Zeus smiled at her, as her deep blue eyes sparkled with curiosity.

"Well, for starters, the poor child had been abused for so long that she could have snapped and shot her mother. She may even have stabbed her father, but he emphatically refuted that his daughter had committed any crime. I believed him."

Freya was shocked that a child could possibly commit such heinous actions against her parents regardless.

"So that's why the father was in the living room and the mother was in the kitchen. She was probably trying to run away from the daughter who had just stabbed her father. But wait a minute Zeus, then why did the mother accuse her husband of the crimes, and not the daughter?"

"The wife's alcohol level was so high; she was close to blood poisoning, so her thoughts were quite muddled. And besides, she may have covered for the child, since she had abused her and didn't want that brought to light, and probably thought she would gain brownie points with her daughter for not snitching on her."

"So which one did the stabbing and which one did the shooting?"

"I guess we'll never really know. The wife was a total nut job, but she's dead now, so that just leaves the daughter—a possibly deranged adult who's snapped once more. But I'm still not convinced she's guilty, and we may be dealing with a third person, I didn't even consider back then."

"What makes you think that?"

"Kassie Driscoll just told me that her daughter received a box of carved wooden dolls depicting horrible things. Just like the one found next to her, nineteen-years ago."

"The unsolved case of the woman stabbed and found by her daughter?"

"Yes, the daughter received one carved wooden doll depicting her attack in college, and then today she received one more. Her mother is very worried about their safety."

Freya looked confused. "What's so strange about receiving dolls?"

"Because the doll depicts where the victim was stabbed, and that detail was never made public. The doll her daughter received depicts an attack in college."

"So, what does that have to do with any of our new cases?" Freya asked perplexed.

"Hang on, I'm getting to that. On that same day the Mackenzie family who lived a few blocks away was attacked, Kassie who did psychic readings from her house was found stabbed by her daughter Ruby."

"Yeah, well, everyone or almost everyone knows that you shouldn't let strangers into your house. And that quack was just asking for trouble. So how does this tie in with anything?" Freya inquired.

"Kassie is no quack; she was and still is a consultant for the police department. In fact, she has helped us solve many cases with her psychic abilities. The connection is that a little carved wooden doll was left by her body, depicting her stabbing, and now the dolls have resurfaced again."

Freya's eyes opened wide. "Just like the ones her daughter says she received. So what are you thinking, the little girl, Giselle, stabbed the psychic, and then went home and tried to kill her parents?"

"Of course not—that's not what I'm saying at all! The girls were best friends and remain so today. But we found some of the carved dolls hidden in Giselle's closet back then. They were little carved dolls hidden in a box, and not depicting horror scenes, but the kind that go in a dollhouse."

"Okay, then explain what the connection is between your old case and today's new ones?"

"I'll tell you what the connection is; one of today's clients is a man named Quinn Masterson. He owns a consulting company called 'Strong Foundations Contractors and Developers.' He's hired us to investigate his girlfriend."

"Okay Zeus, I give up, why is this odd and what's the connection?"

"Well my esteemed colleague, his girlfriend is Giselle Mackenzie; the eleven-year-old child from the crime scene nineteen years ago."

Freya's mouth opened like a fish waiting to be caught. "And why does he want her investigated?"

"The plot thickens here; he had a girlfriend in college who turned out to be a stalker, and he had to file a restraining order against her. He's been very cautious ever since then. Also, he dated Giselle briefly in college, and broke up with her to keep her safe from his stalker ex."

Zeus stood lost in thought staring out the window.

"I sense there's more to your misgivings." Freya commented.

"Yes there's more. Ruby, the daughter of the psychic, Giselle, the stalker—Imogen, and Quinn, were all at the same college together. In their second year, Ruby was attacked, and Imogen was the one who found her. She told the police she was headed back to her dorm when she saw someone lying on the ground, and a person wearing a cloak was holding a knife in the air about to stab her. She shouted and the person ran away."

Freya's eyes grew wider. "I see what you mean. There are too many intersecting lines. But wait, why would Imogen attack a random person and then shout for help?"

"That's a very good question, but one that I could not prove back then. You see, Quinn had been dating Giselle at the time, and Ruby was his study partner."

Freya nodded. "So you're thinking that Imogen thought that Ruby was Giselle?"

Zeus pursed his lips, and grimaced. "Either that, or Giselle attacked Ruby, because she and Quinn were spending too much time together. However, that day, Giselle was also in the library, and Ruby borrowed a hoodie from her because it was raining, and wore it to run back to her dorm to grab a notebook. Maybe Giselle, who had gone to the bathroom, slipped out the back door, attacked Ruby, and then slipped back into the library without being noticed." Freya countered.

"That brings me to another detail in the Giselle saga. Last year, Giselle's aunt, whom she stayed with after the ordeal, was found shot to death in her home. The police report states that it was a robbery gone wrong, but I don't think so."

Freya wrinkled her brow. "Why do you say that?"

"Nothing was missing, and many things of value were left behind, all except one." Zeus informed her.

Freya threw her hands in the air and held up her palms. "Well! Don't keep me in suspense."

"The victim's wedding ring; it was the only thing missing." Zeus leaned back in his chair, laced his fingers together, placed them behind his head, and leaned back.

"Zeus, I think we should take these cases, and that way we may be able to give the clients closure, and you might even gain insight into what actually happened.

"There's one more thing. I also received a call from an old colleague of Jenkins who's sheriff of Twin Pass Junction. His deputy reported some things that has him worried about someone on the force."

Freya laughed at the mention of the town. "So Barney Fife and Andy need help?"

Zeus chuckled. "Something like that, but there's a connection there too."

Freya crinkled her forehead. "Really, another one?"

"Caleb Jones was arrested nineteen-years-ago for shooting his wife Jaimie during an argument. Caleb or CJ as he's called in Palookaville was released early from prison on good behavior, and has gotten his life back together. Jaimie asked CJ for a divorce, which he was only too happy to oblige."

"I'm at the edge of my seat with anticipation." Freya responded drolly.

"Sheriff Hayward told me that Jaimie was a piece of work, known to be wild and reckless. He couldn't derive a conclusion as to why CJ would marry her, and later found out the reason, but never believed it. He's sure CJ was setup at a party, but wasn't able to get enough evidence to the contrary.

"What was the setup?" Freya questioned.

"The suspicion is that Caleb was roofied that night, but there's no proof, since he didn't go to the hospital to get blood-work done, there is no possible way to ever know."

Freya nodded. "I see."

"Sheriff Hayward was informed that after Jaimie divorced Caleb, she moved to Miami, and moved in with a guy named Lenny. The same guy at the party in high school, football player Warren's house, the night Caleb lost consciousness after downing only two beers."

Freya looked confused. "What does all this have to with the calls?"

Zeus smiled mischievously. "The connection dear Watson, is that Jaimie was in the same rehab facility as the late Delores Mackenzie. I'm hoping that maybe Delores confessed her crimes to her before she died that would finally exonerate the daughter. That's what I call killing three birds with one stone, don'tcha think?"

Freya laughed. "Sherlock Zeus, you're over-thinking all these connections. The last one is just an incredible stretch, and you know it."

Zeus laughed too. "You're probably right, but now that I know where to locate her, I want to ask Jaimie Joplin about Delores—it's been weighing on my mind too many years."

"Where will you start?" Freya asked him.

"In the lovely gated neighborhood of Giselle Mackenzie."

"So you're going to nose around her neighborhood for clues?" Freya wondered.

"Yes I am. Her neighbors are the same ladies that lived next door to Giselle when she was stabbed that fateful night. They conveniently live next door to Giselle in this neighborhood too. "Never forget, a nosy neighbor is a cop's best friend."

Freya laughed. "Or in your case a nosy detective."

Chapter 26
The Man With No Name

Stan Davis was not his real name. His unkempt gray hair, beard, and mustache were also fake, as were his eyeglasses, and uneven teeth. He looked sixty years old, and leaned heavily on a cane, but he was actually closer to forty-five. Nobody knew his real name, but in the business he was in, a name was the last thing anyone in his trade used. He was known merely as "The Handyman," and he was one of the highest-paid and most successful contract killers in the underworld.

He had always been a good shot and twenty-five years later, he still was. From the time he was a boy and taught to shoot by his father, he could hit a bull's-eye with one quick shot.

The first time he was contracted to kill someone, he felt ill afterwards, but the compensation had been substantial, and he certainly didn't want to work the fields again for meager pay, so he toughened-up more with every kill. With each executed kill, the images slowly began to fade away, and in time, they all became mere distant memories.

Killing was easy mainly because the marks were strangers, and merely jobs to be solely completed and compensated for, besides, he liked working solo.

He considered himself a detective of sorts, but instead of finding the victim and trying to save them, it was quite the opposite. It was as simple as pushing a button at the arcade and shooting zombies. He felt no remorse, it was likely some of them had done nothing wrong, and for the majority of them, he never knew the motive, nor did he care. It wasn't his place to ask questions, and frankly, he didn't give a shit. Besides, it's not the kind of business in which one asks questions. He had enough money stashed away for several lifetimes, and planned to retire from this profitable game soon.

His employers sometimes had special requests, such as quick or slow, and sometimes they wanted the deaths to look like staged suicides or accidents, posed or gruesome, and some were even done in a specific location.

One of his employers had once told him, "In our world money is easier to obtain by wicked means than by good ones, and since money is power, criminals will continue ruling the world."

Planning could sometimes take weeks of tailing a mark, learning about their routines and outings, and then the hit. He had plenty of patience and understanding, because being hotheaded could put him in danger. He was just doing what was asked, and earned enough to make living in this cesspool world easier. He was a charmer and a detail-oriented planner. He'd study his prey, find their weakness, and use it against them. He'd sometimes pretend to be their best friend right up until the moment he killed them.

His previous mark had been particularly difficult. The woman always stayed locked up in her house and had everything delivered. So broke into in an empty house nearby with 'a for sale' sign out front, and waited. She'd made the fatal error of leaving her curtains parted, and as soon as she stepped out of the shower and entered the bedroom, he took the shot and watched her fall. He packed up and left quickly. No trace of him being there would ever be found.

Tonight, he crouched atop the rooftop of a building across the street, set up and ready for another lucrative hit. He'd been contracted by E to pull off tonight's hit. He was known in their circles as one of the best, and impossible to trace back to either him or the contractor.

His mark stepped out from the shiny limousine, her sleek black hair fell over her bare shoulders and down to her waist. She matched the description exactly, but the photo he had been given hadn't done her justice at all—she was beautiful. The photo didn't capture her voluptuousness, or her full lips and big green eyes. She was dressed elegantly in a long red dress, with a v-cut in the back—it looked expensive.

In other circumstances, he would have flirted with her, and could imagine touching her lips with his. Even in the twilight, he could see she was stunning, *what a waste*. She turned towards her escort, and that's when he saw it. Around her slender neck was the missing diamond necklace from his employer's safe. She had stolen the necklace and a large amount of cash, and it was a shame he was hired to eliminate her. He would have preferred to bed her instead.

She fell without even a cry, one minute she was on her way to a lavish gala and the next she was gone. Her escort thinking she had simply tripped, bent down to help her up, and then let out a shout.

He didn't wait to see the chaos that would ensue. He buttoned the sheepskin lined black leather jacket, which gave him a laid-back biker vibe, clutched the collar to keep warm, and strode up the sidewalk. After he disposed of the untraceable weapon, he boarded a bus, then got off at the next stop and walked towards the station.

Afterwards, he rode the train out of town and settled in a seat with a book. He briefly looked out the window as a whir of indistinguishable shapes resembling ocean mist whizzed by, and thought of his next stop.

He'd preemptively rented a remote cliffside house where he would take some time off. He wanted to disappear for a while and relax somewhere undisturbed.

Once there, he settled into the comfortable chair by the fireplace, and rested. He was still high on adrenaline and wouldn't be able to fall sleep, there would be plenty of time for that later.

He reached for the bottle of Louis XIII Cognac, poured a generous amount in a snifter glass, and gently swirled the amber liquid. He enjoyed the warmth as it slid down his throat effortlessly; the taste was sweet and fruity with woody notes of oak and vanilla, perfect on this cold winter's night. He lit a fresh Cohiba cigar and felt himself relax.

The winds picked up, and he heard distant thunder in the mountains, then lightening illuminated the skies. It would be a stormy night, perfect for the mood he was in after all of the hits he'd been hired to accomplish within the past two weeks. He wouldn't be taking any more jobs for a few months. He planned a vacation in the Caribbean, heck; he might even buy a house and move there. Somewhere he could listlessly sit on a pristine, sandy beach and stare out at the jade colored waters, and forget about his existence.

Chapter 27
Giselle

Giselle awoke before the cloaked figure could reach her. In the dream, she walked in on someone holding an object and the person was angry at the intrusion. The person wearing a cloak with the hood on had swung around holding a knife, and advanced towards her. She had awoken with a start, and wondered what that meant, but shrugged it off to watching a horror movie last night.

She yawned and stretched, and looked at the alarm clock, which read 6:30 AM., then parted the curtains and gazed towards the sky. Expecting to see a subdued Sun, instead the day was golden, and divinely warm upon her chilled skin. The autumn day greeted her with brilliant foliage of cinnabar, papaya, and amber, playful in the morning light reflecting off the small pond, and giving her window a stained glass effect. The leaves had become natures carpet, as if Earth had declared herself queen with the confidence to flaunt such lovely gems.

Giselle looked at the neighboring houses. Her house was identical to all the others, right down to the same shade of paint. Suburbia's finest cookie-cutter neighborhood with homes equally spaced apart, matching lawns, backyards, iron railings, and even landscaping, in endless rows of seemingly indistinguishable homes in a gated community. When her father had moved them in, she'd at first had trouble finding her house, but her neighbors had solved that problem for her.

The house next door belonged to Tisi, her sister Alee, and Meg. Whereas every other dwelling was simply sand colored stucco, The sister's house was an explosion of color, turquoise exterior with an aqua-blue door, and green shutters with terracotta accents.

Their garden was a riot of blooms in every hue, chrysanthemums, pansies, celosias, asters, and violas, giving the once drab exterior a cheery look. Along the picket fence were roses of every color and below the windows were hanging baskets filled with even more flowers.

Tisi and her sisters had moved into their home when Elle was still a child, and when Tisi mentioned the new neighborhood to her father, he had liked it so much that after selling their house, bought one next door to the sisters. Darius felt comfortable leaving Elle with Tisi, and Tisi wouldn't have it any other way.

The sister's home had appeared in the May edition of Fabulous Gardens and Sheds magazine.

Alee was good at woodwork, and made a giant oval-shaped artist painting palette crafted of Maplewood, and filled with seven different varieties of colorful flowers: red, yellow, blue, green, orange, white, and purple, spilling out of the thumbhole on the front lawn.

Meg worked wonders with ceramics, and on front lawn was displayed a large mold of cupped hands with purple flowers in the middle spilling onto the lawn.

In the backyard was a cottage styled shed. Meg had built the main frame from old bricks and broken-up concrete blocks. A close artist friend of hers made the stained glass windows, which he created from her specifications. The windows were fitted with panes designed to resemble Art Nouveau. Inside hung a multi-colored chandelier, comfortable light-brown armchairs, and a small table underneath the French style windows "to enjoy a cup of tea and some gossip with friends." Tisi had told Giselle. And that's where they had enjoyed many afternoon teas. Ruby and Kassie had attended many times as well, and it was the first time in Giselle's young life that she felt insouciant and blithe.

When the sisters had first moved in, Tisi had invited neighbors over as a house warming, and it had been such a success that they'd decided to meet up the third Friday of every month, and hold a potluck.

Giselle hoped the job she had applied for at the Interior Design Firm would hire her soon. Even though she still helped make the little carved dolls with Tisi, the market wasn't as lucrative as it was years ago, but there were still people who collected antique dollhouses and needed the antique-looking carved dolls to go with them. It didn't make her rich, but still paid a few of her bills. She'd received the last of her unemployment benefits last month, and was stressed about acquiring a new job soon. She had already applied to more than five, and had the last interview yesterday.

She'd been working for the same designing firm for the last ten-years, and after the owner had passed away and his son had taken over, things had gone badly. She'd been dismissed over a conflict of interests—his interest in her and her disinterest in him. He'd propositioned her various times and when he tired of her turning him down, he fired her claiming she wasn't a good fit for the firm.

I wonder if that self-entitled jerk called around to the other firms and placed me on a black list. The thought made her livid with anger. The indignation she'd felt when he'd embraced her in the empty employee lounge, while she had her back turned making herself a coffee. She'd resisted the urge to smash him over the head with the coffeepot. Instead, she'd turned

Threefold Dread 128

sideways to get out of his grip, but as she tried to leave the room, he'd backed her up against the wall and tried to kiss her. She'd somehow managed to push him away and slapped him across the face, then ran to the ladies room, and locked herself in a stall. She'd cried for a long time, wondering what she could possibly have done for him to disrespect her—nothing. She'd only been polite and responded to work questions. She dressed conservatively and gave no indication she was interested in him, but he'd gone out of his way to harass her on an almost daily basis. Had she been smarter, she would have applied elsewhere while she still employed, but she had failed to act quickly and now she found herself in the predicament of unemployment.

Maybe I am failure my mother told me I would become, a big stupid failure.

Giselle heard the sound of approaching footsteps. *Hopefully it's today's mail with the check from my last job.* She looked in disdain at the tray with past due bills.

Looking out the front window, she saw no one.

Tisi's door opened a crack and a violet eye peeked out. Two other sets of eyes also watched her house. Shaking her head at the disappointment and sighing, Giselle went into the bathroom for a hot shower, hoping to stop feeling chilled.

Dressed in jeans, a long sleeved tee, a light cardigan, and sneakers, Giselle made her way to the kitchen and prepared coffee, bacon, eggs, and buttered toast.

After clearing the dishwasher, she picked up her purse and car keys from the entrance table, to run some errands. On her way out, Giselle nearly tripped over a neatly wrapped package left on the mat. Flipping it over, she noticed that it was addressed to her in big red letters, but with no return address and no stamps.

She went back inside, and placed the box on the coffee table, then sat on the couch and stared at the box wondering what could be inside.

Tearing off the wrapping, inside was a small wooden box. The exterior had various symbols she didn't recognize. Tentatively opening the top, the interior was black velvet with something hard wrapped in silky fabric.

Unwrapping the crimson silk, there were hand carved wooden dolls about four inches in length—little wooden dolls with secrets.

She removed the first one. The doll was female, with something protruding from her arm, and head. The clothing had red splotches.

What are those, horns?

She rummaged in a kitchen drawer for the magnifying glass, and holding it up to the doll's head, she gasped.

The two objects weren't horns at all, but tiny toy bullets one glued onto its head, and the other in the abdomen.

The second doll was male. It was wearing a pilot suit, with a tiny knife protruding from his lower belly.

The third doll was a little girl wearing bloodied shorts and a t-shirt, with red slashes on arms and hands, a tiny knife sticking out of her leg, and holding a gun glued to the hand.

She gasped, as realization sank in, and dropped the doll back into the box.

The words her mother uttered before falling to the kitchen floor on that fateful night came back to her unbidden.

"I curse you for what you've done."

Thoroughly shaken and trembling, she wondered who had left her those disturbing dolls, and for what reason?

Giselle didn't have any enemies that she knew about, nor was there a reason anyone would hold a grudge against her. She searched through the packaging, and a folded piece of paper fell out.

The neatly typed note read—"No one is as innocent as they seem."

Someone left this on my doorstep earlier. She thought with a shiver.

After placing the box of dolls in the garage, she telephoned Ruby.

"Ruby!"

"What's wrong Elle?" She asked apprehensively.

Giselle told her what she had received, and Ruby gasped.

"I received one too, depicting the horror scene in my house nineteen-years ago."

Giselle was too shocked for words. "Mine depicts what occurred in my house back then too! I've had a trying morning, first I wake up from a nightmare, and now this!"

"I'll meet you at the shop in twenty-minutes." Ruby stated. "Elle make sure your doors are locked and take extra precautions everywhere." Ruby commanded.

After hanging up, Ruby ruminated over the conversation with her friend. She hadn't mentioned to her that she'd also had a particularly disturbing dream. She could still feel the cold blade of the knife against her throat, its sharp edges digging into her smooth skin ready to pierce. She ran her fingers along her neck half expecting to find blood.

She'd been having the same dreadful dream for the past four weeks, and it was always the same. *Apparently, the psycho that attacked me is still out*

Threefold Dread 130

there, but why reach out now, after so many years? And what are my guides trying to tell me? I wonder if these dreams are somehow connected to the gruesome delivery, and how this is all connected Elle?

After waking that morning, Ruby tried to calm the feeling of terror, and her drenched body had soaked the bed sheets. It was just a nightmare, but it left her with a terrible feeling. She went to shower and prepare herself to listen to the same banal queries from lovelorn women.

Giselle entered and looked around appreciatively. She hadn't been here in months, and saw that the expansion looked great. Ruby's original shop was smaller; she had purchased property next door and connected both.

"Yassou," said a melodious voice next to her.

Giselle turned to see Athena who had silently appeared next to her. Athena was tall and willowy; she wore a sky-blue summery dress with embroidered flowers, and royal-blue low-heeled sandals. Her wavy brown hair adorned with burnished highlights from the sun was tied-up in a long ponytail, and her grayish-green eyes surrounded with naturally long lashes stared back at Giselle.

"Hello to you too." Giselle smiled at her friend, and gave her a hug.

"You look agitated. What's going on?" Athena asked concerned.

Giselle told her about the dolls, and Athena nodded. "Ruby received one of those too, but here at the shop."

Giselle and Ruby had met Athena while at university, and the three had become close friends. Athena was studying Greek Mythology. She was adept at creating beautiful works of art using her intuition.

Athena was Ruby's store manager, and ran the daily operations, and also she sold her artwork in the shop.

"I see you're eyeing the totem animals. Is there one in particular that catches your eye?" Athena asked.

Giselle shook her head. "They are beautifully made, but I have no idea how to choose one."

Athena explained, "Totem animals help the spirit, which is essential for success in any venture undertaken. Everyone has a power animal, which is an animal spirit that resides within each individual; it protects and acts as a guardian. It also increases energy fields so that illness or negative energy cannot enter their body. The spirit animal imparts wisdom of its own kind, and also helps guide or protect a person on their journey."

Giselle looked at all the intricately carved animals, some were very small, and some very large.

Athena led her to a shelf. "These are mine, and if you see one you like, I can make a special one for you. Browse the other shelves too, and see if one catches your eye, which means that's the totem for you. Ruby is doing a reading now and her assistant is at a doctor's appointment, so I'm tending the store for a while. Have a look around, maybe you'll be drawn to something."

Athena walked away to attend to a group of customers waiting to pay at the cash register.

Giselle admired Athena's totems. Each animal was beautifully depicted, and she was drawn to a couple: the dolphin and the hedgehog.

Before heading to the waiting room, Giselle perused the various shelves loaded with everything from tarot cards and crystals, to charms and talismans, and the last shelf was lined with little carved dolls, and labeled Katsina Dolls. They resembled the ones she had received, but these were not crude; these dolls were much bigger, intricately carved, and beautiful.

Giselle shook her head; *these certainly aren't the carved atrocities I received.*

Athena returned and stood next to her. "Look, I have no idea who sent you those disgusting things, but I can assure you they are not Katsinas! The ones we sell here are works of art carved by the Hopi Tribe. Hopi Katsina dolls are wooden effigies of the Katsinam, or benevolent spirit beings. They are never used for evil purposes, and the ones you and Ruby received seem to be."

"Just out of curiosity did you bring them with you? I'd like to see them." Athena inquired.

"No way, I left them in the garage. I don't want them in the house or anywhere near me, I didn't know what else to do with them."

"Let me know if you receive anymore of those dolls, I'm already making some inquiries. I'll let you know what I learn. Is it alright if I stop by to have a look at them?"

"Yes of course." Giselle quickly responded.

Athena nodded and giving Giselle a quick hug went to help a customer who was waving her over.

As soon as she walked into the waiting room, there in jeans and a T-shirt sat an extremely handsome man, one she'd never quite gotten over.

They'd met in her first year of college, he in his second. But after going out six months, he'd told her he couldn't see her anymore, because he needed to focus on his studies.

He looked up as she walked in, and realization dawned upon his questioning gaze.

The woman was attractive, in her late twenties. She was wearing conservative flats, medium burgundy pants, an oyster colored Laura Ashley blouse, with a matching burgundy jacket. Her pale blonde hair was shoulder length, which she wore in a tousled look with plenty of volume, and her, eyes a light blue.

"You're the last person I expected to see today." He told her smiling.

She smiled back at him, and nodded. "Same here."

"Are you following me?" Quinn asked mischievously.

"I should ask the same of you," she responded.

"Twice in one week can't possibly be a coincidence, or can it?" He asked her with raised eyebrows.

She sat opposite him in a plushy chair, pretending to look for something in her purse. Her posture was rigid; then her chin rose ever so slightly, studying him.

Quinn went back to the paperwork he was perusing when she walked in, and flipped through various pages.

She wondered what he was doing there. On the weekend, she had run into him at the bookstore and now here.

"I thought you didn't believe in the supernatural." She stated.

"I don't as a matter-of-fact." He replied earnestly, closing the folder and giving her his full attention.

Just then, a disembodied voice that lay beyond the beaded curtain hanging in the doorway called out authoritatively.

"You two, get back here."

He turned slightly, gave her a grin and a wink, and walked through. Giselle followed, frowning at the back of his head.

When Giselle walked into the room where Ruby did readings, she didn't see Quinn.

Ruby poked her head from behind the curtain and grinned. "Looking for someone?"

Giselle shifted her gaze downward, embarrassed, but Ruby gave her a big smile, and Giselle relaxed.

Ruby had removed the robe she wore to do readings and was wearing a short denim skirt, a tan blazer with thick shoulder pads, a green tank tap underneath, and brown heels. Her long auburn hair was cut in feathered waves, and she'd recently added long bangs to complete the look.

Ruby answered her unasked question. "He's in the back looking over some blueprints."

"So Quinn's your contractor." Giselle smiled at her friend. "You could have told me you know, I'm a big girl now, and can handle all sorts of news."

Ruby hugged her tightly, and Giselle felt herself relax.

"It's odd we're both receiving dolls depicting the horrors we suffered through as kids." Ruby stated. Then got up, went into the back room, and returned with a small box. She lifted the flaps, and Giselle peered inside, and then looked up at Ruby, a horrified gasp escaping her lips.

"Do the dolls you received look like these?" Ruby asked.

"Yes, I think so, they remind me of the ones in my dollhouse when I was a child, only, horrible."

"Why would someone send us these…things?" Giselle wondered aloud.

Ruby plopped down in her chair and looked at Giselle, then pressed the button on the intercom and requested two chamomile teas with sugar.

"I'd like to know who the slimeball is too, and then have someone beat the crap out of them."

Giselle looked at her friend with widened eyes. "Ruby!"

"What? You and your father were critically injured, and my mother almost died. Don't you want whoever sent us these hideous things to atone for their grievous error in judgment?"

Giselle nodded solemnly. "Do you think someone thinks this is funny and just wants to see us squirm?"

"I certainly hope not, because if I find out who sent these, there will be hell to pay."

"Should we contact the police?" Giselle asked.

Ruby shook her head. "Yeah, and tell them what? They'll just think some idiot is playing a practical joke on us."

Giselle nodded. "Okay, but promise me that if either of us receives more of these dolls that we'll go to the police."

Ruby shrugged, and nodded. "Yeah, maybe."

"Why don't I do a reading for you?"

Giselle nodded. "Sure why not."

Ruby shuffled the stack of cards on the table and fanned them out.

"Choose four cards and hand them to me."

Ruby turned over the first card.

"The Three of Swords represents a deeply emotional and sorrowful experience. A time in your life full of tears and sadness."

Threefold Dread 134

"Your second card is the Six of Cups, which represents old friends or long-lost family members re-emerging in your life. It can also stand for innocence and nostalgia."

"The third card is the Dark Priestess. This is a warning card, it could be either a man or a woman; it represents an acquaintance pretending to be a friend, but with a hidden agenda. The Dark Priestess has a plan or a goal. Be careful what you say and who might be listening, because this person has a devious plan. You'll know who this is because you'll sense he or she is holding something back. They'll choose their words carefully and will not be upfront. If someone shows up at your door acting friendly, it's because he or she wants something from you. Tell them only what you would want an enemy to know."

Ruby's eyes widened when she turned over the final card. *This is the second time this card has shown up in the same week, and it rarely does.*

"And your fourth card is the Dark Magician. The energy of this card personifies anger, bad intentions, hateful thoughts, and black magic. It can also represent repressed anger that may become destructive. This card is alerting you to an angry and dangerous presence. You might even know who this person is. You are being warned of an enemy, who watches you. There is repressed or carefully controlled anger in this person. The anger behind this energy once reached an explosive level that could have been from jealously, fear, hatred, or disdain. This person expresses these emotions through anger and violence. Remember that an enemy lurks closely, searching for your weaknesses, and for an opportunity to exploit them. Beware of things out of place, or situations that just don't seem quite right. Listen to your intuition warning you of an enemy's presence, or approach. Be suspicious of a stranger at your door, or some casual acquaintance asking personal questions."

Giselle stared at the cards. She hadn't expected the reading to be a harbinger of doom.

"Listen Elle, I won't lie, this is a terrible reading. My advice is that you to take steps to protect yourself, and take notice of any strange dreams or nightmares. You may never see or recognize this enemy, because the work is done behind the scenes, and in the shadows, or even under the guise of a friend. These are obviously not good cards, and are a warning that you have a terrible enemy, who wishes you harm. Do you have any idea who it could be?"

Giselle thought for a moment before responding. "No, I can't think of anyone who would wish me ill. And as far as I know I don't have any enemies."

"I can't stress enough to be very careful, be mindful your surroundings, and be careful what you say around others."

"Thanks for the reading Ruby. If I receive any more dolls I'll let you know, and I promise to be careful."

Ruby nodded. "I hope so for your sake. Let's stay in contact daily okay?"

Giselle nodded, and stood up to leave, but not before hugging Ruby tightly.

"And Elle, watch yourself. I don't like what the cards had to say."

"I'll be extra careful. I promise."

"Are we still on for dinner tomorrow night?" Ruby inquired

Giselle nodded. "Looking forward to it!"

Ruby sat lost in thought. She didn't bother calling in the next client, nor did she want too. They'd probably ask the same vapid questions all her insipid female clientele usually did, which was always about when they'd meet the love of their lives. There was no such thing as a fairy tale ending—idiots!

I hate those stupid dolls for dredging up old memories of a terrifying night long ago. But the show must go on.

"Come in whomever next." She finally called out.

Giselle went back to the store before leaving, and stood before the animal totem display.

Athena smiled at her. "I see you're trying to choose from more than one, and having a difficult time making a decision."

Giselle shook her head. "They're all so beautiful it's difficult to choose only one."

Athena chuckled. "Efharistó polí, I appreciate the compliment. Well, for your particular problem, I recommend the hedgehog or the dolphin." She pointed to the middle shelf.

Giselle laughed. "Those are the two I was considering earlier."

"Those are good choices, but I believe that you need one made with intention, and not just one sitting on a shelf, which will work too, but not as strongly for your particular problem."

Giselle was taken aback. "My particular problem?"

Athena nodded sagely, as if she knew all the evils the world held, and that one was hovering around Giselle.

"Yes, the curse, and the person who is responsible for it affecting you."

Giselle looked at her startled. *How could she know? Not even Ruby knows the last words my mother uttered that night. I've never dared utter them aloud for fear they might come true.*

Threefold Dread 136

Giselle looked at her bewildered—thinking of the last words her mother had said to her. "It can't be—she's dead." She whispered.

Athena looked quizzically at Giselle. "Then you must be thinking of the wrong person, because the person wishing you evil is still in the world of the living."

Giselle was surprised by her answer. "Then I have no idea who could possibly hate me so much to wish me harm."

Giselle stood lost in thought. *Did my mother somehow manage to repeat the curse as she was dying, and somehow it reached its climax many years later?* She thought with dread.

Seeing the look of apprehension on Elle's face. "I can work on a totem made specifically for your needs, and when it's done I'll let you know. Does that sound good to you?" Athena inquired.

"I'm currently going through…." Giselle began, but was interrupted.

"No need to worry about the cost. My spirit guide is most insistent that I need to make a special one just for you, and I can't ignore the request. Although, I can't promise that it will look like the ones you see here. I'll make it at home and give it to you as a gift." Athena told her.

Giselle smiled at Athena. "Alright I trust whatever you decide and accept your offer. Thank you Athena."

Athena "I'll get to work on your totem tonight, and drop it off."

Athena went back to the shelf and picked out an animal totem. "Here take this with you and keep it with you at all times." Athena placed the totem in Giselle's hand and then folded her fingers over it. "I'll see you at dinner next week." Then giving Giselle a quick hug strode towards the customers beckoning her.

Giselle opened her closed hand and looked at the totem Athena had given her. It was a hedgehog. She looked at the shelf.

Written on the hedgehog card: 'It is easy to underestimate this adorable little creature with its spiky exterior and docile expression, but don't be fooled the hedgehog is prepared for anything with its tough exterior. It is no stranger to adversity, and uses its discomfort to protect itself from dangers. When threatened, it survives by rolling into an impenetrable ball, which makes it difficult to be attacked. The hedgehog's protective nature helps steady nerves during difficult periods, and says not to be afraid when facing difficult situations. The hedgehog as a guide can help you face challenges, and teaches you to trust your instincts. When confronted with danger, it does not fight, but instead finds a way to rid itself of the danger, without having to hurt its attacker."

She smiled at the meaning and waved at Athena before leaving the shop.

As soon as Giselle walked outside, she saw Quinn lazily leaning against a car, and clearly waiting for her.

"How did it go?" He inquired while slipping an envelope into his pocket.

She shook her head, pursed her lips, and shook her head.

"That bad huh?"

"What about you and me catch up while we grab some lunch?"

She shrugged and nodded.

He extended his arm, she looped hers through it, and together they walked up the block to Perfect Panini Bistro.

Chapter 28
Clemmy

Inclemencia Maldonado was not a patient woman, and most importantly, hated to be kept waiting. She arrived at The Crystal River Club for dinner with her teenage daughter Elvira, and Quito, husband number five.

As soon as they arrived, the host informed them that their table wasn't ready.

While jabbing a vermilion-lacquered talon into his chest, she leaned towards him inches from his face and clenched the fist of her other hand. Her face had turned the color of a sliced open blood orange. "Do you know who I am?" She asked in a menacing tone like subdued thunder.

The maître d' rushed over, apologized profusely, and led them into the restaurant's bar area, where he seated them at a private table, and told them that while they waited for their table, the drinks and appetizers were on the house. He summoned a waiter, who immediately placed a glass pitcher of sangria on their table, nervously took their drink and appetizer orders, and hurried off. He feared this would be a stressful evening; the very dangerous woman seated with her family reminded him of a coiled cobra ready to strike. The hostility emanating from her had already spread around the room leaving everyone on tenterhooks.

Clemmy was still seething, grumbling about how she had been disrespected and how she would do something about it. Quito, as he often did put his arm around her shoulders, and calmed her down with whispered words of reassurance.

Moments later, a chubby, middle-aged, intoxicated man came lurching over to their table and swayed over them. He leered down at their daughter and pointed at her chest. "Your tits looks great in that skin tight top."

The sentence was barely out of his mouth when the glass pitcher of sangria smashed into the man's face and knocked him to the ground. Shards of glass on the floor haloed the man's bloodied face and his prior white shirt was now a mottled red. The room went completely quiet.

Two burly security guards quickly went over to the dazed man dripping with blood from the gash on his nose and lacerations on his forehead and with one guard on each side dragged him outside.

The man held the towel to his face, the waiter had brought out for him as he was being led out. One of the guards reached into his back pocket, but the man didn't notice.

"She sucker punched me! I never had a chance to defend myself."
The man complained.

"Not really man, you must have known it was coming, but you were just too slow," responded one of the bodyguards laughing.

The waiting taxi was informed to take him to the nearest emergency room, but not before the warning.

"Get yourself fixed up and say nothing about what happened tonight, or those aren't the only inconveniences you'll be suffering. We know where you live." He placed the man's wallet back in his blazer pocket and tossed his identification at him.

The maître d' appeared, seemingly out of nowhere. "Mrs. Maldonado, your table is ready," he said quickly.

The sight and aroma of the food prepared by the Three Stars Michelin restaurant's top chef helped to calm down Clemmy. They enjoyed a sumptuous meal that started with a bottle of Louis Roederer Cristal Champagne, Oysters Rockefeller, golden Caviar, and Foie Gras. The main meal consisted of Chateaubriand with Béarnaise Sauce, Roasted Chateau potatoes sautéed in butter and garlic, and two bottles of Cabernet Sauvignon. Afterwards, they enjoyed a decadent dessert of Belgian chocolate cake with Valrhona cacao ganache, topped with 24-karat edible gold flakes, upon a caramelized white truffle topping. The meal ended with Louis XIII de Remy Martin Cognac and Cuban cigars for both Maldonados.

Clemmy asked to see the chef, and the maître d hurried to the kitchen to let the chef know he had been summoned.

The chef walked over to the table with a worried expression on his face. *This does not bode well. I wonder what I did wrong.* He studied each person seated at the table.

He noticed the husband looked about ten-years younger than his wife did, and was dressed in an immaculate pale gray Armani suit. The daughter looked to be about fourteen, was dressed in an Azzedine Alaia skintight dress, which made her enormous breasts bulge out like squeezing a balloon filled with water, and left nothing to the imagination. As for the matriarch, she wore a black suit with metallic beadwork across the bodice in the shape of an X, which probably meant not to cross her; all that was missing was a veiled fascinator, to hide her puffy, pockmarked face.

"Good evening Mrs. Maldonado. I trust everything was to your liking?"
"That's the reason I wanted to see you."
The chef swallowed visibly, wringing his trembling hands.

Clemmy grinned at his discomfort, enjoying the effect she had on him. She was used to those reactions; they never disappointed her, and made her feel all warm inside—like a celebrity with fans.

"You outdid yourself—the meal was one of the best I've had in a while." Clemmy told him.

She reached over, grabbed his clammy hand, and placed a wad of bills into it. He thanked her, and stood rooted to the spot until the Maldonados walked out, like a soldier showing respect for his superiors. Afterwards, he went to the empty changing room, and checked to see what she had given him. He counted out five thousand dollars in crisp hundred dollar bills. *I hope they return soon. Very soon!*

Quito drove Clemmy and their daughter home in his brand new Maserati Quattroporte—a birthday gift from his wife. Their security detail followed. They drove up Palm Avenue, through the remote controlled gates, past the armed guards, and manicured lawns to a luxurious 6-bedroom, 23,315 square foot Mediterranean-style oceanfront mansion, named Las Palmas de Oro.

As soon as they entered, everyone split up to do their own thing. Clemmy went to the garage, got into her Lamborghini Countach, and sped off. She drove up Collins Avenue towards US 441 south. Clemmy was on her way to check out her newest investment, and to see how new management was working out. She liked to drop in on her employees unexpectedly to see what they were up to, and if she didn't like what she saw, someone would be sure to pay.

She sped along the highway and arrived at the Grove in less than the twenty-four minutes. She drove up Sailboat Bay, and pulled up in front of The Buccaneer Hotel. The doorman immediately strode towards the car.

"Buenas tardes Señora Maldonado."

"Hola Ernesto, cómo está todo esta noche?"

"Todo está bien."

He took her car keys and handed them to the valet, who carefully parked the car in a private parking garage in the back of the hotel. He knew there would be hell to pay if there was even one scratch on it.

Ernesto rushed to open the door for her, and as soon as she walked inside, the concierge appeared by her side.

"Good evening Mrs. Maldonado. I trust you are well."

"I am quite well, but what's occurred? I can tell by your tone you're keeping something from me."

The concierge cleared his throat. "There were a couple of…disturbances earlier, but they were quickly taken care of by security."

She nodded at him and headed towards the office. The newly appointed manager rushed towards her and pulled out a chair.

"Tell me what happened?" She demanded.

"It was nothing we couldn't handle. Jaime and Kimi are still in the club making sure there are no more disruptions, but everything is back to normal."

"I'll go and see if everything is as normal as you say it is." She told him in a deadpan manner, and strode through the heavy brass door and into the lobby.

Kimi was standing by the members-only bar of the Buccaneer Club, wearing a skintight black leather skirt, a silver mesh top, fishnet stockings, and silver stilettos, eyes scanning the room. She was satisfied that everything was back to normal, or what was considered normal. That the guests were enjoying themselves and spending money was all that mattered. She watched as Clemmy walked inside and stood off to the side in the shadows surveying the scene.

In a corner booth, cocaine kingpins Mongoose, Gordo, and Flaco were drinking ninety-five dollar bottles Dom Pérignon and were accompanied by girls in skimpy dresses. Flaco was throwing appetizers at Mongoose, and trying to get one into his open mouth.

Across the thick blue shag carpet Sergeant Martinez, from Metro Intelligence sat at the bar tossing back a Scotch, while taking mental notes of everyone and everything.

Over by the dance floor, Perla Arenas was playing the cello, holding it suggestively between her thighs, and wearing only a G-string, glittery nipple pasties, silver mascara, and a string of pearls. Her eyes were closed as her beringed fingers drew the bow across the strings, as she navigated between vibrato and glissando swaying to emphasize the sexiness of her playing technique.

Barbie Acosta, known as Bubbles, was adjusting her halter gold lamé top over her enormous breasts. She had arrived with César Falcón, a reputed hit man. A tipsy newcomer, who had made a fortune from oil, got up and bumped into Falcón on the way to the toilet. Falcón gave him the evil eye, but decided to ignore the man's mistake, as he had better things to focus on, as he escorted Bubbles to a table, then snapped his fingers for service.

Ex-Federal prosecutor Humphrey Adams was dining with the grass smuggling Bison Boys from upper New York State.

Roger Gilmore, the general manager crossed and let the maitre d' know that one of the bouncers had been sent out to the airport in his personal Rolls Royce. The bouncer had been instructed to pick up a special order from Seattle, the only place willing to ship 30-cases of champagne, and other alcoholic beverages by express freight.

Famous dope lawyer, Joey Beltrán was enjoying filet mignon with a baked potato wrapped in gold tinfoil., as he watched three men all wearing white suits having a hushed conversation—Gilberto and Julio, the Roqué brothers, with CIA agent Edward Wilcox.

"Tell me what happened earlier."

Kimi jumped at the sudden voice close to her ear and bit her bottom lip to stop herself from crying out. She didn't need to turn around to see who it was, as the owner had a habit of unnerving others by sneaking up behind them.

After composing herself, she looked Clemmy in the eye, and related the earlier occurrence that had gotten her out of the Jacuzzi with her latest lover.

"Earlier this evening, I was notified of a disturbance on the third floor. Our $150-a-night Brothel Suite was booked by two low rollers. When the bodyguards and I walked into the room, two men were using fifty-dollar bills dipped in alcohol and cocaine, lighting them up, and then throwing the lit bills up in the air and out the window too. An excessive amount of nose candy was going on there. Then one of the men started crawling across the floor, and dropped his chrome-plated 44. He then rushed to the balcony and threw up over the railing. Another man was screaming incoherently as he followed the vomiting man on all fours, and followed suit. The semi-naked men then made their way to the front of the hotel, by climbing from balcony to balcony, and pounding their chests like Tarzan, and then tumbled onto the second-story awning. Coke was spilling out of their pockets and fell onto the head of the doorman. Two of their friends proceeded towards the members only Buccaneer Club to cause more havoc, but they were dealt with immediately. No one was disturbed, nor did they even notice. Then down the hall in the Badlands Suite, a thief kicked in the door and stole jazz star—Buddy River's solid silver flute. We promised to replace it."

"I see you've had quite a night, and I trust those men are now out of the hotel?"

"Yes Clemmy, they certainly are, and they're not coming back."

"Good girl. If they return, you know what to do."

Kimi nodded. She certainly did; tell one of Clemmy's personal security detail, and those men would never be seen again–anywhere.

Clemmy watched as a few women strode provocatively around the room. The scantily clad hostesses known as "Buccaneer girls" were ready to stash weapons on their bodies in the event of a police raid. They were also available to entertain guests privately upstairs. This had been Kimi's idea, and Clemmy had been impressed that these tramps had been beneficial various times to the club. She was also aware that they made a mint entertaining the rich guests, but paid them top dollar anyway to keep their mouths shut.

"Um, Clemmy, remember the practitioner you mentioned?"

"Yeah, what about her?" Clemmy responded while watching some of the most dangerous people in Miami together in one room, and wondering how they could all be exploited.

"Could I get her number for a consultation?" Kimi asked tentatively, hoping she wouldn't anger her.

Clemmy reached across a table and took one of the napkins, then reached inside her gold snakeskin handbag, pulled out a pen and jotted down a name and telephone number.

She handed the napkin to Kimi, but before letting go of it, looked her in the eyes. "Are you sure you know what you're getting into? This woman is quite dangerous. Not even I would dare cross her."

Kimi nodded. "I'm sure."

Clemmy let go of the napkin. "Suit yourself. Don't say I didn't warn you."

"Where's Jaimie?" Clemmy asked pointedly.

Kimi looked around, wondering what to respond. "She was here earlier and helped with the commotion, but then Lenny arrived and she left with him.

"I see." Clemmy responded with a frown. "By the way…good job." After that, she turned around and left the room.

Kimi sighed; relieved the fiasco was over—for now.

After Kimi was certain Clemmy had left the premises, she made her way back to one of the private suites, and immediately after entering felt one strong arm encircling her waist, while the other stroked her left breast.

She turned around and gave him a deep kiss. This man was one of the biggest cocaine kingpins on par with Clemmy. He was also the best looking one she had ever seen.

"What took you so long babe?" Jimmy murmured in her ear while nibbling her lobe.

"I apologize for making you wait, but Clemmy just left. Earlier, a room full of idiots high as kites made a ruckus, but I'm here now." She turned around and rubbed her body against his.

The provocation proved too much for him, he slid off her leather skirt, then picked her up and with practiced hand easily removed her mesh top, until all she had on was a g-string, garters holding up her stockings, and four-inch designer stilettos.

He gave her an appreciative look, and with a hint of lasciviousness in her eyes slid one slim thigh up his. He needed no more provocation, and immediately dropped the towel wrapped around his waist, and picked her up. She straddled him as he walked both of them towards the orange plush wall of the Moroccan Room. One tanned arm wearing a gold Rolex held up both her wrists, while the other hand with a thick gold bracelet and pinky ring with a giant diamond encircled her waist.

Afterwards, he called room service and ordered two bottles of Dom Pérignon, two bottles of Château Lafite, and Chef Frankie's renowned Lobster Thermidor for two.

Dessert consisted of cocaine lines, cut with the Buccaneer metal membership card that pictured a pirate logo, more champagne and wine, and then another round of straddle and carry. The man was insatiable, and exactly how she liked them—wealthy, handsome, and virile.

Chapter 29
Giselle and Quinn

After meeting at Ruby's three months ago, Giselle and Quinn had begun dating again.

They'd first met in college when Giselle was studying for her Bachelor of Fine Arts in interior design, and Quinn was doing a double major, which included finance, business administration, construction management, civil engineering, and urban development. Both had even discussed the possibility of starting a business together, but by graduation had gone their separate ways.

They returned to his favorite restaurant—Abuela's Kitchen that served the most delicious Cuban food she had ever eaten. The owner, Inez stopped by their table to ask how everything was, and Quinn introduced her as one of his favorite clients to Giselle. She told him that while the location was perfect—what she needed to do now was to liven up the interior.

Quinn looked at Giselle, and then at Inez. "You're in luck then. I'm dining with one of the most talented interior designers on the Gold Coast."

Giselle reached into her purse, pulled out a business card, and handed it to her. Inez took it and placed it in her pocket.

"Come with me dear," she told her. "I'll show you around and you'll tell me your ideas. Anyone recommended by Quinn is always a winner."

Inez pointed out what she wasn't happy with, and Giselle made some recommendations to make the restaurant attract more patrons. Then, Inez made an appointment for Giselle to discuss where to go from there the following day.

Afterwards she rejoined Quinn who was waiting for her return to start on the entrees; she reached across the table and held his hand.

"Thanks for the recommendation! She seemed to like my ideas, and I now have a job lined up."

"It was my pleasure. Remember how we spoke of forming a business together?" He asked her.

"We did have some lofty dreams back then didn't we." She responded.

"Well they don't have to remain a distant memory. I've gathered some expertise over the years, and you have too." He told her.

"If you still think it's a good idea, maybe we should discuss it further." She responded now hopeful. She hadn't been getting any job offers lately, and was constantly worried about bills.

"I really like your portfolio, and the problem isn't where you're applying, but rather with whom." He further stressed. "Having connections in this world is a foot in the door, and I have a few connections that can be beneficial to you."

They lingered over after-dinner coffees; a Café Cubano for him, and a Cappuccino for her, and came up with some ideas about a business while sharing coconut flan. Before either one noticed, closing time had caught them unawares. They exited the restaurant, walked to the car, and he opened the passenger door for her.

As she was about to climb in, he grabbed her and pulled her towards him. His kiss was deep and intense, and she returned his kiss in earnest. They clung to each other tightly, and when they came up for air, he pulled her tighter against him.

"I've missed you," he said into her hair.

She breathed in his familiar scent.

"I've missed you too," she responded.

He gave her the sexy side grin, she remembered well.

"Would you to go to my place for a nightcap, and maybe give me some pointers on decoration? I'm just over the bridge in the Grove."

Giselle nodded her assent and he headed home.

Walking in and looking around, she hadn't expected to find such an austere environment. Even though it looked neat and clean, and the furnishings were in decent shape, many ideas came to mind to improve not only the look, but the quality as well.

Quinn excused himself and went to the kitchen, pulled a bottle of Riesling from the refrigerator and carried it back to the living room, poured two glasses, and handed her one.

"Well what do you think? It could use some improvement couldn't it?" He asked, already knowing the answer.

"I definitely have ideas for some upgrades and changes that can be made." She chuckled.

"Why don't you draw up some of those ideas for me? I've been meaning to make the place more presentable, but I just don't have that skill."

"I can start on some sketches this week." She told him with a smile.

"You've changed a bit over the years." He said admiringly.

"Is that a criticism?" she asked feeling uneasy.

"Not at all, it's a compliment. You look more beautiful if that's even possible."

"You don't look so bad yourself," she responded with a grin. She loved his wide, deep blue eyes, full lips, dimples, and tousled black hair.

"Besides your beauty, you're more assertive." Quinn stated.

Giselle gave him a small smile. "It's taken me years to get this far. When we first met, I was a bit timid because of my past. But I've learned to speak up for myself, and Ruby and Athena helped with the confidence part.

Quinn sat next to her on the couch and linked his hand with hers, looked into her eyes, and gave her a gentle kiss. He placed his wine glass on the coffee table, and did the same with hers. He pulled her closer, and then stood up and held out his hand, and led her towards the bedroom. Quinn looked back at her, and there was no doubting the look of a wonderfully wicked idea, and all it needed was a darkened room and a king sized bed.

Afterwards, they lay naked and draped in moonlight, while listening as the waves crashed on the shore. Giselle turned towards him and kissed him deeply.

"I think I've fallen in love with you all over again?" He told her.

Giselle smiled. Quinn's hand brushed through her long blonde hair, pushing strands away from her face.

"I've never gotten over you Quinn, and you have no idea how long I've wanted to hear those words."

She dropped her gaze; there was so much intensity in it, she was afraid she'd scare him away.

"I have a confession to make about why I broke up with you," he told her.

"There's no need. Let's just focus on here and now," she responded, a little alarmed by what his reason might be.

"No Giselle, I need to get this off my chest; it's also about your safety."

"What do you mean my safety?" She asked alarmed.

"I stopped dating you because I was afraid Imogen would endanger your life."

"What?"

"Before we met, Imogen and I dated for a couple of weeks, but I broke up with her because of her insane jealously. She accused me of flirting with every woman I talked to, even if I just opened a door, or pulled out a chair, or even bumping into a total stranger."

"That's an extreme reaction!" Giselle responded, somewhat relieved by the reason.

"Without a doubt, and afterwards, she started appearing everywhere I went. Then she began asking to get back together, and wouldn't take no for an answer. Basically, she tormented me to the point that I stopped going out with friends, or anywhere just to avoid seeing her."

"Are you saying she was stalking you?"

"That's exactly what I'm saying. I placed a restraining order against her. I even caught her watching us outside the library window one night. I haven't seen her since Ruby was attacked on campus, so I guess she's moved on."

"Imogen is a nice person. Maybe she just has relationship issues, but Ruby, Athena, and I have remained friends with her." She exclaimed.

Quinn eyes opened wide, eyebrows raised, mouth agape, before being able to respond. "I didn't know you three knew her. Are you sure that's a good idea?"

"Don't worry, she's harmless. She's a very nice person when she's not obsessing over you." Giselle teased.

Quinn began tickling her until she called a truce.

"By the way, were you just visiting Ruby or getting a psychic consultation?" She inquired.

"Very funny Elle. Ruby asked me to check into some prime property, she's considering. I was just delivering some paperwork for her to go over. Why were you there? Asking about me?" He asked with a grin.

"Why didn't you ever try to contact me?" she asked, changing the subject.

"But I did for a long time," he responded. "I only recently ran into Ruby, and she told me that you three were still friends. I was hoping to run into you, and just my luck you showed up. But before that I ran into your aunt and gave her a message for you."

She gave him a perplexed look.

"I ran into your aunt Deirdre last year when she was in town shopping, and we had lunch together. I wrote down my number to give to you, and she said she'd relay the message as soon as she saw you. Since you never called, I just assumed you didn't want to speak to me."

Giselle looked away and choked back a tear.

"I'll have to scold her when I see her again." Quinn stated.

"That's impossible." Giselle whispered.

"What do you mean it's impossible?"

"She's dead." Giselle could barely get the words out.

"What happened?" Quinn asked dumbfounded.

"She was murdered last year." Giselle responded with tears streaming down her cheeks.

"That's terrible!" Quinn was shocked at this unexpected news. He held her closer.

"What happened? Was the culprit caught?" Quinn asked, shock showing on his face.

"The police have no clue who was involved, but think it was a burglary gone wrong. I'm surprised you didn't hear what happened–it was on the news for weeks." Giselle questioned.

"I was out-of-town for a good part of last year, working on a big project." Quinn replied.

She nodded, and he hugged her to him, using his thumb to brush a tear from her cheek.

"I'm so sorry Giselle. I would never have brought it up if I had known."

She looked into his eyes, ran a hand over his cheek, and kissed him.

He kissed her back, and held her tight.

⚓☠⚓

Imogen wasn't exactly glad to see Quinn dating Giselle again, but they looked happy and that was all that mattered. It would never have worked between them anyway, especially after he accused her of stalking him, but what else could she do after seeing someone driving an expensive car following them around town. She tried to warn him, but he just wouldn't listen, and then he filed a restraining order against her, but she still kept vigilant.

Imogen thought about that terrifying night on campus. She was walking back to her dorm after picking up some food, when she saw Giselle up ahead wearing her favorite hoodie rushing through the rain. She called out to her, but it began raining so hard she didn't hear her. Then she watched as someone in a cloak pounced on Giselle and knocked her to the ground. Imogen watched as the cloaked figure raised a knife, and she began screaming for security, and then ran towards them frantically waving her arms trying to scare off the attacker. The person fled before she reached them, and she didn't see the face as the hood of the cloak was covering their face, the only thing she noticed was a long strand of blonde hair trailing out of the hood.

When Imogen reached the student to help her up, she realized it wasn't Giselle at all, but a very frightened Ruby wearing Giselle's hoodie.

Imogen helped her up and Ruby hugged her thanking her repeatedly. Then campus security arrived and called the police. Imogen accompanied Ruby to campus infirmary where her bruises were attended to and had their statements taken. The police drove around campus, but didn't see anyone running away or wearing a cloak. They told Ruby she was lucky Imogen happened to be on the pathway.

Ruby told the police she had borrowed the hoodie from Giselle, and was going back to her dorm to grab a notebook. The security guard went to the library to ask Giselle to go to the security office, and a concerned Quinn came with her. Upon seeing Imogen, he reacted strangely. He told the police that he had a restraining order against her, and that maybe she was the one who had jumped Ruby thinking she was Giselle that the police should question her motives.

"I NEVER stalked you. I may have followed you once or twice, but that was because I saw someone following you and Giselle. I tried to tell you, but you refused to listen, and just walked away. What was I supposed to do? And then you slapped a restraining order on me, and that was that." Imogen started to cry.

Imogen couldn't stop crying, and Ruby told Quinn to back off. Ruby told him that Imogen most definitely didn't attack her, since her attacker ran off in the opposite direction, unless of course, Imogen could time travel, or had a twin. Plus, Imogen was the reason she hadn't been stabbed by the psycho.

Giselle was horrified listening to her friend explaining what happened as she held Ruby's hand. She put her arm around Imogen's thin shoulders, handed her a tissue, and glared at Quinn's callousness.

From that night on, Giselle and Ruby became friends with Imogen, and went out whenever they could. They later introduced her to Athena, and the four hung out often, and then kept in touch after graduation.

After Ruby berated him for being an idiot, Quinn was still cautious and didn't completely trust Imogen or her motives. He thought she probably befriended Ruby and Giselle with ulterior motives, but couldn't prove it.

After graduation, Quinn moved away to build his business, and Giselle returned to the house her father had left her after getting married—the one next to Tisi.

Chapter 30
Elizeus Bishop

Zeus rang the doorbell, and listened as it chimed 'Ride of the Valkyries' then smiled. Freya would love this!

Within moments, a short and stout woman with a pleasant face opened the door.

She eyed him with open interest. "Elizeus Bishop, please come in; I've been eager to hear your query."

Tisi led Zeus into the kitchen and told to sit at the table while she prepared tea.

"What can I do for you Mr. Bishop? She asked with a grin.

Zeus couldn't help but smile back. "Miss Furey, I don't know if you remember me from many years ago, when you were living in Coral Point. I stopped by regarding the incident at your neighbor's house."

Tisi looked him over. "Of course I remember you. You're a bit more mature looking, but I'd recognize you anywhere."

Zeus smiled, remembering how straightforward she had been back then too.

Her demeanor reminded him of his grandmother who was loving, kind, caring, and comforting. Tisi was short and slightly plump, probably due to her predilection for sweets. Her thick black hair sported a French braid with dyed blue strands messily woven in, and adorned with tiny rhinestone clips. Her face was round and full, with pink cheeks and full lips. Her age was difficult to ascertain, and he just assumed she was middle aged.

"I have a few questions about one of your neighbors, and Zeus is just fine."

"God of sky and thunder." She simply stated, then sat down, and smiled.

Zeus smiled back at her.

Beneath the table, her calloused hands with nicks and cuts, reached for the beads adorning her red tunic then ran her blue nail polished fingers over each flower. The orange, green, and yellow scarf worn over the blue lined, orange and red striped cardigan trailed on the floor. She crossed one leg clad in blue leggings over the other, while her dark orange boots tapped a slow rhythm to silent music.

"You can call me Tisi. All my friends do." She gave him a big smile.

"Well Tisi, I've been hired to find the person sending some hideous carved dolls to your neighbor Giselle, and wonder if you might have seen the person delivering them."

Tisi gave him a questioning gaze. "Why, has she received more?"

Zeus nodded. "I'm afraid so, and her father is very concerned that she may be in danger."

Tisi nodded thoughtfully. "He may be right, but this is a safe neighborhood and nothing bad will happen here." She stated this rather than making a mere observation.

Zeus watched as she walked back to the stove, poured water from the kettle into a porcelain teapot decorated with flowers, and set it on the table.

"I'm curious, where does the Furey surname originate?"

Tisi smiled as she pulled a tray of freshly baked shortbread cookies from the oven, and began placing them on a plate bordered with flowers. After she set down two cups and saucers, she turned to him.

"Please help yourself. My surname originates from Old Greek. By the way, these cookies are from an old family recipe."

Zeus savored the delicious biscuit. He remembered the cookies Tisi had served him and Jenkins years ago.

Tisi looked at him amused, and happy that he was enjoying her baked goods as he had many years ago.

Zeus licked his lips and a small, delighted smile lit up her face. She pushed her glasses up her nose and tilted her body toward him. "What is it you really want to know Zeus?"

Zeus wiped his mouth and reluctantly placed the second cookie half way to his mouth on his plate before answering her. "I'd like to know if Giselle is the type of person pretending to receive those dolls for attention and actually sending them herself."

Tisi drew her brows together and frowned. "I'm ashamed of you Zeus, for saying such a thing about that lovely girl. I am certain that she did not send those dolls to herself or to anyone else, but the person who did should stop before things get out of hand."

Zeus tilted his head to the side. "You really believe that don't you."

"You're darned tootin' I do!"

He hadn't expected her annoyed reaction or harsh response. "Forgive my asking such a personal question, but I want to make sure I'm not like a dog chasing its tail."

Tisi smiled at the metaphor, and relaxed. "I can only tell you Elle has suffered immensely, and deserves better, but apparently some psycho has other ideas."

Zeus nodded in accordance. "I fully agree with you, and I really want to find out who keeps leaving those dolls on her doorstep. They were not delivered by a service, and I'm hoping someone has seen the culprit walking away."

Tisi abruptly got up from the table, walked to the far wall, picked up the receiver and dialed a number, and asked someone to come over, now. Then she sat down across from Zeus and gestured towards the cookies. They both sat in silence as Zeus bit into another cookie wondering whom she had called.

A few minutes later, a BMW and a Harley parked out front, and two women walked in through the back door. Tisi introduced them to Zeus.

Alee was tall and thin with glossy black hair cut short into a 1920s like bob, and pearl earrings dangling from her earlobes. Her face was oblong and her dark brown eyes quickly darted around the room. She was impeccably dressed in understated elegance. Her tan pants were worn with a cream-colored top adorned with wheat and brown designs, and cream-colored low-heeled pumps, topped off with a camel colored trench coat and a designer handbag.

Meg in contrast to her sisters was muscular and almost as tall as Alee. Her dark brown hair was pixie cut. She wore black jeans with a gray t-shirt, a black leather jacket, and black leather harness boots.

"Zeus, these are my sisters, Alee and Meg."

They both shook hands with Zeus.

"If anyone has seen anything it would be one of us since we like to tinker in our garden and shed when not traveling, but I haven't seen anyone leaving packages on Giselle's doorstep." Alee stated.

Zeus couldn't believe how different each sister was. Where Tisi was kind and friendly, Alee seemed reserved and suspicious, and Meg appeared wild and carefree.

Meg spoke up next. "I believe I saw a woman loitering out front Giselle's house early one morning and later on I heard about the dolls. Those hideous things should have been burned like Ruby suggested." Meg responded.

"I offered to run over them with my bike, but Elle turned me down." Meg looked disappointed.

Zeus was immediately on high alert. "Meg, what did the woman look like?"

Meg's eyes darted to the ceiling, as if trying to conjure the woman's face from thin air. "Well, it was a crisp autumn morning, and I was tinkering with my bike, when I saw the back of a woman quickly walking up the street. I thought it odd at first, but then thought; maybe the person was checking out the neighborhood, there are a few houses for sale after all. So I disregarded it."

"Did you get a look at her fa…?" Zeus wanted to know.

"I sort of did!" Meg interrupted. "I found it odd that she didn't ring the doorbell, but just bent down on Giselle's stoop—I thought she may have been tying her shoelaces. She appeared to be in her mid-twenties, and was extremely thin. I couldn't see her face properly, because she wore a baseball cap pulled down low. I did find it odd she was dressed in business attire, and wearing that type of head gear and sneakers though, but to each his own."

Zeus was intrigued. One of the sisters had probably seen the person leaving the dolls. "Would you recognize her if you saw her again?"

Meg looked thoughtful. "I'm not sure."

Zeus realized something Meg had said earlier.

"You mentioned a person named Ruby?"

Meg nodded. "Yes I did, what about her?"

Zeus nodded. "Would this per chance be Ruby Mason?"

"Ruby is the daughter of a dear friend. We took her in after her mother was in a coma nineteen years ago, and her father couldn't be located. Her grandparents offered to take her with them, but since they lived out-of-town, Ruby wanted to be near her mother, and finish the school term."

Zeus was not expecting this turn of events. "She wouldn't by any chance be the same Ruby Mason whose mother Kassie was attacked?"

All three sisters looked at each other and their postures stiffened.

After a delayed response, Alee looked straight at Zeus, which made him sit up straighter. "Why do you ask?"

Zeus felt uncomfortable under their scrutinizing stares, and resisted the urge to tell them he had to leave for another appointment. "I was one of the officers investigating the attack, and a little wooden doll left by the body; the one I showed Tisi."

There was knock on the back door. "Aunties, it's me Ruby!"

Zeus watched as a tall, beautiful redhead walked in with a look of surprise upon seeing so many people gathered in the kitchen.

Tisi immediately got up and hugged Ruby.

"Ruby, this is Mr. Elizeus Bishop." Tisi introduced him, as he stood up and shook her hand. She looked at him suspiciously, and held his hand a little longer than necessary, causing him to become slightly uncomfortable.

"I see," she said and sat down. "Mr. Bishop what would you like to know about that day?"

Zeus opened his mouth twice and closed it again, before he was able to formulate words. He swallowed, cleared his throat, and asked what she already knew he would.

"Please, call me Zeus."

"I remember you from the most terrible day of my life." She told him with a somber look on her face, although you were younger then."

Zeus wondered how old he actually looked, and was beginning to worry.

"Yes, I was there, but there was unfortunately no conclusion to who harmed your mother. I promise you that we did all we could to find out, and even after the case was closed, Detective Jenkins and I continued investigating, but were unfortunately unsuccessful. There was another incident that occurred years ago around the same time, and something is occurring now that may or may not be connected; I'm trying to find out if there is a connection."

Ruby watched him as he spoke, and feeling he was sincere, seemed to make up her mind.

"Alright Zeus, I'll tell you all I know, and hope this leads to new clues that can finally put the piece of trash behind bars–or worse."

The last word she used had Zeus thinking that he too felt that it would be appropriate if it weren't illegal.

Tisi patted her hand. "Now dear, don't you worry; situations have a way of righting themselves when the right kind of help is summoned."

Zeus was pleased he was considered the right person, and would do everything he could to solve this case.

Ruby sipped her tea, then sat back in the chair and began.

"Nineteen years ago when I was in middle school, a girl in my class would spend her lunch time sitting alone in the yard without anything to eat. I started sharing my lunch with her, and then I began packing two sandwiches, two juice boxes, cookies, and chips, every morning, so she could have lunch too. She looked waifish, was dressed in worn clothing a size too small, and her sneakers had holes. I just assumed she was very poor, and I even began gathering used clothing from my neighbors whose daughters had outgrown them to give to her."

Threefold Dread 156

Giselle was very grateful and polite, and never followed me around as my friends had warned me she would start doing. She just waited for me at a table underneath the tree in the yard, and we ate in silence. Eventually, my friends coaxed her to join us, and Elle acquiesced. She ate in silence listening to the lively conversation but not joining in.   They even tried to get her to respond by being jokey, but she was painfully shy and only smiled back, but spoke very little. I wondered why she always wore long sleeves and pants and a tattered cardigan, no matter how hot the day was.

One day when entering the locker room for P.E., I saw Giselle in coach's office crying. The principle walked in, took her by the hand, and led her away. I was concerned, peeked around the corner, followed them up the hall and saw coach enter the principal's office. Giselle was left sitting on the chair in the hallway, while the principle went into her office and called someone on the telephone.

I walked over and asked Giselle what had happened, but that only made her cry more. I noticed that she wasn't wearing her usual clothing, but the P.E. uniform, and up and down both her legs and arms were purplish bruises. I had to return to gym before I was missed, but I asked to use the bathroom a few minutes later to check on Giselle—I was very worried about her.

While pretending to drink water at the nearby fountain, a pretty, blonde woman arrived. She was taken into the principal's office, and not long after, she began yelling. I peeked in to check on Giselle, and she had stopped crying, but looked very frightened. I uttered some words of encouragement, and asked her if that was her mother, she sniffed and nodded her head. The door to the principal's office slammed open and Giselle's mother angrily stalked out, grabbed her Giselle's arm, and dragged her up the hall. I overheard her whisper menacingly: "wait until we get home."

Giselle tried to pull her arm from the vise grip, but was dragged down the front steps and shoved into the car. Her mother took off so quickly the car's wheels screeched and left tire marks on the pavement. Many things bothered me that day, but I was especially bewildered by the car her mother was driving—a brand new Mercedes. So Elle wasn't poor after all, but neglected. I felt a presence behind me, it was the principle; she placed a hand on my shoulder, and told me to go back to class that there was nothing I could do for Elle.

I never saw Giselle at school again. When I asked coach about her, she told me that Giselle's family had moved away, and that she was attending another school.

I often wondered what had become of her with no food or proper clothing, but I didn't even know where she lived since I'd never been invited over, so I couldn't check on her. She became very happy whenever I invited her over to my house, and especially when asked to sleepover. I was never invited to her house, and when my mom asked about her mom, Giselle made excuses saying she worked late nights."

Zeus sat in silence taking in what Ruby had just divulged.

"Ruby, your mother has always been a great help as a consultant for the police department. She helped us solve many cases where months had passed without any leads, and had again reached an impasse. Without her help, some cases would have remained unsolved, and she once helped save an abducted child. She is well liked and respected."

Ruby sipped her tea before proceeding. "Thank you for sharing that with me Zeus. I'm glad that she's well remembered. But you might not know that she's decided to help with cases again."

"I'm glad she's doing well."   Zeus shared a sympathetic closed lipped smile. "Everyone who knew her thought of her fondly. What happened to her had the department scrambling for answers, and we followed all the leads, but came up with nothing."

Ruby knew he was being sincere and she instantly liked him. "There's more to the story; one day I walked home from school and saw a car parked out front, and knew mom had a client, so I started up the driveway to enter through the kitchen, but noticed there was someone sitting in the passenger seat. The child's head barely made it to the window, so I walked over, and was surprised to see Giselle.

I told her my girlfriends and I all missed her at lunch, and asked her where she had moved to, and what school she was attending. Giselle looked down and whispered she hadn't moved, and wasn't attending school. That her mother told her the new school was still processing the paperwork, and that she would attend soon enough.

I didn't know it at the time, but her mother wasn't planning to send her back to school at all. I asked her if she had eaten, and she shook her head. I asked her if she wanted to come inside so I could prepare some food for her, and she eagerly shook her head. Then we went in and I made some mac and cheese, and we sat down to eat. I had just given her some cookies and milk when we heard raised voices from the living room. Sometimes, clients weren't happy with the predictions and became

Threefold Dread 158

angry, so I wasn't too concerned. But Giselle looked terrified, so I urged her to eat up. She had just finished her cookies and was drinking the last of the milk when the front door slammed shut. We then heard Giselle's name being called loudly, she gave me a terrified look and ran out the kitchen door.

Her mother yelled at her "Get in the car. Didn't I tell you to stay put? Disobedient child." She slapped Giselle hard across the face, and I was just about to run out to defend her, but mom stopped me, and shook her head. I spent a long time wondering what had happened to my poor neglected friend. I really wanted to locate her, but before I could ask my mom…" She trailed off not being able to complete the sentence. The shock from many years ago was easily relived.

Tisi patted her hand.

Ruby took a deep breath and continued. "The following week, my whole world crumbled, and you know the rest. That was the last time I saw Giselle. I always wondered what had become of her until the day mom took me to visit Miss Tisi."

Zeus told them about what had occurred in the Mackenzie house, and how Giselle had been left traumatized.

Meg placed the tissue box on the table, then grabbed one and handed it to Ruby.

"That poor abused child, I can't believe any mother would subject their child to an abusive environment like that, but how did the husband not know?" Questioned Alee.

"I wonder why the husband never saw the neglect and abuse. Maybe he was an idiot and just assumed she was taken care of." Meg wondered aloud.

Tisi shook her head. "Sometimes humanity is very disappointing. I often wondered why the father didn't intervene."

Zeus could see how others would misinterpret the situation.

"The reason he didn't notice anything amiss about his daughter was because he was a pilot, and not only worked for an airline, but also for private charters on weekends. His wife insisted they live an expensive lifestyle, drive an expensive car, and live well above their means, while she contributed nothing in return. Someone had to suffer in that scenario, and that someone was unfortunately Giselle."

Ruby stared at the wall behind Zeus. "I stayed with Miss Tisi for a bit so I could finish out the school year, while my mother was still in the hospital. My grandparents lived an hour away, and I didn't want to be far from my mother. When Giselle was discharged from the hospital, she also stayed at Miss Tisi's to recuperate while her father returned to work, and figured out what to do next. We forged a long-lasting friendship back then. When my mother was finally discharged she and I went to live at my grandparent's house, and Elle and I stayed in touch.

We applied to the same university and continued our friendship throughout the years.

"Did Giselle hang out with any other students while there?"

"Elle dated Quinn Masterson for a bit, but then they broke up."

Zeus narrowed his eyes at Ruby. "Quinn Masterson from Strong Foundations?"

"Yes that's him. Do you know him?"

Zeus thought of how to respond without giving too much away, since he was a client. "We've met, but how do you know him, if you don't mind me asking."

Ruby shrugged. "We met in college. We were study partners, and became friends. Quinn's my go to guy to check out a structure before I make an investment. Although, he's had his share of woes too."

Zeus was interested in what she had to say, since he knew very little about him, except for his inquiry. "What do you mean?"

Ruby hesitated before responding. "While we were in college, two incidents occurred that may or may not be related. He was dating a girl named Imogen, who turned out to be quite annoying. She was so jealous of every girl he talked to that he eventually couldn't take it anymore, and broke up with her.

Then one night after Quinn and I had been putting together a presentation in the library, I needed to retrieve some notes from the dorm, but it was raining and Giselle who was also in the library lent me her hoodie so I wouldn't get wet. As I was walking back to the dorm, I was attacked by someone wearing a hooded cloak and holding a knife, when someone screamed the attacker ran off.

"Which college did you attend?"

"The Gulf Coast University."

Zeus sat back trying to remember the case, as it would have been reported to the police department by campus security, but it might have been assigned to someone else if was an isolated incident. "Were you hurt?"

Ruby shook her head. "No, because the person who screamed and saved my life was Imogen. She's the one who called the police and stayed with me until they arrived."

"Was the attacker ever caught?" Zeus made a mental note to request this incident record.

"Not that I know of, but I was lucky Imogen happened to be returning to her dorm at the same time. I told Quinn that she had saved my life, and he was surprised. Imogen was a good person she just had trust issues.

Zeus could feel the inner mechanisms running at full speed in his head. *So the three of them had been at the same college at the same time. Could I be right about Giselle, and could she have been the one who attacked Ruby. Although, what could possibly have been her motive? Unless, of course, she was so damaged from her childhood trauma, she decided to attack someone who knew about her past. No, that doesn't make sense at all, but there has to be a connection; as any good cop knows, coincidences just do not exist.*

"Did you see the dolls Giselle received, and do they look like the ones left for you?"

Ruby shook her head. "Wait, how do you know I received one too?" She shook her head again. "Mom contacted you didn't she?"

Zeus smiled. "Yes, Kassie is very concerned about those evil-looking carvings, and asked me to investigate."

"She didn't tell me she had contacted a private investigator, but since you were there all those years ago, it makes sense. If you want to see the carving, my assistant has it locked up in a file cabinet." Ruby told him.

"I certainly would like to see it. I'm headed over to Giselle's now to see hers."

Ruby shuddered involuntarily, feeling a coldness creeping up her spine at the thought of the carving. "It seems that whoever sent that carving to me and to Giselle know about our pasts. It's even possible that this is the same person who attacked my mother, and then me on campus."

Zeus nodded. "The same thought occurred to me as well, but it can just as well be a copycat, except that the carved doll left the day Kassie was attacked was never revealed to the public. Only someone in the police force would be privy to that information."

"This is very concerning. Why would the culprit wait nineteen-years to terrorize me and my best friend?" Ruby questioned.

Zeus shook his head. "I really have no clue at this time, but I will do my damnedest to find out. Your mother's attacker was never caught, and if he or she is back again to intimidate you, Kassie, and Giselle, I'll track whoever it is down and put the person behind bars for a long time."

"Are there any other questions you have for me, I have to leave soon for an appointment, but I'd like to catch up with the aunties before I do?"

"Thanks Ruby, I can't think of anything else at the moment, but where can I reach you in case I do?"

Ruby reached into her designer purse, pulled out a business card, and handed it to him. "You can reach me there. If I'm busy when you call just leave a message with my assistant, and I'll call you back."

Zeus turned over the card. "Bloodworth?" He asked inquisitively.

Ruby smiled. "Professional name. I didn't want my name in any way connected to the past.

"I see. Thanks Ruby, I'll be in touch and thanks for sharing that information. I appreciate your help."

Ruby nodded at him. "Sure, if I can answer any more questions, you know where to find me."

Tisi walked Zeus out, and he thanked her for her hospitality, and her delicious cookies. Tisi blushed with pride, told him to wait, and went back to the kitchen. Within moments, she returned with a paper bag, and handed it to Zeus.

"For the road," she winked at him.

Chapter 31
Giselle

Giselle awoke soaked in sweat. The same dream again. A faceless person dressed in a cloak, and advancing towards her with a knife.

She looked around, trying to get her sleepy eyes to focus. The alarm clock read 6:45AM, and Quinn was still asleep.

She decided to try and go back to sleep, but felt a chill run up her spine making her shiver involuntarily as if in forewarning, and then she heard it; a rustling sound in the bushes under the bedroom window.

Quinn woke up and yawned widely.

"Good morning beautiful." He kissed her cheek.

He looked at her frightened face. "What is it Elle?"

"I think someone is outside near the bush by the window?" She whispered.

Quinn shook his head, but sat up and pulled on his robe.

"I'll go and check." He whispered back.

She got up and put on her robe, pulling it tightly around her. Quinn held a finger up to his lips, and went to investigate. Elle stood still in a corner of the room.

Sounds of hushed whispering seemed to be coming from the green striped wallpaper. Was she going crazy? *This can't be happening. This isn't real,* she told herself. Yet, it felt nothing but real and absolute to her.

A breath, hoarse and faint echoed around her, coming from the opposite corner of the room. Giselle slowly turned her head, and the whispering stopped. The air felt icy, and her labored breathing became the only sound. Someone was sitting in the chair, dark and brooding.

"Who's there?" she whispered.

There was no response, but the shadow got up and came towards her. She held her breath.

I'm still dreaming, she thought to herself.

It was Deirdre, she was holding a gun in her left hand, and a cloak draped over her other arm.

Giselle had found her that horrible day. She had gone over visit her aunt. The police surmised she had probably walked in when the thief or thieves were still ransacking the house.

The first bullet had hit her chest. The second bullet had gone through the left eye socket; the dark red blood pooled around her was already blackening when Giselle arrived. Some brain matter had exploded from the back of her skull, and splattered on the otherwise immaculate kitchen. Her body had slumped to the floor like some ungainly life-sized doll. The remaining eye remained open, staring blankly.

Giselle's mouth opened in a silent scream, and her unblinking eyes wide like an old-fashioned doll. A bead of cold sweat dripped down her back, and her skin cold as the steel of the gun that flashed before her.

Terror froze her to the spot. *Where is Quinn?*

"Auntie Deirdre," she whispered. "What are you trying to tell me?"

She then heard a crash in the living room, and forced herself to move. As soon as she did, the apparition disappeared.

"Quinn," she called is everything okay?"

He appeared in the hallway holding a small box.

"Yes, I knocked over the umbrella stand. Looks like the noise outside was just a delivery person dropping off a package."

"I'm going to make us some breakfast." He yawned sleepily.

"Okay, I'll be downstairs in a few." Giselle went into the bathroom, turned the water faucet in the sink to hot, and held them there for as long as she could stand the heat, hoping it would warm her trembling hands.

She inhaled the wonderful smells wafting through the house, and saw as Quinn placed freshly made blueberry pancakes on two plates, which already held bacon and eggs.

"Everything smells and looks delicious, thank you for breakfast."

"My pleasure." He kissed her on the cheek, then sat down and began to pour warmed maple syrup on his pancakes.

"Where's the delivery?"

"I placed it on the counter."

She got up, and scowled when she looked at it.

"What's wrong?" He asked.

"I received a box two months ago, and like this one it was also addressed to me in red ink, but with no return address, or stamp. Meaning someone left it on my doorstep."

"What was in the first box?"

She got up, walked to the garage, and retrieved the first box, then placed it on the kitchen table.

"See for yourself."

He looked inside and examined both dolls, then replaced them in the box.

"That's odd. Any ideas who could have sent them or why?"

She shrugged and shook her head.

"Let's see what's in the box delivered today. Do you want me to open it?"

She shook her head. "No, let me do it."

She cut through the brown wrapping, and inside was another box similar to the first one she'd received. The exterior had various symbols like the other one, only these were different, and the interior was all black.

Quinn stood behind her as she lifted the top object wrapped in crimson colored silk.

The first doll was female, and when she picked it up the tiny leather jacket, jeans, and the t-shirt, she wore fell away in tatters, purposely burnt, and the doll was lying upon a broken and burnt toy motorcycle. Elle dropped it in revulsion.

She unwrapped the next bundle and out tumbled a male doll. This one was wearing blue jeans, a button-top shirt with a blazer, and loafers; he was holding miniature wire cutters.

Quinn studied both dolls and shrugged. "Somebody has a very sick sense of humor." He stated and sat back down to finish breakfast.

"I don't see the humor in this at all." Giselle responded. "And I don't understand the implications. Besides, I don't know anyone who rides a motorcycle besides Meg. And who is the male doll supposed to be?"

She was about to stuff the dolls and wrapping back into the box when a piece of paper fluttered to the floor. She picked it up and noticed some writing on it.

The note was typed: What do you really know about him?

She watched Quinn as he finished the rest of his pancakes, and wondered.

After Quinn left for work, she considered calling the police, but what could they do. They'd probably laugh at her expecting them to hunt down a whittler.

She was still feeling shaky and agitated, but decided to call her father and hoped he was still in town. After four rings, he answered.

"Dad, I'm so glad you're home."

"Giselle what's the matter? You sound upset."

"I received another box of dolls"

"Giselle honey, you should have called the police the first time, and now you've received more. A very sick person is tormenting you with these things, and that person already knows where you live."

"No dad, the police won't take this seriously. They'll just think it's a prank."

"Honey this is quite worrisome. What do those dolls even mean? This seems like the doings of an insane person."

"And the more reason not to contact the police. Giselle responded.

"I disagree." Darius replied emphatically.

"Besides dad, you sent over PI Elizeus Bishop, and he took photos of the dolls I received the first time. He's looking into it, and the ones Ruby received too." Giselle told him. At least he's taking it seriously."

"Just promise me that you'll be extra careful while you're out, and make sure all your doors are locked, both at home and in your car. And that you'll let me know if you receive anymore, and also contact Zeus if you do." Darius insisted.

"I promise dad and don't worry I'll be extra careful.

"I almost forgot to ask, how's Aurora?" Giselle asked.

"She's well; you know her, always busy cooking up a storm, and keeping our home impeccable."

"I'm glad you found each other dad. She's a good person, and you deserve to be with some who loves you."

Her father had remarried when she was in middle school, and Giselle had immediately liked her. She'd gotten to know Aurora before her father sat her down and told her he was planning to propose to her, and asked for Giselle's blessing. Giselle had been very worried at first given the past, but she liked Aurora, and felt comfortable around her. After their marriage, she had come to love Aurora, thought of her mother, and for the first time was able to experience a happy household. And as a plus her father didn't work as many days of the week as he had before, and they did many things together as a family.

Aurora and her father never had any children, and Giselle used to pretend that Aurora was her real mother. Her clothing was always clean and ironed, and her hair braided or combed back into a ponytail every morning. Aurora had doted on her fed her delicious meals, helped her with her homework, and made baked goods for school events. Giselle was grateful her father had gotten a second chance at happiness, and she had too.

"Stay safe, and keep me updated. Can't wait to see you at Thanksgiving!"

"And I can't wait for delicious homemade turkey and trimmings. Love you dad, talk to you soon. Give my love to Aurora."

"Will do. Love you too baby girl."

As soon as Darius hung up, he opened the top drawer of the telephone table stand where the business card file was located, and flipped through. He found the card he was looking for, then picked up the phone, and dialed the number.

Chapter 32
Clemmy

Clemmy observed as Lenny lazily strolled into the warehouse. She hated that little shit—he reminded her of a ferret, long, lean, and smelly. He'd been distributing her drugs for many years now, and even though she could only trust him as far as she could throw him, which wasn't far, he was the best at getting the job done, and especially at keeping his mouth shut.

She watched him loading crates into vans with the other guys. He must have sensed her gaze, looked back, and waved. Clemmy sighed heavily, resisting the urge to pick up the crowbar she'd just used to open a container, and smash his skull into his neck. She beckoned him over with a finger.

Lenny swallowed, feeling his throat parched, and wishing he'd drunk water when he'd had the chance.

"Clemmy, ma'am, is there anything I can do for you?"

Clemmy stood facing him down expressionless, as if daring him to make just one mistake, so she would have an excuse to kill him.

"I received some unwelcome news this morning, and would like clarification."

Lenny's mouth went even drier. He knew what that look meant and had to stop himself from running out the door. No one crossed her when she was in one of her bad tempers, hell, no one crossed her period, but if he had known about her state of mind, he would have avoided working inside. But now it was too late.

"You remember the incident nineteen years ago in that little shit town Twin Acre Junction where my drugs and my money went missing after your little mishap?"

Lenny remembered quite well. He hadn't forgotten that she had been screwed out of both, and Lenny had paid for his grievous error in judgment. In his haste to get away from the incident with CJ and before the police arrived, he had bolted, and left behind a substantial amount of cash and drugs, both Clemmy's.

She looked at his left hand with the missing fingers, and when he saw her looking at his hand, he almost shit himself. He jammed both hands into his pockets.

Lenny stood as still and straight as a soldier awaiting a command. Clemmy took her time before continuing, enjoying every moment of his discomfort.

"This morning, one of my men informed me that he overheard the Bison brothers laughing about how one of their smugglers used to work for me, and that nineteen years ago made off those two things. Do you have any idea who this could possibly be?" Clemmy asked eerily calmly.

Lenny made a face as if he had just sucked on a bitter lemon. "The last I heard was that the police confiscated everything that night." Lenny replied with a tremor in his voice.

The truth was that Jaimie had falsely accused CJ of dealing, and he had been arrested. Warren, a rookie back had been the first on the scene as he had been nearby, and Lenny suspected that he had taken most of the stash and cash before the sheriff had shown up. Jaimie told Lenny that Warren had handcuffed CJ and left him in the patrol car, and then told her to wait in the kitchen. Afterwards, the coke and money disappeared and only a trace of coke had been found. Jaimie thought the sheriff had taken it, but Lenny suspected Warren.

Clemmy raised an eyebrow and scowled. She wasn't sure, if he was lying or if he actually had no idea. She opted for the first part.

"So you have no idea who stole my coke and money? I don't have all day. So if you know something, you'd better fess up now; it's been a very long time."

Lenny took a deep breath and proceeded. "I actually have no idea who it could be. Except…" He trailed off when she narrowed both eyes.

"It's possible someone else in that town may have been working for our competitors and took it."

"I'm in no mood for bullshit, especially yours! Seriously Lenny, I'm giving you this last chance. If you know anything, you'd better speak up NOW!"

Lenny startled at her sudden shout.

"Well, uh, the only other person, besides Jaimie that I know lives in that town is Warren." Lenny had trouble replying, since his lips were also dry now, and he had to keep licking them with limited saliva.

Clemmy nodded. "That's what I thought. One of my guys overheard that some small time punk was working their distribution from a little hick town called Twin Acre Junction, and had been informing them of cargo arriving for me. This is probably the reason some of my cargo went missing a few times."

Lenny felt vomit rising up into his throat.

Clemmy stared at him, or through him, lost in thought. *It's curious, that one of my ex-employees may just be the culprit.*

"I'll make inquiries and find out if you're telling me the truth. God help you, if I find out you're lying to cover Warren's ass or your own about that long ago incident."

She didn't want to believe she had been lied to and cheated by Warren, and that he was her competitor's informant. He was the only one who worked for her back then that lived in that particular town. She believed him when he told her he was quitting the business and going to college.

If Warren was working with the brothers and stealing from me, while using the college story as a cover, I'll make him pay. No way, she thought, *no one who knows me can possibly be that stupid!*

At least I have Kimi. She's become an asset in helping to hide copious amounts of money in real estate ventures. Kimi was sophisticated, cunning, and savvy. The only thing that concerns me is that there's something off about her—something impalpable. She's proven to be trustworthy, or as much as she could be trusted, so far, and so has Jaimie. I hope Lenny wasn't lying, because if he were I'd need to take care of this mistake myself, which includes him.

"Could it be you're mistaken, or because you want me to believe someone else is guilty of double-crossing me instead of the real culprit?" She tilted her head forward, staring him down.

Lenny seemed to shrink into himself under her fearsome gaze. "It's entirely possible, and I don't know for sure, but that's all I know."

Clemmy continued staring at him without blinking, her expression stoic. "Then why are you still standing there, get back to work."

Lenny didn't need to be told twice. "He saluted her like a sea captain, turned around, ran into towards the last crate, and began loading boxes into the van.

Clemmy stood rooted to the spot. *Either Lenny is lying or he's covering for someone. Nevertheless, I will stop at nothing to find out starting today.*

Clemmy hoped for Warren's sake that he had told her the truth; because all her employees knew, she expected loyalty–forever. *If Warren has been, double dipping, and double-crossing me from way back then that is an unforgivable act that requires extreme punishment. I wonder how Lenny fits into this scenario, because I knew damn well he was somehow involved.*

She called two of her security detail over and gave them strict instructions to follow to a T, and to report back to her daily. She'd get to the bottom of this, pronto!

Lenny finished working for the day, and drove straight towards downtown. He pulled into a space in the real estate building parking lot,

Threefold Dread 170

and ran towards the entrance. That bitch Kimi owned the entire building and the underground parking garage too. He wondered how she'd gotten so rich. He entered the elevator and punched in the fifth floor. The doors opened up into an elaborately decorated office—the professional kind, with expensive furniture, and wall-to-wall plush carpeting. He walked over to the receptionist's desk and asked to speak with Jaimie Joplin, urgently.

The woman looked him up and down and frowned. "I'm sorry sir, but you'll have to make an appointment first."

Lenny asked her for a piece of paper and a pen, which she reluctantly handed to him, making sure their fingers didn't touch. As if merely interacting with him would somehow taint her. He made sure to brush her hand with his two stumpy fingers when she handed him what he had asked for, and was greatly amused when she sucked in her breath, and retracted her hand quickly. He knew as soon as he walked away that she'd run to the bathroom and wash her hands a few times.

He wrote a note, folded the paper in half, and told her to hand it to Jaime, and that he'd wait for a reply.

"Is there something I can get you while you wait, coffee, water, a soda?" *Insect repellent.*

Lenny remembered he'd forgotten to drink something before driving off, in his desperation after his shift to get away from Clemmy. He had to clear his throat before being able to croak out his response.

"Sure, I'll have an orange soda."

The receptionist picked up the phone; within minutes, an office clerk came out with his drink, took his message, and disappeared through the doors leading to the back offices.

Moments later, the same clerk walked back through the double doors, and over to him. "Follow me please."

Lenny was led through the double doors, and into another expensively decorated office. He was told to have a seat that Ms. Joplin would be with him shortly. Minutes later, a tall, slim woman walked in and leaned against an ornate desk.

"Hey Lenn, what's up?" Jaimie asked.

Lenny stared at her. "We need to talk privately." He glanced towards the door. Jaimie quickly walked over, closed it, and sat next to him.

"What is it? Has something happened?" She asked him twisting the ring on her finger.

"We've got to do something to get ourselves away from Warren pronto, before it's too late."

"Relax babe. The money's good and we only have to help him twice weekly, then it's easy street. Afterwards, we attend to Clemmy's business as usual."

"NO!" He shouted.

Startled, she leaned back into her seat. "Why Lenn?"

"For starters," he began, "Clemmy questioned me about the missing blow and money from nineteen years ago."

"What did you tell her?" Jaimie asked with widened eyes.

"I lied of course. I couldn't very tell her that Warren was the one who stole her cash and drugs, because then she'd ask me why I didn't tell her back then."

"Shit!" Was all Jaimie could respond amid the terror she felt.

"I overheard two of her goons talking about a rumor they'd heard about Warren working with the unholy trio, and that they knew it was bullshit that he was quitting the business to go to college. They didn't think he was smart enough to get a degree."

"Shit!" Jaime responded again, turning paler, and twisting the ring quicker.

"Shit is right! I'm sure Clemmy is having him watched, and if we go on another run with him—we'll be seen, and we can kiss our asses' goodbye. Hello Biscayne Bay with cement booties." Lenny responded.

"What do we do then? It's not like Warren will take no for an answer." Jaimie told him her eyes blinking rapidly.

"We'll just have to give him the excuse that Clemmy has us working night and day on her shipments, and hope he swallows the lie." Lenny stated.

Jaimie nodded. "Okay, that shouldn't be too difficult, since he knows nothing about Clemmy's operations lately.

"What about Kimi? Lenny asked.

"What about her?" Jaimie responded flatly.

"Will she tell Warren about us not really being as busy as we say we are?"

"What do you mean?" Jaimie asked perplexed.

"You really don't know do you?" Lenny replied, a smirk spreading rapidly across his lips.

"Know what?" Jaimie asked with a sharp tone, while crossing her arms across her chest.

"They've been screwing for some time now." Lenny arrogantly replied. He saw the surprised look on her face, and was cocky enough to be proud of the fact there was something he knew that she didn't.

Threefold Dread 172

Jaimie sat dumbfounded. "Warren, of all the men she could screw around with, she picked easy to provoke and ill tempered Warren?" She couldn't believe it!

After some thought she replied, "There's no need to be concerned. I know how to handle Kimi. She'll pose no threat to us, because I know things about her that would turn even Clemmy's head." Jaimie told him with an evil smile.

"Okay babe, if you say so, but I think Warren is a loose cannon waiting to fire a heavy projectile, and we need a game plan." Lenny told her solemnly.

"Agreed, let's meet up tonight and discuss what to do about him." Jaimie kissed Lenny goodbye, and after he left, she sat thinking how to kill two birds with one stone.

Kimi buzzed through to her assistant's desk and placed her order. Paige came back with a cappuccino for her boss, and watched as Lenny walked up the hall and into reception.

What the hell is he doing here? Paige wondered frowning.

Kimi shook her head wondering what Lenny was doing in her office too. "I wonder if, Clemmy sent him over to give Jaimie instructions about tonight." *What is that worm really doing here,* she wondered.

Paige nodded as if that made sense. "Is there anything else you require before I go back to my desk?"

"Yes, there is. Go back to the shop and pick up another package for me. I'm running out to an appointment, so just lock it in my desk, and you can leave for the day since I won't be back until tomorrow."

This seemed to perk up her personal assistant. "Really, I can have the rest of the day off?"

Kimi smiled at her. "That's what I said. Now leave before I change my mind."

Paige smiled back. "I'll see you tomorrow then."

She quickly walked to her desk, grabbed her purse, and ran towards the parking garage just in case Kimi did change her mind, as she often did. In fact, her boss was prone to erratic mood swings, and anger was one of them.

She found Lenny leaning against his car. "I was hoping you'd still be here she said to him."

He gave her a lazy smile. "I'm always here for one of my favorite clients. I didn't know you worked for a real estate firm."

She smiled at him, reached into her purse and pulled out her wallet, extracted some twenties and handed them to him, but he pushed her hand away. He pulled out a small plastic bag and held it up. "I'm inviting if you're willing to join me."

She hesitated before responding wondering if this was a good idea, but free snow was worth it, the expense was putting a dent in her earnings. "Sure, but what's the catch?"

Lenny gave her a mischievous smile. "I have a proposition for you."

She gesticulated. "Go on!"

"Let's talk when we get to the motel."

"Alright, I'll follow you."

She got into her car and pulled out of the garage. She'd just have to go on her boss's errand later; there would be more than enough time before the shop closed. But for now, she planned to have a little fun on a much-needed and unexpected day off.

Chapter 33
Perilous Situations

"Giselle, where are you?"

"I'm upstairs." Came the croaky reply.

Quinn ran up the staircase two steps at a time. When he entered the room, he saw that Giselle was still in bed, with a thermometer sticking out of her mouth, and tissues strewn all over the bed.

Giselle removed the thermometer from her mouth, looked at it, and placed it on the nightstand. Then reached over and took two aspirin with some water. Her nose was red, and her eyes watery, but when Quinn advanced towards her, she held up her hand to stop him.

"What, a little cold won't affect me." He told her.

"Possibly, but I'm contagious and I don't want you getting sick too, otherwise, who'll make me chicken soup?" She smiled at him.

"Well in that case, I'd better start cooking." Quinn blew her a kiss from the doorway and headed downstairs.

After opening up a can of soup, and making grilled cheese sandwiches, he poured the soup into a flowery ceramic bowl that had probably been made by one of the sisters next door, he placed napkins and a soupspoon on the tray and went upstairs. They had both finished their lunch, and were lying back watching television when telephone rang.

He picked up the receiver on the nightstand. "WHAT? I'm headed over!"

Giselle looked at him apprehensively. "What's wrong?"

"Ruby's in the hospital." Quinn informed her after replacing the receiver.

"Why, what's happened?" Giselle attempted to get up and immediately felt a wave of dizziness.

"I'm not sure; that was Athena, and she didn't say much except that Ruby was in bad shape."

Quinn gently pushed her back onto her pillows. He was worried about the pallor of her face.

"Then go, don't worry about me. I'll be fine. Tell her I'm in bed with a cold, but call me as soon as you get there."

"I don't want you to be alone—you don't look so hot."

Giselle gave him a feeble smile. "I kind of am." She glanced at the thermometer.

Quinn smiled back at her. "I can't leave you alone to fend for yourself."

Giselle began to protest, but Quinn raised his palm. "I'm going across the street and ask Miss Tisi to keep an eye on you. That way I won't have to worry about you too. I'll give her my key."

Giselle smiled weakly and nodded.

"I'll head over to the hospital. Is there anything I can get for you before I leave?"

"Just some more water, and leave the tray in the kitchen, otherwise, I'm all set."

"Sure thing," he responded.

After getting her more water, he kissed her on the forehead and headed downstairs. On his way out, he double-checked that the front and back door were securely locked before heading across the street.

Tisi unlocked the front door with the key Quinn had left with her and called out, but there was no answer. She made her way upstairs, opened the bedroom door, and peaked inside. Seeing that Giselle was asleep, she went back downstairs, found a pad and pen, and wrote that she was downstairs. Not wanting to startle Giselle when she awoke and heard sound then went back upstairs and taped it on the inside of the door. She went back downstairs, sat in the living room with her sewing basket, and worked on miniature doll clothing.

When Quinn arrived at the hospital, there was a police officer standing outside Ruby's door. He was asked for identification, and then checked his clipboard before letting him enter the room.

Upon entering, he saw a very pale Ruby lying back against two pillows, with bandages on both arms, and a patched cheek and neck, where she had received stitches. He also saw the detective he had hired recently, and Ruby's mother Kassie sitting next to her daughter.

"Ruby, what happened?" He rushed towards her bedside and held her clammy hand.

Her eyes welled up with tears, and fought to gain control of her emotions before she could formulate words.

"After we had brunch yesterday, I went back to the shop, and was just unlocking the door, but felt something wasn't right. So I turned around, and that's when I was attacked."

"I've been warning her various times to set up security cameras, because I've been receiving messages and visions of her in danger, and now look what's happened." Kassie told Quinn tearfully.

"Did you see who attacked you?" Quinn asked.

Threefold Dread 176

"No, because the person was wearing a ski mask. I was grabbed from behind, and a knife was held at my throat."

"That's horrible, how did you manage to escape?" Quinn asked her still holding her hand.

"I took a martial arts course after I was attacked on campus, and used the techniques I learned. Let's just say that the person who attacked me is now walking around with injured ribs, stomach, head, neck, and knees. By the way, where's Giselle. I thought she'd come with you?"

"She's in bed with a bad cold. She practically threw me out because she was worried I'd get sick too. She made me promise to call her when I got here so she could talk to you."

He reached for the phone on the table next to the bed to call Giselle, but Zeus stopped him.

Leaning against the wall across the room, Zeus had been listening to their conversations.

Quinn hung up the phone.

"You're not going to like what I have to say, but we have to consider all possibilities. Quinn, did you notice anything odd about Giselle this morning?"

Kassie looked at Ruby, and then at Zeus. "You're not implying what I think you are—are you?" Asked Kassie annoyed at his suggestion.

Ruby nodded in agreement.

Zeus looked at Quinn quizzically.   "No, not at all. She was wearing a bathrobe, and had the covers over her as well. She was shivering from a fever, so besides that nothing out of the ordinary. Why do you ask?" He replied apprehensively.

"No need for concern. I haven't found out anything untoward, but I still have to ask. She did endure a terrifying childhood with an unstable mother, and an oblivious father. Sometimes people who've lived through trauma suddenly snap." Replied Zeus.

Both Kassie and Ruby stared at Zeus shaking their heads. Quinn looked crestfallen.

Kassie spoke up first. "You're completely wrong. Giselle wouldn't hurt Ruby, or anyone else. She was a gentle and caring child, even after surviving nearly being killed by her own mother, but I'm absolutely sure she would never hurt anyone. I remember her playing in my garden, and picking up snails crossing the stone pathway, and putting them on the opposite side where there was grass. When I asked her what she was doing, she told me that sometimes kids at school trod on them, and that made her sad. She wanted to make sure no one stepped on them accidentally. That they were gentle creatures who carried their homes on their backs, and should be kept safe from harm. Does that sound like a dangerous person to you?"

Quinn felt terrible and guilty for even considering Elle was capable of violence.

Zeus shrugged "Anything is possible Kassie, and you of all people should know that from experience."

Zeus wondered if Giselle was actually ill or faking, and wearing a bathrobe to cover up the bruises.

Ruby who had been listening quietly spoke so low it was barely audible, since she was getting sleepy from the pain medication. "We've been through difficult times together and remained close friends, I'd trust Elle with my life, and no one can convince me otherwise."

She turned to Quinn. "Call Giselle, I want to let her know that I'm okay."

Quinn dialed the number, and Tisi picked up on the second ring.

"Hello, Tisi how is she? I'm glad to hear that. Sure thank you. By the way, I'm at the hospital with Ruby. Sure hold on." He handed the phone to Ruby.

Ruby gave him a questioning look. "I left my key with Tisi; I didn't want Elle left alone in her condition."

Ruby nodded in comprehension, and he passed the phone to her. After speaking with Tisi for a few moments and assuring her she was well cared for, she waited for her to tell Giselle to pick up the phone.

"Hi Elle, I'm okay, just a few cuts and bruises, but otherwise, I'm fine. Don't worry, Quinn told us you're ill so stay in bed, and mom will let you know how I'm doing. Okay, take care of yourself too. Hugs."

Kassie hung up the receiver and noticed Ruby's eyes closing. She pulled the blanket up to her daughter's chin and tucked it in on the sides, then sat down to read Howl's Moving Castle.
Before Ruby fell into an exhausted sleep, she remembered an incident she had witnessed when she was in fourth grade.

Kassie had met Miss Tisi after both participated in the local arts and crafts fair. Tisi's booth displayed various beautifully handcrafted pieces, while Kassie's booth was for tarot and psychic readings. Afterwards, the two women kept running into each other around town, and eventually began meeting for coffee, and became friends.

One afternoon, Ruby arrived from school and Tisi told her that Giselle was in the shed, and handed Ruby a small tray with two plates full of cookies and two glasses of lemonade. Ruby thanked her—she was excited to see her friend. Walking slowly, she carefully held the tray so she wouldn't spill anything on Miss Tisi's lovely cream and gold shag carpet. When Ruby got to the shed, she heard Giselle yelling through the closed door and tentatively approached. She placed the tray on the little table outside and peeked through the window.

Giselle seemed to be yelling at a little carved doll she held in her hand. "You're a bad person Delores!"

Ruby gasped. The doll Giselle held was wearing a red sundress, and had long blonde hair, and Giselle was red in the face.

"You're always so cruel. I HATE YOU!" She yelled at the doll and banged its head against the table.

"I wish you were dead!"

She threw the doll across the room, and then fell onto her knees crying.

Ruby didn't know what to do. She didn't want to interrupt her friend working out an issue about her mother, but also wanted to console her.

Ruby waited a few minutes, then picked up the tray, and knocked on the door.

"Giselle, are you in there?"

Ruby watched as Giselle quickly stood up, and rubbed the tears from her eyes with the backs of her hands.

"Ruby is that you?"

"It is and I've brought us a snack from Miss Tisi. Open the door."

Giselle opened the door. Ruby picked up the tray and maneuvered it through the doorway, then placed it on the mosaic table.

"Whew, I was afraid I would drop the tray before I found you."

Giselle just stood there looking at Ruby.

"What's wrong Elle?" Ruby asked her friend.

Giselle sniffled. "It's nothing."

"You know you can tell me anything right?"

Giselle nodded and sat down. "It's just that I'm afraid of what my mother might do next. I'm not allowed at Miss Tisi's and if she finds out I'm here, well, it won't be pleasant for me."

Ruby got up, knelt down in front of Giselle, and held her hands. "When are you going to tell your father what's happening?"

Giselle looked down at Ruby as if she had asked her to solve the mystery of Cleopatra's burial site. Wide-eyed, she shook her head frantically and pulled her hands from Ruby's grip. Her downcast eyes and furrowed forehead told Ruby what she already knew.

Giselle hunched her shoulders while her arms hugged her midsection. She stared at the floor and bit her bottom lip. "He'd never believe how mean she is to me, she replied sadly. Mama will just blink her pretty, lying eyes at him like she always does, and he'll believe her just like he always does."

Ruby nodded, got up, and sat back down on the opposite chair. She poured Giselle a glass of lemonade and handed her a plate with cookies. They sat in companionable silence each lost in thought while absently eating a cookie.

❦

Zeus gave Quinn a slight head nod towards the door. Quinn kissed Kassie's cheek and silently closed the door behind him.

"Do you still want me to continue investigating Giselle?" Zeus asked.

Quinn ran his hands through his hair. "I don't think that's necessary. There's nothing to make me think she's troubled, and much less a bad person. On the contrary."

After Zeus left, Quinn leaned against the wall and considered his next move. He thought back to the day Ruby was attacked, wondering if had missed anything back then. He remembered it had been heavily raining all afternoon, and that they had reserved a table in the far right corner of the library. At the table were Ruby, himself, and Giselle. That Ruby had forgotten some notes back at the dorm on the project they were working on together, and because no one had an umbrella, Giselle had offered Ruby her hoodie. Ruby wore it with the hood pulled over her head and ran outside.

Earlier, Quinn spotted Imogen lurking in the opposite corner of the library sneaking glances at his table, but just ignored her. Giselle had excused herself to go to the bathroom, and within minutes, there was a commotion outside. Giselle hadn't returned yet, and Quinn noticed that Imogen was no longer in the library.

Everyone in the library suddenly got up and ran towards the windows. Quinn followed suit and watched as Imogen bent over a figure lying on the walkway. Looking closely, the person was wearing a hoodie just like the one Giselle had lent to Ruby. He ran towards the exit.

Giselle had just reentered the library, and watched nonplussed as Quinn ran out the front door. She wondered where he was going in such a hurry, and then noticed all the students at the windows. She went towards them and asked what was happening, and was told that a student had been attacked Giselle rushed towards the exit and ran to where Quinn was bent down talking to someone lying on the walkway, and Imogen standing on the opposite side shivering.

"Oh my god Ruby!"

Giselle fell to her knees when she saw that the person lying there was Ruby. "Are you hurt?"

Giselle and Quinn helped Ruby stand up. She rubbed the back of her head, where she was sure there would soon be a sizable bump.

Quinn looked at Giselle and then at Imogen. "Looks like Ruby was attacked and the only witness is Imogen." He replied accusingly.

Giselle looked at Imogen, who burst into tears, and then at Ruby who grabbed Quinn's arm. "It wasn't her; Imogen saved me from being stabbed. Whoever it was ran off when Imogen shouted, and probably saved my life." Ruby told him adamantly.

Quinn looked over at Giselle wondering if she had actually been in the bathroom. *What was she doing for her hair to be so wet when it's already had stopped raining? Was she outside earlier when Ruby was being attacked?*

Quinn turned to Imogen. "Did you get a look at the person who attacked Ruby?" He questioned.

Imogen sniffled a couple of times. "All I saw was a long strand of blonde hair hanging out of the hooded raincoat."

"Did you see the person's face?" He asked her.

Imogen shook her head. "No. The hood was pulled down low."

Quinn glanced over at Giselle and wondered.

After Zeus left, Quinn telephoned Giselle to let her know that he would be back soon, but had to run a couple of errands first. "Is there anything I can pick up for you? Okay I'll see you soon."

He opened the door to Ruby's room and poked his head in.

He motioned to Kassie to meet him in the hallway.

"Kassie I own a condo that's vacant, and you and Ruby should stay there for a while."

Kassie thought this over. "I'll ask Ruby and if she agrees, I'll go with an officer to grab some of our belongings."

"Okay, let me know so I can get everything set up." Quinn told her. "I'll check on both of you tomorrow."

"I will, and thanks for your offer. I appreciate it." Kassie gave him a hug.

Before he left, Kassie grabbed his arm. "I know what you're thinking, but you're wrong. Elle had nothing to do with any of this. That girl is like a sister to Ruby, and no one will change my mind."

☠

In the emergency room, Kimi was being treated for multiple cuts and injuries. She explained to the officer taking her statement that she had been on her way to an appointment, and after the light turned green, she drove through.

Moments later, her Mercedes Benz W126 smashed into a concrete pole. The front end crumpled with the force of impact, and the windshield imploded, showering her with slivers of glass. Both the steering wheel and dashboard compacted into one mangled mess.

"I'm glad I remembered to wear the seat-belt." She told the officer.

The officer nodded. "Good thing you did."

"The motorcycle came out of nowhere, cutting me off after running the red light, which caused me to swerve and hit the pole. One moment the road was there, and the next there were loud noises, acrid smells, and terrible pain." She continued.

She remembered hearing the sirens from the fire truck in the distance, then the police, and an ambulance arrived. The last thing she remembered was leaning back and closing her eyes.

She told the paramedics she felt a sharp pain in her stomach. That her neck was painful and felt stiff, that she had an immense headache, and it hurt to breathe. Her chest hurt and she couldn't move her legs, and was also feeling dizzy and nauseous; then she fainted.

Kimi was admitted, after a series of tests showed she had broken ribs, whiplash, internal bleeding, and a few other issues. She was told she'd require surgery to stop the bleeding, and was promptly wheeled into the operating room.

When Kimi awoke, a nurse quickly came in and checked her vitals, and then left to find the surgeon that had operated on her.

The surgeon walked into the patient's room, and wondered for the second time where had he seen this woman before, but then most patients looked similar to him these days. He shrugged it off to the long hours of surgery; he desperately needed some time off.

"Good afternoon Miss Darlow. I'm Dr. Curtis; I performed your surgery earlier. How are you feeling?"

Kimi looked at him, choking back the answer she would have preferred to give him, and instead responded. "A bit groggy, but I guess I feel okay."

"That's because we put pain medication in your IV, otherwise you'd be in considerable pain."

Kimi looked at him with widened eyes. "Why? What's happened to me?"

"You suffered three fractured ribs on your left side; the neck injury is possibly from the seat-belt pressed into a previous injury—where I can see scarring, and some whiplash is present too. I had to remove your spleen due to abdominal trauma, which caused a hematoma. There is also considerable swelling and bruising around the front of your left knee. The x-ray shows a dislocated knee and a Patellar Fracture.

"What does that mean?" Kimi asked screwing up her eyes.

"It means you have a broken kneecap." Dr. Curtis explained. "I performed a procedure to put the bone fragments back into place and stabilize the patella. You'll be on crutches for a while. I've placed a cast on your knee until the bone mends. I want your knee immobilized until it's fully healed. That means no standing on it, or bending it for any reason."

"How long will it take for my knee to heal?"

Dr. Curtis looked perplexed as if trying to remember something but couldn't, and quickly snapped back to doctor mode. "About three months if you follow my instructions." He couldn't understand why that was the only injury she was most concerned about.

"You also have a concussion. Do you remember hitting your head?" Dr. Curtis asked her.

Kimi looked bewildered. "To tell you the truth doctor, I don't remember much, except that I hurt all over, but I think I may have hit my head on the steering wheel."

"That's entirely possible. *Although I see no bruise there.* You're in good hands and you'll be looked after by our capable staff. Let the nurses know if you require more pain medication, I've left more prescribed for you. I'll be back to check on you in the morning. Rest is all that's required of you for now. I don't want you getting up for any reason; just call for a nurse, and one will help you with whatever you need."

He turned to leave, but Kimi stopped him. "Dr. Curtis, how is the woman driving the motorcycle doing?"

Dr. Curtis stopped mid-step and hesitated before responding.

"What is it doctor?" Kimi asked

"She didn't make it." Dr. Curtis responded flatly.

Kimi gasped as her hand flew to her chest, and gave an incredulous gasp.

"If there's nothing else you require I need to see another patient." Dr. Curtis left as quickly as possible. For some inexplicable reason, he just wanted to get far away from this woman as possible.

Kimi nodded and stifled a sob, and watched as the doctor closed the door quietly behind him.

She covered her mouth to stop from laughing aloud, but began feeling the effects of the pain medication, and closed her eyes and fell into an uneasy sleep.

Dr. Curtis glad his shift was over, headed back to his office to grab his clothing, and then to the locker room to change out of his scrubs and shower.

Driving home afterwards, he had a nagging feeling that he had missed something important, but couldn't think what it was.

Chapter 34
Twin Pass Junction

Sheriff Raymond Hayward was parked behind a sign near the town's exit. He watched as Warren's truck sped away, and then put his plan into action. He'd gotten a search warrant from Judge Strickland that same morning, and was on his way to check out Warren's house. He radioed Chief Deputy Mike to meet him there and Sergeant Dwight too; the two men on his force he trusted the most.

He'd received a call from Zeus earlier that Warren had been seen driving into the Keys various times, and then getting onto a speedboat, which took him past a tiny islet full of mangrove and disappeared behind it.

Zeus also informed the sheriff that his guys weren't the only ones trailing Warren and friends. There were a couple of dangerous looking guys watching them too, and that they had gotten on a motorized Dinghy and followed them at a safe distance. Afterwards, Warren and, the guys returned, they loaded packages from the boat, onto a van, while the guys in the Dinghy watched them through binoculars. His team couldn't see the faces of his helpers, but Warren's face was clearly visible, and had taken photos.

After the van drove away, the guys in the Dinghy used a walkie-talkie and two other guys in a truck followed the van. Zeus' surveillance guys also followed and watched the van drive into a warehouse.

Zeus would let the sheriff know as soon as his team radioed him when Warren was headed back.

Sheriff Raymond Hayward or Ray as everyone called him sighed heavily. He wasn't getting any younger, and before retiring, he wanted to eliminate any obstacles that would disturb his quiet little town. That one obstacle was like a splinter he just couldn't remove, no matter how hard he tried, but this might be his saving grace at righting past wrongs. He'd put every plan into action to make sure he had enough evidence against Warren to finally charge him. He had failed CJ in the past and swore he would not fail him again.

His height made him look more imposing than he actually was, and that laid-back demeanor came from living in the same peaceful town where he was born. He ran his fingers through his short gray hair, the style he'd kept from his days in the marines. His handlebar mustache was a new acquisition. He'd almost shaven it off when he realized that it required maintenance and regular waxing and curling, but his wife told him he looked dapper, so he'd kept it. His perpetually narrowed eyes took in everything, but relayed nothing, they only added to his poker face and increased the deep frown on his forehead—the reason he could keep secrets until they needed to be broadcast.

Raymond had always suspected Warren was a bad person, but that wasn't enough—he needed proof. Solid irrefutable proof. Accusations against Warren were never provable as he always had a handy excuse. And because Raymond didn't have probable cause, he had not followed up on his hunches, but now he could thanks to Zeus.

"For a chief deputy you sure look nervous, relax Mike."

"I just don't feel comfortable going inside Warren's house." Mike responded.

Sheriff Hayward turned around and waived the warrant in front of his face.

"This is all the permission we need. If you're worried Warren will find out you were here, I assure you he's occupied at the moment hundreds of miles away. Besides, if he shows up and raises hell, we have just cause to arrest him."

"You go check the garage and I'll check inside with Dwight." He told Mike pointing to the house with his thumb over his shoulder.

Sheriff Hayward walked in and looked around, but there was nothing remarkable; it was just an average furnished home.

He checked the living room, and besides a nice set of furniture, nothing out of the ordinary stood out to him. He checked the kitchen, and it was the same, nice and clean, just ordinary.

Chief Deputy Mike entered the front door, apprehension showing on his face. "Uh, Sheriff, there's something you need to see in the garage."

The sheriff followed him, and Mike led him to a box he had found hidden in the back of a cabinet. When the sheriff looked, he saw a stash of weapons and ammunition.

"Well, I sure hope he has permits for those." He told both deputies.

Mike looked at him amused. "Those don't look like hunting weapons to me." He picked up a semi-automatic and held it up in his gloved hand.

"Nope, it sure doesn't." The sheriff replied. "Mike I want you to write down the serial numbers on those, and have them checked."

"Let's head back to the house. Who knows what surprises we'll find stashed in there."

"Yeah, I'm curious too." Replied Sergeant Dwight.

Mike nodded, and proceeded to check the serial numbers.

"I've already checked downstairs, and everything seems normal. Let's go upstairs." The sheriff told Dwight and they both headed up.

They climbed the stairs and went into the guest bedroom, but found nothing remarkable, just furniture and a blue oval rug. Then they went into the master bedroom. As soon as they walked through the door, they found this room was very different from the rest of the house.

There was a big waterbed, and on the ceiling was a mirror, which in itself wasn't a big deal, but in front of the bed was a camera on a tripod. They both looked at each other and shrugged their shoulders.

"Let's keep looking." Sheriff Hayward told Dwight.

Dwight headed to the closet, and within moments walked back through the room and went downstairs. He returned with a hammer, and walked back inside. A loud metal sound reverberated throughout the room.

Sheriff Hayward wondered what Dwight was doing. As he was walking towards the closet, he stopped mid-step. The painting on the wall was tilted, and he instinctively went to straighten it. Then he noticed that it wasn't flush with the wall, but actually covering something. Maybe a hole, or a water spot.

He removed the painting and behind it was a wall safe. Dwight walked back into the bedroom, and stood beside him looking at the safe.

"It's not illegal to own a safe." He told Sheriff Hayward. "But you really need to check the back of the closet."

Sheriff Hayward looked at him. "No it's not, but get a locksmith pronto to open it anyway so we can see what's inside."

Dwight went downstairs to call the locksmith, and the sheriff went to inspect the closet.

There was a door in the back wall of the closet, and the sheriff understood the thwack he'd heard—a lock lay on the ground. He pushed the door open, and there were shelves filled with packets that he suspected were drugs. The other shelves held enough weapons and ammunition to start a small militia.

Mike who had finished in the garage, walked in and stood behind the sheriff, and whistled under his breath.

"Sheriff, there are no serial numbers on any of the weapons in the garage." Chief Deputy Mike informed him.

Sheriff Raymond stood looking at everything on the shelves, not wanting to believe this was all in Warren's house. He finally understood why Warren never had applied to any of the openings in the department, and had chosen to remain in the starting rank of deputy. Warren had told him he didn't want the responsibility of being in charge, but Raymond knew that was hogwash. It was probably due to the numerous complaints he had received about him over the years.

Ben the local locksmith arrived and began to work on the wall safe, while Mike checked for serial numbers on the weapons in the closet. He wasn't surprised to find that there were no serial numbers on any of the weapons there either, because they had all been filed off.

There was a shout from the room that the locksmith had gotten the safe open. The sheriff thanked him, and the locksmith left, grumbling that it was too late to be out, and that he wasn't happy about leaving his warm bed on a cold night.

They peered into the safe and saw many sealed envelopes. Pulling out the top one, they saw it was dated, and labeled with locations. The sheriff opened it by unwinding the string, and pulled out an 8×10 glossy photo. A woman sat astride a container posing in barely there lingerie with a machine gun suggestively held between her legs, and a cigar in her mouth. He wondered who the woman was, maybe she was the drug runner he was working for, but he'd have to check. He'd look through the mug book and see if she was in one of the shots. He called Sergeant Dwight to photograph it, and to replace the original in the envelope afterwards.

Mike returned from the patrol car with a camera, and proceeded to photograph the photo of the woman, and all the other evidence too.

For now, Sheriff Raymond needed to think of a strategy for dealing with Warren. He didn't know how deeply involved he was in illicit dealings, and who he was involved with that could be dangerous. He went downstairs to make a phone call, and after he hung up, he called in Mike.

"After you finish photographing everything, put it back exactly as you found it, then go out and buy an exact lock and place it back on the door. I found the key in the night-table, so you'll need to replace that one with the new one."

Mike and Dwight nodded acknowledging they understood, and got to work.

Warren returned to town the following morning and drove up Sherry's street.

"Son of a bitch!" He pummeled the steering wheel with his fists. "It's too early to deal with this shit." His tried to calm the rage he felt, and was about to drive away when he saw CJ walking down the steps.

Within seconds, he left the truck running in the middle of the road, stormed up the sidewalk, and blocked CJ's path. The startled look upon CJ's face gave him an adrenaline rush. He quickly grabbed him by the collar and pulled CJ towards him.

"What the hell do you think you're doing asshole? I thought I warned you about bothering Sherry."

"She's not yours to protect Warren." He shouted back.

Sherry hearing the shouting ran out the front door, and when Warren saw her, he quickly let go of CJ.

"What the hell do you think you're doing Warren?" Sherry yelled at him.

"I have every right to be here. This is a public street, and I'm investigating a public disturbance."

"Which you're causing! You're off-duty and I see you're stalking me again, and that's an offense. Do you want me to file a restraining order against you?"

Warren looked at her incredulously. "You'd really do that to me Sherry? I mean we've known each other since grade school."

She stared him down. "Yes, yes I would, and if you don't leave immediately, I'll scream for help, and have you arrested for assault."

Warren looked as if he'd been struck. He began to walk away, but then turned around and pointed at CJ. "You stay away from her if you know what's good for you. I'll be watching."

Across the street, Emily hid behind some bushes taking photographs of the entire altercation with the camera she had left ready for just such an incident.

Warren slammed the truck door and took off burning rubber, then sped up the street and towards his house. *I should have tried harder to remove CJ from my life permanently—years ago. I need to come up with a definitive plan this time.*

His rage left him unable to see the car that pulled out a few car-lengths behind him following him up the street.

Chief Deputy Mike watched as Warren exited his truck and slammed the door, then reopened it and slammed it again.

Boy is he angry. I'm glad I didn't provoke him years ago when he broke into my house and appeared in my room. Mike radioed the sheriff that the suspect had returned, had an altercation with CJ and Sherry on the street, and was presently at his house.

The response: "Stay on his tail Mike, he's got the entire weekend off, and I want to know every move he makes, even if it's just throwing out the trash and what he's throwing out. When you need to take a break, Dwight will replace you otherwise don't lose sight of him."

"Understood sheriff. Over and out."

Chapter 35
Lover Boy

Phil parked his truck, fed the parking meter, and stood on the sidewalk looking at the shop window. A beautiful and sexy woman was just walking out and he winked at her. She turned away, deeply annoyed, and hurried up the sidewalk. He shrugged. *What a stuck-up bitch.*

Sighing heavily, he pushed open the door, entered the shop, and looked around. *She's following the same damned path as her mother,* he thought dismayed. The look on Athena's face didn't look very pleased to see him.

"Hello Athena, how's life treating you?"

Athena stared him down, and frowned. "Life always treats me kindly; in response to the same way I treat others." She told him pointedly. "Why are you here Phil?" She asked him with suspicion.

Phil smiled at her. "You're as blunt as usual."

Athena gave him a sinister smile, but did not respond.

Phil sighed heavily again, as this was the same unwelcome he always received from her. "I need to speak with Ruby is she here?"

Athena walked behind the counter and picked up the phone. "I'll check."

She watched him walk towards the gemstones and pick one up.

"Ruby are you in? Your dad is here and wants to speak to you. Yeah sure, okay I'll tell him."

"Phil, Ruby says to go on back, and wait until she calls you in, she's just finishing a reading."

Phil nodded, put the stone back, and walked through the adjoining hallway towards the waiting room. He sat in one of the chairs and nodded at the two other women waiting their turns, and they smiled back.

Athena watched him walk away and shook her head. *He might be forty-eight, but still acts as if he never escaped teenage-hood.*

Phil was dressed in tight jeans that left nothing to the imagination, and a white t-shirt that showed his tanned, bulging muscles. He wore his brown hair longish, giving him a youthful air. She glanced outside at his truck, *yep, bright red that's beyond mid-life crises, which makes people ditch some of their responsibilities in favor of makeovers, fun, flashy cars, and lovers. Nope, this had been an ongoing lifetime endeavor. Self-serving, Immature asshole!*

She knew what he was bothering her friend about—again. She said a silent prayer. *Ruby don't give in!*

As soon as a woman walked out through the beaded curtains, Ruby stuck her head out and motioned to her father. She led him past the reading room and into a small back room that served as her office. She motioned to a chair and sat behind the desk.

"I know why you're here dad, and the answer is still no."

Phil rolled his eyes, and counted to ten before he was able to respond.

"First of all, I want to know how you're feeling."

"I'm doing better. I still have a few bruises, but I'm managing."

"Ruby, why hang on to a house with bad memories?" He questioned.

Ruby gave him a piercing look. "Mom's not selling the house and that's final!"

Phil sighed heavily for the third time that day. He looked at his daughter resignedly, and shook his head sadly.

He thought back to that terrible day and felt the same mixture of sadness, remorse, and guilt that he'd felt all those years ago.

Ruby had called the construction site where he was working, to tell him Kassie was in surgery, but he'd left early that day and was at the party in Delores' house. After being discovered by her husband, he was too flustered to go home and face Kassie, so he just began driving around with no direction, and then pulled over to make a phone call. The enthusiastic response he received, mollified the dread he'd felt earlier, and soothed his frazzled nerves, somewhat.

It was the weekend anyway and besides Kassie didn't want him around, and this way he wouldn't have to put up with her glaring at him.

He drove straight towards the Keys and into Candace's open arms, eagerly waiting for him at the Conch House. At Candace's insistence, he succumbed to her demands and decided to stay a few days longer.

When he finally returned home, there was yellow tape across the entrance of the house. A patrol car was parked out front, and he was asked to go to the station. After being questioned by the police, Phil was permitted to go to the hospital

He'd found Ruby in the waiting room sitting next to her grandparents. She'd run to him and hugged him, and then he'd gone to ask for an update.

The surgeon informed him that he'd been able to repair the damage from the wound, but that Kassie was in a coma. He imagined a coma was better than her being dead. He'd visited her daily, mostly because he'd felt guilty and obligated. Then he only visited her weekly, then monthly, until he finally stopped.

Ruby was staying with an old biddy friend of her mothers, and that suited him just fine. Seeing Ruby was a daily reminder that she had been the one to find her mother half-dead, while he'd been in Delores' bed, and afterwards in Candace's.

After the insurance money had run out, he'd paid to have Kassie taken care of in a private rehab facility, and continued to pay for it with his salary from the construction job. Then he'd talked to Ruby about selling the house, to use some of that money to pay for the facility, and some of it to get himself a smaller place. But Kassie's parents had told him that they still held the title to the house, weren't planning to sell it, and that they would take over the rehab payments.

Twelve-year-old Ruby had consulted her grandparents about how to pay the ongoing nursing charges after her father told them he couldn't keep up the expense. They decided to rent out the house, and used that income to pay for Kassie's ongoing round-the-clock care.

"Ruby sweetie, times are tough, and I could really use a rent-free place for a short time."

Ruby looked down at the deck of cards on her desk, and then at her father.

"Mom needs the rental income from that house to get by. Don't you remember that she was left with issues after the attack, and doesn't work full time anymore? Besides the property belongs to gran and gramps, and 'they' were the ones letting us all live there rent-free."

"But you know the construction business comes and goes, and at this time it's dwindling. Can't I at least live in the house temporarily?"

The truth was that the women Phil dated had extravagant tastes, and most of his salary went towards appeasing their needs, in exchange for satisfying his.

Phil knew this was a losing battle; he'd been down this road before, and the answer was always the same. He now understood why Kassie had written a will, months before the attack, leaving her parents to make the final decision about her well-being and also Ruby's, should anything happen to her, and then it had.

The culprit had never been caught, and the crime remained unsolved to this day. The police had speculated that it might just have been a random crime, but the lead detective believed otherwise. He wanted to know if Phil knew any of his wife's clients, since the crime could have been committed by one of them. He didn't have a clue who any of his wife's clientele was, and he didn't believe in any of that psychic crap either, and let the detective know it.

"I can see we're not going to agree, so I'll leave you to your—ah, work." He rolled his eyes.

"The trouble with you dad, is that you never supported mom's work, and now you don't support mine. It doesn't matter whether you believe in it or not, it's what I'm good at, and I'm not going to change it, for you, or anyone else."

He looked at the determined look on his daughter's face so like her mother's, and got up to leave. "I'm sorry you think that I don't support your line of business. It's true I don't believe in any of this hocus pocus, but I respect your drive and ambition. I mean look at what you've accomplished on your own, and without any help from me. You're mother should be as damned proud of you as I am!"

Ruby got up, walked towards her father, and gave him a hug. He hugged her back.

"Mom has always been damned proud of me." She said into his shoulder.

"Let's have dinner soon. I'll pick-up some takeout." Phil told her.

"Sounds like a plan. Let me know when." She responded. Although, she knew he would flake out as he always did.

Phil walked towards his truck and drove off; he was hungry and annoyed. Glancing at the clock, he saw it was late afternoon. Spotting a Cuban restaurant up ahead, he pulled into the parking lot.

The hostess welcomed him to Crystal River, offered him a table near the window, and handed him a menu. He glanced through and ordered a Media Noche Sandwich with fries and a large iced tea. The server wrote down his order and went to the kitchen to place it.

Bored, he looked around, and was surprised to see the same woman he'd seen walking out of Ruby's shop earlier. She was seated three tables away facing him, holding a glass of water, and staring absently out the window. She reminded him of someone he'd known long ago.

The delicious aroma coming from the kitchen caused his stomach to grumble in anticipation. He was disappointed when the tray bearing food went to another table instead of his.

Phil looked over at her again, and caught her looking at him. She blushed and quickly turned away. He didn't see a ring on her finger and without hesitation got up and walked over to her table.

She looked up at him, eyes widened in alarm; her perfectly made up face apprehensive and grim.

He gave her, his signature sexy smile, with one side of his mouth raised just a bit, and crinkling his gray eyes.

She bit her bottom lip gently, and looked up him questioningly. She found him extremely attractive. From the casual stubble that littered his face, to the tight jeans in all the right places, and the t-shirt that made his tanned muscles bulge. She imagined herself embraced in those arms, and trembled with anticipation at the thought.

When she was able to compose herself enough to return to the present moment, she noticed that he had said something. "I'm sorry, what did you say?"

He pointed to the chair across her and repeated the question. "Is this chair occupied?"

She knew that he damned well knew it wasn't, but she was up for the game he was playing too. "No, you're welcome to it."

The server walked over to his table and set the plates down, but as she was turning to leave noticed that the man was now seated with the woman, and motioning her over. Inwardly sighing, she picked up the plate and iced tea, put them back on the tray, and placed them in front of him. She inquired if either of them wanted anything else, and when they both simultaneously said no—she walked away grinning.

When they finished their meals, the server removed their plates and took their dessert orders. In a few minutes, she returned with a couple of flans, a cappuccino for her, and a Cortadito for him.

She looked at him and grinned. "I see we have the same taste in food and dessert."

She wasn't fooling him for a minute she looked a bit older, but still beautiful. Phil recognized those blue eyes, blonde hair, and lustful gaze. Without looking at her, he kept spooning flan into his mouth.

"Just like we used to."

Her face paled. "Excuse me!" She responded indignantly.

He wiped his lips and smiled at her. "You heard me."

She stared at him. "I think you're confusing me with someone else."

He turned his head and looked at her. "I could never confuse you with anyone else. I remember every inch of that sexy body of yours."

His look unnerved her. "Stop saying inappropriate things and stop looking at me like that."

He thought for a moment. "For starters, where have you been all these years, and what are you doing in this neck of the woods?"

She stared at him intently, trying to come up with an explanation. She hadn't expected to run into him after all these years. "I had to go into hiding to protect myself. Then I moved as far away as I could, but thought it was safe to return, and here I am." She replied nervously.

He reached across the table and held her hand, and a tear ran down her face. "You should have called me; I could have been there for you."

She wiped her face and leaned towards him. "You can protect me now."

Seduction was what she did best, moving into his personal space with the look of heat in her eyes. She didn't just look at him; she looked into him knowing his desires.

His closeness brought back memories of how he used to kiss her neck, making her resistance instantly crumble. After just a few delicate touches of his warm lips, his hands would travel all over her body. His gaze told her he was also remembering their past together.

He paid for their meals and walked her to her car.

He brushed her hair back over her shoulder, and noticed a scar on her neck. "That bastard do this to you?" He asked indignantly.

She nodded sniffling, and he moved in closer, and brought her to him in an embrace. She pressed her body against his and hugged him tightly. She felt his warmth and the world around her became noiseless, with only him to fill her senses. He could feel her heart thumping rapidly against his chest. He wanted her lips, her kisses, and her body. Then he cupped her face in his hands and gave her what he knew she wanted. A slow, deep kiss that made her body tingle all over.

She looked at him expectantly. "Do you have anywhere else to be?"

He looked back at her and lustily replied. "I'm all yours babe."

She smiled at him. "Then follow me."

He got into his truck and followed her out of the parking lot.

On the way home, she thought of the reading she'd gotten from the psychic hours earlier, and smiled. She was right, someone from my past has definitely come back into my life, and what a wonderful surprise— one of the best lovers I've ever had.

Phil wondered, *what has she been up to all these years, but what the hell does that matter now. She looks like she's doing well and far away from that psychopath.* He couldn't shake the feeling that this was a big mistake, but his body disagreed, and he looked forward to what awaited him.

Chapter 36
Retribution

Six weeks after the accident, Kimi debated going back to the office; she was exhausted from her all night lovemaking session with Warren, but it was now past eleven and she wanted to retrieve what Paige had picked up for her weeks ago. The man was insatiable; she smiled to herself while applying eyeliner. She got into her rental car and drove off.

Kimi walked into her office and saw Paige seated in the chair at her desk.

What the hell is she doing?

Kimi quietly walked up behind her, and saw that Paige had opened the package in her drawer, and was inspecting its contents.

Feeling flushes of heat throughout her body, Kimi edged closer and whispered in her ear. "Find what you're looking for?"

Paige jumped in the chair, causing her to drop the box on the carpet, and the contents spilled out.

"I was just trying to reseal the box. I remembered that it was open when I received it, and I didn't want anyone else to come snooping in your personal things." She stammered.

"How very thoughtful of you Paige; just leave the box on my desk and get back to work. I'll make sure everything is set right."

She watched Paige scurry back to her desk like a rat caught rummaging through cupboards; amused that she had frightened the hell out of her. Then she picked up the box, dropped its contents into her purse, and threw the box into the trash bin. She was glad she had come to work after all and caught her in the act. Kimi wondered what else her assistant had had been up to. She bit her bottom lip deep in thought and came up with a plan.

Back at her desk, Paige tried to calm her trembling hands, and was glad when lunchtime finally arrived. She called Lenny.

"Meet up with me now. I have something to tell you that you'll find very interesting."

"Alright I'll be at our special place in fifteen." Lenny responded.

"Hurry, I only have one hour for lunch." Paige told him quickly and hung up.

Someone else was listening to Paige's conversation—all of it. Paige's intercom buzzed and Kimi told her she was on her way home, and wouldn't be back until the following day. Paige sighed with relief and picked up her things. She wouldn't have to rush back, and could take a long leisurely nooner. She didn't notice a car following her out of the parking garage.

Twenty-minutes later, back in their usual motel room, Paige told him what she had discovered in the box.

"Those things freaked me out." She said with an involuntary shudder. "I have no idea what they mean, but it can't be good. Maybe they're voodoo or something. That's something you can tell your boss." Paige told him in between snorts of cocaine.

"That's stupid Paige. If I give that information to Clemmy, she'll kill me for stupidity."

"What the hell does she care if one of her employees is into voodoo?"

"You don't understand. She's sent me to leave small packages on two doorsteps without being seen, and I complied. She told me it was a warning to the real estate agents spreading false rumors about her around town. But I'm almost sure that's not true. What if I've been leaving these hideous voodoo things at people's doorsteps, and I'm cursed instead?"

Lenny shook his head. "You really are stupid, there's no such thing as a curse. And what makes you think it's those dolls you've left on the doorsteps?"

"She somehow found out about my...habit, and has been using that to keep me quiet about the deliveries, and other things too. I always open the packages, and inside each one was one of those voodoo dolls, and sometimes more than one. I forgot to check the last box because I picked it up late since I was with you that day. Today, I just wanted to confirm that the last box I picked up for her contained the same voodoo dolls, and she caught me snooping. What do I do Lenny? I'm freaking out!"

"Shh." He rubbed her arms and began opening her blouse. "Just let Lenn take away your troubles."

He removed the tiny spoon from her hand, and placed it on the nightstand. Then he handed her a freshly rolled joint, which they shared, and she felt herself relax.

Lenny removed the rest of her clothing and gently pushed her onto her back. Afterwards, he tried to wake her, but she was too out of it, so he let himself out of the room, and drove off.

Moments later, the door reopened, and someone entered the room. Biting her bottom lip, she quietly placed her purse on the table and removed three items.

Paige stirred on the bed, but didn't awaken.

Wearing disposable gloves on both hands, she went to the bed, placed a pillow over Paige's face, and pushed down hard. Within moments, the flailing limbs ceased, and she removed the pillow. She got a small mirror from her purse and held it up to Paige's nose, but there was no breath. She lay an ear against her chest, but her heart was no longer beating. Taking the syringe from her purse, she quickly injected the contents into Paige's left arm, and placed the needle in her right hand.

That'll teach her to meddle in my affairs.

Then peeking out the side of the heavy curtain and seeing no one around, readjusted the black haired wig, quickly went down the stairs, and walked up the street.

She removed the gloves and threw them into an open dumpster, then got into her car and calmly drove back to the real estate building. She entered thorough the back entrance, and went to her office. No one had even noticed that she had left.

She practiced what her reaction would be when someone told her that Paige was dead, and chuckled quietly.

Chapter 37
The Letter

Quinn had just stepped out of the shower when the doorbell rang. He toweled off, and grabbed his robe. The ringing was incessant.

"Hold your horses, I'll be right there!"

He opened the door.

"What's happened?"

They looked at each other, and then at him.

"What makes you think something's happened? The younger officer asked him suspiciously.

"What kind of a stupid question is that?" Quinn responded. "When cops show up on someone's doorstep first thing in the morning, it isn't for donations."

The older officer shook his head, and apologized. "He's new."

"Are you Quinn Masterson?"

"Yes, why?"

"A few years back you filed a restraining order against an Imogen Ainsley?"

"Yes I did. What is this about? Has she been following me again?"

"No sir, she was in a traffic accident, but didn't make it."

"That's terrible, but why are you telling me, shouldn't you be notifying her next of kin?"

"We're treating the accident as suspicious, and when we searched her apartment, we found a letter addressed to you."

"A letter? For me?" Quinn couldn't imagine why she would have written him a letter after so many years.

The officer handed him the letter, and stood waiting. The envelope was addressed to Quinn Masterson, but never mailed: Open In Case Of My Unexpected Death, all written in red ink.

Dear Quinn,

If you are reading this, I may already be dead or mortally injured. I know you believe I was stalking you, but unfortunately, I was never able to convince you otherwise. When your study partner was attacked, you immediately accused me, just because I was the one who found her.

I know I behaved like a lovesick schoolgirl and did follow you a few times, but it's not what you think. I was looking out for you, as I feared your life was in danger too.

I regret any actions that led to the end of our relationship. Please understand that it wasn't what it seemed. Someone else was following you, but it wasn't me.

Lately, I feel like I'm being watched, and someone has been following me. A month ago, I received a pair
of hideous little carved wooden dolls, one resembling me and the other possibly you. I filed a police report, but they weren't able to determine who had left it on my doorstep, and disregarded it as a prank. So please be careful, as I fear for my life and for yours as well. I thought of contacting you many times, but feared you wouldn't listen or believe me, so I didn't.

I have no idea who has been stalking me but it's quite frightening, and now I understand what you must have been going through.

The only clue I have of the person stalking me is long blonde hair that I saw late one night when the hood of her jacket fell back, as she quickly ran away from my bedroom window. I never saw her face, but the person is of tall stature, and reminded me of the person that attacked Ruby near the dorms.

Be careful, take care, and stay safe.

Respectfully, your friend,

Imogen

Quinn reread the letter to make sure he understood what he had just read.

"This is unbelievable. So the stalker was being stalked." Quinn said incredulously.

"It appears that way."

"Have the police followed up on what she wrote in this letter?"

The officer shook his head. "We just wanted to know if you have any idea who could possibly have been following her."

Quinn shook his head. "I really don't know, since I haven't seen her in many years, and there's been no contact between us either."

"Well, thanks for your time anyway," the older officer told him, and turned to walk away.

"Officer, what about those carved wooden dolls mentioned in the letter."

The officer turned around and shook his head. "We didn't find them at her home during the search, but she might just have thrown them away. Why do you ask?"

The officer didn't mention that they had found them still in the box on her kitchen table.

Quinn was just about to mention that Giselle and Ruby had both received the carved monstrosities too, but changed his mind.

"I was just curious if you had found them, since Imogen mentions that one resembles me. If you do find them, could you let me see them?"

The older officer pursed his lips and nodded. "Sure, if we find them, we'll let you know."

They left taking the letter with them, and leaving Quinn wondering about poor Imogen. *Have I been wrong about her all these years?*

He went back into his bedroom and got dressed. Before going to the office, he telephoned Ruby to see how she was getting along, and if she or Kassie needed anything. He didn't want to tell her about the morning's police visit, but felt he should.

"Quinn what the hell is going on and why is this happening now?" Ruby asked shocked.

"I have no idea, but I'll take extra precautions myself from now on. I also don't want someone following me to see you, so I'll have to come up with another plan how to do so. Say hello to Kassie."

Quinn went to his safe, extracted a revolver, and loaded the chambers with bullets, then strapped on a holster. He took out his wallet, pulled out the business card of Elizeus Bishop, and dialed the number.

After telling him about the police visit and Imogen's letter, Zeus told him he'd look into the details and get back to him.

Zeus gave him the number to a private security company, and Quinn dialed them as soon as he hung up. The appointment was set for early afternoon; there were four places he quickly wanted safe and secure.

Chapter 38
Ruya

Kimi drove over the bridge into Key Biscayne. The top of the convertible was down and she was enjoying the sea breeze and the briny smell. The address of the practitioner Clemmy had given her was a waterfront condominium in Emerald Towers. The condo was steps from the sandy beach with stunning ocean views. She wondered how this woman could afford to live in such an expensive place.

After Kimi was cleared by security, she left her car with the valet and was buzzed into the lobby. The concierge welcomed her and rushed towards the elevator to press the button. She was impressed and still a little bewildered. When she exited on the twenty-second floor, there was a young man dressed in a white jacket, white shirt, and white pants, who ushered her into the hallway. He relocked the elevator, and led her into the penthouse.

She looked around the living room in awe. The floors were pristine white marble and the furniture was also white; it was reminiscent of a wedding cake. The big open spaces were uncluttered and beautifully decorated with gold accents, and ocean scene art. She followed the young man up the hallway and into an office; he told her to take a seat in one of the chairs in front of the glass desk. Kimi looked out at the ocean and wished she had a place like this one.

She'd ask Jimmy if he owned property in one of these buildings, and maybe he'd give it to her It wasn't as if he hadn't offered before, but she didn't want to be tied down to him. She entertained a variety of lovers, and he wouldn't be very happy to find one of them with her.

A woman dressed in a flowing Moroccan style caftan of deep emerald green with fine gold embroidery walked in through a side door. She was petite; her golden brown curls were piled atop her head and held in place by an open turban. Her oval face, deep brown eyes, small narrow nose, and flawless skin, gave her the appearance of a model.

"Good morning Kimi. I'm Ruya. What brings you here today?"

"I have a problem I don't know how to resolve and need your help." Kimi told her.

The woman studied Kimi for a moment and then shook her head. "I very much doubt that. Aren't you already dealing with the problem yourself?"

Kimi couldn't believe what the woman was saying; it almost seemed she knew what Kimi had been up to. *Dammit!* The assumption made her insides boil. She gazed intently at the woman with barely contained contempt, while clenching the armrests of the chair tight enough to turn her hands a sickly yellow.

She watched as Ruya narrowed her eyes, tilted her head back, and scrutinized her. She felt as if every inch of her was being examined, and didn't care for the feeling.

Ruya immediately disliked the woman, sensing she was trouble, and if it was trouble she had brought with her, then she would send it back to her tenfold.

She knew why Clemmy kept sending her lackeys over. The couple who'd had their appointment before Kimi had only asked for protection; they were a disparate twosome; she tall and pretty, and he scrawny and slippery, but still paid a big fee. She would work on their mojo bags tonight as those were simple and easy, but this one was a contradiction.

The woman before her was dressed in a purple, skintight short skirt, with matching blazer and low-cut camisole with her ample bosom pushed to the limit, and purple high-heeled pumps. Her long blond hair cascaded down her back, and her flawless features were meticulously made up. She was quite beautiful, and no doubt attracted many men, but there was something disconcerting about her, something Ruya couldn't quite figure out. But whatever it was, she didn't want this woman in her presence any longer than necessary.

"I don't know what Clemmy told you, but I do serious work here. I can counsel you, and prepare a spell to your specifications, but following the advice is entirely up to you. I also don't come cheap, and require payment upfront…in full, before I begin any spell-work."

Ruya leaned forward, entwined her fingers and folded her hands underneath her chin, and stared at Kimi awaiting a response.

Kimi relaxed her grip on the chair. "What I'd like is to place a curse upon my enemies, to stop them from making my life miserable." Kimi informed her. *Miserable by being alive.*

Ruya continued to watch her through narrowed eyes. "By enemies, how many people do you have in mind?"

Kimi didn't need to think this one through, "Two from my past who tried to kill me, and another one who also poses a serious threat to me, so three in total. It would have been four, but she passed away not long ago. If they died, no one would miss them, they're horrible people."

Ruya leaned back and studied the person asking her to curse three people, and wondered what perceived grievances they had actually committed against her. The woman appeared cool on the exterior, but she sensed Kimi was a ticking time bomb just waiting for the right moment to explode.

"What you are asking for is hoodoo, which is dark magic. I want to make sure you're aware of this before proceeding."

Kimi nodded her assent.

Ruya continued. "Two things. One, this will cost you $20,000 up front. I will need their full names, the dates, and places of birth if you know them, and if you have photos, I will also need those. I will offer protection against those wishing to harm you, meaning I can stop them from coming into contact with you, or maliciously attacking you. However, I must warn you again that this can backfire… on you. Reconsider before this process is begun, because you may be the one to suffer instead, by wishing harm upon others. Two, if these curses you want me to prepare for you are placed on innocent people—the harm will befall you instead."

Kimi was silent taking in her words. "I thought you were a witch, don't witches perform evil against others?"

Ruya looked at her as if she were considering squashing an offending insect with her sandal, or simply sweeping it away out the window.

Ruya ignored being called a witch "Like I said before this type of magic carries consequences. Are you prepared to cross that threshold and suffer the repercussions?"

Kimi wondered what would happen if she suddenly got up, advanced towards the woman, and strangled her. That was something to think about afterwards, as she preferred no witnesses to her crimes. Then she considered who had recommended her—Clemmy, and she didn't want to seem rude or ungrateful to her.

Maybe the protection being offered was a plus, and might just keep her hidden from those pests, until she could dispose of them when the time was right.

"When can you start?" Kimi responded, a synthetic smile forming on her lips.

After the payment was taken care of and the details given, Kimi was on her way back to the Buccaneer, where Jimmy would be in the Moroccan room later tonight, and another night of hedonistic pleasure awaited her. She was high on adrenaline, thrilled that the she would be invisible to the irritating obstacles in her life. She needed to devise a strategy to eliminate those pesky hindrances that continued to annoy her very existence–like an untied shoelace. *Whatever it takes. Knowing the dolls are causing them worry and stress makes me happy.*

As soon as Kimi left and her assistant locked the private elevator, Ruya returned to her office deep in thought. The client hadn't batted an eye when she'd told her the amount she required upfront for the work. On the contrary, she'd been eager to sign a check and hand it to her.

Ruya expected upfront payment from her clients, and they never protested—this was the reason she had accepted the woman's petition, but mostly because Clemmy had recommended her. She felt this one was unstable, and she flat-out didn't like her. Her intuition was never wrong, and she would have turned her down, but this was easy money, and her lifestyle demanded these chumps invest in her expertise. She would do some extra work to keep this one under control, just in case. Ruya made a quick phone call to let Clemmy know the details of the three she had sent to her.

Clemmy's private line rang, and she locked herself in her office to take the call. She was informed of what had transpired at the meetings with the three she had sent Ruya's way.

After hanging up, Clemmy sat back, and wondered: *why am I surrounded by morons and crazy people? The two idiots seemed harmless enough and had only asked for protection; in this line of business, they needed all the protection they could find. And if they ceased to be loyal in any way, she had many ways to keep them in line, or make them disappear—their choice.*

Kimi is a different story altogether. Clemmy wondered: *who does she need protection from and who she is cursing? Sure, she is competent, but sometimes I sense something brewing deep beneath those fake smiles, and also a blatant disregard for rules. I'll be keeping a very close eye on her. Just one reason to doubt her loyalty and…I'd have to give that some thought.*

Ruya stood at the floor-to-ceiling window, and stared out at the ocean. She hoped the waves would bring an ideal solution to her dilemma. Ruya wondered what she could do to sever certain tedious ties. Her assistant appeared in the doorway as if mentally summoned, holding a tray with a frozen strawberry Margarita in a frosted double-bowl glass.

Ruya looked up and smiled as he approached her with the tray. "What would I do without you, Bastaq?"

Bastaq smiled and bowed then quietly walked away, and silently closed the door behind him.

Ruya marveled at the gullible fools who willingly gave her any amount of money she asked for. Most clients asked to either vanquish their perceived enemies, revenge upon an ex-lover, or to gain a lover. Clemmy apparently told those she sent her way that she was a voodoo priestess, but that wasn't even close to what she really did, and it certainly wasn't dabbling in the dark arts. Although, if she wanted to she could certainly go that route.

Ruya was spiritual, and gifted at working with plants and herbs for healing; she could cast magick to reverse bad luck, and to gain good health. She could dream-walk, and go on quests, but she did not practice black magic, that, she left to others. She believed in karma, and no good ever came out of performing evil practices. She'd seen the destructive forces of the dark arts, and had warned practitioners she'd met along the way not to dabble in the occult, but they wouldn't listen. All four were dead now, and those deaths could have been avoided had they heeded her warning, but their path towards self-destruction was their own. *Some lines just shouldn't be crossed. Not if you value your life.*

Ruya picked-up the Margarita, licked the salted-sugared rim, took a sip, and savored the perfectly mixed drink. Then, reluctantly got up, picked up her drink, locked the door, and pulled a book from the shelf that opened a secret door.

Once inside, she knelt before her altar and lit four candles. The first one was white to cleanse her surroundings, repel negativity, and provide protection, the second was black, to absorb and banish negative energy, the third candle was red to draw in fresh energy, the final candle was purple, which was for opening her third eye and invite visions to enhance her intuition.

There was one more candle, but that one she would light later. It was a silver candle, used to neutralize any negative energy directed at her, which would also help her gain discernment and wisdom.

Ruya whispered a short prayer for retribution against those wishing to cause harm to innocents, a protective one for herself, and then began preparations for the petitions.

Chapter 39
The Man With No Name and From Nowhere

He listened intently for any sounds, but only unnerving silence greeted him. The doors of the tomb-like place were suddenly thrown open—the jarring sound loudly clattering against the interior. An intense sound echoed off the walls like an empty crypt—evoking visions of a void left by those who had been and are no longer. It was akin to the shock of a bucket of ice water being poured over his head.

Huge torches gave their meager light, which reflected on the prisoner's terrified face. His fearsome torturers entered one-by-one—their gray faces expressionless and pitiless as if carved by a mad sculptor, on their backs dark wings fluttered.

He had come to, with a thudding headache, eyes closed against the intense pain. The back of his skull throbbed as if he was inside a giant speaker playing extremely loud music.

The last thing he remembered was sitting by the fireplace reading a book and holding a glass of cognac, when he saw lights in the distance. He went to the window and watched as flickering lights neared the cabin. He grabbed his gun and hid, but then everything went dark. Upon awakening, he seemed to be in some sort of dungeon, with sconces on the wall holding torches.

A hooded figure pronounced him guilty.

"Erik Slater. For the crime you have committed, you are sentenced to the depths of hell." The figure stated emotionless as if bored.

What the hell? He wondered. *Which crime—there had been many.*

As if reading his thoughts. "You will know more soon." Was the response.

I suppose my past has finally caught up with me. The thought made him shiver, but then he considered the consolation that it would be over quickly. *The condemner being condemned that's ironic. Whoever these people are, I suspect someone placed a hit on me, and I'm now the mark. Who could have found out where I was....or more importantly, who I am.*

He received a blow to the head and everything went dark.

Hooded figures entered tapping their canes making hallow, thudding sounds on the wooden floor, and brandishing whips. The twang of their whips made sharp sounds as they sliced through the air. The explosive reverberation echoed off the walls causing the man to flinch with each crack.

Hellish torment filled his mind as he awaited the next blow—he could not detect where they were coming from.

One of the hooded figures removed his blindfold, and he squinted trying to adapt to the darkness.

He cracked open one eye to survey his surroundings.

"I see the prisoner is awake," one of the voices stated, the voice echoing off the ceiling, raw and rasping, like the threatening growls of hell-hounds, the whip dragging along the floor as the person drew nearer.

The remnants of his clothing were soon tattered and hanging in long strips. The twang of the whip crackled like explosive thunder reminding him of a shotgun. The man winced and jerked as a long gash opened on his side. He let out a sharp, high-pitched wail that pierced the air like a well-sharpened blade echoing off the walls.

A screeching voice next to his ear made him cry out in anguish.

"You seem to have gotten away with many killings, but murdering the woman with the stolen necklace was a big mistake! She has a vengeful sister." One of the voices taunted him.

Who contracted you? I'll double the payment. Tell me what you want, and let's negotiate a fair deal!"

He was being subjected to incredible and insurmountable torment; at least he killed his victims in one clean shot with no suffering….usually.

Who the hell are these lunatics? His muddled mind was disoriented and on the verge of hysteria. The excruciating pain was making his eyes water and his muscles cramp.

"What is going on is your comeuppance. Our special retribution." Was the reply to his unspoken question.

"Designed just for you." Another voice explained with indifference, and followed by the sound of mocking laughter.

"You must have known you couldn't continue your line of work forever, without repercussions. Did you?" Questioned another voice.

He writhed in agony as the stabbing, ripping, and tearing continued. He wondered what time it was, as the pain began ebbing away to a dull throb, like late-morning fog lifting off a lake.

Then just as quickly, more pain shot up his other leg and it felt as if he had been seared with a burning fireplace poker. He cringed as he felt his leg explode with agonizing pain like ice melting upon molten lava. It made him dizzy with pain and for the first time in his life—fear.

The hooded figure lifted the whip again. Crackle. A bloodied strip of skin tore from his torso and hung limply, like a tree shedding its bark.

He compared the pain to electric needles dipped in alcohol then jammed through his injuries, and directly into his into exposed nerves. Each crackle created a mini-shock wave, a sonic boom as it broke the sound barrier.

He bit out a curse and once more tried to move his hand to inspect the damage, but it wouldn't move. Something was restraining his wrists, and found that his legs too were immobilized. His hands were above his head. *Manacles?* Old styled medieval ones made of heavy iron. *What is this place?*

Then the blows began in earnest, each slash falling on the next, and peeling away more flesh until he resembled a road map, badly drawn by a child with a crayon.

It's just a nightmare! I'll wake up any second! This isn't real!

He tried to calm his desperate mind and think how he could escape the maniacs who had captured him. His mind raced with uncontrolled thoughts. *How long have I been here? How did I get here?* He tried to clear his throat, but it was parched and caused agonizing pain to swallow. His stomach growled. *When did I last eat?*

He squinted, trying to see his aggressors, but darkness engulfed him, disallowing him sight, and he closed his eyes. He was exhausted and terrified. Then all went silent.

Where are they? Maybe they went away and left me here to suffer and die from my wounds.

A scraping sound on the floor alerted him that someone was still there. A tremor of panic vibrated through his being.

Terrible things were screeched in his ear, then again whipped repeatedly. Suddenly, the lashings increased in intensity until his body shook and his muscles trembled.

Once more, he tried to wrench his limbs free of the restraints, but all that did was dig the shackles deeper into his flesh, and he cried out in pain. He heard the howling laughter of one of his aggressors.

His every instinct forced him to fight these unseen enemies, to escape the bonds, and run to safety, but there were restraints and fetters attached to all four limbs.

He yelled a panicked shout. The suffocating heat caused him difficulty in breathing. He choked and swallowed the metallic taste of blood against the back of his throat causing him to gag.

The attack stopped, and his aggressors suddenly began humming a strange melody. The vibrations triggered intense feelings of guilt and remorse in him, and tears ran down his cheeks.

What the hell is happening to me? Why did I kill all those people? He sobbed uncontrollably. He would give anything to be given the chance to atone for all the evil he had committed, but he knew there would be no absolution. It was too late for remorse now.

As he felt the last of his strength beginning to fade away, he drew in one ragged breath after another and felt death was imminent. He tried to cry out, but his throat was raw from screaming and his lips were dried and crackled; only a gasp uttered from his mouth instead.

He felt cloth brush his hand and braced himself for the next blow, but none came.

He listened with all the attention he could gather, but not a sound was heard. Maybe they weren't coming back to continue torturing him. Then realization hit him like an epiphany, as Sir Isaac Newton had when discovering gravity from a falling apple; *they aren't coming back at all, and have left me alone the darkness—to die of my wounds.*

A line from a poem of the book he was reading came to mind. It was Hesiod describing Tartarus as *"a vast chasm, both dismal and dank and a place of decay. It was the lowermost region of the Universe, a separate entity lower than Hades."*

This is where I suppose I am, in hell.

He continued unsuccessfully to free himself, but the struggle only managed to exhaust him more, and he gave up. The binds tightly constricted with his every movement. He let out a tortured sigh, and felt the immense pain of his broken body on what he assumed was a slab of stone.

The scream in his left ear took him by surprise and he let out a strangled cry. He tried to plead with the pathetic strength he had left, but if was pointless. He was impotent against his aggressors, so he closed his eyes and rested, trying to recuperate some strength to fight back later if he got the chance. He tried slowly opening his eyes, but could only squint. The torment he had endured from the agonizing torture had left him in misery and hoping for a quick death.

Three hooded figures materialized from the shadows and advanced towards him. He held his breath. They surrounded him and slowly walked around where he lay, like vultures circling their prey, and then they descended upon him with all their fury.

Standing over the badly beaten and bruised man, the trio looked at each other, and decided that their rage had not been abated, because he still breathed, and the person he killed no longer did.

The aggressors grew even more brutal in their attacks until blood had dyed their cloaks crimson.

The man lay listless, barely alive, and through the haze of agony, he heard one voice conferring with the other two.

"Let's check if he's still alive." He was prodded with a swift punch to the stomach, making him vomit.

"More punishment must be vetted out." Another shrieked.

They watched the man twist, squirm, groan, and writhe in time to the spasms of his mutilated body. Then they watched as his eyes rolled into the back of his head, foam coated his lips, and his entire body shivered in violent spasms—all the fight suddenly gone from him.

He gasped and groaned one final time, before succumbing to his destiny. As his limp body went into oblivion—the clenching grasp of death came to collect him. His final fleeting thought was that there would be no coin in his mouth to pay the ferryman.

Chapter 40
Ruby and Ruya

Ruby sought protection, and this time she would do the ceremony correctly. No more shortcuts with hallucinogenic substances as those left her feeling lousy afterwards. The last time was a fantastical mushroom trip that led to an exploration into dream walking, which allowed her to enter someone else's dream where she could either observe or control the dreamer. It hadn't been a pleasant experience. She could never forget what she had seen, and promised she would never go that route again.

Ruby was terrified that she and her mother were in imminent danger, and needed to act quickly.

She contacted her friend Ruya for help.

Ruya explained earlier that no drugs were involved in her process. "It is a common misconception with Shamanism that plant medicine or psychedelics must be involved. I prefer to reach a state of being where the rational mind fades into the background, and allows intuition to step into the foreground."

Ruby wanted a Shamanic journey with a connection to the spirit world, to receive guidance and protection.

She agreed to meet Ruya at Biscayne National Park that night, where Ruya's boat would take them to an isolated islet only reachable by boat. The place was located in the shadow of Miami's shores, and yet a world away.

In preparation, Ruby locked herself in her room with a do not disturb sign on her door. Relaxing in a reclining chair in her quiet, calm space, and wearing cordless stereo headphones, she listened to the tape Ruya had given her.

It was chilly tonight and Ruby wore a thick cardigan while waiting in the car with Kassie. She opened up the sunroof and looking up at the sky, thought of the old adage 'Red sky at night, sailors delight; Red sky at morning, sailors take warning.' The night sky was ablaze with hues of orange and red, making it look both frighteningly surreal and beautiful.

She knew good weather would make the journey a tranquil one, or so she hoped.

As night fell, the clouds retired, revealing a clear sky filled with stars that resembled twinkling fairy lights, surrounded by the interminable vastness of eternal space.

Ruby had always been a night owl, and felt that this was closer to the truth of who she was, a nocturnal being connected to far away entities that perhaps gazed back at her through their telescopes. She pictured the night resembling a curtain pulled back, where she could see through the window into the endless Universe.

Ruya arrived shortly after with Bastaq at the helm; she stood at the bow and waved Ruby over.

"I'll be back in one hour to pick you up." Kassie waved at Ruya and drove off.

Ruby exited her car, climbed aboard, and embraced Ruya. They sat in the stern and Ruya waved at Bastaq to steer onto their destination—Crystal Key.

The shallow waters were calm tonight, only small waves as the boat glided through the darkness, guided only by the light of the full moon. They rode on in silence and watched a gray lump floating in the water. Bastaq slowed the boat almost to a stop.

They looked over the side of the boat and saw that it was a manatee taking a power nap with only its head exposed. Bastaq immediately slowed the boat to a crawl.

Ruya laughed, "It's only a sea cow guiding us on our journey."

"Why is it doing that?" Asked Ruby amusedly.

"Manatees need to breathe air to survive and the reason they come to the surface frequently. This one is apparently a natural acrobat, and looks like it's standing on its tail to keep its nostrils out of the water."

"I think it's a sign for our mission tonight." Ruby mused aloud.

Ruya nodded. "These gentle giants have a tranquil disposition, and are the embodiment of peace, harmony, wisdom, serenity, and patience. In ancient civilizations, manatees were considered deities, and were revered creatures. They move steadily and purposefully which reminds us to remain mindful of our feelings. Their symbolism includes nonaggression, tranquility, change, and intuitive awareness. So yes, I see this as a positive sign."

All three reached over and rubbed its head.

When they neared the islet, Bastaq eased up and let the boat drift towards the shore. He jumped off and tied the boat to the nearest palm tree, and helped both women over the seaweed garland adorning the beach, and onto the gentle hue of golden sands that shimmered in the moonlight like millions of shattered Christmas ornaments.

Bastaq waited by the boat and kept watch, secretly armed as per instructions. Ruya led Ruby past the mangroves that secluded the area from outside view and into the thickly forested area. She placed the portable radio cassette player on a tree stump, and pressed play. The hypnotic sounds of drumming and flutes emanated around them.

Ruya unfurled a blanket, spread it open on the ground, and sat down. She motioned for Ruby to sit next to her. Ruya then reached into her French wicker basket adorned with embroidered colorful straw flowers, and pulled out a thermos. She opened the top, poured liquid into a cup and handed it to Ruby.

"State the reason for this journey, then drink this, breathe deeply, and lie down."

Ruby smelled the liquid and detected chocolate, and looked questioningly at Ruya.

Ruya smiled. "Don't worry—it's ceremonial cacao. I added some cardamom, ginger, maca powder, and a little bit of raw honey for sweetness, to help you on your journey,."

Ruby nodded and sipped the liquid, feeling its warmth slide down her throat. It was tasty, yet not like hot cocoa, as it had an earthy taste. After she finished it, Ruya helped the already sleepy Ruby lie down.

"I am here to seek my spirit animal to keep me from harm, guide me along my path, and offer any advice." Ruby stated. She thought her voice sounded far away and felt herself slipping into a dream.

Ruya instructed, "Think of the roots of an ancient tree, and follow them down to lower earth, where spirit animals dwell."

"Describe what you are seeing." Ruya asked.

Ruby dropped into a trance, her breath was steady, and her spirit helper appeared quickly: she saw a female black bear. The bear reminds her of her childhood teddy bear, her cuddly nighttime companion that protected her from bad dreams as she slept.

"The bear has thick black fur and amber eyes, she is growling loudly, exposing her neck."

"Exposing her vulnerable neck is a sign of trust." Ruya explains.

Then Ruby and the bear gaze upon each other as equals, but she begins to feel her analytical mind attempt to pull back from what is happening, and immediately, the bear places a giant paw on Ruby's forearm as if gently saying, stay with me.

The bear then turns around and points to a trio standing in the distance, watching the ceremony. The faceless beings wearing long dark robes frighten Ruby, but the bear is adamant she stay and face them.

Ruya asks Ruby to describe how she feels. "I feel this is my spirit animal and would like for her to stay with me in this world, but I don't understand what she is showing me in the distance."

Ruya explains, "black bears symbolize protection, and defense against danger, mystical journeys into the underworld, or to other realms, and also symbolize the need to adapt to your surroundings. It is also associated with inner strength, the ability to face challenges, and overcome obstacles. I feel this is the right spirit animal for you at this moment in your life. As for what she is showing you in the distance, I feel they are protective towards you in some way, and why they have appeared at the same time as the bear. Since the bear is remaining calm with their appearance, then take that as a sign that it does not feel threatened by them, and neither should you."

"Do you accept her?"

Ruby responded, "Yes, I do accept this bear, I feel a connection with her."

The drumbeat changed, indicating the end of Ruby's journey.

"This is the call back, it is time to return." Ruya instructed.

"Thank your spirit guide for the advice and guidance." Ruya instructed.

Ruby bowed to the bear, and watched as the bear raised a big paw as if waving her goodbye, then she slowly came out of the trance-like state, and sat up.

Ruby and Ruya sat in companionable silence, each lost in thought. After a few minutes, they walked back to the boat and headed to shore.

On the ride back, Ruby reflected on the image the bear had shown her, and wondered who they were, and why they protected her.

Chapter 41
Revealed

A tanned man with a thick beard, driving a beat-up 1967 Camaro, tailed a line of over-sized vans headed over Seven Mile Bridge. He stayed in one-lane three cars down following one in particular.

He watched the vans trek over the bridge with the massive shipment Warren and the trio had unloaded all night from the islet overrun with mangrove. The entourage split up into different lanes to avoid attracting attention and the man followed, but changed lanes frequently.

The man had spent the night in the water in a wetsuit, clinging to a branch of mangrove He watched as they unloaded a large shipment from ten boats on the far side.

The man maneuvered into traffic, and followed Warren's procession across the bridge, always keeping a safe distance until the convoy arrived at its destination. Then he parked on a hill, and watched them through binoculars. He attached a long lens to his camera and photographed them unloading their booty into the warehouse. He then headed south, to have the film developed, and to give a report to one of the most dangerous drug dealers in Miami.

Clemmy couldn't believe what her guy was telling her and showing her, but she wasn't completely surprised. Warren had been a good worker, but she never trusted him–never. How his underhanded treachery had gone unnoticed for so many years she had no idea. She viewed the photos and shook her head—a frown wrinkling her forehead and causing deep creases.

She turned to Lenny who was cowering behind a stack of crates. "Thanks for finding out where he would be. I was starting to wonder where your loyalties lie, but now I know. Say nothing to Warren; I'll get this mistake corrected, quickly."

After she walked away with the tanned man, Lenny let out a long sigh, and mopped perspiration from his forehead with his shirtsleeve. He then continued hauling bags into crates for distribution while whistling a tune under his breath. He hoped Jaimie had also played her part, so they would be free of Warren—for good.

Kimi was at her two-month checkup, and after the doctor looked over her x-rays he declared, her ribs were fully healed, and the splenectomy site had also healed well. She was still getting around with a cane, since her gait was a bit unsteady, but otherwise, she was in good spirits. She was still annoyed that she had lost one of her prized possessions—the Mercedes, but that was just collateral damage. She was waiting for Phil to pick her up and drive her to the dealership to choose a new car.

When she had first been released her from the hospital, Phil had practically carried her up to the condo. He'd helped her change out of her clothing, bathed her, and assisted getting her into pajamas. He was a sweet man, albeit a clueless one, as most men in her life had been so far.

Phil then ordered takeout and had gone to pick it up. Kimi carefully got out of bed, the pain, and discomfort in the surgical site made her wince. She opened a bottle of pain medication and downed one with the glass of water Phil had poured for her. Then shuffled over to the cabinet, unlocked it, and retrieved the last box Paige had picked up for her, before her untimely death. Pulling out one of the little carved dolls, she studied the detail. One was wearing a red cape and had long red hair. The other doll had long blonde hair, and was dressed in a business suit. Smiling, she replaced the box in the cabinet and locked the door, pleased with how the carvings had turned out.

Kimi got back into bed and turned on the television, but nothing good was showing so she turned it off. She began thinking of what her next move would be. She reached for the phone and dialed Clemmy's personal number.

"Hi Clemmy, yes, I've finally had been given the green light, and am resting at home per doctor's orders. No, I won't be able to work full-time for another week. Yes, I'm sure Jaimie is fully capable of managing in my absence. I promise not to stop by the office again until I'm fully healed. Thank you Clemmy. Good bye"

Jaimie she thought. I'll be glad to see the last of her, but she is useful…for now. As long as Clemmy was happy, that's all that mattered. Of course, she'd have to have another doll made—sooner or later.

As soon as she could get around with less pain, she'd go back to work. She didn't need a two-bit whore usurping her place at the business she had built from the ground up, and one in which she excelled.

She heard the front door open and smelled Thai food. She wished she could have some wine with the meal, but the doctor had specifically told her not to drink with the medication. Plus her body was still adjusting to not having a spleen, and alcohol would be a bad idea during the recovery period. She would have plenty of time to drink anything she damn well pleased later on she thought, but for now, she'd behave.

Ruby was enjoying spending time with her mother, but was starting to feel like a caged animal. She was lucky to have a friend like Quinn with extra real estate to house them, but how long was she expected to stay hidden away?

"I see that look in your eye and you know this is for your own good." Kassie scolded her daughter.

"I know mom, I just want to get back to the shop and do more readings, but I'm holed up in here, hoping the crazy person who attacked me is caught, and that's a long-shot isn't it?"

Kassie nodded. "It seems like an impossible task, but I just spoke to Zeus, and he told me that he has a plan. He made me promise to be very careful, and that he or Freya would get back to me very soon. So go, get some rest, because you're still recovering."

Ruby nodded. "Fine, but I'm only staying until I feel well enough to go back to work. I know you want to join me at the shop too."

Kassie smiled. "You're right, I've been away too long, and I'm really looking forward to doing private consultations again. I just want to feel safe afterwards."

Ruby hugged her mother. "I know mom, me too. I'll go over some paperwork, then I'm going to take a nap, and you should too. You've been tending to my needs for a week, you must be exhausted."

"Why don't I make us some lunch while you're going over that stack, and then we can both take naps?" Kassie suggested.

"Sounds like a plan." Ruby agreed and kissed her on the cheek.

After Kassie, left the room to prepare lunch, Ruby looked around and thought that maybe her mom could put the house up for sale, and buy a condo like this one. It had good security and felt much safer than their apartment.

"Mom?"

Kassie walked back into the plush living room.

"What do you think about selling the house and buying a condo like this one?"

Kassie's eyes opened wide. "I think that's a wonderful idea! I've been contemplating that thought myself. The small apartment is a bit cramped, and something like this is much nicer."

"But what about Giles?" Ruby questioned.

Kassie laughed. "Giles has been trying to convince me to move in with him, but I don't know. It's probably too soon."

Ruby cocked her head to the side. "Really mom, too soon!"

Kassie smiled at her daughter. "Not too soon, but too soon for me."

Ruby got up and hugged her mother. "I don't think dad will be very pleased though. He's been bugging me to convince you to either sell so he can get his share, or let him live there rent free."

Kassie shook her head. "Your poor delusional father. That is one of the houses left to my mother by her parents in their will. It is one of the many properties they invested in decades ago. The house was never his to get a portion of, and he never even gave a thought about how I would live after I was left incapacitated. It's always been about him." She sighed deeply.

"Then the house is still in grandma's name?"

"Yes, your grandparents wanted to deed the house to me, but didn't after I married your father. Your grandparents never fully trusted him. They warned me if he were to get his hands on the house that I could very well be left living on the street." Kassie confessed.

"They're probably right," Ruby replied sadly.

"After the divorce, your grandparents deeded the house over to me to do as I pleased with it, and they told me to sell it and buy another property. They understood that I wouldn't want to live in a house where I'd feel unsafe."

"I agree with them, I never want to step foot in there again, and much less live there. Dad is going to have to fend for himself, and find a way out of his extravagant lifestyle, and rethink his spendthrift ways."

"Your father lives in a fantasy-world, and doesn't take responsibility for his actions. Not too long ago, I saw him walking cozily next to a blonde woman, and shortly after that, he was with a brunette. He's aged, but never matured, and that's the reason I divorced him. When you were a child, he'd go off with other women and spend most of his paycheck on them. I had to borrow money from my parents to make ends meet. Thank goodness I didn't have to pay rent too."

"Oh mom that's terrible. I always knew dad was irresponsible and immature, but not how much. I'm glad you've finally decided to sell that house. I'm sure Quinn can help you find a place."

"I'll ask him what the best options are the next time he calls." Kassie responded.

"And I'll talk to a real estate agent this afternoon and get the house listed. The tenants lease is up in three months." Ruby told her.

"Ruby that's an excellent idea, but maybe I'll just keep the money from the sale in the bank, and give more thought to Giles suggestion."

Threefold Dread 220

Ruby grinned. "I support that decision, and I think it's a good idea for you to move on with your life, and with a loving partner. That way, I won't have to worry about you living alone."

Kassie smiled widely and nodded. "I think I'll give him a call and give him my decision. It's time I lived in the present. But what about the shop?"

"Mom, it's our shop, and besides, you'll be there accompanied by Athena when I'm out. I can take care of anything that comes up with the house, while you two tend to the store and readings. I can enlist Giselle to spruce it up and get it sales ready."

"Okay then you handle the sale and I'll tend to the shop with Athena. I can't wait to get this done and over with, and start my new life free from the past." Kassie replied, thinking of all the possibilities open to her.

Ruby hugged her mother for the third time that day and felt happier than she had in a long time. Her mother had lived in fear since that fateful day, and was just now becoming interested in making some changes—big ones.

Chapter 42
Bad News

Warren raced his Corvette Stingray up the turnpike and turned onto a dirt road. The house he was seeking was at the end of the lane; he parked out front and rapped on the door. There was no answer, so he just let himself inside. He heard muffled sounds from the bedroom, and pounded on the bedroom door for her to come out.

Jaimie wrapped in a blanket walked out to see Warren pacing in the living room. Moments later, Lenny also walked out of the bedroom, wearing pants, but no shirt.

"What's going on man?" Lenny asked him—knowing damned well why Warren was angry, but asked anyway.

Warren stopped pacing, turned around, and faced them. "What is it with you two always boning?"

Lenny gave Jaimie a sideways look.

"Why did you want us to include you too?" Jaimie responded playfully.

Warren reached her in two steps his face mottled with anger, and grabbed her by the throat.

"I wouldn't touch you with a ten-foot pole, you filthy skank." Warren yelled in her face.

Lenny grabbed Warren's arm and pleaded for him to stop. Warren reluctantly let go and started pacing.

Jaimie's face blanched with horror, as she clutched her neck with both hands and coughed uncontrollably.

Lenny went to the kitchen, brought back a glass of water, and handed it to her.

"What the hell Warren!" Lenny spat at him.

Warren walked towards the couch and fell heavily onto it.

"Do either of you know why Clemmy called me out of the blue to have a chat?" Warren asked accusingly.

Lenny glanced at Jaimie and shook his head. "No man, we have no idea."

"I didn't think either of you would be stupid enough to know and not warn me. But I still have another problem." Warren stated, staring straight at the wall.

"It's the thorn in my side since middle school." Warren raked his fingers through his hair making it stand straight up in peaks.

"Ah, CJ strikes again." Lenny responded with a sigh.

"He infuriates me by merely existing and this time he's gone too far."

"Why, what's he done?" Lenny asked while nodding to Jaimie to go back to the bedroom.

Jaimie left to get dressed and out of harm's way, just in case Warren got angry again. She was tired of his violent reactions, and wondered what solution she and   Lenny could come up with to get Warren out of their lives—permanently.

Warren didn't notice Jaimie leaving the room, and continued. "He's circling Sherry like a vulture, and that's not okay with me. I need to employ drastic measures to get him to stop....forever."

Lenny didn't like where this was going. One thing was to set up the poor sucker, but another is what Warren is implying.

"What makes you think Sherry will want to be with you if CJ is out of the picture?" Lenny inquired.

Warren glared at Lenny before responding. "Because after pretty boy is gone for good, I'll be around to console the grieving girlfriend, and eventually, I can charm her into falling for me. I mean, we've know each other since kindergarten, and I've had a crush on her since the fifth grade. But along came pretty boy and lured her away from me."

It took an immense amount of effort not to roll his eyes at Warren, but Lenny knew better.

"I mean, what does she even see in that dweeb?" Warren said more to himself.

"What did you have in mind?" Lenny asked tentatively. *What a freaking moron!*

Warren looked up at him. "I want an irreversible solution, one where he is gone for good. I have a plan, but need Jaimie's help to pull it off."

Jaimie walked out of the bedroom and stood next to Lenny who put his arm around her.

Warren looked over at her. "Sorry about earlier, I let my temper take over."

"I'll help you one last time, but under one condition." Jaimie stated.

"Name it." Warren responded.

"That you never place your hands on me again. Not even for a high five." Jaimie stated.

Warren shrugged. "I'll try my best."

"What do you want me to do?" *Dimwit.* Jaimie hated helping Warren set up the nicest guy she'd ever known—again. But if she didn't agree to help him out, he had enough dirt on her to ruin her life.

Warren gave them both the detailed plan he had in mind, one that was guaranteed to eliminate CJ forever.

After Warren left, Lenny and Jaimie sat down to discuss what had occurred. They were tired of his violent ways and his threats. Lenny already lived in fear of Clemmy, and adding Warren to the mix was nerve-racking.

Months ago, Jaimie and Lenny had agreed that it wasn't worth it to keep working for Warren behind Clemmy's back; especially after Lenny reminded her what would happen if Clemmy discovered that they had been working for the opposition. They'd given excuses for months, lying to Warren that Clemmy was keeping them very busy late at night.

Jaimie's hand trembled as she placed her iced tea on the table.

Lenny stared at the red stripes forming on her throat. Yeah, something has to change and soon.

"Maybe Clemmy will take care of our problem and we'll have to do nothing." Lenny stated.

Jaimie nodded slightly, swallowed, and winced.

The phone rang and Lenny walked across the kitchen to answer it. "WHAT!"

Jaimie looked over at him alarmed. Lenny ended the call and looked over at her.

"That was Kimi. She wanted me to tell you the bad news as a heads-up before you went in to work tomorrow. Paige was found dead in a motel room this morning by a maid."

"Kimi's assistant Paige?" Jaimie asked incredulously. "What happened to her?"

"Apparently, she died from a heroin overdose; the needle was found in her hand. That's very odd." Lenny stated.

"What's so strange about that, I mean, she was a druggie after all."

"It's surprising, because I only sold her coke and weed. She was hooked on coke, not heroin. Hell, she could barely afford the tiny packets of snow I sold her. So I made a deal with her to spy on Kimi, and give me any info she found out in exchange for blow."

"And did she find out anything interesting. Something she can be blackmailed with?" Jaimie asked.

"Nah, she thinks, or thought her boss was into voodoo." Lenny responded mockingly.

"What do you mean Kimi is into voodoo?" Jaimie asked incredulously.

"Exactly what I said. She found some hideous carved dolls in a box, and jumped to the conclusion that Kimi is some kind of voodoo priestess." Lenny laughed at the idea.

Jaimie joined him and both laughed until they cried, until she forgot about her throat. She quickly got up, grabbed the kitchen towel, pulled an ice cube tray from the freezer, wrapped some ice in the towel, and held it at her throat.

"Can you imagine perfectionist and pristinely dressed Kimi cutting off a chicken's head, and dancing around a fire pit while chanting curses at her enemies?" Jaimie said in between laughter.

Lenny roared with laughter. "I've only come across her a few times, and she strikes me just as you described, but you forgot to add stuck-up and uppity."

"And conniving and crooked too." Jaimie added. "She's just a stupid witch."

Lenny nodded in agreement. "You're probably right; she poses no threat to us."

Jaime nodded in agreement. "No, she doesn't." She said adamantly.

They sat in the kitchen discussing different ways to go on with their lives—one that didn't include Warren.
Both agreed the plan was fail-safe. One they would soon put it into motion, and finally eliminate the nightmare she had been dealing with since high school.

Chapter 43
Revelation

The phone rang and was picked up on the second ring.

"Zeus, Raymond returning your call. What have you got for me?"

"Some very disturbing but intriguing news; I'm just waiting for Freya to return from Clear Lake General Hospital, and then we'll head over." Zeus replied.

An hour later, Freya walked through the door and made it to Zeus' desk in two quick strides, bouncing from foot-to-foot.

Zeus looked up and raised one eyebrow questioningly. "You look like you've just discovered the secret burial place of Genghis Khan."

"Better." Freya replied. "I just received confirmation that the woman in the photo found at Warren's house, is the same woman hospitalized after being involved in a motorcycle accident. Now ask me who the person in the accident was?"

Zeus playfully rolled his eyes at her, "Okay, I give up, whom?"

"Kimi Darnell." Freya responded.

"Kimi Darnell, the real estate tycoon?" Zeus asked.

He took the photo from Freya's hand and looked at it. He'd never met this woman, but somehow she reminded him of someone. In his line of work, he must have come across numerous women that resembled the one in the picture.

He shrugged and handed back the photo, which Freya placed in her briefcase.

"Yes, that's her, but you'll never guess who was riding the motorcycle, which supposedly cut Kimi Darnell off." Freya told him.

"Please enlighten me the suspense is getting to be too much." Zeus responded drolly while holding a hand over his chest.

Freya waited a few moments, making Zeus become uncomfortably anxious waiting for the information.

"The woman who wrote the letter Quinn called you about—Imogen Darlow." She relayed.

"I don't know how all of this fits together, but I don't believe it's just mere coincidence, do you?" Questioned Freya.

Zeus sat deep in thought.

"So what's our next step?" Asked Freya excitedly.

"We'll have to pay Jaimie Joplin a visit." Zeus replied.

"Why her, and where will we even find her?" Freya questioned.

"Because Jaimie has been friends with Warren Bullard since grade school, and she might know who the woman in the photo is." Zeus replied.

"I asked Sheriff Hayward to let me know if Jaimie showed up, because I wanted to ask about her time in rehab. He phoned me just before you walked in that she showed up in Twin Pass Junction this morning, so we'd better get a move on before she leaves again."

"Well that's convenient?" Freya responded.

"Indeed it is." Zeus opened the top drawer, pulled out his gun, and slipped it into his holster, and Freya followed suit.

"Now let's get go some answers." Zeus said walking towards the door.

Jaimie was disappointed that Lenny refused to accompany her to Twin Pass Junction, because CJ might recognize him, so she was there alone to save both their asses. Warren had already seen her, waved to her from across the street, and smiled; he was pleased she had begun to play out his plan. She knew he wouldn't be there long, as his shift was ending soon, and he'd head out to the Keys—there was an extra large shipment arriving, and he'd be there all night.

As soon as she saw Warren driving out of town, she crossed the street, and looked around before entering the building. Jaimie was led into an interrogation room, and asked to sit down that the sheriff would be with her soon.

Jaimie looked around the austere room painted a dull gray, and felt her head pound with tension. Across the table, there was a cushioned chair the exact opposite of the stiff and uncomfortable one she sat upon. She noticed her chair was bolted to the floor, and included cuff bars. There was also a chair in the corner, probably for an observer.

She kept hoping someone would bring her water—her throat was very dry and still painful.

She fidgeted with her hair, clothes, nails; the scarf tied around her throat, and purse zipper, until she heard the door open, and held her breath.

Sheriff Hayward, and a young woman in uniform she did not recognize entered the room.

"Hello Jaimie, long time no see what can I do for you today?" Sheriff Hayward asked her as he sat down. The young patrol officer sat in the chair in the corner.

Sheriff Hayward reminded her of the western actor—Sam Elliott. He had the same deep voice with a long mustache, and he was tall, thin, and wiry. He was soft spoken and polite—the perfect gentleman. She wished she'd had a father figure like him while growing up, but instead she'd had a crude, beer guzzling, hit first and ask questions later stepfather. After her loving and caring one passed away unexpectedly one Christmas Eve, when she was ten and her trailer-trash mother quickly remarried other trailer trash.

On the day she turned twelve, he'd entered her bedroom late that night, stinking of beer, and forced himself upon her. It was a night she tried to forget, but never could. The following day, she'd told her mother what had happened, and her mother slapped her hard across the face, and accused her of lying and trying to break up her marriage. That day, Jaimie stole a door bolt from the hardware store, and asked her only friend—Warren to help her install it. That night, her stepfather tried to get into her bedroom, but the bolt stopped him. He walked away angry, and took it out on her mother. The following morning, Jaimie found her mother crying at the kitchen table with a black eye, but she didn't ask her what had happened, because she darned well knew and didn't care, then skipped happily all the way to school.

Jaimie painfully swallowed the lump at the back of her throat, and asked for water. The sheriff looked over to the officer, and she got up, opened the door, and asked someone to bring in a glass of water. Within moments, there was a knock on the door, and Dwight walked in and set a glass of water in front of Jaimie. She nodded at him and gladly picked up the glass and took small, painful, sips.

The sheriff turned on the recorder and looked at her expectantly. "You can start whenever you want."

Jaimie pointed to the recorder. "Is that absolutely necessary?"

Sheriff Hayward nodded. "It certainly is. You know this station does everything by the book. Just begin as soon as you're ready."

Jaimie told him every detail of the night of Warren's party, and how Warren had prepared two beers with roofies and given them to CJ. How afterwards, she had helped him set up CJ with a bogus rape accusation and then a fake pregnancy and that CJ had never even touched her.

The night of the shooting, her boyfriend had fired the shots. He had been spooked by CJ suddenly showing up, thinking it might be Warren. That her boyfriend really meant no harm, but she had agreed to back him up anyway, because Warren had threatened her when he'd shown up as first responder. The drugs they found that night were actually Warren's,

Threefold Dread 228

and that he forced her and her boyfriend to sell them in other towns, and why they were stashed in CJ's house.

Jaimie further explained that Warren had tried to choke her the day she returned from rehab, and he had told her to say that it was CJ. She didn't want to do that and after asking CJ for a divorce left town. She then removed the scarf and showed the sheriff the bruises recently inflicted by Warren.

"He did this to me yesterday, because he was angry that CJ was with Sherry."

"Why have you waited so many years to confess all of this Jamie? You could have come clean years ago and cleared an innocent person, but you just continued to let everyone believe he was dangerous?"

Jaimie looked down at her hands as her fingers pulled at the thread of a button coming loose.

With her voice thick and unsteady, she responded. "Because sheriff, when I threatened to do just that, Warren threatened he'd tell you that what had occurred to CJ was my doing. That I used him to live an easy life and that I thought he'd by my ticket out of this town, but all of that's a lie. I was never planning to stay in this town anyway, and didn't need CJ or anyone else to help me do that."

"Then why now—why not years ago? I don't think it's because of Warren threatening to spill the beans, because if you haven't noticed that would also implicate him as an accessory; since he was the mastermind and you the willing accomplice."

Jaimie chewed on her top lip as ominous thoughts squirmed at the back of her mind. Then she looked at the sheriff and replied. "Because sheriff, now he has a new plan, and I refuse to help him, but if I don't he threatened to kill me."

"What new plan?" The sheriff asked her wrinkling his brows.

"Warren wants me to show up at Sherry's house when CJ is there, and start an argument that gets out of control, and CJ gets shot dead. Warren told me that he'd just wound me, but hell if I trust him to keep his word."

The sheriff's eyes opened wide. "So you've actually considered going through with this?" He asked incredulously.

Jaimie looked him in the eyes. "Warren frightens the hell out of me! He used to beat me up whenever he had a bad day, just like my stepfather. What makes you think he would think twice before shooting me dead too?"

"What is this pull Warren has over you?" The sheriff asked her bluntly.

Jaime wrapped her arms around herself. "That's something I cannot divulge without implicating someone very dangerous, and that'll get me killed much quicker than Warren. At least with Warren you'll find my body afterwards."

"Stay put. I'll be right back." Sheriff Hayward got up and left the room.

Jaimie drank the rest of the water. Her sweaty armpits were making dark circles under her arms, and her hands felt clammy against her bouncing knees.

Minutes later, the door reopened and Jaimie turned around to see six people walk into the room: CJ, Sherry, Elizeus, Freya, Captain Dwight, and Chief Deputy Mike. They had all listened behind the two-way mirror, which the sheriff had setup so there would not only be witnesses, but so that CJ would finally learn the truth.

Jaimie looked wildly from one face to the next, and felt the blood drain from her face. "What's going on here? I never agreed to a full room confession. I'm leaving." She got up from the chair.

Chief Deputy Mike stood in front of the door and pulled out his handcuffs. Jaimie turned around and cowered in front of the sheriff.

"Are you arresting me?" She asked through nervous breaths. "Wait a minute; you can't arrest me, I know my rights. The statute of limitations ran out years ago." She gave a grunt of satisfaction.

Sheriff Hayward calmly looked at her and gave her a small smile. "But not on the crime you just confessed to that you came back to commit with Warren. Now you've returned as the conspirator, collaborating with Warren to commit a future crime."

Jaimie swayed slightly where she was standing and then sat back down. "What do you all want from me?" She asked in a low voice.

"I just wanted confirmation of what I had guessed long ago.' Sherry responded.

CJ just pursed his lips and shook his head. "But why Jaimie. Why has Warren done all of this to me?"

Jaime looked over at him, ashamed for the first time since the night of the party.

"Because he's jealous of you. Jealous of Sherry liking you and not him, jealous that you got the football scholarship instead of him, jealous that your parents cared about you and stood behind you, even after all the accusations. Jealous that you have your family business and didn't have to resort to selling drugs for pocket money, jealous that your father wasn't a drunk who beat you up, and a mother who didn't care enough to

Threefold Dread 230

save you from those beatings, and who ran off with the first person she could. Does that answer your question?"

CJ sighed heavily. "Those are all ridiculous reasons to ruin another person's life. Warren's just seeking excuses for his life's circumstances that have nothing to do with me, but he made me his target. I've suffered nineteen years of this insanity because of him. My parents have also suffered needlessly, and my relationship with Sherry too because of his lunacy."

CJ looked at Jaimie and then at Sherry. "I've heard enough, let's go."

CJ held out his hand and Sherry held it tightly as they left the building. For the first time in many years, he felt vindicated. They headed to his parent's house to tell them the news.

Sheriff Hayward introduced Elizeus and Freya, and told Jaimie that they had a couple of questions for her.

Jaimie rolled her eyes thinking she would have to repeat herself, but the sheriff pointed to the machine still recording.

Resignedly she looked at Zeus and Freya. "What is it you want to know?"

Freya pulled the photograph out of her briefcase, and slid it across the table in front of Jaimie. "Have you ever seen this woman with Warren? Is she involved in the drug trade with him?"

At the mention of drug trade, Jaimie felt an ache in her belly, as ominous thoughts cluttered her mind, and making her head pound. *Shit, I have to pretend I have no idea what she does for Clemmy, otherwise, shit!* Dozens of scenarios raced through her cluttered mind of what would happen if Clemmy found out she was in the sheriff's office being asked about Kimi and their connection. The terror she felt thinking what could happen felt as if icy, spider-like fingers were racing up and down her spine, and she shivered.

Jaimie looked at the photograph. "Yeah, I work at her real estate office in Miami. There's a rumor she's Warren's lover, but I've never seen them together, and I have no idea about any drugs." *Shit!*

Sheriff Hayward had just returned with another photograph and placed it on the table in front of Jaimie. "What about this one. Any idea who she is?"

Jaimie picked up the photograph and squinted. She smirked at the barely there attire and suggestive pose, and shrugged her shoulders. "Yeah, that's also Kimi."

Zeus nodded. "When you were in rehab after getting shot do you remember a woman named Delores?"

Jaimie's wrinkled forehead relaxed, as her lips formed a smug smile. "Oh I definitely remember her. Why do you ask?"

Zeus exchanged a look with Freya before responding. "I want to know if she ever told you what happened at her house the night she was shot. Was it her daughter or her husband who shot her?"

Jaimie looked at Zeus and then at Freya. "You're kidding right?"

"Kidding about what?" Freya asked immediately alert.

Jaimie gave a short laugh. "She told me plenty, but I think you've got it all wrong."

"How so?" Freya asked her.

"How long have you got?" Jaimie asked.

"As long as necessary." Zeus responded.

"Good, before I tell you anything more I want a lawyer present." Jaimie informed them.

"Mike read her, her rights and lock her up after she makes a phone call." Sheriff Hayward instructed.

She made the call, and afterwards, told the sheriff that her lawyer wouldn't be able to make it until the following morning.

"Jaimie Joplin, I'm arresting you on suspicion of conspiracy to commit a crime."

Jaimie couldn't believe he was arresting her, but on the other hand: *Warren can't get to me. I'm safe in here, and it won't be on my conscious when he does something stupid.*

Chapter 44
Girl's Night Out

Giselle parked behind the shop, looked around to make sure no one was lurking in the shadows then got out of her car and locked it. Walking towards the shop, she put her hand in her pocket and was reassured by the cold steel. She kept looking around to make sure no one was following her, and knocked on the door while facing the lot. Athena peeked through the peephole, and unlocked the door to let her inside. Then she quickly relocked it as soon as Giselle entered.

"How have you been holding up?" Athena asked her.

"Looking over my shoulder regularly what about you?" Giselle responded.

"Same here, we're being extra careful." Athena told her. "Did you hear about the gruesome discovery of a mutilated corpse two hikers found over the weekend?"

Giselle nodded. "I heard on the news that the police are treating the death as accidental. Seems the hiker fell from a great height, probably from one of the peaks, and afterwards, wild animals got to him."

Giselle shuddered, "It's creepy and frightening—the horrible things that happen to people."

Athena nodded. "Indeed it is, hang on, I'll grab your special order it's in the back room."

Athena reemerged with a box, removed a wrapped package from inside, and placed it atop the glass case. After unwrapping the bundle, she turned to Giselle and noticed her perplexed look.

"I thought I was getting an animal totem, but this isn't one. What is it?" Giselle asked Athena.

Athena tilted her head to the side and looked at Giselle. "You are correct it is not. I did carve a small one for you to carry in your purse though, but my guides told me to specifically carve this one for you."

"But what it supposed to be. I can see three figures, but who are they and how does this protect me?" Giselle wondered.

"They remind me of Greek goddesses. I did my thesis on them. The Greeks sometimes refer to them as The Kindly Ones, because they are so terrifying that they don't want to mention their names directly." Athena informed her. "Legend tells these goddesses seek vengeance and retribution against anyone who has committed an evil act, especially crimes of murder. The victim seeking justice can call down the curse of the Erinyes upon the criminal, and they torment them. They are an eye for an eye type of vengeance against those that have committed crimes against others."

Giselle stared at the scary looking carving. "I still don't understand what this has to do with me?" She asked bewildered.

"I'm not too sure myself, but they are responsible for punishing crimes." Athena continued and pointed to each one. "The first one is Alecto—the unceasing; next is Megaera—the grudging, and finally Tisiphone—avenger of murder. They are described as winged women with hair, arms, and waists entwined with poisonous serpents. As you can see, they are wearing long black robes, with serpents coiled around their waists, and wielding whips."

Giselle gave Athena a questioning look. "Where do I place them? I certainly don't want them in my bedroom."

"Anywhere you want really that's up to you, but there is one more thing. If you find yourself in danger, you can call upon them to help you." Athena explained

"Okay, so if I find myself in dire straits then I can just call upon them, and they come to my rescue?" Giselle asked in disbelief.

"That's what the lore implies. All you need to do is to ask them aloud or even whisper your plea when you need them to come to your aide. However, any plea for vengeance is enough to summon them, and once they're invoked, they show no mercy." Athena explained.

"Wow, that's something." Giselle told Athena for lack of better words.

"And not to be taken lightly; they can only be summoned in a desperate situation, or when an evil person has gotten away with a crime or crimes." Athena stated.

Giselle nodded still not comprehending.

Ruby appeared through the beaded curtain and stretched. "It's been a long day. What are you two up to?"

"I was just explaining to Elle how to summon the Erinyes in case the psycho sending you the dolls shows up."

Ruby nodded. "Yeah, she gave me the same grotesque carving, and made me promise to summon them if I find myself in a desperate situation."

Athena pretended to look offended. "You'll thank me later."

Before opening the door, Athena once more scanned the parking lot through the peephole, then poked her head out and checked all around. Feeling it was safe; they walked outside, locked the door, and together walked towards their cars.

Threefold Dread 234

"Where shall we grab a bite to eat?" Athena told them with a grin.

"I know what you're thinking," Ruby responded smiling.

"To the Grub N' Stuff Diner it is!" Giselle responded enthusiastically.

They each got into their cars and drove to their favorite eatery a few blocks away.

As soon as they walked inside, they heard the booming voice of the proprietor.

"Well as I live and breathe, it's three of the four Musketeers!"

Angie the owner advanced towards them, and gave all three a hug at the same time.

"I haven't seen you since…forever! Welcome back!"

"Always up for some of your comfort food and especially your witty humor!" Athena told her.

Angie threw her head back, slapped her thigh, and gave a hearty laugh. She grabbed three menus, and with a twinkle in her eye, led them to the corner booth with a view of the entire restaurant.

"Then you've come to the right place. Maybe I should have named the place 'Zingers and Steaks." She gave another guffaw.

Angie was jovial, with a ruddy complexion and short of stature; what she lacked in height she made up for in personality. She wore a long-sleeved plaid shirt, a vest with fringe, a matching skirt with fringe along the bottom, a belt with a big rhinestone buckle, red cowgirl boots covered in red rhinestones, and topped off with a western hat held in place with a chinstrap.

They slid into the bright red and white seat of the booth, and rested their elbows on the long red table.

Angie handed each a menu. "Hey, one of you is missing. I can't remember her name. She was a little slip of a girl, always nervously giggling, but the four of you looked quite close."

All three looked solemnly at their menus, but didn't respond. Athena found her voice first.

"Sorry Angie, but Imogen was involved in a terrible accident not too long ago, and didn't make it."

Angie shook her head. "I'm real sorry to hear that girls, my condolences. Just flag me down when you're ready to order." She walked away rapidly as if not wanting to feel the sadness that had overcome the table.

They checked the menu for new additions, but ordered their usual, classic cheeseburgers with the works, chili-cheese fries, and milkshakes.

"Feels like we're back in school," chuckled Ruby.

Giselle was deep in thought as she sipped her strawberry milkshake.

"What's on your mind?" Ruby asked.

Giselle looked at both women apologetically. "I was thinking of the dream I've been having almost nightly, and trying to figure out what it means."

"Well, give us the details, maybe we can come up with an answer." Athena responded.

Giselle nodded. "I've been having dreams, nightmares really about my aunt Deirdre."

"The one you lived with for almost a year, before your father bought a new house?"
Athena asked.

Giselle nodded.

"I thought she was loving towards you. So why the nightmare?" Ruby asked her.

"It's just that I can still see her after I've awakened, but covered in blood. Giselle told her friends.

Ruby gasped, she knew her friend had found her aunt after she'd been attacked, and now she was reliving that terrifying day. She reached over and squeezed Giselle's hand.

"Seems like she's trying to tell you something." Athena told her.

Ruby nodded. "Seems that way to me too, but what? Does she show you anything?"

"She shows me different things. Sometimes she'll show me an empty picture frame, and at other times, she'll show me a cracked mirror, or a bottle of wine in one hand, and a cloak draped over her arm." Giselle informed them.

"A broken mirror can reflect two halves, so maybe she's trying to tell you to beware of someone two-faced." Ruby told her.

"The empty picture frame could signify someone missing or no longer alive." Athena stated.

"Cracked mirrors also mean bad luck." Giselle added.

"Or a distortion of self-reflection." Ruby replied.

"Romans believed that the soul regenerated every seven years. Essentially, when you break a mirror, you're waiting for an entirely new soul, to rid yourself of bad luck." Athena chimed in.

"That's interesting," Giselle replied, "and much better than seven years of bad luck."

"Mirrors can also reflect energy in the form of light. They can reflect the positive energy of beautiful objects, or the negative energy of gloomy

Threefold Dread 236

objects. Depending on how you use them, mirrors can activate or deflect different energies, and let you multiply different elements as well." Athena continued.

"As for the wine and the cloak, I'm stumped." Giselle told them.

"Yeah, I've got nothing." Responded Ruby.

Athena responded after careful thought. "I wonder if the wine and cloak are things she owned and were taken by her killer, but not noticed at the time."

"But why would the killer steal those specific items?" Ruby asked. "It just doesn't make any sense at all."

"The killer did steal the wedding ring off her finger and nothing else. Nothing was taken from her purse or wallet—they were still on the kitchen table." Giselle added.

Athena shook her head. "That doesn't make any sense at all. Why not steal the wallet too or the entire purse for that matter?"

"Who knows, maybe the thief, panicked and didn't see the purse." Ruby explained.

"So we have an empty picture frame, a broken mirror, a cloak, and a wine bottle, being shown to me in a semi-awake state by my murdered aunt; I have no idea what all of this means?" Giselle wondered aloud.

"Let me draw some cards tonight, and I'll let you know what I see, but for now let's enjoy this decadent meal, then you can tell us all about you and Quinn getting cozy again." Ruby told her.

Giselle blushed and took a few bites to think through an answer before responding. "There's nothing much to tell, except that he saw the error of his ways, and decided I was better than the other women he's dated."

Giselle told them trying to keep a straight face.

All three burst out laughing, and they enjoyed the rest of the meal only discussing non-serious topics.

After listening to a few comical anecdotes from Angie, the girls paid the bill. Angie walked them outside, and made sure they were all safely in their cars before they took off in opposite directions.

Parked across the street, someone that had followed them from the shop slumped down to avoid being seen. The person had watched as they enjoyed each other's company over dinner, seething, watching them enjoying themselves without a care in the world.

Chapter 45
Twin Pass Junction

Sheriff Raymond Hayward had been working with Miami PD and they had set up a task force in the Florida, Keys.

Zeus still had his surveillance team keeping an eye on Warren. He wanted to make sure there wouldn't be a change of plans at the last minute, and end up empty handed.

Zeus called Sheriff Hayward to warn him Warren was headed back to Twin Pass Junction. His team had followed him all the way back to town, and were awaiting instructions.

The task force reported Warren was seen roaming the streets, and asking if anyone had seen Jaimie. He was spotted at the back of a building and seen punching a wall; then he headed home. Within minutes, Warren had changed into all black clothing, complete with a jacket and hoodie jumped into his truck, which he parked a block away, and then walked up the block. He was headed towards Sherry's house.

"Don't lose him, whatever you do. I'm counting on you to catch him in the act." Sheriff Hayward told Mike and Dwight. "Everything's in place and the players are waiting for the lights to go up on stage."

"I'm a block away and headed your way." Sheriff Hayward responded.

Warren lurked in the shadows and hid behind trees and hedges. Making sure no one saw him. He saw CJ's truck parked out front and Sherry's car in the driveway, and stifled the urge to shoot holes in the car, but instead slashed the tires for good measure.

He looked in the window. The gun in the pocket of his jacket was poking into his side, so he pulled it out and grasped it tightly in his hand. He heard the telephone ring and watched as CJ walked over to pick it up. Made himself at home I see.

I could just shoot him right there, and CJ would never know what hit him. I want to see Sherry suffer too over her poor judgment in picking the wrong guy.

One of the SWAT members lay on the roof next door with a Remington Model 700 rifle with Unertl scope pointed at Warren, and Chief Deputy Mike and Sergeant Dwight were in the house ready to take action. Two officers were recording everything; one was outside behind a tall bush and another was inside the house.

Sheriff Hayward wanted to catch Warren in the act, so he couldn't pretend he was just out for a walk and stopping by for a visit. I want to catch the lousy bastard red-handed once and for all.

After making sure that neither Sherry nor CJ were in the kitchen, Warren snuck around the back and tried the door, it was locked. He quickly reached for a case in his pocket and pulled out a tool from the lock picking kit. The lock clicked open without a sound, and he smiled that it had been easy to get in without using force. He made his way towards the living room, and looked around the corner. CJ was looking through a pile of records, and Sherry was pouring them both a glass of wine.

Warren entered the room, pulled out his gun, and pointed it at CJ. Sherry screamed and dropped the wine glass.

He swung the gun towards her. "Shut up!" He yelled at her.

CJ held up both hands. "Look man whatever your problem is, this isn't the way to solve it. I can give you all the cash I have. Just don't hurt us."

Warren threw his head back and laughed then pulled off the ski mask. "What makes you think this won't solve my problem once and for all?" He responded pointing his gun at Sherry.

CJ was about to tackle him, but Warren was quicker and pointed the gun back at CJ.

"Whoa there cowboy this ain't a toy gun and this isn't a rehearsal. You're both gonna die tonight, and I'll make it look like a murder-suicide. Here's the narrative, life got to be too much for poor CJ, and he just couldn't take it anymore, so he shot his girl and then out of remorse killed himself. How does that sound?" Warren taunted.

Warren released the safety and pressed the trigger.

Sherry screamed as CJ staggered backwards and fell against the record player, causing the needle to make a scratching sound before toppling over and crashing to the ground.

Chapter 46
Dixie Cove Springs

Giselle stood outside the two-story, two bedroom, two and a half bath Tudor Revival home constructed in 1926, nestled between a couple of mature oak trees. It had been one of her favorite places to go to after school besides Miss Tisi's house. She wanted to visit the Plumeria tree in the backyard one last time, as a sort of farewell to some fond memories from her childhood. The carport had been swept clean of cobwebs, and the concrete pathway leading into the backyard with the previous surface cracks resembling shattered glass had been repaved and looked as good as new.

She entered the house using the key Kassie had given her and looked around. Plenty had changed since her last visit as a child, but some things were still the same. She climbed the stairs and looked in the bedroom that used to be Ruby's, and pictured her friend sitting at her little desk under the window doing her homework, and herself sitting on the shag carpet working on hers. She'd had the carpet removed, and the original pinewood flooring was now visible.

She checked Kassie's bedroom, the carpet had also been removed as per her instructions, and the prior flowery wallpaper was now painted a pretty sage green.

Further, up the hallway, she checked the bathroom with the claw-foot tub, and satisfied the carpet had been removed and the walls freshly painted, closed the door, and headed downstairs. She walked into the kitchen, which brought back pleasant memories of Kassie baking, and she and Ruby enjoying the baked treats. The kitchen had been painted a light yellow and the counter-tops were pristine.

Exiting through the backdoor of the kitchen, Giselle remembered the vegetable patch that had once been there, but was now a grassy area instead. The flowerbeds were no longer overgrown with weeds and were growing proudly in the soil. *The gardeners did an excellent job.*

She remembered how Kassie had cared for the flowers, and the small vegetable garden that she and Ruby tended to, and picked vegetables for Kassie to cook for dinner. The exterior of the house had been painted a pale blue and the shutters a medium blue. Satisfied, she proceeded into the backyard.

Walking towards the middle of the yard, she sighed—the small Plumeria tree had been cleaned up and stood in all its glory. She walked over, closed her eyes, and inhaled the sweet aroma of the pink blossoms of Frangipani. She remembered the fun times she'd had playing in the garden with Ruby. After one last look at her former sanctuary, she relocked the door, pulled up the collar of her raincoat, and drove to the grocery store to purchase food for tonight.

Kimi hadn't been this excited since she got her first payment for services rendered from Clemmy. The 1926 Tudor Revival was up for sale, and it was in pristine condition. She noticed the garden was freshly mown, the bushes trimmed, and the prior cracked pavement had been repaved.

As soon as her new assistant hammered in the for-sale sign, the calls had started flooding in, and appointments were set to view the property for the next two weeks. But she didn't think it would take long to sell the house. Sure, it wasn't her usual million-dollar listing, but this property in an expensive area of town would sell for a hefty price. *I know I'll make a lucrative killing on this sale.* She laughed quietly at her choice of words.

It was a cold and rainy November night, the kind where small animals were burrowed wherever they could seek shelter.

Giselle was busy cooking dinner, while Ruby and Athena were setting up the table.

The atmosphere was welcoming and jolly. The friends had the music turned up and were dancing around the living room. Giselle opened two bottles of Cabernet and left them airing on the table. Ruby stopped abruptly causing Athena to bump into her.

"I see Giselle gave the hideous carving a special place on the entrance table." Ruby exclaimed."

"Ahem, remember that was carved by yours truly." Athena informed her trying to sound severe.

"I just don't think they should be placed in an exposed area. Ruby said incredulously.

"Mine's in the closet."

"They're protective carvings." Athena explained. "So they're supposed to be visible."

"I've never known you to carve anything not beautiful, so why not prettier versions?" Ruby wondered.

"My guides told me to carve one for Giselle and one for you, and that's all I know, apparently, there's some kind of connection." Athena explained.

"I can't imagine any association to something so grotesque. Maybe your guides were high that night?" Ruby teased.

"Don't be disrespectful Ruby, my guides have never lead me astray, and felt strongly that this would be more beneficial than just a totem. Who am I to question their wisdom? They've never been wrong before." Athena responded solemnly.

Ruby held up both hands. "Okay, okay, I believe you. Take a chill pill." Ruby teased her.

Athena playfully punched her in the arm.

"Okay, you two quit goofing around and let's eat." Giselle called them from the kitchen while removing her apron.

They sat down to homemade Lasagna, salad, wine, and tiramisu for dessert. Afterwards, board games were brought out, and a couple of hours later Ruby and Athena went home.

As Giselle was turning off the lights throughout the house, she passed by Athena's carving and patted each head. "Thank you for watching over me." She whispered before going to her bedroom.

She didn't notice the car parked across the street with the lone passenger who had been watching her and her friends all evening, finally leave. Neither noticed the three sets of eyes watching them all.

Jaimie's lawyer arrived the following morning, and advised her to accept the plea bargain, or risk a lengthy sentence for prior and current crimes that were interconnected. She was surprised to learn that the statute of limitations would not work in her favor, because she had just confessed to a new crime that was connected to the previous ones; the sheriff hadn't been bluffing. Her lawyer also informed her that her confession was admissible, because she had made it voluntarily, which could be proven in court. She had confessed to having aided and abetted Warren in the crimes. The attorney made it clear that the goal was to come to a mutually agreeable resolution without taking the case to trial, since the outcome of which would be uncertain.

Jaimie's was crushed. "So you're telling me that I'm screwed if I don't admit to wrongdoing from nineteen-years ago, in between, and up to the present?"

"That's exactly what I'm telling you. If your case goes to trial, you could be doing considerable time in prison for conspiracy to murder. I'll give you some time to think about what you want to do."

Jaimie didn't need extra time to think about anything at all. "I'll accept the plea bargain, and come clean about everything." She replied all in one breath.

"I'll prepare the paperwork." He told her. "I'll be back soon."

"I want you to ask the sheriff to contact the private investigator for me…urgently; there's something he needs to know. I think others may be in danger." Jaimie told him.

Within minutes, Sheriff Raymond placed a call to Zeus, and told him Jaimie's request. Zeus told the sheriff that he and Freya were headed back to Twin Pass Junction, and would be there within forty-five minutes.

Jaimie felt she had atoned for her prior errors. I've probably saved CJ and Sherry's sorry asses, and now to rid myself of another anchor dragging me down.

After listening to Jaimie's confession, Zeus made two quick phone calls.

Zeus and Freya were speeding back to Dixie Cove Springs hoping they weren't too late. Kassie had told him that Ruby and Giselle were at her house meeting with the real estate agent. They were still twenty-minutes away, and hitting rush hour traffic. Zeus told Freya to call their contact at the police department from the car phone, and to fill him in as much as necessary. They needed backup now!

As they neared the highway exit, six police cruisers were behind him, turned on their flashing lights, and three sped up and eased in front of Zeus' car.

"I'm glad they sent a police escort to get us there quicker." Zeus told Freya.

Zeus had called Kassie earlier to verify if his suspicions were correct about a prior client of hers.

"Her name was Kim Darlow, why do you ask?" Kassie asked him.

"I'll let Freya fill you in, but right now I'm headed towards your house; the girls may be in grave danger." Zeus told her.

Zeus couldn't believe Jaimie had kept that information to herself all these years. The chief of police told Freya that he and his team were headed to the house in Dixie Cove Springs, and would meet them there.

Chapter 47
Final Sale

Kimi paced back and forth waiting for Giselle and Ruby in the kitchen of the Tudor Revival to choose from stack of the prospective buyers and agree on the final sales price offers. Kimi had arrived earlier than their 3 PM appointment to make preparations; she wanted everything to be perfect.

Giselle arrived and let herself in, and walked towards the kitchen.

"You must be Giselle. I'm Kimi Darlow. Nice work you've done with this old wreck."

Giselle was about to protest that the house had never been a wreck, when she heard a car door slam out front.

Giselle shivered involuntarily hoping that Ruby would make a decision today, so she wouldn't have to deal with this woman again. The real estate agent had been abrasive from day one, but was considered the best, and she wanted Kassie to get a good deal on the property.

Giselle dropped her keychain before reaching the extended hand of Kimi, and Kimi bent down to retrieve it.

"Ouch! Your stupid keychain pricked me!" Kimi, sucked on her index finger, grabbed it with her other hand, and flung it across the room.

Giselle eyed her questioningly and went to retrieve the little hedgehog Athena had given her that she had attached to her keychain.

Ruby entered the house, said hello to Giselle, and said hello to Kimi.

"I was wondering if I should disclose that someone in this house was murdered." Kimi asked without emotion, but inside she was laughing at the expressions on their faces.

Giselle didn't know what to say, but Ruby spoke up first. "What makes you think there was a murder committed in this house?" She asked her with narrowed eyes.

"Everyone knows that the woman who lived here was attacked by an unknown assailant and stabbed to death."

Ruby choked back the urge to strangle the woman, who was casually mentioning her mother's terrifying ordeal. What the real estate agent didn't know was that her mother had gone into hiding, and was given a new identity. The police thought it would be a good idea to publish her demise in case the attacker returned.

Kimi caught Giselle staring at her. "Is something wrong hon?"

"Have we met before?" Giselle asked Kimi.

Kimi smiled widely. "Yes, we absolutely have. Don't you remember?"

Giselle shook her head. "No, I don't think so."

Ruby was starting to feel uncomfortable and annoyed.

Kimi stood there smiling at them as though nothing had transpired.

"Are we here to discuss matters with the house, or to reminisce?" Ruby retorted.

"We're here to do both." Kimi informed her.

"I have no idea what you're talking about?" Ruby responded.

Kimi opened her purse and pulled out three small bundles, then slowly unwrapped them, and placed them on the kitchen counter. Ruby and Giselle both leaned in and stared at the carved dolls. One had long red hair with a knife protruding from the chest, the other had long blonde hair with a bullet in the head, and the third was a tanned man in jeans and t-shirt holding a gun. They looked at each other and then at Kimi.

Ruby spoke up first. "If this is some kind of a joke, it isn't funny!"

Giselle had gone pale. "No Ruby, I don't think she's trying to be funny. We should go." She grabbed her friends arm and began walking towards the door.

"Stop right there. Not another step." Kimi warned them.

Kimi pulled a gun out of her purse, then opened the kitchen drawer and pulled a butcher's knife. "I think it's only fitting that Ruby should get stabbed, and Giselle shot."

"Are you crazy?" Ruby yelled at Kimi.

"Crazy, no, angry and seeking revenge, yes." Kimi pursed her mouth in a self-satisfied smirk.

"I don't understand what's going on here?" Ruby told her.

Kimi looked at Giselle. "Do you know what's going on here?"

"It can't be you're…." Giselle began trembling, and spoke with her childhood stutter.

"I'm wha….wha...what?" Kimi goaded.

Ruby wondered if this was the person who had attacked her, and if she was, then she'd know where to kick and punch her again. She also wondered how she could disarm her.

There was a sound at the back window and Kimi turned her head wondering who had stopped by.

"Babe, are you here?"

Kimi laughed. "I'm in here hon the more the merrier. I thought it would be a nice touch to have him here too."

"Here you are. Hi Ruby, what are you all up to? Who's your friend?" He leered at Giselle.

"Dad, how do you know this woman?"

Phil looked at Ruby perplexed and nodded. "I've known her for many years."

Giselle felt a flash of recognition. This man was one of her mother's party friends, the one who stayed over whenever her father was out of town. Although older, he still looked the same. *Good grief, he's Ruby's father!*

Giselle looked at the woman, but couldn't believe it—*it can't be.*

Phil had just noticed that Kimi was holding a gun in one hand and a knife in the other.

"Kimi what's going on? Was an intruder here? Where did he go?" He began to look around, searching for any movement.

"Poor ignorant Phil. Great in bed, but clueless about life." Kimi responded.

"What the hell does that mean?" Phil asked her.

"It means dad that she plans on killing us and making it seem like we killed each other."

Phil looked wildly at her. "What?"

"Your daughter's astute." Kimi told him. "Unlike you."

Kimi waved her gun at him and motioned for him to stand next to Ruby.

"You never really cared about me, it was just about sex." Kimi told him.

"What are you talking about? I've always cared about you!" Phil stated.

"Really, because that terrible night you high-tailed it, and I never heard from you again. Not even in the hospital where I almost died. Your wife was already dead, so you could have come to me, but instead, you disappeared."

"What are you talking about, my wife's…"

Ruby interrupted him before he could continue. "Dead, thanks to you I'm guessing?"

"That's right hon. I'm the one who stabbed her to death in the upstairs bedroom, moments before you got back from school. Hope you enjoyed the pose I left her in.

Ruby's face turned scarlet as fury roared through her mind. *I'll strangle this bitch!*

Giselle feeling the hatred emanating from her friend, held onto her wrist to stop her from advancing towards the woman.

Swallowing hard and trying to push down the swell of disgust. "Why?" Ruby yelled with a shaking, rage-filled voice."

Kimi stared at her and shrugged. Scorn narrowed her eyes in silent judgment. Her lips curled in a sneer.

Slowly, a horrid thought crept through Giselle's mind, her eyes widened in alarm and she gasped. Her mind flashed back to all the previous times the woman standing in front of her had abused her.

"Because she's not who she claims to be."

Ruby looked at Giselle "Who the hell is she?"

"Go ahead tell her who I am." Kimi urged.

Giselle paled and mumbled. "Her real name is Delores; she's my mother."

"Very good hon." You are as stupid as I remember. How you didn't recognize your own mother is a mystery to me."

"Maybe it's because you've never been a real mother to me." Giselle retorted.

Delores shrugged. "You never really understand a person until you consider things from their point-of-view."

"That still doesn't explain why you stabbed my mother." Ruby told Delores.

Delores rolled her eyes. "Because she knew too much, and had something I wanted."

Delores' mocking tone infuriated Ruby.

"Please don't say it was because of me!" Phil replied running his hands through his hair.

"Of course it was because of you. Kassie wasn't only an accurate psychic, but she was also astute. She somehow found out about us and was threatening to tell my husband unless I promised to stop seeing you. I, of course, disagreed. I tried to persuade her to keep quiet, but she was adamant that she was not going to change her mind. I just couldn't have that happen and lose my lavish and fun lifestyle." Delores informed Phil.

"You've got to be kidding me. You lied to me! You told me your husband abandoned you and I believed you."

"It wasn't entirely a lie. My husband did leave me…weekly—to fly around the country." She countered.

"I can't believe what I'm hearing. You've been lying to me from the beginning. I destroyed my marriage over you. I thought you actually cared about me." Phil yelled at her.

"If had a dollar for every smart thing you say. I'd be poor." Delores retorted.

"I may not be very clever, but I was there for you!" He spat back.

"Were you really Phil? I could have used your help that night, but instead you ran, tail tucked between your legs like the coward you are. You left me there to face an angry and dangerous man, and his accomplice daughter. If you had stayed, we could have left together, but instead I nearly died. This is all the fault of your interfering wife." Delores retorted with condescension.

"You're a damned liar Delores, and you'll pay for this!" He yelled back at her with an ugly twist to his mouth, and walked forward to disarm her, thinking she would back down.

Delores shot him in the leg.

Ruby screamed, the blood drained from her face.

Giselle froze, trembling. Fear locked her feet to the floor. Dozens of terrified thoughts raced through her mind; all of them were of the abuse she had suffered from the woman she thought was dead. The very same woman boldly standing in front of her now.

"Move again and the next one goes in your head." Delores warned him.

"You vindictive lunatic!" Phil spat at her.

Delores ignored him. "I can see the headlines now. Daughter finds best friend with her playboy of a father in a compromising position gets stabbed by friend, then bereaved father kills best friend, and then kills himself out of remorse." Delores replied with a mocking, challenging expression.

"Why are you doing this?" Giselle asked her as blood pounded in her ears. Her panicked thoughts growing wild.

"Because you tried to kill me nineteen-years ago, and your father attacked me to defend you."

"You're remembering that night incorrectly. You attacked dad and stabbed him, and then you tried to kill me when I tried to run for help. Had it not been for the gun left on the kitchen table, I wouldn't be here today." Giselle informed her.

"Semantics," responded Delores. "Besides, you were an accident; I never wanted children—especially you, you just didn't fit into my lifestyle, but along you came anyway…uninvited."

"Why did you have to hurt my mother! You could have agreed to stop seeing my father. She would have been reasonable." Ruby stated.

"Your mother threatened me, and I don't react well to threats." Delores informed her.

Threefold Dread 248

"Sane people don't murder others because of a difference of opinions. You're crazy!" Ruby yelled at her.

"Crazy no, vengeful, yes. I almost got you twice, and one night you even surprised me with some karate moves, and that was unexpected. You caused me considerable damage, and I had to up the ante, by causing the meddlesome Imogen to die in a terrible traffic accident. Otherwise, how would I have been able to explain all the injuries?" Delores informed her mockingly.

Ruby paled at the revelation. Giselle grasped her friend's hand tightly as an anchor, trying to quell her shaking.

"I wasn't sure if she had seen my face when I attacked you on campus thinking you were Giselle. That obsessed and meddling idiot was always skulking around, and one night she did see my face. She had to go."

Giselle thought of another person who might also have been a victim of her psycho mother. "What about aunt Deirdre?"

Delores turned to her and smiled widely, held up her left hand and wiggled her ring finger. "What about her?"

Giselle gasped. "Why would you do such a terrible thing to her. She never did anything to you?"

"Because she also crossed my path. You see she made an ill-fated shopping trip, and bumped into me. I couldn't have her blabbing to your uncle, who would then blab to your father, who would then call the police. I couldn't risk being discovered. So she had to go."

"Why did you take her ring?" Giselle asked in a small trembling voice.

"I would have left a wooden doll, but I didn't have one on me, so I improvised and took a memento instead." Delores responded unemotionally while glancing at the ring on her finger.

"Looks better on me anyway."

Just then, Delores' Motorola DynaTAC 8000X phone on the kitchen counter rang. She held up a finger to her lips, while she answered the call, still pointing the gun at them.

Giselle and Ruby bent down to tend to Phil. Ruby removed his belt and tied it around his leg.

"Yes Clemmy, I understand, but I have no idea why Jaimie's been gone since yesterday. I'll be there in thirty minutes after I close this deal. See you at the club tonight. Buh-bye"

Giselle made eye contact with Ruby and silently mouthed 'the summon.' Ruby thought of what Athena had told them in case of dire circumstances. Ruby pressed down on Phil's leg, while Giselle held his hand, and they whispered for help.

"I call for the Erinyes to come to my aid. Do not permit Delores' wicked deeds to remain unpunished. Come to our aide now. Help us!"

Ruby looked up as a shadow crossed the room, and saw the outline of a big bear on the wall; her eyes opened wide in amazement. She felt as if a shield had been placed around her and Giselle and her father, embracing them in a protective hug.

Delores finished the call and pointed the gun at Giselle. Before she could pull the trigger, she screamed while holding the gun to one side of her head, and the knife to the other. She continued screaming, and dropped both weapons on the ground, while holding her head with both hands.

Ruby and Giselle stared open mouthed as they watched a trio of hideous creatures materialize. They had blood dripping from their eyes, and wore black cloaks with serpents entwined in their hair, and also wrapped around their arms, while surrounding Delores. One was poking her with a knife, another was yelling in her ear, and the third was pointing a gun at her while yelling in her face. All three wielded whips in their opposite hands, which they brandished at Delores continuously.

Ruby was the first one to react, she sprang up and kicked both weapons away, and then she forcefully shoved Delores until she backed her into the pantry. Giselle grabbed one of the kitchen chairs, and pushed it underneath the doorknob. They could still hear Delores screaming behind the closed door.

Phil pushed himself on his elbows when Delores screamed, and stared wide-eyed and speechless, then slumped back to the floor.

Moments later, sirens were heard in the distance and a long line of police cars pulled up outside.

In another car, Freya and Zeus arrived.

Chapter 48
One Month Later

Warren was locked-up in jail for attempted murder and awaiting arraignment. Jaimie's case was dismissed, but only after a stern warning from the judge and a hefty fine.

Clemmy was informed that her real estate agent and manager, Kimi Darlow was currently being held in a psych ward, and that Warren was in jail.

Interesting, Clemmy thought. *I've always suspected there was something off about Kimi.*

"Now I know exactly where to find him." She told Lenny and Jaimie.

Clemmy owned majority shares in Kimi's real estate agency, had it renamed and put Jaimie in charge. Lenny was promoted to warehouse manager, running shipment and distribution. She valued loyalty and those two idiots had remained loyal to her. Warren, however, was another story. He might talk to save his ass, and that was something she couldn't risk.

Ruby was finally able to sell her mother's house to a nice couple expecting their first child, and Quinn had gotten Ruby and Kassie a good deal on a lovely condominium. It was within walking distance to the shop, but Kassie told Ruby she'd still drive there to be safe.

Kassie was seriously contemplating a relationship with Giles, but was still old-fashioned and didn't want to move in with him. Until he surprised her at home with baked goods and freshly brewed coffees, a bouquet of Red asters, signifying undying love and devotion. After she sat down to enjoy the surprise breakfast, he had gotten down on one knee and proposed.

At first surprised, she had remained speechless. But seeing the expectant and loving look on his face, thought of a hundred possibilities in her future with this loving man.

"Yes!" Kassie responded enthusiastically. She kissed and hugged back an ecstatic Giles.

After all these years, Kassie knew she would finally feel safe—especially with the help of her fiancée.

Phil had suffered a non-threatening leg wound, and swore to stop womanizing—that is until a cute nurse showed up to change his bandages.

Giselle finally relaxed, knowing that her psychotic mother would be locked away in a high-security ward for the criminally insane.

❦

Aunt Deirdre appeared to her one final time, but this time she looked normal, blew her a kiss, and waved goodbye. It was then Giselle understood what her aunt had been showing her and that it was all connected to Delores. The wine bottle to signify her heavy drinking, and the cloak and knife are what she used to attack Ruby, thinking it was her.

❦

Giselle's father Darius had informed his brother Gordon about what had actually occurred to Deirdre that wretched day. Gordon had never been able to move on, or much less date again. He had retired to the coast and begun writing to pass the time; his stories were published in the local magazine. A publisher read his stories and convinced him to let them publish his writings, and he had become a famous author.

Darius was upset that his crazy wife had devised such a heinous plan and waited many years to take revenge. Delores had not only murdered his kind and loving sister-in-law, but almost killed his only child too. To find out that he was still married to the psycho-murderess and not to his loving wife was incredibly shocking. He quickly filed for divorce, and then immediately proposed to Aurora—again. Their wedding was planned for the following month, and Giselle had already begun making preparations.

❦

Giselle's house was a hubbub of activity. The doorbell rang again, and when Giselle opened the door, her neighbors, the three sisters who supported her throughout the years were standing there holding various boxes.

Athena arrived moments later.

Giselle introduced Athena. "These are some very dear friends of mine—Miss Tisi, Miss Alee, and Miss Meg."

Athena shook their hands, immediately taking a liking to them. Upon hearing that Athena had Greek heritage, they began a conversation about delicious Greek pastries.

Miss Tisi had been very worried about the dire situation Giselle and Ruby had been through, and kept giving them hugs. Meg and Alee were also very concerned, and kept patting Giselle and Ruby's arms and shoulders.

The doorbell rang again, Darius and Aurora arrived and rushed towards Giselle, and both embraced her at the same time. Introductions were made and Darius hugged Tisi, and thanked her for looking after Giselle throughout the years.

Tisi blushed deeply. "Never you mind Darius. It's been my pleasure to do so."

He shook hands with Zeus, and they talked about how everything was finally resolved.

Freya sat with a full plate of food talking to Athena about different cultures and mythology, which was something she was interested in— especially the Vikings.

The sisters had brought over boxes full of food. They had made a chicken and potato casserole, lasagna, a chili-mac casserole, and an apple pie, just like when Giselle was a child.

The sisters had also prepared finger sandwiches and an assortment of little cakes. Tisi brewed coffee in the kitchen, while her sisters laid out the plates and napkins on the dining room table.

All the fusing and care had Giselle reminiscing about her childhood days, when she had taken refuge at Miss Tisi's house, and finally felt herself relax.

Ruby smiled at the scene of the fussing aunties, and was glad Giselle had someone else to go to when she most needed it all those years ago.

When Giselle went to check if the sisters needed her help, they practically threw her out of the kitchen.

"Giselle, would you mind looking in on our house while we're away?" Tisi asked her.

"Of course, anything you need." Giselle told her and hugged her.

Tisi responded, "We just need to check on some acquaintances and make sure they're well taken care of, and after that, we're taking a much needed vacation."

Quinn arrived amidst the ado with a bouquet of roses for Giselle whom he hugged tightly. He hugged Ruby, Kassie, and Athena, and then he hugged Miss Tisi, and thanked her for watching over Elle. The sisters assured him that it had always been a pleasure, and hoped to watch over her, always.

Everyone was enjoying the treats the sisters had brought over, and the sisters told Giselle that the plants would need watering and mail brought in, but not much else needed to be done.

Giselle nodded, but inwardly thinking: *I'll be dusting and cleaning too, so that you can return to as clean a house as you left it in, and a meal cooked for your return.*

When Quinn gave her a questioning look, she explained. "The sisters are going on vacation, and asked me to check on their house while they're away. I'm always more than glad to do this small thing for them. They've been like mothers to me since I was a little girl. Miss Tisi's home was like a sanctuary for me, and I love them dearly. Besides, they travel often, and are always coming up with a new place to visit."

After a couple of hours, Tisi, Alee, and Meg got up to leave. They wanted to begin packing since they had an early morning flight.

"Do you need a ride to the airport?" Giselle asked.

The sisters looked at each other and smiled. "No dear, we've already taken care of that no need to worry." Tisi responded.

They hugged Giselle and Ruby, said their goodbyes to everyone else, and began walking back to their house.

Athena chatted with them while seeing them out, and before Tisi walked out she pointed at the carved sculpture on the entrance table.

"Interesting sculpture by the way, but the likenesses are a little off." She smiled and winked at Athena as she walked out the door.

Athena stared at Tisi, and then at Alee, and then at Meg. As realization dawned upon her, she opened and closed her mouth like a stranded fish flapping desperately on the sand, and gasping for breath.

"Giselle, what is the sister's surname?" Athena asked.

"Furey." Giselle responded.

It can't be! Athena thought.

Her dissertation thesis was on Greek mythological goddesses—The Erinyes, which she entitled, 'The Wrath of the Furies.' The goddesses were servants of Hades and Persephone in the underworld, and when not punishing wrongdoers on Earth, they lived in the underworld, or land of the dead, and tortured the damned. Apparently, they do not live in the underworld, but in my world.

She watched as the three sisters walked next-door whispering and giggling while looking back at Athena.

Athena wondered if her interest in mythology, and vast knowledge of myths had made her fanciful. It's all a coincidence, these is no such thing as the realm of Hades.

No way, she thought shaking her head, and smiling at her silliness headed back inside.

Chapter 49
One Grave Two Names

Zeus stood solemnly next to Darius at the cemetery gravesite containing the remains of Kim Darlow, and watching as Delores' gravestone was replaced with a new one stating the correct name.

Ten minutes later, a man arrived by taxi holding an arrangement of crimson roses and forget-me-nots, and walked towards the two men.

"Brennan Haines?" Zeus asked.

The man nodded and held out his hand. "You must be Elizeus."

Zeus nodded, shook his hand, and introduced the man next to him. This is Darius Mackenzie. The men shook hands and stood looking down at the grave.

As soon as the workers had finished installing the new gravestone, Brennan bent down and placed the flowers upon it.

"I want to thank you for changing the headstone." Brennan said to Darius.

"It was the least I could do." Darius responded.

"And thank you Zeus for tracking me down, and putting an end to the misery of not knowing what became of Kim.

"I'm just sorry it took so long to find out the truth." Zeus responded.

Brennan sadly looked down at the grave. "We were engaged to be married you know, and then one night, her ex shot her in a fit of rage, because she had moved on, and he hadn't. The last time I saw her was in the hospital, the day before she was discharged. The following day, after attending to one of her clients, when I went to pick her up, and I was informed that she had already left."

He continued: "I drove to the home we shared, and found she had packed and gone. She'd left a note for me explaining that she needed time to herself and would contact me when she was ready. After two months passed and I hadn't heard anything, I grew concerned, and hired a private investigator, but he was unable to trace her whereabouts. Until weeks ago when I received a call from you asking if I knew a Kimi Darnell. How were you able to track me down, when my detective failed?"

"Well that's because your investigator never searched beyond Canadian borders. I put a trace on Kimi Darnell and could not find much on her in the U.S. My partner, Freya, did a search outside the U.S., starting with Canada, and bingo, there was a missing persons report on a Kim Darnell filed by you."

"Then a photograph was sent my way from the sheriff handling another case we were investigating here in Florida. The face looked familiar. I was sure I'd seen her before, but couldn't be sure." Zeus informed him. Then I had a déjà vu moment that transported me back to a crime scene from 1967, and when I contacted her ex-husband Darius, and showed him the photo, he confirmed my suspicions." Zeus explained. "The woman in the photo whom others knew as Kimi, was actually Delores masquerading as her."

Brennan looked bewildered. "But how did this woman acquire Kim's identity?"

"The real Kim arrived at the rehab center on the same day that Delores, and another woman named Jaimie who was unintentionally involved was sent. Jaime was the one who was able to fill us in on what actually occurred that day.

The morning they arrived at the rehab center, there had been a series of urgent situations. All three women were left in a waiting room, while the staff tended to one crisis after another.

Jaimie was the first one taken to her room, while Delores and Kim were left in the waiting area, while the staff attended to the second emergency. Then the alarm rang for the third time, just as they were about to wheel the other two women to their rooms.

Brennan looked from Darius to Zeus. "But what was the cause of Kim's death?"

Zeus looked at Darius before proceeding. Darius nodded for him to proceed.

"When the staff returned, they found Delores had died, and Kim was asleep. They informed the head of administration about the death, and he then informed Darius that his wife had died. This is the reason the staff at the rehab wasn't aware of who was who."

Zeus cleared his throat and continued. "Since the staff had never seen the women until they were wheeled in that day, they had no idea who their new patients were until after the emergencies ended, and even then were rightfully mistaken. Delores fearing she would be sent to prison for the crimes committed against her husband and daughter decided to obtain a new identity, and used the commotion to commit yet another crime. What she didn't know was that someone had witnessed her wicked actions, which were held over her head should Delores ever try to try something similar on her."

"Jaimie the first person wheeled to her room filled us in on what occurred. She had gone back to the waiting room to see if her hospital-

Threefold Dread 256

mate Delores had been assigned to a room yet, cracked open the door, and watched as Delores placed a pillow over Kim's face until she was no longer breathing, and then switched her chart with Kim's. That's the reason Delores was listed as deceased. Jaimie kept what she had witnessed to herself, first at first out of fear, and afterwards as leverage, because as a con-woman herself, she never trusted Delores."

Brennan shook his head incredulously.

Darius who hadn't heard the full story before today, didn't think he could be more shocked by what Delores had done, but he was wrong.

Tears streamed down Brennan's face. Zeus and Darius walked away and stood under a tree on the opposite side, and left him to grieve.

After a while, Brennan walked towards them.

Zeus drove him to his hotel and waited at the bar with Darius until he was settled. Then the three of them ordered drinks and spoke of nothing in particular.

Chapter 50
Atonement

Delores had failed the competency evaluation, and was deemed unfit to stand trial. She was in the wing of the county mental institution locked away in isolation.

After her arrest, Zeus and Freya arrived at the institution, and watched as three deputies were struggling to restrain Delores so the doctor could inject her with an anti-psychotic drug. Odd thing was that she kept swatting at invisible people, and screaming at them to go away and stop tormenting her. Then she'd hold her head and start screaming.

Locked in a room and woozy from the injection, she could still feel her tormentors. There was a scream from deep within forcing its way from her mouth, as if her terrified soul had unleashed a demon. She cowered in a corner of the room curled up in a fetal position.

CJ was lucky Sheriff Hayward had convinced him and Sherry to wear bulletproof vests, as Warren had managed to shoot him in the chest. The sheriff had explained, "If he manages to get a shot, you're most likely going to have the wind knocked out of you, and land hard on your ass."

CJ sustained a grapefruit sized contusion to his bruised sternum. He told Sherry that it felt as if he'd been hit in the chest with a sledgehammer. Sherry nodded and gingerly touched the side of her head.

She'd panicked when he'd fallen to the ground, and ran to him, but Warren had reached out and grabbed her ankle causing her to fall and hit her head on the coffee table.

She'd crawled over to CJ, and then she watched as Dwight tackled Warren knocking the gun from his hand, and Mike, tased him to make sure he stopped attacking like a wild boar. As soon as Warren was down Dwight quickly handcuffed him. He didn't waste any time since Warren was a big, burly guy, and the taser would only briefly incapacitate him for up to five seconds, and that's all he had.

After CJ was discharged from the hospital, Emily who had been nervously pacing in the emergency waiting room drove both Sherry and CJ back. They spent the night at Dwight and Emily's house across the street, where Emily fussed over them until they fell asleep with a belly full of food, and tucked in and feeling safe.

While waiting in county jail for the trial date to be set, Warren began experiencing nightmares. Three winged women with serpents-entwined in their hair, and blood dripping from their eyes, and serpents wrapped around their arms descended upon him wielding whips, and wearing red robes dripping with blood, and serpents coiled around their waists. He hadn't slept in over two-weeks and felt like a zombie.

Nightly, Warren felt an overwhelming mixture of guilt, fear, and remorse, followed by rage, and what the guards would later describe as madness. They were summoned to his cell nightly, because of his screams of anguish, and they'd watch him hold his head and moan in agony. The doctor had already examined him and found nothing physically wrong with him.

"Probably faking it." One of the guards told the other.

"Yeah." The other guard nodded, and they both walked away and left Warren to scream in his cell.

On the third night, the guards just ignored the screaming, and instead had coffee and pastries. They turned the television volume up higher to drown out the lunatic's screaming and howling.

The following day, just before dawn on a gloomy morning, the last thing Warren saw was the graffitied wall over the toilet, and then he was stabbed to death.

"Clemmy sends her regards," were the last words he heard before blacking out into permanent oblivion.

⚜☠⚜

Clemmy got the call that Warren had been taken care of, and this brought a big smile to her twisted features, making her acne scarred face take on the semblance of a puckered old lemon.

She took off speeding in her vermilion Lamborghini on US 441 south headed towards the Grove. She was singing along with Queen to Another One Bites the Dust blasting on the radio, and failed to notice that a car had been following her since she left home, suddenly slow down and pull off the road to the shoulder.

She began hearing a screeching sound, and turned the knob to another radio station, but that did nothing and every station the same effect, so she turned it off. Then, she began hearing tormenting voices yelling obscenities and felt something poking at her. Looking in the rear-view mirror, she saw three cloaked figures sitting in the back seat, causing her to swerve into the opposite lane.

"The man you tried to have murdered was driving somewhere with his young son and pregnant wife. His son, wife, and unborn child perished, but he survived. He summoned us." One of the figures screamed.

She shook her head thinking, *shit I must have used some bad coke, I swear I'll personally murder whoever sent it to me,* and then veered back into her lane.

As she neared the exit, the car exploded with a loud and echoing boom. The explosion sparked a blaze that quickly engulfed the entire car.

Clemmy was lying in a pool of blood. Her ears were ringing from the blast, and she could smell a deadly cocktail of agricultural fertilizer, diesel fuel, and other chemicals she couldn't identify. Her feet were in pain maybe they were blown off she thought, but she couldn't move to check them.

The conflagration caused by the explosion was so intense that it could be seen from miles away. The smoldering wreck lurched to a halt in the middle of the road, its windows were blown open, and the entire floor panel was gone. The police officer who arrived first on the scene saw lots of blood and debris, and a human foot in the roadway. A fatally wounded woman lay on the pavement; both legs were missing from above the knees.

A driver a few cars length back who had witnessed the explosion described the fiery impact of the blast to the police: "I actually saw the car drop out of the sky." He relayed incredulously.

Clemmy was airlifted to the nearest hospital barely alive. She had a skull fracture, various fractured bones, a head injury, deep wounds, severe burns, open injuries to her chest, an abdominal hemorrhage and perforation, pelvic injuries, amputations to both arms and legs, spinal injuries, and her left lung had collapsed. Her prognosis was dire, and she kept coming in and out of consciousness. She couldn't see because the outer membranes of both eyes were burned off, and her ear's tympanic membranes were ruptured causing middle ear damage, which made her hear mumbled voices from afar.

The cloaked ones continued their torment until she flat-lined.

Just as they were about to head out, a plea was heard, but they ignored it.

Clemmy's daughter wanted vengeance for her mother, but ironically, her mother had already accomplished that before she died.

"Two birds with one stone," one of them said.

The sisters looked at one another and emitted mirthless laughs.

Threefold Dread 260

Epilogue

They'd heard the supplications loud and clear, and preparations were already done. It would be a much longer journey this time, but afterwards they had something to look forward to.

The content of their suitcases was well packed with the necessary items to be used.

The sisters arrived early the following morning, checked into their rented three-room villa, and admired the view from the window.

The shimmering sunbeams made the sand sparkle like thousands tiny gems. Beyond the pristine sandy beach was an aqua-blue sea of gentle waves; the sky shimmered like a curtain of pale blue silk. They watched as a child posed next to a golden sandcastle glistening in the sun, while his mother focused the camera to take a picture.

The sea-song of the waves was soothing, and they closed their eyes to the melody.

Alee opened the living room window wide, and inhaled the briny air deeply. Meg pointed to a squabble of gulls fighting over a piece of bread left by beach-goers. The sisters laughed at the mundaneness of their surroundings.

They turned around and unpacked their suitcases—before they could plan any fun activities, there was work to be done.

Tisi placed her suitcase on one of the beds and removed a false bottom, then pulled out a cane, a whip, a thick chain, and a cloak.

With a wicked grin, she turned to her sisters she asked. "Whom shall we visit first?"

"I think the psychotic murderess witch should be our first visit." Alee stated solemnly.

Tisi nodded in agreement.

"Then let's get a move on, so we can begin our much deserved vacation." Meg grinned.

The following morning, with their missions complete, the sisters donned bathing suits and sarongs, went to the beach, applied sunscreen, and lay back on lounge chairs listening to the calming ocean waves. Sipping Piña Coladas and listening to the vibrant, rhythmic melodies of tropical Caribbean beach music–they began their vacation.

"Where shall we dine tonight? I'm in the mood for a thick, juicy steak." Tisi wondered aloud.

Alee and Meg looked at each other and chuckled. "Why to Persephone's Chophouse, of course!"

The sisters rose from their chairs, and holding their drinks, danced in a circle around the fire-pit to the happy beats of bass guitars and steel drums.

"THE END"

Elodie Stirling is a writer of supernatural mysteries. Her stories explore the unseen forces beyond the visible world, mysterious occurrences, and people with unexplainable abilities—drawing readers into worlds filled with emotion, intrigue, and suspense.

As a young girl, Elodie spent countless hours reading books and dreaming of becoming a writer. After living overseas and traveling through Europe, she eventually settled in the Pacific Northwest, where she studied creative writing and honed her unique voice. Her work is influenced by Nancy Drew, Agatha Christie, and J.R.R. Tolkien.

When she's not writing, Elodie enjoys creative projects, music, and reading. She believes stories have the power to spark our imaginations and invites you to join her on unforgettable adventures through her words. She is currently working on her next story.

For more information visit: www.elodiestirling.com

Cast Of Characters Name Meanings

Athena: Goddess of wisdom, courage, arts, crafts, inspiration
Kallistos: Best

Brennan: Sadness; sorrow
Haines: Wretched

Caleb (CJ): bold
Jones: Son of John

Darius: Possessing goodness
Mackenzie: Fire-born

Deirdre: Sorrowful; broken-hearted

Delores: Pain and sorrow

Elizeus: One who can seek and comprehend truth
Bishop: Overseer

Freya: War goddess; noble lady
Shepherd: Guardian; town watch-keeper

Giles: Kind
Bonham: Good man

Giselle (Elle): Hostage; a solemn promise

Gordon: Spacious fort

Imogen: Innocent
Darlow: Secret love

Inclementia (Clemmy): Cruel; Cruelty
Maldonado: Badly given; ill favored

Jaimie: Supplanter; taking the place of another

Joplin: To cause pain and suffering

Kassandra (Kassie): Messenger of truth
Driscoll: Descendant of the messenger

Kim: Noble
Darnell: Hidden away

Lenny: Brave
Craven: Cowardly man, one who begs for his life when conquered

Paige: Minor servant
Carter: Transports goods

Phil: Loves horses
Mason: Ardor; stone worker; bricklayer

Quinn: Wise and reasonable
Masterson: Son of the master; superior one in charge

Ruby: Precious red gem

Sherry: Darling
Townsend: someone who lives at the edge of town

(Sheriff) Raymond: Wise protector
Hayward: High guardian

Warren: Guard; watchman
Bullard: Fraud; deceit

Characters With Only One Name Provided

Emily: Laborious; Eager

(Sergeant) Dwight: White or blond

(Chief Deputy) Mike: Valiant and strong; defender against evil forces

Ruya: vision and sight; the act of seeing or perceiving beyond the physical realm

Bastaq: attendant; servant

The Three Sisters
Their names were already explained by Athena. I thought it would be fun to portray the Erinyes as people living in the human world, and what they would look like, act like, and dress like.

www.ingramcontent.com/pod-product-compliance
Lightning Source LLC
Chambersburg PA
CBHW051421170626
46809CB00006B/2268